Brenda Minton lives in the Ozarks with her husband, children, cats, dogs and strays. She is a pastor's wife, Sunday-school teacher, coffee addict and sleep deprived. Not in that order. Her dream to be an author for Harlequin started somewhere in the pages of a romance novel about a young American woman stranded in a Spanish castle. Her dreams came true, and twenty-plus books later, she is an author hoping to inspire young girls to dream.

Avid reader, coffee drinker and chocolate aficionado **Jessica Keller** has degrees in communications and biblical studies and spends too much time on Instagram and Pinterest. Jessica calls the Midwest home. She lives for fall, farmers markets and driving with the windows down. To learn more, visit Jessica at www.jessicakellerbooks.com.

Small-Town Redemption

Brenda Minton

&

Jessica Keller

Previously published as
The Rancher's Texas Match and
The Ranger's Texas Proposal

HARLEQUIN® LOVE INSPIRED®

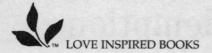 LOVE INSPIRED BOOKS

Recycling programs for this product may not exist in your area.

ISBN-13: 978-1-335-46852-9

Small-Town Redemption

Copyright © 2019 by Harlequin Books S.A.

First published as The Rancher's Texas Match by Harlequin Books in 2016 and The Ranger's Texas Proposal by Harlequin Books in 2016.

The publisher acknowledges the copyright holder of the individual works as follows:

The Rancher's Texas Match
Copyright © 2016 by Harlequin Books S.A.

The Ranger's Texas Proposal
Copyright © 2016 by Harlequin Books S.A.

Special thanks and acknowledgment are given to Brenda Minton and Jessica Keller for their contribution to the Lone Star Cowboy League: Boys Ranch miniseries.

www.Harlequin.com

Printed in U.S.A.

CONTENTS

THE RANCHER'S TEXAS MATCH   7
Brenda Minton

THE RANGER'S TEXAS PROPOSAL   229
Jessica Keller

THE RANCHER'S
TEXAS MATCH

Brenda Minton

Dedicated to the workers who tirelessly serve,
helping children and families in need.

Pure and genuine religion in the sight of God the Father means caring for orphans and widows in their distress and refusing to allow the world to corrupt you.
—*James* 1:27

Chapter One

The Silver Star ranch was one of the prettiest, most peaceful places Macy Swanson had ever experienced, from the stately oaks that lined the fenced drive, to the white-sided, two-story home. Behind the home was a red barn. In the background were the three cabins that made up the Lone Star Cowboy League Boys Ranch.

The Silver Star, on first glance, looked as if it might be a family ranch. On second glance, a person noticed the boys. From ages six to seventeen they were the reason the ranch existed in its current state and the reason she had come there. Because one of those boys was hers. Her nephew, Colby.

As she parked under the shade of a twisted old oak tree, she caught the tears before they could fall. She took a deep breath, to let go of the pain, the grief. The guilt. It took more than one breath. It took several. It took a swipe of her finger under her eyes to brush away the evidence. Even now, at the first of October and almost a year since the accident that had taken her brother and sister-in-law, the grief still sneaked up on her.

She missed her brother, Grant. She missed Cynthia,

his wife. They should have been here, raising their son. Instead she was the one trying to fill their shoes after the crash that ended their lives. She was the one trying to put the pieces back together for Colby, only seven and still angry and hurt that his parents weren't coming back.

The guilt sometimes outweighed the grief because she didn't know how to help her nephew. She had always wanted children. Now she doubted she knew how to be a mom. After all, she didn't seem able to fix this one hurting little boy.

Someone tapped on her car window. She jumped a little, moving her hand to the steering wheel and managing to smile up at the man looking in at her.

Tanner Barstow. Wonderful. The rancher and volunteer at the boys ranch stepped back from the door as she pushed it open. He'd posed as Mr. January for the calendar the community put out as a fund-raiser for the ranch. The Cowboys of McLennan County calendar had been a hit, she'd been told. She had a copy hanging in her kitchen. It had been there when she moved in last winter, after the accident.

Her life had become segmented, broken in two distinct halves. Before the accident. After the accident.

Before the accident she'd been engaged to Bill, an attorney in Dallas. She'd been a librarian, managing several libraries in the Dallas metro area.

After the accident… She was still trying to find the person she was after the accident. She now lived in Haven, where she was a librarian at the local library, a substitute teacher at the high school and a volunteer at the Silver Star. Most important, she was the aunt of Colby, determined to find a way to make that little boy smile.

"Are you okay?" Tanner asked as she stepped out of her car.

He was a full head taller than her five-feet-eight inches. He was rangy, lean and powerful. His jeans rode low on his hips. The button-up shirt tugged at his shoulders. His dark chestnut hair was wavy, and she could tell that when it curled, it bothered him. Maybe because he couldn't control it. He seemed to be a man who liked control. Dark blue eyes caught her attention. He was giving her a skeptical look, as if he was positive she couldn't be okay.

And maybe she wasn't. Maybe she was so far out of her depth here in this small town that she didn't know if she would sink or swim. Mostly, she felt as if she was sinking.

"I'm good." She cleared her throat and gave him a smile that wavered; she felt it tremble a little.

"It's going to get better. Give him time. Give yourself time." He said it like he meant it. She nodded and closed her eyes, against the brightness of the sun and against the pitying look he was giving her.

"I know," she finally answered, and she thought it sounded as if she meant it or believed it. She added a hopeful smile for punctuation.

"Come, watch him ride. We're in the arena today. He's doing great."

His hand brushed her back to guide her in that direction. The touch was brief, but the comfort of the gesture couldn't be denied. She could really use a friend. She could use a hug. She shook off that thought as one that went too far. After all, she'd made friends in

Haven, through work and through the Haven Community Church. She wasn't alone. Not completely.

But the idea of a hug wasn't wholly without merit. What would Tanner Barstow, vice president of the local Lone Star Cowboy League, self-made rancher and horse trainer extraordinaire, do if she asked him for a hug? He'd probably do the man-hug, quick and from the side, and then head for the hills.

Movement in the arena caught her attention. She watched as the boys, all younger, rode around the enclosure. They kept their horses in an easy lope, right hands on the reins, left hands at their sides.

"What are they doing?" she asked as they walked in that direction.

They stopped a few feet from the white, wood fence of the arena. She kept her attention focused on Colby. He was such a tiny little guy, with his mom's dark hair and his dad's green eyes. The ranch hand in the arena called all the boys to the center. A young teen stood next to him. The boys rode their horses and lined up so that boys and animals were facing the ranch hand.

"They're practicing showmanship, for Western pleasure classes at local events. It takes control for the horses, and for the boys."

"This is such a great place. I'm so glad it was here for Colby. I don't know what we would have done."

He nodded, acknowledging the comment. His gaze remained on the boys and the men working with them. "It's the best. It was truly inspired. When Luella Snowden Phillips started this ranch, she probably didn't realize how long-lasting and far-reaching the ministry would be. But it's been here for seven decades. I just wish we had more room and could take more boys."

"They were praying about that at church last Sunday," she offered. "Someone mentioned that boys had been turned away. And wouldn't it be an amazing thing if no child was ever turned away from this program?"

"That would be amazing." He walked away from her, moving a little closer to the fence. "I heard Colby had a hard time last weekend."

He shifted, settling his gaze on her just momentarily before turning his attention back to the boys in the arena.

Was that an accusation? Or was she just being unduly sensitive? Colby had been allowed a twenty-four-hour pass to go home with her. She'd had to bring him back to the ranch early.

"It's hard for him to be at home. I keep thinking that it will get easier, that he'll want to be there."

"Don't give up." He stepped away from her, heading toward the gate. "If you'll excuse me."

She nodded as he walked away. From the arena someone shouted. She saw the ranch hand who was working with the boys move quickly. As she watched, the boys dismounted and started tugging their horses away from the center of the arena. Tanner was through the gate, leaving it open in the process.

"Close that," he called back to her.

She reached the gate and closed it as she went through. The boy at the center of the ruckus was yelling at Jake, the ranch hand who'd been instructing them. The other boys, most of them under ten, were backing away as Tanner hurried to help. It looked like chaos about to be unleashed. The teenager who'd been helping was trying to get control of the nearly half dozen boys left to fend for themselves as the adults focused on the one youngster who was causing the problems.

The boy at the center of the trouble had hold of his horse and was backing away from the two men. The horse, wild-eyed and jerking to be free, kept moving. The boy held tight to the reins.

Colby hurried toward her, dragging his horse along with him. He had tears in his eyes. His friends didn't look much better.

"Hey, guys. Let's see if we can get these horses in the barn. We'll put them in stalls." She looked to the teen helper for guidance. "You're Ben, right? Do the horses go in stalls?"

He grinned, showing crooked teeth but a charming dimple. His hair was light brown, and his eyes were warm hazel. "Yes, ma'am. I can put the horses in the stalls."

"Why don't we do that?" She looked at the group of boys surrounding her. Big eyes, sweet smiles. She glanced back in time to see that Tanner had hold of the poor horse being dragged about the arena.

"Come on, guys, let's see if we can have fun." She clasped her hands together as she stared at the expectant faces.

Colby didn't look convinced.

"Colby, what story do you like the best?" she asked.

That got his attention. That was their common ground. Stories.

"The one with the dragon slayer," he said as he reached for her hand, his other hand holding the reins of his pony.

"The dragon slayer it is." She only hoped she could remember the story she'd made up on a Saturday night when neither of them could sleep. She smiled down at her nephew. If she couldn't remember, he would help.

In the background she heard a young voice raised in anger. Or hurt. A calm, reassuring voice spoke; the words were lost, but the tone carried the meaning.

Macy felt that reassurance, even though it wasn't meant for her.

"The dragon slayer knelt in prayer, knowing his kingdom would stand forever and that it was a greater power than his own that kept them safe from the evil..."

Tanner stood just outside the open barn doors, unwilling to go in and interrupt. He'd taken Sam Clark back to the cabin where he lived and to the house parents, Eleanor and Edward Mack, who would make sure he was safe until he could regain control of his behavior.

The eleven-year-old had been at the ranch for six months. He was a good kid who had seen the bad side of life. The result was a lot of anger. Edward and Eleanor could handle it; with degrees in counseling, and their involvement in the local church, they were experts on the kids at the ranch.

Kids wanted people to connect with. Even when they fought the people who cared, they still wanted to be cared about.

Tanner got it. Until the age of ten he'd lived that same life. His parents had been abusive to each other and their children. They'd been drug addicts who couldn't hold down jobs. There hadn't been a safety net until the state sent the three Barstow kids to live with Aunt May in Haven, a community just on the outskirts of Waco. The move had saved his life. His older brother, Travis, had struggled a bit more and had lived at the boys ranch for a while. Their little sister, Chloe, hadn't been much more than a baby when they were sent to live with their dad's aunt May.

Young voices erupted as the story being told ended. He peeked inside the barn and watched as those five young boys moved closer to Macy Swanson, her nephew included. The little boy had recently turned seven. Colby's hand was on her arm, and he stood close to her side. From thirty feet away Tanner could see her nerves. It was easy to perceive that she was afraid to move, afraid to lose the thin thread of connection between her and her nephew.

But the story she'd been telling had enthralled the kids. They were still asking questions about the dragon and the dragon slayer. She was telling them about faith in a way that a kid could understand.

He didn't know Macy very well, but he had to admire how she could calm a group of rowdy boys with a story. If he was being honest, there were other things to admire, things a man couldn't help but notice. He sure didn't mind admiring or noticing. Sunlight danced through the center aisle of the barn, the beams of light catching in the blond hair that hung loose to the middle of her back. She was tall and classy. Beautiful, really.

And all city.

Things transplanted typically did better when transplanted into a similar environment. That was what he knew from living in the country. A water oak didn't tend to do well in hot, sandy soil. Cacti thrived in the desert. That was just the way it was. City folks thrived in the city, and country people tended to stay in the country.

Macy looked up as he approached, her smile touching her green eyes with a warmth that took him by surprise. The boys remained circled around her. They had avoided the worst of Sam's outburst and had been entertained with a story; they were on top of the world. Even Ben had lurked at the edge, listening to the story.

Ben, fourteen, tall and lanky with a shock of light brown hair, had been at the ranch for two years. He was a good kid. He'd had one failed attempt at going home. He'd been adopted as a preschooler, and the experts said he had trouble bonding because of his early childhood. That made sense to Tanner. The boy was sometimes angry and tended to push away when he started warming up to people.

But he was doing better. They could all see that.

Time. For so many of these kids it took a lot of time to heal. With that thought, his gaze fell on Colby Swanson. The boy's parents had died in a car accident, and his grief had turned to anger that made him act out at school and be difficult to handle at home.

When a spot had opened, Macy placed him at the ranch.

"You boys get all of your stuff gathered up." Tanner let his gaze fall on Colby. The little boy was holding tight to his aunt Macy. "And maybe we can get Miss Swanson to finish her story, or read to you all when you have library time."

His phone rang. Rotten timing. He would have ignored it, but the caller ID flashed the name of the president of the local chapter of the Lone Star Cowboy League, an organization started over a hundred years earlier to help ranching communities. Since Gabriel

Everett didn't call just to shoot the breeze, it had to be important.

Jake, about the best hand around, had entered the barn from a side door. The big bonus was that not only could he break a horse to saddle, he also had a knack with the kids on the ranch.

"Jake, can you and Ben go ahead and take these guys on down to Bea?" He didn't have to spell it out. Beatrice Brewster, the no-nonsense director of the LSCL Boys Ranch, ran the show. She'd watch the kids until she got the all clear from house parents Edward and Eleanor, who had their hands full with Sam.

Jake gave him a thumbs-up and started organizing the boys for the march to the main ranch house. Without asking, Macy fell in with Jake and the boys. She volunteered in the ranch office, helping with accounting. She'd also become pretty adept at finding donations and writing up grants. She didn't usually help with the kids. But at times like this, everyone pitched in and helped out.

"Gabriel, what can I do for you?" Tanner watched as the small troupe marched toward the big ranch house, and then he headed for his truck.

"Tanner, we need to have an emergency meeting of the League. Can you be here in about fifteen minutes? Bring Bea with you. And Katie will probably need to attend so she can take notes for the ranch."

"I'll be there." He glanced at his watch. "What's going on?"

"I'd rather make the announcement when you get here. Let's just say that some prayers are answered a little quicker than others."

Interesting. "I'll be there in ten minutes."

When he pulled up to the ranch, Bea was already on her way down the stairs. Tall and in her fifties, the former social worker for the state was all heart. She adjusted her glasses and smoothed her hair, turning to give a "hurry up" look to the person following her out the door.

Macy Swanson?

The two climbed in his truck, Macy opening the back door and getting in the backseat. Beatrice clicked her seat belt and settled her purse on her lap.

"Katie is staying to help Jake with the kids. I asked Macy to come with us to take notes. I'm going to want my own person there so that we have a record of our own." Beatrice shot him a questioning look. "Do you know what is going on, Tanner Barstow?"

Like he was one of her kids and someone had TP'd the house.

"No, Bea, I don't. I got the call the same as you."

"Gabriel said it's a good thing. But, Tanner, I'll have you know, I'm not a fan of surprises. Even of the good variety."

"I'm sure it'll be fine." He glanced in the rearview mirror and caught a glimpse of Macy looking out the window, bottom lip caught between her teeth. He cleared his throat, and she shot him a look. "I'm sorry I put you on the spot back there. So, do you think you'd be interested in spending time reading to the kids? They enjoyed the story you told them."

"I'm not sure," she finally answered. "I mean, it would be good, wouldn't it? The boys enjoyed it. Colby enjoyed it."

He slowed to make his turn. "Think about it."

The Everett Ranch, owned by Gabriel Everett, was a

big spread located between the Silver Star and Haven. Tanner parked next to a half dozen assorted trucks and SUVs. He got out quickly so he could hurry to the other side and open the door for the ladies. His dad hadn't taught him to be a gentleman, but Aunt May had. She'd told him someday he'd appreciate the manners she instilled in him. He'd be thankful.

He was, and he wished she was alive so he could tell her how much she'd meant to him and his siblings. But she'd passed about eight years ago, getting them mostly raised, all but Chloe, who had been not quite fifteen. May had at least seen Tanner's business get off the ground. She'd known they would be okay without her.

Eight years later Haven Tractor and Supply was well-established, and Aunt May's small ranch had quadrupled in size. He didn't mind feeling proud of that accomplishment. May had sold off land to get him through college. He'd put the family spread, the Rocking B, all back together for her. It had taken him a few years, buying back the land as it came up for sale or as he convinced neighbors to sell it back to him.

He opened the door for Bea. She stepped out, not needing the hand he held out for her. He reached to open the door for Macy, as well.

"Thank you, Tanner." Beatrice patted his arm, as if he wasn't thirty-two and just twenty years her junior. With Bea they were all kids.

The ladies preceded him to the house. He didn't mind. A few more minutes meant a little more time to think; maybe he might come up with some reason they were all being called to the Everett place for a meeting. But by the time they were shown to the library, where the meetings were held, he still didn't have a clue.

A gavel pounded on the table. Tanner sat back and gave Gabriel his full attention, but then his gaze shifted to the right of the league president. The man sitting in the seat of honor was Harold Haverman, attorney and member of the Lone Star Cowboy League, of which Tanner was vice president. It seemed to him that if there was something going on, Tanner should have been told ahead of time.

Tall, with a black Stetson covering his gray hair and metal-framed glasses on the end of his nose, Harold had presence. And he had a document in his hands that looked far too official.

"Meeting to order." Gabriel glanced around the group. He cited the date, the time, the emergency status of a meeting of the Waco district Lone Star Cowboy League chapter.

The formalities were taken care of with some seconds, a vote, and then on to new business.

"I would like to recognize our guest, Harold Haverman."

Harold stood, pushed the silver-framed glasses back in place and shifted the papers he still held. He gave them all a look, serious as could be, no hints as to what this was all about.

"I'd like to thank you all for coming today. I know this is unexpected." He peered at them over the top of those glasses. "As you all know, we lost a respected member of our community. Cyrus Culpepper passed last week. I know several of you attended his funeral. Today I have the honor of sharing with you his last will and testament."

"What does this have to do with me?" Bea started

to stand, but Gabriel shook his head. "I have children at home."

"Bea, this won't take a minute." Harold cleared his throat and shook out the papers. "If you'll just give me five minutes to read this. And then we can take care of the details."

He started to read. Silence held as the members looked from one to the other, clearly astonished. Tanner glanced across the table and made quick eye contact with Macy Swanson and got caught in those green eyes of hers. She looked wary and like she was pretty sure she shouldn't be involved. She also looked like someone still hurting. The grief for her brother had turned to pain for a little boy still missing his parents.

Listening as Haverman read the final will of one Cyrus Culpepper, curmudgeon and stirrer of the pot, Tanner thought that maybe they'd all just been tossed in the middle of a big old mess.

I, Cyrus B. Culpepper, am writing this on my deathbed with, per my doc of over forty years, only days or weeks to go. I may be about to meet my maker, but I am of sound mind and hereby bequeath the bulk of my estate to the Boys Ranch, as I was once a resident myself back when the ranch first started in 1947. Yes, that's right. I might be an old curmudgeon who can't tolerate a thing, but since I was once a troubled kid who was turned around by the Boys Ranch, I want to do something for the place. However, I have conditions. When I lived at the Boys Ranch, there were four other original residents who I lost touch with. I would like you to bring them together for a reunion at the ranch on March 20th, a party on my birthday for the 70th anniversary celebration of the Boys Ranch. That gives you six months. Now, now, quit your bellyaching—given all the newfangled technology, search engines and social media nonsense, you'll probably find them lickety-split. Though I never tried, so who knows? I suppose I've gotten a bit nostalgic in my old age and leave it up to you whippersnappers to do my bidding.

Oh—and one more thing. I had a son, John Culpepper, who I didn't get on with too well after his mother passed. We were estranged, but I know he had a child, a girl—Avery—who lost her mother. I heard, well after the fact, that my son died when the child was young. I have no idea what happened to her, and I'd like to invite her to the ranch to receive an inheritance.

If the terms of my will are not met, I've instructed my attorney, Harold Haverman, to bequeath the estate, minus a small endowment to the Boys Ranch, to Lance Thurston, a real estate developer, to build a strip mall bearing my name. Sometimes you have to provide the right incentive.

Now for the boring part. The "bulk of my estate" is to include my ranch house and all the outbuildings, livestock and land except for the cabin in which I grew up and the five acres of land it sits on. That cabin, five miles from the ranch on the outskirts of town, and land is bequeathed to Miss Avery Culpepper, to be given to her in March. I was a self-starter and believe everyone

should be, but I also believe I did wrong by Avery and want her to have what she likely would have garnered over the years as my granddaughter. The rest of my bank accounts and investments are bequeathed to the LSCL Boys Ranch.
Yours, Cyrus B. Culpepper

Everyone was talking at once. Outrage. Shock. The library fairly rattled with raised voices. Fletcher Snowden Phillips, last remaining kin of the founders of the boys ranch, was the loudest. He was crowing that the ranch was meant to be at Silver Star and nowhere else. For a man constantly trying to litigate against the ranch, that rang false.

Gabriel Everett pounded the gavel on the table, and a hush fell with just a few last-ditch remarks from those wanting to voice concern.

"It looks as if we'll need volunteers." Gabriel looked over the group that had gone suspiciously quiet. No surprise. Everyone had something to say until they were asked to contribute more than words.

Macy Swanson raised a tentative hand, and Gabriel gave her the floor. Tanner leaned back in his chair, wondering what she planned on saying…and why he was so interested to hear it.

Chapter Two

"I'll volunteer to help find one of the people on the list. If anyone needs use of the library computers, they're available. Social media is probably a good place to start searching." She made quick eye contact with the people at the table, and when she got to Tanner, she faltered. Their gazes connected and she felt her cheeks flush.

Gabriel Everett sat down at the head of the big table. He looked too relieved when Macy volunteered. And she felt a little apprehensive. She wasn't a part of this group, of this town, or their lives. Every single day she woke up in Haven she felt like a fraud. She could buy boots, show up at church, even cook a decent dessert for the monthly potluck. But she was as far from country as a person could get.

And she'd never been a part of a community, not a tight-knit place like this. People asked questions, they prodded, they wanted to be involved in her life and have her involved in theirs. She'd never been that kind of person. She'd grown up in a sprawling neighborhood, but she hadn't known her neighbors.

So why in the world had she raised her hand to volunteer? Because Gabriel had looked like a lost giant standing at the end of the table waiting for someone to say something?

Now that she'd opened her mouth to volunteer, everyone was staring. Tanner Barstow, blue eyes and too-handsome face, wore a frown as he studied her from across the table. She glanced at Bea, hoping for a little moral support.

Bea patted her arm and smiled big. "Well, there you go. We're all sitting here stunned, and Macy is jumping right in. Gabriel, give us that list again so that Macy can write them down, and we can figure out who is doing what here. It seems to me that we don't have time to waste. We need that ranch."

"And what if we can't find those four people and the granddaughter?" Fletcher Snowden Phillips stood. He was tall, middle-aged, with thinning hair and a scowl that could have put off the most well-intentioned person.

Macy shivered in reaction to his growling voice. As a lawyer, Fletcher knew how to back people down. And she knew that he had long wanted the boys ranch closed. She found that hard to believe, considering his grandmother Luella Snowden Phillips, along with the Lone Star Cowboy League, Waco Chapter, had started the boys ranch. His own father, Tucker, had been the *reason* for the ranch. A neighboring rancher had helped put Tucker back on the straight and narrow, and later on, mother and son had done what they could to save other boys.

"What if these people have passed, or are too sick or just unwilling to come to this event Cyrus wanted us to plan?" Seth Jacobs, a rancher from closer to Waco, asked. Macy had met him at the boys ranch.

Harold Haverman tapped the pages of the will on the table and stood, sliding the papers back into a folder. "If you don't find the people he has asked you to find, well, we'll cross that bridge when we get to it."

"I think the will clearly states that the property will be turned into a strip mall." Gabriel shook his head as he made the observation.

"That's a mighty big strip mall," Tanner drawled in that low, easy voice of his. He grinned at Gabriel. "I find it hard to believe Cyrus would do that to his pride and joy."

"It isn't for us to say what Cyrus would or wouldn't have done," Beatrice chimed in. "We have to make sure that ranch becomes the property of the League because we have boys waiting to be a part of our program."

"I get that, Bea, but it seems a little like a wild-goose chase to me." Flint Rawlings, foreman of the boys ranch, swept a large hand through his dark blond hair and then settled his hat back on his head. He rested his gaze on Fletcher. "And, Fletch, don't get all excited. The boys ranch isn't going to come to an end if we don't get that property. We still have the Silver Star."

Fletcher shook his head and then clamped his mouth closed. It was well-known around town that Fletcher used his legal might against the ranch. No one really understood why.

Gabriel cleared his throat. "We have five people to find, if you include Cyrus's granddaughter, Avery."

"And who are they?" Beatrice prodded.

Gabriel picked up a piece of paper. "Avery Culpepper, the granddaughter, and then we have Samuel

Teller, Morton Mason, Edmond Grayson and Theodore Linley."

Bea coughed a little, and Macy saw her shoot a look in Tanner's direction. "Well, Gabriel, you should be able to help us find Theo."

Gabriel pushed the paper aside. Macy was lost. She didn't know these people or their stories. She waited, watching each person at the table as they reacted to the list.

"My grandfather and I haven't spoken in so long, I wouldn't recognize his voice on the phone. I'm not sure I'd know him if I saw him. And I doubt he wants to talk to me." Gabriel glanced around the room. "I have one volunteer."

"I'll look for Theodore Linley," Tanner offered into the silent room.

Gabriel gave a curt nod. "I appreciate that."

"I'll look for Avery Culpepper," Macy offered.

Next to her, Beatrice tapped her fingers on the table and hmm'ed. "Well, I have the most at stake. Or should I say, my kids do. I'll look for Samuel Teller and Morton Mason. It seems as if I might have a few emails or letters from former members. It might be easier than we think."

Flint, sitting closest to Gabriel, reached for the paper. "I guess I'll look for Mr. Grayson. That name is common, but I have a friend with the same last name."

Beatrice smiled big. "So, the good Lord willing…"

"And the creek don't rise," someone muttered from the other end of the table.

Bea shot the offending party a look. "I've been praying for a bigger place or for money to build more cabins. The church has been praying. God has opened this door, and I, for one, intend on going through it."

"Amen," Gabriel murmured. "When does the Triple C become the property of the boys ranch and the LSCL?"

Mr. Haverman looked at his notes. "Possession begins one month from the reading of the will. Although you understand if the stipulations of the will aren't met, you'll have to return the property and move the boys back to the Silver Star. And Miss Avery Culpepper will be allowed to move to her property in March. And, please, don't question me, because Cyrus had his reasons."

Gabriel closed his eyes and ran a hand over them. Finally he looked out over the group that had assembled. "And with that, we will adjourn the meeting. If any of you want to stay and plan how to proceed, feel free to use this room. I'm afraid I have another appointment."

With that, he picked up his briefcase and left.

Macy made eye contact with Bea. The other woman just shrugged and adjusted her horn-rimmed glasses but then turned her attention to Tanner.

"Well, Tanner?" Bea prodded.

The room had cleared, leaving only the four of them. Macy, Tanner, Flint and Bea. Tanner got up and headed for the coffeepot and Styrofoam cups.

"Coffee?" he offered.

He started pouring cups before anyone could answer.

"This Culpepper ranch is large?" Macy asked as she took the offered cup. She didn't mean to notice Tanner's hands, long-fingered, tanned, calloused, but when their fingers touched, she couldn't help it.

Flint laughed at the question, but his smile was genuinely friendly. "The Triple C is a big spread. The house has three wings. There are plenty of buildings. And there's room to grow."

Beatrice got up to make copies of the list of names. "And that property is going to be our new ranch. I'm just not willing to give up on this. Every day I get a call from the state. There aren't enough foster homes or residential facilities. Macy put Colby on the list last winter, and it took us several months to get him a bed. It breaks my heart each time we have to turn away a child in need of a home, or counseling."

Tanner stopped behind Beatrice and placed a hand on her shoulder. "We won't let you down, Bea."

He took one of the papers she'd copied and returned to his seat. Macy pulled out her phone and typed the name Avery Culpepper into the search engine. A slew of entries appeared. She held the phone up for the others to see.

"It isn't going to be easy, but it won't be that difficult. There are dozens of hits for the name Avery Culpepper. I'm sure you'll have the same experience with your names. And then it's a matter of tracking down the correct person."

"I hope it's that easy," Flint grumbled.

"Me, too." Bea stood. "I'm not sure what else we can do here today. I have a dozen boys waiting to be fed, and I guess some kind of chaos Tanner created before we left."

Tanner grinned. "Yeah, that's what I do, create chaos. But the kid whisperer, Macy, calmed them all down with a story."

Kid whisperer. She wished that were true. If it were

true, she wouldn't be a failure with her own nephew. As they stood to go, Tanner stepped in close.

"He'll survive this." He said it with conviction.

"I'm sorry?" She looked up, unsure what he meant.

"Colby," he continued. "I know you worry about him, but give it time. He'll come around."

"I hope you're right." She prayed he was right. Because she didn't want to lose her nephew. For Colby she would stay in Haven. She would manage to be the person he needed her to be in this small town with people who commented, gave advice and offered help.

What other choice did she have? She'd given up her life and her career in Dallas. She'd given up the fiancé who didn't support her decisions.

This was her new life.

As they left together, Tanner touched her back, a gesture that comforted. She was sure that was what he meant by the fleeting contact. But it did more than comfort her; it made her aware of his presence.

In all the months she'd been here, he'd struck her as a man who didn't get involved. He was a successful rancher and business owner. He sometimes showed up at the boys ranch. He rarely took time to socialize.

Today she was in a vulnerable place, worrying about Colby and missing her brother. Tomorrow she would be back to normal and Tanner's touch, his kind words, would make sense.

Tanner strode through the doors of the Haven Tractor and Supply. His sister, Chloe, looked up from the counter and smiled. He felt immediately on edge because she was wearing that look, the one that spelled trouble for him. She wanted something. And he'd probably give in and get it for her. If he could.

"Been busy?" he asked as he walked behind the counter. He saw that she'd been doodling on a piece of paper. Pictures of dresses. The wedding variety of dress. He cringed. She was twenty-four and old enough, but he didn't think she was ready. As an older brother he doubted he'd ever be ready to see her walked down the aisle, by either himself or their brother, Major Travis Barstow.

"Not real busy. Larry has a customer on the lot, looking at a tractor. Or a stock trailer. I'm not sure which." She tapped the pencil on the counter and sneaked a look at him.

He pretended not to notice, but he almost couldn't hide a smile. She was pretty, his sister. Dark hair in a ponytail, she was all country with beat-up boots, faded jeans. She made it all feminine with a lacy top she'd probably spent a day's wages on.

"Are you selling off steers this weekend?" She hopped up on a stool and slid the doodles under the cash register. Like he hadn't noticed.

"Are you buying wedding dresses?"

She turned a little pink. "No. I'm a girl. We dream about weddings."

"You've only been dating Russell for a few months."

Her smile dissolved. "He's a good guy, Tanner. He's made mistakes, but he's got a job, and he's trying to make things right."

"I know that. I'm willing to give him a chance, but I'm not willing to let him hurt you."

Her smile returned. "I've been thinking that maybe you could let him volunteer at the Silver Star. They're going to need help moving, and it would give you a chance to get to know him."

"I'll talk to Beatrice. But, Chloe, I'm not going to put up with nonsense when he's around the kids."

"I know and I appreciate that. Tanner, he made mistakes when he was young. His parents' divorce really upset him. He did things he shouldn't have. But that isn't who he is."

"He stole a truck and a stock trailer full of cattle."

"He was seventeen. He hasn't been that person in a long time."

"People in town have their suspicions."

Before he could finish, Chloe slid off the stool and closed the distance between them. Yeah, he was in trouble. She'd always known how to work him. With a soft smile, she kissed his cheek and then patted it.

"You're the best big brother a girl could have."

"And you always say that when you get what you want."

She didn't move away. Her blue eyes glistened with tears, and his own throat tightened in response because he knew she was going to drag them back into the past, into memories she didn't have because she'd been too young.

"You've been taking care of me for a long time," she started. "Since I was a baby you've been the one feeding me, changing my diapers and keeping me safe."

"How would you know? You were a baby."

"Travis told me. And Aunt May. She said she had a hard time getting you to let go and just be a kid. You were always the one. You took care of us. And then you took care of May."

"Do you have a point?" he asked, his voice more

gruff than he'd intended. It didn't seem to bother her. No, not his little sister. She smiled and dug her heels in, intent on some emotional rabbit trail.

"Yes, I have a point. Find someone to love, Tanner. You're not getting any younger, you know. And I'm past the age of really needing a caretaker."

"Thanks for that reminder of my advancing age."

She grinned at that. "It's the truth. You are getting a little long in the tooth. But, seriously, you'd make an amazing dad and a great husband. So why not let yourself be loved? Stop thinking you have to be there for everyone else, and let someone be there for you."

"Words of wisdom?"

She scooted around him and headed for the door. "I am wise. I'm also right. It's time for you to find a wife. Travis is happy in California. I'm eventually going to get married. And then you'll be alone in that castle you've built."

"It isn't a castle."

"It's your kingdom," she countered. "Fill it with kids."

She left, and he didn't have a thing to say in response to her lecture. It was almost closing time. He walked to the front door and watched as his salesman and mechanic, Larry, walked past the building to an old farm truck. The customer was old Joe Falkner, known to be worth millions. Joe still drove a truck he'd bought new a couple of decades ago. He lived in a house that appeared to be falling apart. But he raised some of the best Angus in the state.

He joined Larry as Joe drove off.

"Don't tell me Joe is thinking of getting a new stock trailer."

Larry laughed and pulled a stick of gum out of his pocket. He'd been trying to quit smoking for six months. So now he chewed gum. A lot of gum. He offered a piece to Tanner.

"Yeah, he's going to have to buy a trailer. The floor rotted out of his. The guy who normally fixes it said no more, he isn't fixing that trailer again."

"Did you close him on one?"

Larry shook his head. "He won't turn loose of a dime. He said in 1970-something he could get that trailer for, I don't know, a ridiculous amount."

"I guess if he decides to haul some cattle to auction, he'll come back and buy a trailer."

"Knowing Joe, he'll go hire some drovers and herd those cattle to the auction like they did a hundred years ago."

"Don't give him that idea." Tanner glanced at his watch. "I'm going to take a drive. You'll be here for a bit?"

"Yeah, anything you need me to do?"

"Yeah, pray. We've got six months to find some people, or old Cyrus Culpepper's place is going to be paved over."

"I'd heard rumors about a crazy will. You can't pave over that many acres, and Cyrus hated those types of developments."

"Tell that to his will."

Larry adjusted the bent-up cowboy hat he always wore. "He was an ornery old cuss. It's hard to tell what he was thinking, but I'm sure he had some kind of angle when he came up with this plan."

"I'd sure like to know what it was. If I don't get back, will you close up?"

"You got it, boss." Larry headed back to the building.

Tanner didn't really have a plan when he left, but he found himself heading up the drive of the Triple C. It wasn't too far from his own spread. When he pulled up, he saw another car in the driveway. He got out of his truck, surprised to see Macy sitting on the hood of her car looking at the old Culpepper place.

For a long minute he stood watching her. Her blond hair was pulled back with a headband, and sunglasses perched on the end of her nose. She looked out of place in jeans, boots and a plaid shirt, as if she was trying to fit, but she didn't. She was city, from her manicured nails to the way she stepped around mud to keep it from getting on those boots of hers.

He admired that she wanted to blend, that she wanted to transplant herself in this community for the sake of a little boy who had already lost too much.

Admiring was as far as he wanted to let his thoughts take him on a sunny day in October when his sister was looking at wedding dresses, his brother was currently on temporary duty somewhere in the Middle East and Cyrus had strung them all up by their toes, asking for something that might be impossible. "I came to pray," she finally said without turning to look at him.

The words took him by surprise, but they weren't uncomfortable the way they might have been if someone else had said them. She was simply stating a fact.

He closed the distance between them.

"I came to take a look around. I haven't been here in years. I don't know if anyone has been up here. Cyrus kept a loaded shotgun, and he made it pretty clear he'd shoot first and ask questions later." He grinned at the memory of the old guy.

"He didn't like people?"

He leaned a hip against the hood of her car, leaving a good bit of space between them. "I guess he liked people okay. He just didn't want anyone messing around up here. He must have liked people, because he's making a big donation to the LSCL Boys Ranch."

"He isn't making it easy."

"I guess that's true. But we'll work it out. Like most of us, Cyrus had baggage. I never knew he had a kid, let alone a granddaughter. I didn't know he'd lived at the ranch."

"There are several Avery Culpeppers in the area."

It hadn't taken her long to get started. He hadn't even thought about where to start his search for Theo Linley. He doubted Gabriel would be much help.

"We'll find them all," he assured her. Or maybe he was hoping to assure himself.

They sat in silence looking at the big house with the pillared front porch. There were three wings. Plenty of space for kids to run and be kids. He'd looked over the will, and it said they could go ahead and begin moving. It would take weeks to get the process started. There would be supplies to purchase, as well as volunteers to organize. A place like this meant more of everything. More staff. More furniture. More food. More time. But it would be worth it.

It would be good to have the boys in this house so they could celebrate Christmas in their new home.

"I should be going." She slid off the hood of her car.

"Me, too." He paused, watching as she dug her keys out of her pocket. "Have you thought about what I asked you earlier? About reading to the boys?"

She glanced away from him, her hand going up to

brush strands of blond hair from her face as the wind picked up a bit. "I don't know."

"Something troubling you?"

"No, not at all." But the worried look in her green eyes said that something about the offer did worry her.

"It isn't something you have to decide on today. The library as it is will be packed up and moved over here. We just got it put together. Now we'll have to take it all apart and do it all over again."

She moved to her car, and her hand settled on the door. "I can help with that, with getting things packed and then getting the new library organized."

"That would be good. I hate to overwhelm you, since you're new to the area, but you might have noticed if we get a willing volunteer, we use them."

"I don't scare easily. And I don't mind helping."

He reached past her to open the car door, the way Aunt May had taught him. A hint of something soft and floral, like wild roses on a spring day, caught and held him a little longer than was necessary or safe.

Chloe would have told him to stop living his life off a list he'd made twenty years ago. He couldn't. That list had served him well. It had taken him from the gutter to the life he had now, and someday he'd find a woman to share that life with him.

He closed the car door and watched Macy drive away in her little economy car, and he smiled. She wasn't at all the woman he was looking for. But something about her made him think about finding someone.

Chapter Three

Macy juggled her purse, book bag and keys in order to get her front door unlocked. As much as she wanted to just crash, she had more work to do and she was going to need a cup of coffee to get her through the rest of the day. It had been a few days since the reading of Cyrus Culpepper's will. She'd been substituting at the Haven high school, so she hadn't had much time to think about finding Avery Culpepper or even going out to the Silver Star.

Entering the house, she was met by silence. It was peaceful. But lonely. Colby should be here. He should be running to the kitchen to grab a snack, plopping in front of the TV to watch his favorite afternoon shows.

But then, in a perfect world her brother and sister-in-law would be here to greet him. Macy would still be in Dallas. Maybe she'd even be planning her wedding.

Instead she was standing in her brother's kitchen fighting the familiar doubts that had assailed her since she'd learned that he'd named her guardian of his son. In the beginning she'd believed they would make it, she and Colby. His anger had proved her wrong. It had proved she wasn't a parent, or even something close to a parent. She was twenty-eight, single, and hadn't even begun the process of thinking about kids.

Grant's and Cynthia's deaths had changed everything. For Colby. And for her.

It had amazed Macy that her brother had found his way to the small town of Haven. Their mother, Nora, had insisted he could do better if he stayed in the city. He would have moved up, made more, had a nicer home than the remodeled craftsman house with its large front porch, complete with porch swing.

Grant and Cynthia had been happy in Haven.

She worried that she didn't have it in her to be the small-town librarian, mother of Colby.

She turned on the coffeemaker and found her favorite mug. As she waited for the water to heat, she stood at the window and looked out at the small but wooded lot behind the house. Not a high-rise in sight. No sirens in the distance. Not a sound could be heard.

She missed Colby.

The ready light flashed, and she put her mug under the spout and pushed the button. Coffee poured into her mug. She opened the book bag that she'd brought home from school, and as she pulled out her organizer she noticed another book. She tugged it out, trying to decide where she'd picked it up and when. Yes, she'd been distracted today. She didn't think she'd been *that* distracted.

A note fell out of the book. She picked up the yellow piece of paper. A creepy, crawly feeling shivered down her spine.

The book was a middle grade book about a ranch. There was nothing remarkable about the title or the story. She set it down and turned her attention to the note. The feeling of apprehension eased.

Could you read this to the boys? Thanks, Tanner.

How in the world had the book gotten in her bag? Maybe when she'd stepped out of the room to make copies? But surely one of the students would have told her. She thought about the fifteen English literature students. No, they wouldn't have told her. All that aside, why would Tanner Barstow have a sudden desire to get her involved with the boys at the ranch? She couldn't even raise her own nephew.

Every single day she questioned why she was in Haven. She'd given up her career, her friends and her fiancé to be here for a little boy who only wanted his parents back.

She slid the note back into the book.

Maybe Tanner thought that if she spent more time with children, she would grow into the role of Colby's mom. That made sense because Tanner seemed to be a natural with children. He'd practically raised his own sister. He was the type who would get married, have a half dozen kids and never miss a step.

Macy worried that she didn't have that parenting gene. There were days that she loved the idea of raising her nephew, of someday being the person he ran to at the end of school, eager to tell her about his day. There were more nights that she lay awake, scared to death that she would never be able to fill that place in his life, and that he would never want her to be that person.

Beatrice had told her to take her time. In family therapy she'd learned to give him space and to not react when he pushed her away. It was hard, because every time he pushed her away, her heart took it personally.

When it hurt, like it did just then, she reminded herself that her pain was nothing compared to Colby's.

Her coffee was finished. She put a lid on the thermal mug and grabbed the book Tanner had left for her. She had thirty minutes to get to the ranch. She'd promised Bea she would put some finishing touches on the ranch library, and she wanted to apply for another grant.

When Macy pulled up to the main house of the Silver Star, Beatrice's car was in the drive. Flint, the ranch foreman, was just walking down the front steps. He tipped his hat in greeting but went on, heading for the barn. Macy got out of her car and strode up to the house. Beatrice met her at the front door.

"Hey, Macy, I wasn't expecting you today."

Macy held the book out, and Bea took it, perplexed, her eyes narrowed as she studied it.

"What's this for?" Bea asked.

"I thought you might know. Tanner must have brought it to the school." She handed over the note.

"You didn't see him leave it?"

She shook her head. "No. I found it in the book bag I carry."

Bea motioned her inside. "That doesn't sound like Tanner. He doesn't do things willy-nilly like that."

"He asked me if I would read to the boys. I told him I'd have to think about it. I thought maybe he left it, hoping I'd say yes."

Bea led the way to the big kitchen at the back of the house. "Would you like a cup of tea?"

"That would be nice."

Bea put the teapot on to boil, and then she leaned against the counter, still giving the book her full attention. "Tanner should be here in a bit. We're going to see what we can find on our missing ranch alumni. You can ask him if and why he would leave a book for you. But if he did do this, don't feel as if you have to do what he's asking. I think you already do enough."

"I love doing what I can for the ranch, Bea. It's my way of giving back. You all rescued us. I'm not sure what would have happened to Colby if he hadn't gotten a spot here."

"I think you would have found him help. Go easy on yourself, Macy. Colby isn't the only one who has suffered. You lost your brother."

Unexpected tears burned at the backs of her eyes, and her throat constricted. Macy nodded, because if she opened her mouth, she might cry.

Bea placed a comforting hand on her arm. "Give yourself time to grieve. I think you have a tendency to go full throttle, fixing things. Some situations need time."

"I know. I'm just afraid. What if I can't be the person Colby needs me to be? What if he never gets over being angry? Eleanor Mack and I have discussed this several times. We understand anger and sadness at the loss of his parents, but it seems like the anger is magnified, and we don't know why."

Bea poured water in two cups. The fragrant aroma of herbal tea filled the air with hints of cinnamon and clove.

"I would agree with Eleanor. Colby is an especially angry little boy. But give it time. We'll figure out what is going on. Once we get to the root of the problem, we can start working on making the two of you a family. I know you're afraid you can't do this. We all feel that way when we are looking a problem head-on and thinking that this is our future. In time you come to a place where you realize you've survived it, and that, through it all, God made you a little stronger."

"Thanks, Bea. I hope you're right."

Bea chuckled, "Haven't you been told? I'm always right."

"And if she isn't, she'll find a way to convince you she is." Katie Ellis, in her twenties and receptionist of the boys ranch, entered the room. She got a cup and added a tea bag before pouring water.

"Katie, you know I'm always right." Bea pushed the sugar jar to the pretty blonde receptionist. "Oh, did I tell you that Pastor Walsh is coming by for Bible study with the boys? He has a new video series he wants to do with them."

Katie turned a little pink at the mention of the Haven Community Church pastor. "I'll make sure the meeting room is ready."

"That would be good. And you might offer to help him out." Bea grinned as she made the suggestion.

"I would, but I have to do laundry tonight." Katie headed for the door with her tea. "I'm going to head home. Is there anything else you need?"

"Nothing at all," Bea called out to her. And then to Macy, "That girl. Pretty as they come and sweet, but she's never really dated."

Dating, the last thing Macy wanted to discuss. She smiled and reached into her purse for the information she'd found on the many Avery Culpeppers.

"I found all of this last night. Maybe one of these will be Avery Culpepper, granddaughter. A few of them even live in Texas."

"You've been busy," Bea said as she looked over the list.

"I don't have much to do in the evenings."

Bea looked at her over the top of her glasses. "That's going to change when we get Colby home to you."

"I hope so, Bea. I really hope."

"It'll happen sooner than you know. I realize the two of you had a rough visit when he tried the weekend pass. But that was a big event, going home for the first time since coming here. There are a lot of memories, a lot he has to deal with. We'll try another pass soon, but for now we'll stick with day passes. He might do better with a few hours just to let him get used to being at home with you."

Macy must have made a face, because Bea patted her hand. "And that will give you a chance to get used to being the mom. He's going to need you, Macy."

She nodded, unable to give voice to her concerns. Booted footsteps interrupted the conversation. A moment later Tanner appeared in the kitchen. He was tall and broad-shouldered, ruggedly handsome, and for the better part of the year Macy had lived in Haven, he'd ignored her.

She could think of several reasons. Folks in small towns weren't always eager to welcome outsiders. Or maybe he didn't like that she'd made a mess of her relationship with Colby. He was protective of the kids on the ranch. She couldn't fault him for that.

"Are we having a meeting about our missing alumni?" He cut a path to the coffeepot and poured himself a cup, taking a whiff before adding sugar.

"It's a couple of hours old, probably a little on the bitter side," Bea informed him. "And, yes, an impromptu meeting. Macy got the surprise you left in her bag."

He turned, eyes narrowed as he looked from Bea to Macy. From that look, she knew he hadn't left the book.

Tanner leaned against the counter, not sure what to say to the two women who obviously thought he should know what they were talking about. He barely knew Macy Swanson. And he didn't make a habit of forming relationships with parents of the boys at the ranch. "Surprise?"

Macy pushed a book across the counter. He reached for it and gave it a long look. "Never seen it before."

She handed him a note with handwriting that definitely wasn't his. "This was attached."

He shook his head. "Again, I've never seen it before, and that isn't my writing."

"But you asked me to read to the boys." Macy's voice trailed off at the end, and she took the book back from him. "Who else would have done this?"

"Interesting question. But I just saw Pastor Walsh on the front lawn because he was told the boys want Bible studies on Friday afternoons. That's the first I've heard of that. Not that our boys aren't good kids, but they don't typically reach out to the local pastor wanting more church. More often than not, they complain about Sunday and Wednesday services."

Bea rubbed a finger across her chin and hmm'ed. "You know, I got a note next to my phone, like someone had left a message after talking to Pastor Walsh. It said he was interested in spending more time here with the boys and thought that perhaps Katie Ellis could help lead a Bible study with the boys. Of course I called him and asked when he'd like to do this."

"And here I was going to blame you, Bea." Tanner sat down next to the older woman.

"Well, it wasn't me, Tanner." She gave him an arch look over the top of her glasses.

He winked at Bea and then glanced at Macy. She sat with her gaze lowered, focusing on the book and not on him.

That gave him a few seconds to study the woman sitting across from him. A curtain of blond hair fell forward, slightly hiding her expression. She was slim and graceful; even her hands seemed delicate. Delicate but capable.

He cleared his throat and cleared the thoughts from his mind. "But now that you have the book, are you interested in reading to the boys? I've lost track of the ages, but I think we have several under the age of ten who would enjoy a little quality time with you. Colby being one of them."

"I'll read to the boys. We'll combine reading with a lesson on how to use the library, and they can also help me start packing it up."

Bea clapped her hands together and shot him a beaming smile. "That sounds like a great idea. And I think this will give you some real quality time with Colby. He does love your stories. He talks about them, you know."

Macy's expression changed, her teeth worrying her bottom lip. "He always seems to draw back just as I think we're getting closer."

"Maybe he's afraid of getting close?" Tanner offered. "I remember when we first came to Aunt May.

We'd been on our own, and suddenly there was this woman wanting to be involved in every moment of our lives. It wasn't easy to let her in."

"But he wasn't used to being on his own. He had parents who loved him and cared for him."

Bea sighed at the reminder.

"Yes, and then they were gone and you were there trying to fill their shoes. It hasn't been easy for either of you," Bea said, her arm around Macy's shoulders. "Now, Tanner, what brings you to the ranch this late in the day?"

"I wanted to arrange for the group of us looking for the lost residents to meet for dinner tomorrow evening at the steak house. I'm buying. We can look at any notes we've found and see what we need to do next."

"What time?"

"Six okay for everyone?"

"That sounds good," Bea said as she gathered their cups.

Tanner headed for the door, but then he remembered one other item on his list. "Oh, I forgot something."

Bea set the cups back down on the counter. "What is it?"

"Chloe wants to see if Russell can have a job helping out around here. I understand if the answer is no."

Bea laughed at that, taking him by surprise. "That girl can still wrap you around her little finger."

"Yes, she has a gift," Tanner acknowledged. "And she thinks I need to get to know the man she plans on marrying."

"We'll find him something to do. And try not to worry. We all know Russell. We know his past. After all, Tanner, the boy spent six months here."

"Of course. I just don't want any problems for you or the ranch."

"Don't you worry about us, we know how to handle young men like Russell."

Yes, if anyone knew how to handle Russell, it would be Bea. As he started to turn to go, his gaze landed on Macy. He didn't know what to say to her about the book and the note. Someone obviously wanted to push her into spending more time with Colby and the other boys at the ranch. Maybe Bea? Could even have been Flint or Jake.

Maybe he would ask Jake. He'd been there yesterday. Maybe he'd overheard Tanner ask Macy to help out, and he'd taken off with the idea in order to get her over here more often.

But the book and story time were low priority. The LSCL Boys Ranch needed Cyrus Culpepper's property. Still, as Tanner left the Silver Star, the Culpepper place wasn't on his mind. Instead his thoughts had turned to Macy Swanson and the strange turn of events that had her front and center in his life.

Chapter Four

The print of the grant Macy had typed up blurred a bit as she stared at it. She rubbed her eyes and leaned back in her chair. She'd been at the Silver Star since shortly after three, and she had three hours to go until the dinner at the steak house. If she hadn't agreed to the plan yesterday, she would back out and go home. But she had volunteered, and she wasn't canceling on people who were counting on her.

Things might seem a little brighter if she hadn't woken up that morning to a car that wouldn't start. She'd walked to school from her house. After work, Katie Ellis had given her a ride to the ranch. Macy would have to see if the other woman was still around to give her a ride back to town.

All in all it had been a long day. The kind of day that deserved another cup of coffee. Or a really long nap. And she was getting neither of those things. Instead she was sipping on a cup of herbal tea that Beatrice had brought her, something to soothe her, she'd been told.

A light rap on the door interrupted her musings. She smiled at the woman standing in the opening, her auburn hair pulled back. A floral shirt stretched tight over her belly. For a few months Josie Markham had tried to hide her pregnancy. Or maybe the young widow had been in denial. Her husband, a county deputy, had been killed in the line of duty. Only after his death did Josie learn that she was pregnant.

The two of them, Josie and Macy, had bonded immediately. They were both grieving, both trying to figure out the next step in their lives.

"Are you busy?" Josie asked as she stepped into the room and lowered herself into a chair. She was petite and even now seemed to be all belly.

"No, not really. I'm writing a new grant for a playground. But I have to decide how to word it. I'm trying to have faith that we'll get the Culpepper place. That changes things a bit."

"I guess that would complicate the grant process."

"Yes, a bit." Macy slid the grant paperwork into the filing cabinet and locked the drawer. "How are you feeling?"

Josie shrugged, but she briefly looked away and dashed a finger under her eye. A sign she wasn't as great as the chipper smile she always managed to show the world might indicate.

"I'm good." She sighed, and her hand went to her belly. "Good, meaning I'm waking up each morning. I'm moving forward, even though sometimes I feel like I'm stuck in quicksand."

"Josie, I'm so sorry." Macy reached for Josie's hand and gave her fingers a light squeeze. "If you need anything…"

The smile reappeared. "I know. And the same goes

for you. We're quite a pair, aren't we? Neither of us planned parenthood this way. How's Colby doing?"

"I'm not sure. When I see him here, he seems fine. But when I tried to take him home, he was lost and then angry."

"He has been through so much for someone so young. Give him time."

"It's been a year, Josie. What if he needs more than I can give him?"

"What do you mean?"

Macy closed her eyes just briefly. What did she mean? How could she put these thoughts into words? "I worry that I'm not the right person to raise him. Would he be better if there was someone else, and I just went away?"

Josie leaned forward and placed a hand on her arm. "Oh, Macy, don't. He needs you. He might be pushing you away, but in time he'll let you in."

"I hope so. And if that isn't the case, I hope God will show me what our next step is."

"Colby was always a good little guy." Josie sat for a long moment, looking out the window of the tiny office Macy used. "Maybe there's something else, something more. Does he say anything in therapy or their group sessions?"

"Not really. They've had a hard time getting him to open up about that night. I understand. Sometimes I'd like to brush it under the rug and pretend it didn't happen. But he's been stuck in the 'anger' stage of grief for so long. I just worry we won't get him to acceptance."

"And on top of that worry, now we have Cyrus's will to contend with. I don't know why his lawyer didn't try to talk him out of it."

"Do you think he could have talked him out of it?" Macy asked, already knowing the answer.

"Not a bit. And now I have to run. I'm helping Abby and John Garrett with the boys in their cabin. We're having a cookout and game night. But Bo Harrington is attending, and his son, Christopher, is already a pill without his parents there to make it worse."

Macy knew a little backstory, that Christopher Harrington was sixteen and spoiled. The state juvenile office had placed him at the ranch, and his parents were still determined to get him out.

"Have fun. I heard he waxed the windows of Abby's car. And he's pulled a couple of the other boys into his antics."

Josie groaned as she stood. "He's rotten. I think he has potential if his parents will learn to allow him to suffer consequences. See you later. And let me know how it goes with the meeting and the big hunt."

"Of course I will." She smiled and waved to her friend. She had thirty minutes to work in the library. She wanted to start organizing things for the move. With the goal of moving at the end of the month, Bea was in overdrive, trying to get everyone and everything organized.

The library would be one of the easiest rooms to pack. It was fairly new and already somewhat in order. The rest of the ranch, she shuddered to think of that process. Decades of accumulation and living and only a month to box it all up.

As she wandered about the lovely old room with the high ceilings and dark stained woodwork, she heard footsteps in the hall. Light footsteps. Not the heavy booted footsteps of one of the hands or the soft swish of Bea's sensible shoes.

She turned and caught sight of a slip of a boy, his

dark hair mussed and his sneakers scuffing back and forth on the wood floor, as if he wasn't sure of his welcome. She knelt and held out her arms.

Colby ran into her embrace.

"Hey, sweet guy, what's up?" She wrapped her arms around him, wishing she could take away all of his pain, all of his anger. She would. She'd do it in a heartbeat because she knew she could process it, figure it out and move on. She had been moving on for the past year. Losing her brother, Grant. Losing her fiancé, her job.

But gaining Colby.

If only she could find a way to help him move on.

He shuddered in her arms, and his hand raised to swipe at tears rolling down his cheeks, dampening her sleeve. She tried to pull him back against her, but he stiffened, unwilling to have the embrace a second longer.

"Are you okay?" She stayed on her knees, her hands on his arms.

He nodded, but his green eyes swam with tears he was fighting to hold back. She bit down on her lip, trying to think of the right words. A mom should know what to say. A mom would know how to help him. She closed her eyes and admitted her failings in this area.

"Colby, I want to help you. I want to make it all better. If you could just tell me."

He shook his head, but he stepped a little closer.

"I love you," she whispered close to his ear. She brushed a kiss across his head, and he didn't move away.

"I love you, Aunt Macy." With those words her heart grabbed hold of hope.

"Did you sneak away from the cabin?"

He nodded and again swiped at tears that threatened to fall.

"Did someone upset you or hurt you?" Stupid question. Of course he was upset and hurt. But was this a new hurt or lingering pain?

It was like trying to put together a puzzle, but without all of the pieces. How she wanted all of the pieces! She wanted him whole. Sometimes she saw glimpses of the Colby she'd known before the accident. But the glimpses were fleeting.

He sat down on the floor in front of her, and she took that as an invitation and sat next to him.

What would a mom do? She desperately wanted to think like a mom, be a mom. She scooted close, but she didn't put her arms around him. She waited, knowing he needed time.

"Diego called me a big baby."

Diego, not much older than Colby. But with a different story and different baggage to work through.

"He's wrong," she told her nephew. "You're tough. Really tough."

"Ben took up for me. He told Diego to be nice, but Diego said that I'm not nice to you."

"You are nice to me." She covered his hand with hers. "We're going to make it through this."

"Because we're family now. That's what Eleanor says."

Eleanor Mack was counselor and house mother of Cabin One. Macy smiled and told herself to thank the other woman.

"Yes, we're family." She wanted to hold him. He smelled of the outdoors, of hay and livestock. He had red cheeks from playing in the sun. He was everything to her.

"I have to go." He stood, looking down at her with

such a serious expression. For a moment she saw his father in him. Grant's seriousness. Her heart ached at the thought. "I'll walk you back."

He reached for her hand. It might as well have been her heart.

"Eleanor says I can have a pass to go to church on Sunday."

"I like that idea." Macy glanced down at the little man leading her through the house.

"Me, too. Do you think you can tell me another story?"

"I'm sure I can."

"Ben says you're going to read stories to us. He said he'd come with me."

She surprised herself by smiling. "That's fine."

"He's not too old for stories?" Colby asked as they walked out the front door. It was warm for the first week of October, but a light breeze blew, bringing country scents of cut grass, livestock and drying leaves.

"No. We're never too old for stories."

"That's good." They walked along the path to Cabin One, Colby swinging his hand that held hers. "Ben said we're going to move to another ranch. I don't know if any of us want to move. We like it here."

"But moving can sometimes be good. There will be more room for more boys at the new ranch."

Colby stopped walking and looked up at her, his green eyes narrowed against the glare of the sun. "But if they come here, it means there's something wrong in their homes."

"That might be true, Colby. But it's good that there's a place for them to go."

He continued walking, his hand still holding tight to hers. "But it would be better if moms and dads…"

"If they never went away?" she asked quietly.

He nodded, but he didn't answer.

"You're right, that would be better." She kept walking, trying hard not to give in to the tears burning her eyes. "I'm not going anywhere."

He didn't answer.

She left Colby with Eleanor. That moment, walking away from him, was as painful as the first day she'd left him at the ranch. The difference was that this time he hugged her goodbye. That first day he'd walked away without a word, without even looking back.

That parting hug gave her hope.

When she got back to the main house, Katie Ellis was waiting to give her a ride to the meeting where they would hopefully find that it would be no trouble to track down a few men who hadn't been seen or heard from in decades.

"How was Colby?" Katie asked as they pulled up to the restaurant.

The Candle Light, Haven's claim to fine dining, was on the main road. The building with the stone exterior had a long, covered porch with rocking chairs and potted plants. The parking lot was crowded. Typical for a Friday night in Haven.

"He's good," she answered Katie. "He was upset with Diego, but that's to be expected when you have so many kids living under one, or three, roofs. He hugged me goodbye."

Katie pulled the keys out of the ignition and gave her a quick and easy smile. "He's such a sweet boy, and he does love you."

"I know. And I love him. I hope he knows how much."

They got out and headed for the entrance to the restaurant. A dark blue Ford truck pulled up to the building. Macy knew that truck. She knew the man getting out, adjusting the cowboy hat he wore so naturally.

And it was just as natural to take a second look. But that was all she was doing, looking.

Tanner tipped his hat to the two ladies standing on the sidewalk of the Candle Light.

"Looks as if we're the first to arrive," he pointed out for no good reason. "I have the back room reserved, so we won't have to answer a million questions. I know people in town want to know what is going on. Until we have real answers, I'd prefer to keep things quiet."

Katie stepped through the door he opened for them, leaving Macy to slide in, brushing against his arm. He leaned in a little, just enough to catch the scent of wildflowers. "We've been getting calls at the ranch," Katie responded as he led them through the already crowded restaurant. "I'm not sure what to tell people."

"Tell them we'll release a statement to the local paper."

He stopped at the door to the private meeting room to wait for Macy. She'd stopped to say hello to the Macks, counselors from Silver Star, who were having a rare evening out. They waved when they spotted him.

He'd lived in this small town long enough to know that an innocent gesture had just been turned into a connection between himself and Macy. Because he looked like a man waiting for a woman, not a man merely holding the door the way he'd been taught.

He disliked small-town gossip, the constant speculation, pairing people up, marrying them off if they were seen having a cup of coffee or even walking in the same store. A few years back he'd dated Nina, a secretary at Fletcher Snowden Phillips's law office. She'd left town for a job in Houston. Neither of them had felt the need to keep the relationship going.

But the town had practically had them married off.

Macy parted from the Macks and hurried to join him.

"You didn't have to wait," she assured him as she slipped past him into the meeting room.

"I didn't mind."

She glanced up, her smile tipping her lips and crinkling at the corners of her eyes. "Oh, I think you did. You looked cornered, standing there with the door held open."

"I'm not sure why you think that," he countered, his hand going to her back to guide her to the table. There was an easy back-and-forth between himself and the woman who had taken him by surprise several times lately.

It was easy to touch her. Too easy.

He pulled a chair out for her. She accepted the gesture, sitting and scooting herself in as the door opened, and they were joined by Gabriel Everett, Beatrice and Flint. Fletcher followed them in. Tanner hadn't expected to see him at this meeting. It seemed the local lawyer had developed a habit of showing up uninvited.

It wasn't that Tanner disliked the other man. It was just that Fletcher did things that got under a person's skin. Although he should have felt a connection to the boys ranch, he seemed more often to be in favor of shutting the place down. He found fault with the boys, tried to pin petty crimes on the kids and turn them into juvenile delinquents, and he had opposed several grants that Macy had gotten for improvements.

It stood to reason that if Fletcher could find a way to keep them from getting a bigger property, he would. Or maybe he'd like to see them move after all. Tanner thought there might be a legal matter that would turn the Silver Star property over to Fletcher if the boys ranch closed or was no longer there.

Before he could say anything, a waitress entered with glasses of ice water and a coffeepot. She smiled big as she surveyed the small group, but then she went to work, handing out water, filling cups and setting menus on the table.

After she left, Gabriel pulled a piece of paper out of his pocket. "I guess this isn't a meeting of the LSCL, so we don't have to call to order. Fletcher is here because he thought we might need his advice."

Gabriel shot the lawyer a look that said he didn't buy it. But Fletcher ignored the glance. He was probably used to making enemies.

Beatrice squeezed the lemon into her water and stirred, the spoon clanking against the edge of the glass. "I haven't had a chance to start digging too much. But I do have some information on a few of our men. I'm sorry, Gabriel. I don't know much about your grandfather."

Gabriel's slim smile completely disappeared. "Yeah, neither do I. In the past we've looked, but we haven't been able to locate him. And after a while we stopped trying."

"I'm sorry." Bea stopped stirring. "Gabriel, it's no

shame that your grandfather was at the ranch. Tanner's brother, Travis, was there, and look how he turned out. The ranch has a purpose. It turns lives around and gives young men an opportunity to make something of themselves."

"Not every life can be saved." Fletcher said it quietly, smoothly. "And some just bring trouble to our town. I'd like for Haven to be more than the community that supports a ranch for troubled boys."

Flint practically growled. "Fletcher, I can show you to the door if your purpose here is to cause problems."

Fletcher held up hands of surrender. "I'm not. I'm just making a statement."

Flint picked up his menu. "Keep your statements to yourself."

"I've found several promising leads on Avery Culpepper," Macy offered.

The waitress returned, a notepad in hand. They ordered and she left again, closing the door behind her.

Macy stopped twirling the silver bangle bracelet that circled her slim wrist. "I have an Avery in Dallas, one in Austin and two in Houston. Those are the most promising leads, although I've also found one or two out of state."

Beatrice went next. "I think Samuel Teller will be easy to find. I have a letter from about ten years ago. It seems he did turn his life around, and he wanted to contribute to the ranch." She made a point to stare Fletcher down until he turned a little bit red. "I tried to call the number in the letter, and it's been disconnected. But I think it won't take long to locate him."

A phone rang. Katie pushed aside the notebook she'd been taking notes in and dug around in her purse. She gave them all an apologetic smile and hurried out of the room. When she returned, it was to gather up her things.

"I have to leave. My cousin is in crisis. Macy, maybe Bea or someone can give you a ride home?"

"Of course. For that matter, I can walk. It's only a few blocks, and the weather is great."

"I'll see you all Sunday at church."

She left, and the meeting continued until their steaks arrived. An hour later they were leaving. To Tanner it seemed as if they had a chance. And that meant the ranch had the chance to expand and bring in more boys.

Bea had left early, but she'd parted letting them know she'd had a phone call that day asking her to take another boy. She'd put the child on the waiting list because she didn't have a spare bed, and she already had close to twenty boys waiting.

Tanner was climbing into his truck when he noticed Macy walking away from the restaurant. He started the engine and shifted into Reverse, pulling out and then slowing to idle next to her. He rolled the window down. She stopped walking and looked up at him.

"It looks like rain."

"It's a five-minute walk."

He could have shifted back into Drive and gone on, but he didn't. "Where's your car?"

"It wouldn't start this morning, so Katie picked me up."

"I can take a look at it."

She stood there at the side of the road, the wind coming up and whipping her blond hair across her face. She brushed it back and glanced up at the sky. A light mist had started to fall. He'd been guessing about the rain.

"I guess I'll take that ride." She headed around the front of the truck.

He leaned across the seat to open the door for her. "I don't typically predict the weather with that kind of accuracy."

She smiled at that, brushing her hands down rain-dampened arms. It wasn't cold, but in the air-conditioned truck, she probably felt chilled. He reached in the backseat for a jacket and handed it to her.

"Thank you." She wrapped it around her shoulders and pulled her hair free. "Are you as good with cars as you are with the weather?"

"Almost." He glanced her way and saw her hand wipe at her cheeks.

Weather and cars he could handle. Tears were another thing altogether. Especially when those tears were the quiet, stoic kind that made him want to charge to the rescue.

He reminded himself that she'd accepted his offer for a ride, and she was willing to let him look at her car. She hadn't asked to be rescued, and he didn't need to get tangled up in something that would hit a big dead end as soon as she realized she wasn't a small-town girl.

He glanced her way as another tear slid down her cheek. The last thing he wanted to do was get tangled up in something that was temporary. He didn't want to push his way into her life only to find out she wasn't going to stay in Haven.

Those tears were a pretty good—or maybe a pretty bad—sign.

Chapter Five

Macy blamed the rain for the tears slipping unbidden down her cheeks. Just a few drops, easily brushed away. If it hadn't rained, she wouldn't have cried. She would have taken the five-minute walk home, maybe a little melancholy, but she wouldn't have let the tears slip loose.

It wouldn't have been so bad if she hadn't been in Tanner's truck, knowing he had glanced her way and seen her brush the tears away. At least he didn't comment. She was glad for his silence.

What would she have said if he'd asked why she was crying?

It seemed as if, lately, every time it rained, something bad happened. She shook off the thought because it didn't allow for faith. And she had faith. But it had been raining the night the hospital called asking if she was related to Grant Swanson. It had been raining the night Bill broke their engagement. And it had rained the night she'd come to terms with the reality that she couldn't help Colby.

All coincidence, of course. It had been a rainy year in Texas. The news had covered the stories of downpours and floods. So her small story of heartbreak and rainstorms would mean nothing to the outside world.

The truck slowed and drove into the driveway of the craftsman-style home that had belonged to Grant and Cynthia. Tanner pulled next to her car and parked. For a long moment they sat there in silence, neither of them looking at the other. Finally she shrugged out of his jacket and reached for the door handle. Belatedly she grabbed the dessert she'd brought home from the restaurant.

"Thank you for the ride home. I guess it did rain."

In the dark interior of the truck his teeth flashed white in his face. "Just a little. I'll take a look at your car while I'm here."

He was out of the truck before she could tell him it wasn't necessary.

"You don't have to do this," she told him as he headed for her car.

"I don't mind. It's probably something simple. Go ahead and release the hood."

She opened the driver's-side door and pulled the release. From under the hood she heard him saying something about a hose.

"Go ahead and start it," he called out.

She turned the key, and the car roared to life without a sputter. Tanner pushed the hood down and walked around to join her.

"What was it?"

"Do you always leave your car unlocked?" he asked as she got out, closing the door behind her.

"Sometimes. Why?"

"Someone pulled a hose loose."

"Maybe it just came loose?" She hoped that was the case. It didn't make sense that anyone would tamper with her car. It definitely left her feeling unsettled.

"It didn't just come loose, Macy. Someone unhooked it. I know Haven is a small town and we like to think we're insulated from real-world problems, but crime does happen here. Make sure you lock the car. And your house."

"I will." She lifted the bag she'd brought from the Candle Light. "Join me for dessert. It isn't much, but since you're standing in the rain fixing my car, I should offer something."

The invitation had slipped out, surprising him. Surprising her.

"I should go," he started. And then he glanced at his watch. "What did you get?"

She grinned at the question. "The giant chocolate turtle cheesecake. It sounded great, and then I couldn't eat it."

"I can't turn down chocolate turtle cheesecake. Do you have coffee?"

"Of course."

"I'm in."

She led him inside, flipping on lights as they went. The house was quiet, but empty without Colby. There were times that it felt like home. But it was still Grant and Cynthia's home. Their furniture, their photographs and their pictures on the walls.

In the kitchen she started the coffee. When she turned, Tanner was pulling plates out of the cabinet.

"You seem to know where to find things better than I do."

He pulled open a drawer and handed her a fork. "I visited a few times. My sister and Cynthia were friends. Grant kept the LSCL informed on school functions and needs in the community that he was aware of through the school."

"I feel like a visitor here," she admitted, and then she was surprised by another round of tears. She brushed away the moisture and turned from his steady, curious gaze. "I'm sorry, I don't know what's wrong with me tonight."

"You lost your brother, your sister-in-law and what was probably a settled life in Dallas."

Not to mention her fiancé. But she was starting to see that as more of a near miss than a loss. If a man wasn't willing to make changes for a child in need, well, she didn't need that man.

"Yes, I suppose. It might feel different if Colby was here, if we were making ourselves into a family. I know that's what Grant wanted, and yet, here I am, and Colby is at the ranch. And the house still feels like their house, like I'm borrowing it. It feels as if they should be coming home any minute, and I'll go back to my life, and Colby will come home and be happy again."

"I'm sorry." He said it softly, and it wasn't a platitude, just a simple acknowledgment of her pain.

"Me, too."

"Make it your own," he countered. "Maybe it's time to pack up what was theirs and make this a home for you and Colby."

"They said to go slow."

"It's been a year. I'm not a therapist, but I think

Colby needs to be allowed to move on, too. Maybe it would help him to do this with you. The two of you could go shopping together for new things."

She poured them each a cup of coffee, and he cut the cheesecake into two pieces. They sat down together at the island in the center of the kitchen.

For a few minutes they ate, and she thought about his suggestion. "It might work, you know. If we did this as a team."

"Talk to Bea and to the Macks," he suggested.

"I will."

The cheesecake was chocolate, caramel and pecans. She took a bite and realized Tanner was chuckling. She gave him a sharp look as she slid another bite into her mouth.

"What?" she asked after the next bite.

"It is good, isn't it?"

"Amazing."

His eyes twinkled, and he took another bite of the cake.

"You're still laughing at me," she accused.

He reached for a napkin and turned to face her. "Because you have a little bit of chocolate—" he dabbed at her chin "—right there."

They froze, sitting there facing each other. Her breath caught, the moment taking her by surprise. His hand stilled, and she knew by the way it lingered, by the way his blue eyes darkened to a smoky hue, that he felt it, too.

Slowly he slid from the stool. She looked up, unable to speak her fears, to tell him this was a bad idea. Because in the moment, it felt like the perfect idea.

His hand slid to the back of her neck. His other hand cupped her cheek, tilting her head so that when he leaned in, his mouth met hers with ease.

The fork in her left hand dropped on her plate with a clank as she let go and moved her hand to his waist. His lips stilled over hers, but neither of them broke the connection.

Eventually he pulled away, his calloused but gentle hand slid from her neck like a caress, and his lips brushed hers one last time. And she wanted him back, holding her, making her feel safe. A kiss had never made her feel so cherished.

"That wasn't what I'd planned." He said it quietly, and she was glad for that.

She didn't want to be jarred from the moment.

"No, neither had I." She clasped her hands in front of her, afraid they would tremble if left to their own devices.

"I don't want to complicate things," he continued.

She put a finger to her lips. "Then don't say anything, or you will. It was a kiss. And a very nice one. I don't think either of us expected it, but, please, don't say it won't happen again or some other mature and noble thing."

Pushing aside mature, she reached for his hands and gave him a little pull in her direction. Her face tilted toward his was an invitation, and he leaned forward, taking it, dropping another sweet kiss on her lips before pulling away and breaking the connection again.

"I'm not always noble."

She laughed at his words. "I'm glad to hear that."

"But I should go, because this is complicated."

"Hmm," she said, because who could deny the truth? And the second half of that truth was that her heart was still bruised from Bill's rejection.

At least she knew she still had a heart. It could beat wildly and yearn for more than a solitary life.

She walked him to the door. He considered a few dozen ways to apologize, but in the end he decided against what would surely have been a lie. He wasn't at all sorry he'd given her a ride home, and he wasn't sorry he'd kissed her. She was beautiful and kind, and all wrong for him.

He guessed if he was sorry, it was for himself. Because he knew better than to chase something that wasn't meant to be. Sitting in her kitchen, he'd realized just how unsettled she was. She lived in Haven, but it looked as if she might be days away from packing up and leaving.

She wouldn't leave Colby. He'd watched her with her nephew. Maybe she doubted herself, but that little boy didn't doubt her. He just had something buried deep that he needed to work through.

"Good night," he said, standing on her front porch. The rain was coming down in earnest. Somewhere in the distance a siren blasted the quiet of the night.

She reached out, trailing a finger down his cheek. "I wish…"

She shook her head.

He took her hand, kissed her palm and let go. He had to get out of here and get back to the reasonable sanity that usually kept him from making the moonlit night kind of mistakes.

"Good night." She stepped back inside the house.

He took the long way back to his ranch. He drove past the Blue Bonnet Bed and Breakfast. Then he turned and went down Main Street in Haven, past the coffee shop, the library, the grocery store and a few other businesses.

This was his town. He was a part of Haven, and it was part of him. He wouldn't change that for anything. When he thought of the city, he thought of Houston, his parents and chaos. He remembered too well what it had sounded like in that apartment on any given night. The hungry cries of his little sister, the yelling, the fights. And the smell of drugs.

He knew he was biased because of his experiences, but he couldn't undo his past or the way he felt. Cities were just fine. They served a purpose.

As did small towns. This small town had saved his life.

Aunt May. He smiled, remembering a woman who had never married, never had children of her own. But she'd taken in three kids she barely knew, and she'd taken all of their baggage, as well. The fears, the rebellion, the independence.

Travis had been the rebel. Tanner had found trusting a difficult thing to do. He'd kept on doing what he'd done before Aunt May, trying to keep his sister fed, never trusting that Aunt May would have food the next day, or that she'd see to their needs. It had taken trust on his part and patience on hers for them to work past his issues.

He guessed he still hoarded, always fearing that he'd

wake up one day and everything would be gone. It was baggage left over from his childhood.

He kept a pantry stocked with food. He kept money in a safe box. He kept to his goals. The list had made sense when he came up with it. College. A career. Buying back the ranch for Aunt May. Savings and a backup plan. And a relationship, someday. The right relationship. A woman who wanted to be a wife and a mom. One who enjoyed life in a small town and understood ranching.

His brother, Travis, had teased him for that list, telling him he was courting trouble. Trying to keep his life to some kind of schedule only meant the schedule was sure to fall apart. But Tanner had stuck to it, needing the security a plan provided. He maintained his life without entanglements that would drag him back into chaos.

Thirty minutes after leaving Macy, he pulled into the garage of his house. His castle, as Chloe called it. He'd built the house a few years back. It was two-story, stone and stucco, with heavy wood trim. It was open and light, with big windows. Light was important to him.

Open spaces were important.

As he walked through the kitchen and the family room, Chloe appeared. She studied him a little too closely, and then she plopped on the leather sofa and crossed her arms, her head cocked slightly to the side.

"What?" He picked up a book he'd left on the table and pretended he was walking away from her.

She stuck out her leg and stopped him. "Where have you been?"

"Dinner at the Candle Light. We're working on the

people we have to find in order to keep the Culpepper place for the boys."

She stood, going on tiptoe to study his face. And then she reached to wipe his cheek. "Since when does Bea wear that shade of lipstick?"

He rubbed his face, and she laughed.

"Gotcha, big brother. Nothing on your face except a guilty look."

"That's nice," he grumbled. "I'm going to my office."

She grabbed his hand. "Don't go. I'll play nice. I was driving by as you all left the restaurant. I saw Macy Swanson get in your truck."

"You're impossible."

"I'm a little sister. I think impossible is part of the job description. So, she's pretty. And nice. That's a good combination."

"I'm not having this discussion with you."

She sat back down on the sofa. "No, you only want to discuss *my* relationships."

He let it go. He'd learned a long time ago that he wouldn't win if he engaged in an argument with his little sister. "I need to decide which yearlings we're going to put on the website to sell. Do you want to help?"

The question put a smile on her face. "You don't fight fair. Of course I'll accept the distraction and help."

He'd known it would work. Mention horses, and everything else was forgotten.

After raiding the refrigerator, they headed for the computer in his office. Chloe pulled up a chair next to his.

"So, about these people you have to find. Do you

want me to help with that?" Chloe asked as he pulled up the inventory of their livestock.

"I might. I'm looking for Gabriel's grandfather Theodore Linley."

"Have you found anything?"

Tanner pulled a few notes out of his desk drawer. "Not much. He hasn't lived around here in years. Gabe doesn't know much about him, other than that he wasn't much of a provider, got into some petty crimes even when he lived around here."

"I hate to ask, but have you checked the prison system?"

No, he hadn't. He let out a long sigh. He didn't want to find his friend's grandfather in a state prison. "I'll take a look."

"You might also check death records."

"Yeah, I will."

"Tanner," she said hesitantly, and he doubted he wanted to hear what came next.

"Yes?" He glanced away from the computer because he knew she'd want his full attention.

"I've been looking for our parents."

"I'm not sure why." He wouldn't even call them parents.

"Because I need to know where they are. I know the word is overused, but I need closure."

He brought up the file of yearling quarter horses. "I understand that."

"Do you know where they are?"

"No, I don't. I haven't tried to find them."

"They visited once, didn't they?"

He leaned back in his chair and allowed the memory

he'd been pushing aside for a good many years. "Yes, they came to visit."

"I was four."

"Yes, you were four. And they were…" He shook his head. "Chloe, they were strung out. They wanted money. They weren't here to see their children. They showed up to play on Aunt May's good heart."

"I know, but still. What if they're out there somewhere? Don't you want to know where they are?"

"I don't want to sound coldhearted, Chloe, but you and me, we're coming at this from different places. I remember too much. You don't remember enough."

"But you understand."

That she needed closure? "Yeah, I do."

But that didn't mean he could help her find them. They all had their own version of the past. His version was about parents who let him down, who left him to be the adult when he'd barely had a chance to be a kid.

She pointed to the file, the conversation about their parents at an end, thankfully. "We had a good crop of foals, didn't we?"

"We did. And I know you hate this part, when we have to let some of them go."

"But that's because we're a working ranch," she mimicked him with a gruff voice. "And if we don't sell our animals, we can't afford to feed them."

"I'm glad you've been listening."

"I've been listening." She moved her chair closer to the computer. "I do want to keep Daisy."

The buttery-yellow filly with a white blaze down a dainty face. "What are you going to do with her?"

"You let me pick one filly a year that I think is special and that will add to our program. She's the one."

"Okay, Daisy is ours." He pointed at the screen, at a light gray colt. "Frosty?"

"He'll grow up to be a good horse for someone."

They worked through the list, and fortunately, the conversation didn't return to their parents. Or to Macy Swanson. Both were topics he wanted to avoid. One was old news.

The other had taken him by surprise.

Chapter Six

Macy showed up at Cabin One on Sunday morning feeling more than a little apprehensive over the pass with Colby. It was the first one they'd had since the failed attempt at a weekend pass. As she walked up the steps, she could hear chaos inside. Someone shouted, and then a loud cry pierced the quiet country morning.

Hand at the ready, she hesitated short of knocking. Before she could make a decision, the door jerked open, and an angry teen stood on the threshold. His eyes widened in shock when he saw her there.

"I'm sorry." His voice was gruff, and he made a move to get past her.

Before he could, Edward Mack was there. The tall redhead was midforties, normally quiet and always concerned with the boys at the ranch.

"Johnny, when we're talking, you're not to walk out that door."

Macy took a step back, unsure of her next move. Should she go inside and collect Colby or step aside and wait out whatever was taking place? Edward answered her unspoken question.

"Macy, Colby is in his room. Give us a few minutes, and we'll allow them all out." Edward had a hand on Johnny Drake's back. "Johnny, let's take a walk."

Edward and the boy stepped out the door, and Macy moved aside to let them pass. From inside she heard Eleanor call out, telling her to go ahead and come in. Macy walked through the cabin and found Eleanor in the hall.

"I think I came at a bad time."

Eleanor waved off the apology. "No, it's okay. Johnny has been doing so well, but he still has his moments. He and Ben had a disagreement. We put the boys in their rooms until we know the episode is over, and everything and everyone is safe again."

"They're all okay, though?"

"Yes, they're fine. They're unfortunately used to this. They go to their rooms, play with toys, color or read. When the crisis is over, we give the all clear. Which I think is right now." Eleanor cleared her throat. "Boys, come on out."

Two doors opened. Ben peeked his head out and looked down the hall. "He's not waiting for me?"

"No," Eleanor assured him. "He's outside with Edward. But I'm sure we'll all sit down and talk."

The other door opened. Colby stepped out and, behind him, eleven-year-old Sam Clark with his pale blond hair and serious blue eyes.

"Aunt Macy!" Colby rushed forward and wrapped thin arms around her waist. Macy pulled him close, her heart taken by surprise at the greeting.

"Hey, sweetie, you ready for church?"

He nodded against her stomach. As she slipped past,

Eleanor patted Macy's shoulder. "You two have a good day. Be back by five this afternoon."

"We can do that." She separated from her nephew. "Is there anything you need to get?"

He hurried back into his room for a backpack and came out with it slung over his shoulder. "I'm ready to go. See you later, Sam."

Sam stood in the door to the room they shared, solemn and worried. "You'll be okay, Colby?"

"Yeah, I'll be okay," her nephew reassured the other boy, and then he took her hand and led her from the cabin.

The weather was perfect for the first part of October. It was still warm, but with less humidity and a light breeze that made it ideal for the time of year. And with Colby holding her hand and talking a mile a minute about a new cow he'd fed and the big move, it was easy to believe everything would be okay.

They arrived at church as the bell was ringing, and people were hurrying inside. Macy parked, and she and Colby ran together, the backpack swinging at his side. Chloe Barstow was entering just ahead of them. The younger woman held the door.

"I'm late, too. We had a mare foaling. I didn't want to leave her," Chloe explained. She ruffled her hand through Colby's hair. "Hey, Colby, good to see you."

Colby grinned at the other woman. He'd been raised in this church. His parents had taken an active role, working with the youth. Like the house, the church had been theirs. Macy often felt like a placeholder. She could handle that at church, even in the house, but she wanted to be so much more to Colby.

"Can I sit with the Wayes?" Colby asked as they entered the sanctuary and looked for a place to land.

The Waye family had been Grant and Cynthia's closest friends. And it was easy to see Colby's connection with them. It was easy to see that Laurie Waye, the mother, had natural instincts.

Macy envied her that gift.

"Of course you can," she answered when she realized her nephew still stood waiting for her to respond.

He skipped away, leaving her to find a seat alone. A hand touched her elbow. Chloe Barstow nodded toward a few empty seats. "Sit with me? Tanner is at home with the mare and new foal. He probably won't be here."

"Thank you," Macy whispered, following the other woman to the empty spots.

"No problem."

They sat and the music started. Chloe touched her arm.

"Colby loves you," she said in hushed tones. "I know you worry, but don't."

"It's hard not to." She tried to focus on the music, but her gaze kept straying to her young nephew. He seemed so happy with the Waye family. There was a mom, a dad and several children. A real family. A dad to play basketball. The kind of mom who knew how to bake cookies without burning them. They probably had a strong extended family with grandparents, aunts, uncles and cousins.

Macy had no one, really. Her dad had passed away years ago. Her mom, Nora, lived in Arizona. She'd come to Texas following the accident and then the funeral. But then her husband, Macy's stepfather, had called and asked her to come home. And she'd gone.

For a few weeks after she'd gone back to Arizona, they'd talked on the phone every day. Now they talked once a week. Every Sunday at seven.

"I know it will get easier. Just give it time," Chloe offered.

Of course, she nodded, because she had to believe that things would get better.

Again her attention focused on the Wayes. A real family. Maybe that was what Colby needed? And it was something she couldn't give him. It was just the two of them. She closed her eyes, praying away the pain and wishing God would give her a clear sign.

What if she wasn't meant to raise Colby? What if someone else could do this and make him happy? She shuddered, thinking about letting go. It hurt too much to even contemplate. But could she do it if it was the best thing for her nephew?

"You okay?"

The service was ending. She gathered up her Bible and purse. "Yes, I'm good."

Chloe opened her mouth to respond, but Colby raced back to them, a coloring page in his hand. "I colored this for you."

She took the page and held it up to study the image of Jesus calming the storm. *Why are you afraid?* it said in bold letters at the top of the page.

"Well, I guess that's a direct message," Chloe said with a hint of laughter. "Hey, why don't the two of you join us for lunch at the castle? I mean, the ranch."

"Castle?" Colby perked up.

"That's what she calls my place," Tanner said, appearing at Macy's side. "It's actually my kingdom. Sometimes she forgets."

"You have a kingdom?" Colby, still amazed by the castle, now had a kingdom to imagine.

Chloe nodded. "He does. And he's the king. But I thought he was at home taking care of horses."

The last sentence was obviously directed at her brother, and Chloe gave him a look to let him know.

He shrugged. "The new foal is doing great. I slipped in after the service started. And if Macy and Colby want to join us for lunch, that's fine with me."

"We shouldn't," Macy started. Chloe cut her off.

"If you have other plans, that's okay. But it's just the two of us and a big roast in the slow cooker. Someone should help us eat it. And we might need help naming that new foal."

Macy caught a look between brother and sister. She started to give excuses why she and Colby couldn't join them, but Colby grabbed her hand.

"Could we go?"

Tanner smiled down at her nephew. And then he raised his gaze to meet hers. Something in his dark blue eyes unsettled her.

"You should join us. If you don't, we'll be eating roast all week." Tanner touched a hand to Colby's shoulder.

That settled it for her. Colby needed people. He needed men who would be role models and do things with him that a father would have done. She could toss a ball, she could teach him to drive, but he needed male role models in his life.

"We'd love to join you all. Is there anything I can bring?"

"No, we have everything," Chloe responded. "You can follow us."

Colby could barely contain himself. As they followed the dark blue Ford truck in the direction of the Barstow ranch, her nephew talked nonstop about castles and kingdoms. She gave up trying to convince him that they were just going to a regular house. He wanted to believe that they were on their way to Tanner Barstow's kingdom and that the rancher was some sort of king. Or worse, that he was a knight in shining armor.

Macy tried to picture that knight with a cowboy hat. She smiled at the thought, until she remembered the way he'd held her just days earlier.

She might need a rescuer, but she thought it more likely she needed someone to rescue her heart from memories of a kiss.

Tanner turned up his drive and shot Chloe a look that she happily ignored. She saw, but she shifted away and pretended she didn't. Instead she sang along to a George Strait song and dug through her purse for a piece of gum.

"What are you up to?" he finally asked.

She looked up, a flash of guilt quickly dissolving into an innocent smile. "Up to?"

"Inviting Macy to lunch?" He let that thought ruminate for a few seconds. "Did you put that book in her bag?"

"Book?"

No, of course she didn't. Now he was getting paranoid. "Macy has a lot on her plate. The last thing she needs is you trying to involve yourself in her life."

Anger flashed in his sister's blue eyes. "Really? Did it ever cross your mind that I might like Macy? She's new in town, and she's had a tough year. She needs

friends. So does Colby. If it feels like I'm trying to manipulate your life, maybe you should think how I feel."

"Touché," he said. "I'm sorry."

"You should be. And would it hurt you to take a look
at a really nice woman?"

"I've looked," he admitted.

That made his sister happy. "Well, isn't that surprising. And?"

"I'm busy, Chloe. Yes, I want to get married and
have a family." Lately, he'd thought about it a lot. A
wife. Kids. It was what he'd always wanted. "I don't
want to get involved in a relationship with someone
who might not stay in Haven."

Her eyes widened. "Why don't you think she'll stay?
She has Colby, and this is his home."

"Several reasons," he said, and he had to make it
quick because he was pulling into the garage. "She's
from Dallas. I learned something in plant sciences and
that's that a plant doesn't do well when taken from its
native surroundings. She's all city. I can't see her lasting in our small town. And second, Colby has a lot of
memories here. It could be that a fresh start elsewhere
would help him to move on."

"I hadn't thought of that. But would it be good to
take him from what he's always known?"

"Sometimes a fresh start helps."

"Sometimes you have to give people a chance," she
countered as she got out of the truck. "You could at
least play nice."

He shook his head as he got out to follow her inside. Yeah, he could play nice. As a matter of fact, he'd
tried, and he'd actually enjoyed it. It didn't take much
to remember the way it had felt to hold Macy. He could

imagine the scent of her hair, the way it had felt to kiss her, the way her hands had touched his face.

He hadn't been prepared for the attraction. And it went beyond attraction. He liked her. Liking her added a whole other level of complication.

"She's the mother of a resident at the ranch," he grumbled at his sister's retreating back. "That changes things."

She glanced back at him, a frown in place. "She won't always be the mom of a resident. Colby will go home. And I think Macy will stay and make Haven her home.

"I'll go let them in," she offered. "Do you want to turn the oven on so I can heat the rolls?"

Anything to stay busy.

He was pouring tea in glasses when Macy, Colby and Chloe joined him. Colby was wide-eyed as he look around the kitchen and up at the high ceilings.

"Wow. It is a castle."

"Colby," Macy cautioned. "Why don't you wash your hands? And is there something I can do to help?"

"You can put the glasses on the table," Tanner suggested. But he wished he hadn't. He should have told her to go ahead and sit down. That would have put her a good thirty feet from him and out of reach. But instead she was next to him, her arm brushing his as she grabbed a couple of glasses. And he couldn't help but lean a little in her direction. That shift brought him close enough that he caught the herbal scent of her shampoo.

She didn't notice, but across the room Chloe did. A wink told him she'd caught the move.

Colby finished washing his hands and hurried past

them, nearly bumping into his aunt. Tanner caught the boy up in his arms. "Slow down, buddy, or you'll take someone down."

The kid grinned, but he nodded affably. "Okay. But after we eat, can I see that new horse?"

"Yeah, you can see the new horse."

"Is it a black stallion?"

"Yes, and when I ride it, I'm going to wear armor and carry a sword."

Colby laughed. "You're not really a knight because my aunt says this isn't a castle. It's a really big house. Too big for two people."

The aunt in question was on her way to the dining room with glasses of tea, but he heard her gasp. She turned, her cheeks faintly pink. "Colby."

Tanner considered rescuing her but decided against it.

Chloe jumped in. "It is too big for two people, Colby. That's why Tanner needs to get married and have a bunch of kids."

He should have known.

"He could let kids from the ranch live here with him," Colby suggested.

"That's a great idea," Chloe continued. "Tanner, why don't you do that?"

"I'm going to get the roast." Tanner turned tail and ran. He'd never considered himself a coward, but any man would be if he had to face his sister. Add Colby and the pink-faced Macy, and he was outnumbered.

He was a man who liked goals, and today's goal was clear. Finish this meal as quickly as possible, before Chloe could take meddling to a whole new level.

Chapter Seven

Monday, after a long day substituting for the high school algebra teacher, Macy headed for the Silver Star. She had a bag with treats for the boys and the book that someone thought she should read. It no longer mattered who had left the book in her book bag. What mattered was that it would give her time with Colby. The other boys would enjoy it, too.

She pulled up to the ranch house, waving to Flint as he headed out to the barn with a few of the older boys. As she walked toward the house, a loud explosion shook the air. From a distance she heard screams. The horses in the field took off at a dead run. Heart pounding, Macy ran for the cabin where Colby would be with the Macks.

Edward Mack was running in that direction, too. They met on the steps, and she followed him inside.

"What was that?" she asked as they hurried through the door.

Edward closed the door behind her and locked it. "I'm not sure. But we aren't taking any chances."

Eleanor was in the living room with Colby, Sam and Ben. "What was that?"

Edward shook his head. "Where's Johnny?"

The fifteen-year-old with the quiet demeanor, curly brown hair and easy smile was missing. Eleanor had an arm around Colby and Sam, the two taking comfort in her strong presence. Macy stood there, not knowing what she should do. She had known only that, when she'd heard that explosion, Colby was somewhere, and she needed to make sure he was safe.

"Johnny is with Doc Harrow. They're working with sick calves."

"You all stay here. I'm going to see what I can find out." Edward headed for the door. Macy followed, locking the door behind him.

"So, what will we do, boys?" Eleanor asked with a smile that was probably meant to tell them everything was okay.

"I have a book I planned on reading," Macy offered. "Unless you have something else?"

"A story is a great idea. Boys, what do you think?"

Colby and Sam nodded and moved from her side. Ben looked unsure.

"Ben, it's up to you," Eleanor told him.

"I'll stay with Miss Macy," he said quietly, a little unsure. He was in his early teens but still a boy. Macy motioned him toward the furniture, a big sectional and two recliners that filled the small room.

"I like this story," Colby said. "It's one of my favorites."

Macy sat down, Sam and Colby on either side of her and Ben in one of the recliners. It gave her pause that the mystery person had left one of Colby's favorite books for her to read.

The front door unlocked as she started to read. Edward stepped in with a few more of the younger boys and the house mom from Cabin Three, Laura Davidson. She was in her fifties, and she and her husband had been at the ranch for quite a few years. They'd never had children of their own, but she loved the ranch kids as if they were hers.

"Laura and the boys are going to join you all for story time," Edward informed her, and then he was gone again.

Laura herded in her boys. "Morgan, Billy and Jasper, do you all know Miss Macy?"

The little boy she knew as Jasper stepped forward, his sandy-colored hair a mess and his eyes twinkling with orneriness. "Yes, ma'am. She told us a dragon story."

"Okay, let's have a seat, and I'll go see if Eleanor needs any help."

Jasper gave her a sweet smile and sat down on the floor. She knew the little boy from the library and wouldn't doubt if he had superglue hidden somewhere on his person. He'd glued a book to her desk a few weeks ago.

"Is Colby going home with you?" Morgan Duff asked as she opened the book. He looked up at her so seriously, his brown eyes luminous behind his glasses.

"Of course he is," she replied. And then she wondered if that was the right answer. Morgan looked away, his hands clasping at his side.

"Morgan, are you okay?" She leaned toward him, and he looked up.

"Yeah. I hope he does go home. He's just a kid."

Her heart broke a little on those words. Morgan was about ten, and a child himself. He was someone's broken little boy with anger issues and a hurting heart.

"You're a good friend to worry about him," she told Morgan.

"We're more like family than friends," he said.

"Yes, definitely."

Jasper groaned. "Could we read now?"

"Yes, we can read."

She started the story, and the boys moved closer, even Ben, who pretended to be too old for stories. She wondered about the teenager. He was quiet and respectful, always looking out for the younger boys. And yet he was here at the ranch. Someone had mentioned parents on drugs.

Each child had a story. And they had the ranch to help them change their stories for the better.

She was on page twenty when Eleanor stepped back into the room. "I have cookies and hot cocoa if anyone is interested."

The boys jumped up and hurried from the room. All but Colby. He remained at her side on the sofa, his head tucked against her shoulder.

"What do you think made that noise, Aunt Macy?" His voice was small and worried.

"I think probably a car backfiring." Or she would like to believe that was the cause.

"What's a backfire?"

"Hmm, good question. I guess I don't know what causes a backfire. I can look it up, and then we'll both learn something new. But it happens sometimes. A car will be driving and suddenly make a loud sound."

"Oh. I've heard that before. My dad…" His voice trailed off.

Macy held her breath, waiting. He almost never mentioned his parents.

"Colby, it's okay to talk about them."

He shook his head. "I'm mad at them."

The response took the air from her lungs and made her heart ache. She wanted to tell him that was wrong. Instead she asked, "Why?"

He shrugged slim shoulders and pulled away from the arm she'd put around him. "They shouldn't have left."

"No," she agreed. "They shouldn't have left. But they didn't have a choice."

"Yes, they did. They didn't have to go out. They didn't have to leave me."

Tears were streaming down his cheeks. He curled into a ball on the sofa. Macy touched his shoulder and tried to pull him close. He stiffened and wouldn't budge.

Eleanor appeared at her side. She briefly touched Macy's shoulder, and then she got down on her knees at Colby's side and put a hand on his back.

"Care to talk, Colby?"

He shook his head. "I don't want to talk. Talking hurts."

"Yes, but sometimes it hurts and then makes it better. Did you ever cut your finger, Colby, and just when you thought it was getting better, it started to hurt and itch?"

He nodded.

"That's when it's healing. It hurts, but it's getting better. Your parents didn't know that, when they left, they weren't coming back. Do you think if they'd known, they would have left? I think they would have stayed home with you."

He shook his head and wouldn't look up.

"Do you have a reason to think they wanted to go?"

He nodded, but he wouldn't talk.

Eleanor brushed a hand across the top of his head. "Do you want your aunt Macy to hold you? Sometimes when I'm sad, it helps if I get a hug."

Without a word he turned and crawled into Macy's lap. And he cried. She tucked his head under her chin and allowed her own silent tears to fall.

Eleanor grabbed a few tissues out of the box on the end table and handed them to her, and then she left them alone. Macy cradled her nephew in her arms and told him everything would be okay. She hoped he believed it, because sometimes she wondered.

Edward unlocked the door to Cabin One, and Tanner followed him inside. He knew the kids were safe, and with Eleanor and Laura on the job, the kids were probably seeing this as a great adventure and nothing to worry about. He didn't expect to see Macy on the sofa cradling Colby in her arms as the little boy cried.

He also didn't expect the crazy urge to go to them and make their problems his. As a matter of fact, when Edward kept moving, giving them privacy, Tanner told himself to keep on moving, too.

For the first time in a long time, he didn't listen to his better self. Nope, he headed right into the situation, settling himself in a recliner that had been pulled close to the sectional. Macy looked up, her green eyes swimming with tears.

"Hey, Colby," he said quietly.

"Hey, Tanner," the little boy said in a tearful voice.

"Bad day?" Tanner guessed that was an understatement.

Colby nodded against his aunt's shoulder. "I miss my…"

But he wouldn't say it. He never did. Not a mention of his mom or his dad. Tanner had noticed. He'd heard other people comment on it.

"You miss your mom and dad?" Tanner prodded. He wasn't a therapist, but he knew all about being a kid and wanting his parents.

In his case he'd wanted his parents to actually *be* parents. And he'd even kind of hoped that once the state took custody and placed them with Aunt May, that their parents would get their act together.

He'd taken a few classes and even gone through foster parent training because he wanted to know the laws and the emotions of the kids at the ranch. He knew that, no matter how bad a home situation might have been, kids always wanted their biological parents. Colby hadn't been taken from abusive parents. He'd had his parents taken from him.

"Yeah," Colby finally answered. "I miss them."

"That's okay, you know."

Colby nodded and pulled away from Macy to sit up. He wiped his face with his hand, and Macy handed him a tissue.

"How's your new horse?" Colby asked, done with the tears.

"He's real good. One of these days, your aunt Macy can bring you out to see him again." He'd shown Colby the horse the previous day, after they'd finished lunch.

Colby looked up at her. "Today?"

Tanner laughed. "I think we're going to be kind of busy today."

"Because a car backfired?" Colby asked, sniffling and brushing his hand across his eyes.

Tanner looked at Macy, and she arched a brow and gave him a well-meaning look. Okay, backfiring cars. Why not?

"Yeah, because of that."

Macy gave Colby a hug. "How about cookies and cocoa now?"

Colby slid off her lap and headed for the kitchen. Tanner didn't know what to do after the boy left and it was just him and Macy in the living room. She looked about to fall apart. He wasn't sure what he'd do if she picked his shoulder for that event.

But she didn't fall apart. Instead she took a deep breath.

"I want to fix him," she said in a quiet voice, her gaze on the door her nephew had gone through.

"Of course you do. It takes time. But he's turning to you. That's new, isn't it?"

"Yes, it is. I can't describe how it felt when he crawled onto my lap and let me hold him. He doesn't often do that."

"That's a starting place." He stood, needing space. "The police are on their way. Tell Edward I'll be at the barn waiting."

"What happened?"

"Someone shot a hole in the barn. Fortunately it lodged in a support pole."

Her face paled. "I was hoping it was just…"

He grinned. "A car backfiring?"

"Yeah."

"I wish it had been." He glanced at his watch. "And Chloe's fiancé is going to be here in an hour. He's going to volunteer. It's a chance for me to get to know him."

"Chloe seems to love him."

Tanner brushed his fingers through his hair, surprised by this conversation. "Yeah, she seems to. Bring Colby by when you can to see Knight again."

"Knight?" Her voice had a teasing quality to it.

"A castle needs one, don't you think?"

"Yes, I guess it would."

He left. As he headed for the barn, Gabriel Everett was pulling up. Behind him were county police. And Fletcher. Great.

Gabriel was out of his truck first. "What happened out here?"

Beatrice came out of the barn, her eyebrows drawn together in worry. "We were shot at, that's what. And keep it down, Gabriel. We don't want to scare the boys."

Fletcher was upon them. "And how do we know it wasn't one of your boys, Bea? I keep telling you all that this is getting out of hand. Fifty years ago, troubled boys were a lot less dangerous. We live in different times. These boys have different problems. And we don't need those problems in our community."

"Fletcher, this is a level one facility. We don't take boys with serious behavioral problems, and you know that."

"Bea, I think you take any kid that the state brings you."

"Maybe I do, Fletcher, but the state also knows what we're equipped to handle. We don't have the facilities for truly troubled youth, and so the state takes those boys to placements that can handle them."

Fletcher shook his head. "We need to have a meeting and discuss this."

Gabriel stepped forward. "Fletcher, the last time I checked, you weren't a member of the LSCL, and so you don't get to call meetings. I'm the president. I call meetings."

"Then call one," Fletcher said. "Call one, or I'll call the state and find out what we can do to close this place down."

"Don't threaten this place." Gabriel issued the warning in a stern voice that no one should ignore.

Fletcher ignored it. "I'm not threatening..."

Tanner held up a hand. "Please, don't say it was a promise, not a threat. Because if you do, I'm going to laugh."

Bea chuckled. The moment slid into a less hostile one. The deputies were out of their cars and taking notes. Tanner stepped back, not wanting to get in their way. Fletcher, on the other hand, was in the middle of everything.

Gabriel stepped close to Tanner. "This is getting out of hand with him."

"I know. I'm just not sure what to do about it. I think once we get to the Culpepper place, he'll have to stop because it won't have anything to do with him."

Gabriel adjusted his black Stetson. "I'm afraid he'll fight us legally and try to close the ranch."

"We'll fight back. We can outspend him."

"True, but..." Gabriel started but let his words trail off.

"Gabriel, don't tell me you're rethinking the ranch."

"No, I'm not. I'm just worried. What if a boy had been in the path of that bullet?"

The reality of that settled over Tanner, turning him cold.

"I'd rather not think about that." Because thinking about it brought an image of Colby Swanson for some reason.

Tanner cared about the kids at the ranch. All of them. He saw himself in each of them. Colby was different. Maybe knowing Macy made the difference in how he felt about the boy.

"Someone is going to get hurt," Gabriel continued.

"Then we have to find who did this."

"Yeah, I hope we can."

Tanner heard a door. He looked back and saw Macy leaving Cabin One. He let out a sigh and shook his head.

"If you feel like you need to stop her, go." Gabriel jerked his head in Macy's direction.

"I don't." Tanner shot another look her way. "I wanted to see if the two of us could sit down to discuss your grandfather. I know this is bad timing, Gabe. I know you've got reasons you don't want to discuss him. But we have a dozen kids moving at the end of the month, and I sure don't want to take a chance that we might have to move them back over here."

"We can talk. After the meeting at the end of the week."

"That works." He glanced back over his shoulder again.

"Go."

Tanner stood there a full minute, watching the officers, watching Bea soothe Fletcher's ruffled feathers, and then he walked away.

When he caught up with Macy, she was standing in the yard of the cabin, her back to him.

"We have a shooter on the loose, no idea who it is and where they are, and you're standing out here in the yard." He jerked off his hat and looked around.

That was when he noticed the slight tremble in her shoulders. He shoved his hat back on his head and reached, letting his hand hover above her shoulder for a second before allowing it to settle. She turned, and he lost the battle to remain detached.

But he also wasn't going to stand in the yard and be the next target. He took her by the hand and led her at a fast walk toward his truck. Tears were streaming down her cheeks, her eyes were puffy and her nose was red. A woman in crisis. She wasn't his problem, he reminded himself on the short trek to his truck.

For the life of him, he couldn't walk away from her. Even when he reminded himself that he didn't get involved with parents who had boys at the ranch.

He opened the door of his truck and motioned her inside. Once she was in and buckled, he drove away.

"I'm sorry," she said softly with a hint of a sob.

"What happened?" And with that question he knew he was digging a deeper hole.

"Nothing." She shook her head. "Not really. It's just a roller coaster. And I want to fix this all for him, and I can't. I'm mad at my brother, too. But I don't get to be angry because I have to find a way to help Colby get past his grief and his anger."

"You have a right to be angry."

"I also have a car back at the ranch."

He chuckled. "You can get it later."

She leaned back in the seat and covered her face with her hands. A growl, muffled by her hands, split the silence of the truck. "I am angry. I'm so mad at him for leaving. I'm mad because I don't know what to do for Colby. And the person I always went to for advice is gone. Grant is gone. I think Colby and I were both in a delusional state, thinking they would come home. But they're not coming home. I'm not getting my brother, my best friend, back. Colby isn't getting his parents back. They're just gone. And it isn't fair. It isn't fair that I had to—"

Her eyes closed, and she shook her head.

"Macy?"

She pinched the bridge of her nose. "No. I'm not going to say that. I lost a job and gave up an apartment. Colby lost his parents. What I lost doesn't amount to anything. I lost things I don't miss."

"I think you're wrong. I think you miss your life. There's nothing wrong with that. Accept it, or it'll eat you up."

He pulled up to her house.

"I miss my life." She said it on a sigh. "I wouldn't be anywhere else. But I have to admit, there are days I wonder if Colby would be better off with someone else, with anyone but me. But I'm his family. We have each other."

"Yes, and in the end, that matters."

"But…" She bit down on her lip and glanced away from him, not finishing.

"But what?"

"What if I'm not a mom? What if I can't do this?" She looked young sitting next to him, her green eyes troubled. "I'm sorry, you didn't ask for this, to be the person I pour out my insecurities on. I lost the person I always went to when I was upset. I don't know how to do this, and Grant isn't here for me to talk to. If he was, I'd tell him I'm not sure if I know how to be a mom. And what if I hurt Colby in the process of learning?"

"I think that anyone would question their ability. I'm guessing that even a mom who planned on having a child would still question if she could do it."

She reached for the door. "Thank you. I'm sorry that you had to leave when there were probably things you needed to do."

He raised a hand to stop her apology. "No trouble. If I'd stayed, I might have been arrested for hurting Fletcher."

He got out and walked her to the front door.

"I would have bailed you out," she said with a hint of a smile. "If you'd punched him. Oh, what about my car?"

"I'll have Flint help me get it over here."

The car reminded him. She'd been vandalized. He couldn't help but wonder if the person who had disconnected that hose on her car was the same person who had shot at the barn. When he got back to the ranch, he would mention that to the police.

"Macy, you need to be careful. Just keep an eye on things around here. Keep your car locked."

"I will. Thank you for letting me talk about Colby."

"Anytime." He said it, and then he realized the door that had opened.

She laughed. "Don't worry. I won't be calling at midnight to talk about my feelings."

"If you did, I'd answer."

She stood on tiptoe and touched his cheek to bring it down to her level. When she kissed him, he felt floored by the unexpected gesture.

He also felt like a man wading into quicksand, because he wasn't satisfied with that sweet kiss on the cheek. Standing on her porch in broad daylight, he turned and brushed his lips against hers.

"See you later," he said as he stepped back to leave.

"Yes, later."

He drove away thinking about that old saying "Out of the frying pan and into the fire." This was one of those situations, he realized.

Macy had soft hair, soft gestures and a soft heart. She was easy to like. He guessed if a man wasn't careful, he'd find himself falling a little in love with her.

Chapter Eight

Macy pulled up in front of Lila's Café on Tuesday morning. She was meeting Josie Markham for breakfast before she headed out to the ranch for family therapy with Colby. Since she was early, she walked down the sidewalk and stopped in front of the secondhand shop. The store had a cute selection of shabby chic furniture. Old dressers, desks, chairs and tables that were painted light colors.

Maybe, she thought, she could purchase a few pieces to lighten up the darker colors in Grant's house. No, not Grant and Cynthia's house, her house.

"Hey, that's a long sigh for such a pretty day."

She turned, managing a smile for Josie. "It is a pretty day. I'm window-shopping."

"We should go in."

"No, I don't think so. Moving forward isn't easy, is it?"

The humor in Josie's eyes dimmed. "No, it isn't. What does that have to do with furniture?"

"It isn't my house. It's my brother's house. He and his wife decorated it."

"And you haven't made it your own?"

They were walking toward the café. "No, I haven't. It feels as if they will walk in any moment, so it would be wrong to change their home. It feels wrong to move into their home, their lives and their shoes."

"And that's something I can understand. Moving on is difficult."

They entered the café that was less than crowded. They'd purposely missed the morning rush. The waitress, a young woman with a bouncy ponytail and braces, hurried forward to take their order.

"I'll take coffee and a cinnamon roll." Josie turned her coffee cup for the girl to fill it.

"I'll have the same."

Macy waited until the waitress left. "I'm so sorry, Josie. I get so caught up in my life. How are you doing?"

Josie shrugged a slim shoulder. "Some days better than others. Today is a good day. I can talk about it today. I can think about the baby and being a mom, and I don't feel as if my whole life is a nightmare that I can't wake up from. And today I'm trusting God instead of being angry with Him."

"Have you picked a name?"

Josie grinned and wagged a finger. "No, and I'm not telling."

"I'll get it out of you yet."

The door opened. Macy looked up, surprised to see Fletcher Snowden Phillips walking in. He shot her a look, shook his head and headed for the front counter, where the waitress was bagging up a to-go order. She didn't have a clue why he'd be upset with her. And really, she didn't care. Fletcher seemed to have a lot of his own baggage to deal with.

"He's called a meeting of the LSCL," Josie informed her, pausing as the waitress returned with their breakfast. She waited until the girl left to continue. "I heard Gabriel Everett wasn't happy about it and told him he didn't have the right to call meetings. But Fletcher is determined. He says the Silver Star has become something other than what it started out to be, and he won't have it being a blight on the community."

"I can't imagine someone knowing that place the way he does and still believing it should be shut down."

"He's always been against it. For as long as I can remember, he has disliked the ranch and the boys."

"I don't know what Colby and I would have done without the ranch."

"How is Colby?"

Macy pulled the cinnamon roll apart with her fork. "I'm not really sure. Some days I think we'll make it. And then there are days that I'm positive I'm doing the wrong thing for him. There are days I just know that he needs more than I can give."

"More?"

"A real family," she admitted. "I don't know the first thing about being a mother. So how could I be mom and dad to a little boy?"

Josie touched her belly. "And do you think I do? Parenting is on-the-job training. And you already have the most important part. You love him."

"Yes, I do. And I am already at a place where I don't know what I'd do without him."

"Then give it time," Josie encouraged.

On his way out Fletcher stopped at their table. "Good morning, ladies."

"Fletcher," Josie responded. "You know Macy. Her nephew is at the ranch."

Fletcher gave her a long, steady look. "I'm not sure that's the safest place for a young child."

"I believe it is," she responded. "It's been a great place for him."

"Aren't you also on the LSCL committee to help find the missing members of the ranch?" Fletcher asked.

Macy looked up at him, a bite of cinnamon roll on her fork. "Yes, Mr. Phillips, I am. And I intend to find them and make sure the boys get that bigger ranch."

"You will have your work cut out for you." He inclined his head.

Fletcher left, and Macy shuddered as he walked out the door. Josie's eyes were big, and her lips twitched with a suppressed smile.

Macy's phone rang, and she reached into her purse for it. The number was out of state. She answered.

"Hello, my name is Avery Culpepper. I received a message from Macy Swanson," the chipper voice on the other end announced.

Macy set her fork down. "I'm Macy Swanson. And I left that message, Miss Culpepper."

"Yeah, well, you found me. Old Cyrus was my grandfather. I didn't know him, though. My dad left years ago."

"I see. Mr. Culpepper was very interested in finding you." She hesitated, unsure of how to proceed because part of this message would include telling this young woman that her grandfather was deceased.

"Was interested? Did he give up?" Avery Culpepper had a jarring voice. Macy told herself it was just the phone.

"No, he didn't give up. He passed away, and it was in his will that we should try to find you."

"Did he leave me something? He had a ranch, didn't he?" The voice was definitely jarring. No blaming the phone for that tone.

"Yes, he did own a ranch. Miss Culpepper, I really can't go into this on the phone, and it isn't my place to give specifics. I was just asked to find you."

"Right, okay, well, I'm kind of tied up right now. It might take me a week or so to get there. Haven, right?"

"Yes, right outside Waco. But there's really no need for you to come here yet. March is when everything will be settled. Let me give you the name of the lawyer so you can touch base and he can tell you what you need to do." Macy sent a grimace in Josie's direction because the other woman looked too hopeful, too excited.

"Yeah, well, I'll be there as soon as I get some business taken care of."

"But there's no need for you to—"

The call ended. Macy looked at the phone, amazed.

"Well, was it her?" Josie asked.

"I guess it was."

Josie's smile disappeared. "What's wrong?"

She shrugged, "Nothing. She was just very…harsh?"

"Maybe she'll be better in person. And we don't have to like her. We just have to find her," Josie reminded her.

"That's true."

They were finishing their cinnamon rolls when the front door opened. Macy's heart stuttered a little when Tanner walked in, taking off his hat as he approached their table.

"Tanner, how are you this morning?" Josie shot Macy a questioning look before she offered the greeting.

"Good, Josie. How are you doing?" He reached for a chair and pulled it to their table.

Macy was glad when he sat down. Craning her neck to look up at him hadn't been comfortable. As he sat down, he turned his attention on her.

"We're having a meeting of the LSCL to address Fletcher's *concerns*. We're also going to discuss our search."

"Oh, I just got off the phone a few minutes ago. With Avery Culpepper."

"That's about the best news I've had today. The way this has been going, I wondered if Cyrus just wanted to mess with us all."

"I think we've all been feeling that way."

He stood again. "I'm going to meet early with Gabe. If you could be at his place in thirty minutes, we're gathering in his library."

"I can be there."

"Good." He inclined his head. "Josie, if you need anything…"

"Thanks, Tanner." Josie smiled at him as he left, and then her inquiring gaze landed on Macy, her eyebrow arched; she tapped her fingers on the table.

"What?"

Josie stopped tapping. "That was interesting."

"Interesting?"

"Macy, Tanner is a nice guy, but he doesn't typically come in and sit down. He issues orders and moves on."

Macy could have agreed. That had been the Tanner she'd first met when she came to Haven. He'd been busy. He'd rushed in the day she arrived, telling her he was sorry, asking if she needed anything. He'd left a casserole on his way out the door and a card with his business number.

This new Tanner was an enigma. And she liked him.

"You're quiet," Josie said.

"I'm sorry." Macy shook her head. "I was thinking."

"About Tanner Barstow, no doubt." Josie wiped sticky fingers with a napkin. "Chloe says he wants nothing more than to get married and have a bunch of kids. He's been so focused on building the ranch and his business, she thinks he's kind of gotten sidetracked."

"I really like Chloe, but I doubt Tanner wants her sharing his life with everyone in town," Macy answered. At Josie's widened eyes she realized she'd messed up. "I'm sorry. I'm just being overly sensitive. I'm worried about Colby, the ranch and what I'm going to do to make things right. And Tanner is…" What was Tanner?

"A distraction?" Josie replied, unrepentant, it seemed. "A very gorgeous and super wealthy distraction."

Macy shook her head at her friend's tenaciousness. "Yes, he is that. And I think I've already proved that I can't be on a list of 'wife and mother' candidates. I can't even manage to make one little boy happy."

"Don't be so hard on yourself."

"Tell that to my heart," Macy replied, glancing at the clock on her phone. "I should get to that meeting. A rain check on shopping?"

"Deal. But do me a favor. Give yourself a chance. And give Colby a chance."

Macy gave her friend a quick hug, and then she hurried out the door. She had twenty minutes to get to the meeting. Twenty minutes to prepare herself to face Tanner. She'd kissed him. She'd taken the first step. She'd never been that person. Not once in her life had she been the initiator in a relationship.

But it had seemed so natural to stand on tiptoe and kiss his cheek. It had seemed just as natural when he'd turned into the kiss, and their lips had met.

It had been a mistake. She had a list of reasons why. At the top of the list was Colby. He needed her. She doubted herself. When nothing was making sense or working out, how could this possibly be the right thing?

The library was starting to fill up. Tanner glanced at the paper in front of him, a letter sent by Fletcher, letting them know that the Silver Star had to be in compliance. They had a duty to keep the community safe. He wanted to blow it off, ignore it, but he couldn't. Fletcher knew the law. He knew how to make problems for an organization that wanted to do good.

Tanner shoved the letter aside and leaned back in his chair just as Macy walked through the door with Bea. He'd noticed earlier that Macy looked tired today. But that was the last thing a man ought to say to a woman.

He noticed everything about her. When a man was trying to maintain a professional relationship with a woman, he shouldn't notice her smile, or the way her eyes translated every mood. He also noticed that the tightness in his chest loosened up a little when she smiled a greeting.

He took a deep breath and relaxed.

Gabriel walked through the door, tense as a mountain lion about to pounce. He moved to the end of the

table and then paused and turned toward the door as
Fletcher entered. The two stared each other down.
Fletcher lost that match. His gaze shifted, and he adjusted his tie and quickly took a seat at the opposite
end of the long table.

Macy was still standing, looking unsure. Tanner
pulled out the chair next to him. She glanced around the
room, as if looking for a better option. When she found
none, she moved in his direction. Across the table from
him, Mayor Elsa Wells peered at him from over the
top of her glasses. In her fifties, she'd been his Sunday school teacher twenty years ago. And he guessed
she still felt the need to keep him on the straight and
narrow. At least that was what he would surmise from
the look she was giving him.

A lesser man might have flinched under the fiery
look from the redheaded mayor of Haven. He managed a smile.

"Let's bring this meeting to order." Gabriel Everett didn't have his gavel, but his voice was firm, and
everyone knew to end their personal conversations.

The door opened, and Seth Jacobs, from a ranch
close to Waco, hurried in. Behind him was Lena Orwell from the neighboring community of Fieldton. She
served as treasurer of the group. Seth was the LSCL
secretary.

"Sorry I'm late," Seth said as he took a chair on the
opposite side of the table. "I've been doctoring cows
with pinkeye."

Gabriel sat down in his seat at the end of the table.
Tanner leaned back in his chair and waited because
a quiet Gabriel Everett was a dangerous Gabriel. He
let his gaze slide to the other end of the table where

Fletcher was looking a mite uncomfortable. He had to guess he was severely outnumbered in this ridiculous task of trying to destroy an organization that had helped so many kids.

"I'd like to start this meeting by discussing Fletcher's claims." Gabriel drilled his gaze into Fletcher, and the lawyer at least had the sense to look chastised.

"These are not claims," Fletcher started. "These are facts. The incidents of violence are on the uptick, and it is only a matter of time before someone gets hurt."

"And you know it is tied to the boys ranch, how?" Gabriel asked.

Fletcher leaned forward, his gestures mirroring Gabriel's.

"I know it is tied to the boys ranch because the crime in Haven is generally low. It is steadily getting worse..."

Tanner couldn't take any more. "Fletcher, crime is getting worse everywhere."

"Fine, if that's what you think. I believe the boys at the ranch are hurting our community."

"Then what should we do about it?" Gabriel jumped back into the conversation. "We aren't closing the ranch, so try to come up with something else."

Fletcher let his gaze drift around the table, from person to person, more than likely looking for anyone who might be on his side.

"I only know that we have to do something. We can't allow our community love of that place to interfere with the safety of our citizens."

Bea cleared her throat, and Tanner knew that look on her face. She was about to blow. He guessed a person could say what they wanted or do what they wanted to Bea, but they'd better have sense to leave the boys on the ranch alone.

"Fletcher, I've just about had it with your nonsense. One time a few years ago a boy soaped your windows. You haven't gotten over that. And maybe it's time you forget and forgive something that was really just a silly kid prank."

"I had to replace—" he started with a sputter, and then he waved his hands. "That has nothing to do with this. I want our community to be safe."

"And I want to change lives. As do the other people in this room. When or if you find evidence that incriminates one of our boys, you let me know."

Gabriel cleared his throat and looked around the room.

"Well, I guess that takes care of that. Now we'll discuss our searches for the missing alumni of the ranch."

Fletcher stood, pushed his chair in and stared them all down. Tanner didn't mind at all. He gave the local attorney the same look, daring him to really say too much.

"I think you all will regret this." With that, Fletcher turned and left.

"Wow," Macy said. "I guess he's not a fan of the ranch."

"That's an understatement," Katie Ellis added.

Gabriel rapped his fist on the table. "We need to discuss our searches. Anything new to share?"

Tanner pointed to Macy and drew Gabriel's attention to her. She raised her hand just slightly.

"Macy? You were searching for Avery Culpepper?" Gabriel jotted down a note on his paper.

"Yes, and she called me." Her words hung in the

air, and a murmur spread through the room and then died down.

"And?" Bea pushed.

"She's actually very eager to come to Haven. I explained that she doesn't really have to get here so quickly. But I think she might show up sooner rather than later."

Bea murmured, "Thank You, God."

"How do we know we have the right people?" Lena Orwell asked, a pencil stuck behind her ear and her red hair a bit of a mess.

"We'll have to check identification and backgrounds," Katie piped up.

Lena pulled the pencil out of her hair and tapped the table. "We'll just have to be careful."

"We will be," Bea assured her. "And I have a lead on Samuel Teller. He has actually donated to the ranch. It's been several years, but I don't think he'll be hard to find."

"Anyone else?" Gabriel asked, looking first to ranch foreman Flint Rawlings and then momentarily to Tanner. And Tanner got it. No one wanted their skeletons dug up.

Flint shook his head. "I'm following a few leads, but so far nothing."

Tanner shook his head. "I'm still looking."

Before he could say more, a loud ruckus ensued. Footsteps sounded in the hall, and someone shouted. Gabriel hurried to the door. He opened it to one of his ranch workers.

"Something wrong out there?" Gabriel asked, his normally unflappable demeanor in evidence.

"Yes, sir, someone put a rock through the windshield of Miss Bea's car."

Tanner pushed back his chair and stood. They were miles from town, and very few people, other than the ones in this room, knew about their meeting. This was definitely getting personal.

Gabriel turned back to the room. "I guess this meeting is adjourned. Bea, let's go see what's going on."

They were all standing, moving toward the door, and Tanner realized Macy was next to him. She was planning to walk out the door with the rest of them. And he couldn't let her do it.

"Do you think it might be a good idea if the women waited inside until we see what is going on?" Tanner suggested, knowing the women would protest and maybe even rebel.

Gabriel glanced back, but then he came to a dead stop in the hall. "I do think that's a good idea. Something we all need to remember is that, so far, no one has been hurt. And we don't want that to change. I agree with Tanner. The fewer people we have out there, the better."

"It's my car, Gabriel." Bea moved to stand next to the man. "You can tell the rest of them to stay. Or you could ask, because I know these women, and they don't want to be ordered around."

Gabriel gave the group a long, steady look. "If you all don't mind waiting inside, I'm going to check Bea's car and probably call the police."

"I need to go," Macy said, not really objecting but not really acting as if she intended to agree with the plan.

"We can't keep you safe if you leave," Tanner told

her. "Considering the fact that your car was tampered with last week, I think it would be better for you to stay until we know there's no one out there."

All eyes were on them, and he couldn't seem to care what people thought, or even what they would say. He stood face-to-face with a woman whose green eyes were unsure. Her mouth was a firm, stubborn line.

While they lingered there, Gabriel headed outside with a half dozen people following him and Macy still shooting daggers because he'd tried to stop her from going out that door.

"You're not my keeper," she said when they were alone.

"No, I guess I'm not. I just want to keep you safe. Colby needs you."

"I know that." Her resolve weakened. He could see it in her expression. "I don't want to let him down."

"No, of course you don't." He led her to the front door. The group had gathered around Bea's car. Obviously they were going to ignore his warning that they shouldn't all be out in the open.

"Who do you think would do this?"

Tanner led her down the steps and across the lawn. "I don't have a clue. But it seems it has escalated since the details of Cyrus's will were revealed."

"Someone who doesn't want a boys ranch?" She stopped to look at Bea's car with its cracked windshield.

Someone who didn't want a boys ranch. The words, the accusation, were loud and clear. One person didn't want the ranch. One person knew where they were today. Fletcher.

But one thing Tanner knew about Fletcher Snowden

Phillips—he supported the law. That didn't mean he wouldn't break the law, but Tanner couldn't see him going to this extreme.

Tanner took Macy by the elbow and led her to the car he and Flint had delivered to her place the previous day after she'd left it at the ranch.

"I don't think Fletcher would do this," he assured her. "That doesn't mean you're wrong. Maybe the right theory but the wrong person."

"Yes, maybe." She looked up at him, green eyes serious as she bit down on her bottom lip. Her blond hair framed her face, lifting a little as the breeze picked up. The herbal scent perfumed the air.

He let out a breath and took a step back from her and from temptation. "I think it's safe to go."

Safer if she left than if she stayed, he decided.

She smiled, as if she knew.

Chapter Nine

There were no clues about who might have thrown a rock through Bea's windshield. But the incidents were putting a damper on the entire moving process. People in the community were concerned. People at the ranch were more concerned. They all cared about the safety of the residents. They were also worried about public opinion, always such a tenuous thing.

Macy pulled up to Cabin One on Wednesday afternoon. She and Colby were scheduled for family therapy with Eleanor Mack. Macy had a list today. There were some issues to tackle. She felt it was time. After all of these months of struggling and grieving, it seemed to her that in the past few weeks Colby had been improving.

For herself, she struggled between wanting Colby home so they could move on with their lives together and worrying that she wasn't the mom he needed. Those doubts were magnified after the visit she'd had the previous evening with Laurie Waye. The other lady had stopped by Macy's house to have coffee and talk. She wanted to know how Colby was doing, and how

Macy was settling in. During the visit she'd revealed that at one time Cynthia had mentioned the Wayes taking custody of Colby. She went on to say they'd obviously made the best decision, though. It was clear Macy loved her nephew and he loved her. As she'd left, Laurie had offered her help, should Macy ever need it.

The cabin dog, a mutt of unknown breeding but with a sweet face and wiry brown hair, met her as she got out of her car. His tail thumped, and he whimpered as he pushed up against her.

"Hey, Paulie, good to see you, too." She brushed a hand over his wiry head, and he looked up with limpid brown eyes. "Yeah, you have a tough life."

The front door of the cabin opened. Colby grinned at her, his sandy-brown hair a mess, his eyes sparkling. With unshed tears?

"Aunt Macy, you're here."

"Of course I am." She wrapped him in a hug and kissed his head, but then she smoothed down his hair. "Did you think I wouldn't be here?"

He shrugged and then ran off, leaving her to follow.

Eleanor greeted her with a smile and an easy hug. "Good to see you, Macy."

"Is he crying?" she asked, watching after her nephew.

Eleanor gave him a minute to get out of earshot. "He was a little upset. He watches the clock, and sometimes he is afraid that you won't show up. Let's go in the playroom."

Of course he was afraid. Macy ached on the inside, thinking of him waiting for his parents to come home that night. And they never made it. Instead she'd shown up in the middle of the night. He'd been asleep on the couch, the babysitter holding him tight.

They had so much to work through.

The playroom served many purposes. The boys did play in the big room with shelves, boxes, a foosball table and television with game sets. It was also the room used for counseling sessions.

Colby was already in the room. He drew on the chalkboard wall. First he drew a dog. Probably Paulie. And then he started drawing his family. Him, his mom, his dad. As an afterthought, a woman with long hair. Macy guessed it was probably her. He wiped a hand across his parents.

"Colby, why did you erase your picture?" Eleanor asked.

"Because they're gone, and they aren't coming back."

Eleanor sat on the edge of a nearby table and motioned Macy to a chair. "No, they aren't. And how does that make you feel? Use your 'I' words, please. I feel…"

"I feel angry. I'm mad at them for leaving. I'm mad, and sometimes I'm sad. And I have nightmares."

"I'm sorry." Eleanor pulled up a small, kid-sized chair and sat. "How do you feel about Aunt Macy?"

He glanced back, and then he shrugged and started drawing again.

"Colby?"

"I feel like she doesn't want to be here."

Macy closed her eyes and shook her head. "Oh, Colby."

"Macy, tell Colby how you feel about that."

"I wouldn't be anywhere else. Colby, I love you."

"Why do you think your aunt Macy doesn't want to be here?" Eleanor asked.

"Because."

"Because why?" Eleanor prodded.

He wouldn't tell her. For the next five minutes very little happened. Eleanor let him draw, and then she pulled him back into the conversation.

"How do you feel about going home?"

He shrugged.

"Can you draw your house, Colby?" Eleanor asked. "Is there anything you would change about your house? Maybe there are things you would like to get rid of. Or things you would like to get. Some people don't like white walls. They might want blue or brown. Some people like red or blue furniture."

He drew a dog in the middle of his house.

"You would get a dog?" Eleanor asked. "What if Aunt Macy wanted to get new furniture or different pictures for the walls?"

He shrugged, but this time he looked back, as if remembering her presence. "What do you want?"

"I don't know, Colby. I just thought it might be fun if we redecorated."

He nodded and turned to draw a picture of a cat. Macy laughed a little. It felt better than crying.

"So the changes you would make would be animals?" Eleanor asked.

"Yep," he said.

"How would you feel about Aunt Macy's changes?" Eleanor asked.

"I guess it would be okay. It's her house."

"No, Colby, it's our house." She wanted to reach for him, but she didn't.

"I live here," he told her. "I live here."

"Yes, you do. But you won't live here forever, Colby. You will go home. Boys always go home. Once they feel better, they go back to their families." Eleanor touched his arm to get his attention. "You know that, right?"

"Or to new families." He sniffled as he said it. "I didn't want them to go."

"I know you didn't," Eleanor answered. She motioned Macy forward. "But they did. And we can't change that. And it's okay to be sad. It's also okay to be happy. It's okay to have fun. It's okay to love Aunt Macy."

Macy touched his arm. "And it would be okay if I hugged you, right?"

He hugged her, tight. He held on and held on until she thought he would hug the breath out of her. She kissed the top of his head as he let go.

"I think that's enough for today." Eleanor pushed herself up from the miniature chair. "Why don't the two of you go outside? I think we're getting a new horse today."

"Could we?" Colby was already pulling Macy toward the door.

Eleanor laughed. "Oh, I think definitely."

Colby led Macy out to the barn, moving fast for a seven-year-old with short legs. The truck and trailer at the barn looked familiar. Tanner's truck. She hadn't ever realized how much he was around until recently.

As they approached, they saw the new horse, a pretty bay. Tanner led the animal toward the corral. Chloe was with him, and a young man that she guessed might be Russell.

"Let's not rush in too fast, okay?" Macy tried to slow Colby. "The horse is new and may be a little unsure of his surroundings."

Colby gave her a look that said he didn't think too much of her horse knowledge. As they approached the corral, Tanner turned and saw them. He waved, and the horse pranced around him.

Chloe smiled when they stopped next to her, first at Colby and then at Macy. "Hey, Colby, you're the first one to meet Captain."

"Do you think I can ride him?" Colby asked.

"I'm sure you can. Not today, though. He'll have to get settled in."

Colby looked at the horse and then at Macy. "Aunt Macy, do you know how to ride?"

She shook her head. "No, Colby, I don't ride."

"We'll have to fix that," Chloe said. "Tanner, Macy doesn't know how to ride."

Tanner led the horse in their direction. "That's a big problem, Macy. You can't live in Haven and not know how to ride."

The young man with them returned from the barn. He smiled at Macy and winked at Chloe. "I put away the tack."

"Thank you." Chloe beamed. "Macy, have you met my fiancé, Russell?"

"No, I haven't." Macy held out her hand. He took it in his. The handshake was brief and nothing that would recommend him. She didn't want to make a snap judgment, but she didn't like him.

And from the look Tanner gave him, he felt the same way.

She met his gaze, and something passed between

them. It felt strangely right and frightening all at the same time. Right because she knew the chemistry, had felt it in his arms. She felt it when she trusted him with her fears. It was frightening because she thought she wasn't passing this test of motherhood. It was frightening because she remembered the night her fiancé, Bill, had thrown everything away because he didn't want to give up his life. That was how he'd put it. His life. His dreams.

All her life she'd felt confident. She hadn't tackled anything without believing she could overcome it. But this parenting thing was a whole different ball game. And she was learning that doubt could snowball and touch every area of her life if she allowed it.

As her gaze collided with Tanner's, the doubts grew and got tangled up with fresh emotions she hadn't expected.

As they stood next to the corral, Tanner had to shift his focus from Macy and Colby to his sister's fiancé. Russell was tall and lanky, with dark hair a little too long. And he didn't impress Tanner, but he was trying to step back and stop judging. Chloe was right; he'd run off a few boyfriends of hers. Usually for good reason. But she was old enough to make some decisions— okay, maybe all decisions—on her own. She was also old enough to make her own mistakes.

"So, about those riding lessons." He turned his attention to Macy, because it was easier, less complicated. No, he took that back. It was possibly more complicated. "You don't ride?"

"Only if you count the carousel at the fair."

"I don't think that counts," he said. And he regretted

it. She was all city. From her new boots to her manicured nails, she was as far from country and what he
needed to focus on as a woman could be.

And yet...

"I think it's time you try a horse that does more than
go in circles," Chloe said, taking her fiancé's hand.

Tanner turned away because he couldn't focus when
he was thinking how happy he would be to send Russell on down the road. He was about to respond when
one of the newer ranch hands, Jay Maxwell, came out
of the barn and into the corral. Jay was good with the
horses, better with the kids. He was going to school
to be a therapist, but he liked the ranch and wanted to
work in a residential setting.

"Want me to take the horse and put him up?" Jay offered as he reached for the lead rope. "I'll stick him in
a stall tonight and put him out in the field tomorrow."

"That should work. Thanks, Jay." Tanner patted the
horse on the neck and watched as Jay led the animal
away.

"Colby and I should go. Eleanor suggested a walk,"
Macy explained as she started to back away. And that
was when Tanner decided he wasn't ready for her to go.

"About those riding lessons," he pushed.

She stopped. That had been his goal.

"I don't know about that."

Colby yanked on her hand. "But I can ride. If you
can, then we can go together."

He watched her pause and consider her nephew's
words. Her green eyes focused on the little boy, and
her smile was gentle, full of love for the little guy. Finally she nodded.

"Okay, riding lessons."

Colby practically danced a jig. And she laughed, although a bit tensely.

"Friday, late afternoon at my place," Tanner told her. "And don't forget to wear boots."

"I won't forget. We should go."

Tanner opened the gate and walked through, ignoring the curious looks of his sister. "Mind if I walk with you? There are a few trails that are best. And you want to be…"

Safe. He didn't say it. But with the recent incidents, she didn't need to be away from the ranch alone.

"You don't have to," she told him. She reached for Colby's hand. "We'll stay close."

"But I want to show you the spring. There are big fish." Colby was pulling on her hand. She shook her head, and he stopped.

"I can get a pole out of the barn," Tanner offered.

"Fishing?" Her eyes got big, and she looked as nervous as she had when he mentioned learning to ride.

He barked out a laugh. "Let me guess, you haven't been fishing?"

"Not by myself. Not with, what? Worms?" She made a face, half disgust, half fear.

"Yeah, worms," Colby said with a little too much excitement.

She closed her eyes, scrunching them together. When she opened them, she managed a tight smile. "Okay, fishing. But you're going with us, right?"

"I'll bait the hooks," Tanner assured her.

"Well, I guess I'm going to leave now." Russell stepped away from their group.

The abrupt statement took Tanner by surprise and distracted him from Macy and Colby. He looked past

Russell to his sister. She looked just as surprised and not too happy.

"I was going to show you around," she said, not letting too much emotion into the statement.

"Yeah, but I remembered that I have somewhere I have to be," Russell, the gem, informed Chloe. "Sorry, honey, gotta run."

He kissed her cheek. She pulled back. "Fine, go. I'll see you later."

"Of course you will."

"I'll go in and get the fishing gear." Tanner glanced at his sister, giving her what he hoped was an encouraging, not judging, look. "Sis, you want to go fishing?"

She was watching Russell as he walked toward the main house and the old truck he'd parked there. She shook her head. "No, I don't think I do. I'm going back to the shop. Should I close up for you this evening?"

He looked at his watch. "I might be late. So, yes, if I'm not back, go ahead and lock up. Tell Larry I'll be there all day tomorrow."

She nodded and started to leave. Jay must have settled the horse and left the barn by the side door. He was heading in their direction with a backpack.

"Hey, Chloe," he called out, stopping Tanner's sister from leaving.

She looked back, and he held up the backpack. "Did you leave this in my car?"

Her eyes widened. She didn't quite look guilty, Tanner thought. But she didn't look innocent. The ranch hand, probably a guy Chloe would have given a second look if not for Russell, appeared completely innocent but a little confused. He headed her way.

"Interesting," Macy whispered. She was standing

next to him, her arm brushing his in an easy way that felt a lot like friendship. "Did you see that coming?"

"I'm not even sure what I'm seeing. She looks cornered, and he looks clueless."

She chuckled. "Well, men usually are."

He looked down at the woman next to him, and she lost that amused look. "I promise you, some of us are not clueless."

She opened her mouth, a lot like those fish Colby was wanting to catch. But before she could say anything, Chloe returned with the backpack, and Jay was heading toward the cabins, whistling a country song.

"Did you do that?" Chloe pointed a finger at Tanner.

"Do what?" Okay, now he was clueless.

"Did you put my backpack in his truck? Because if you did…"

"Why would I?"

Chloe let out a sigh and looked a little lost. "I have no idea. But it was in my car."

"Unlocked car?" Tanner asked.

"Yeah, of course. I never lock my car. He went down to his truck to get some special salve he has for one of the horses, and my backpack was in there. Fortunately it has my name on it because it's one I used in college."

"Maybe it dropped out of your car and someone saw it and just put it in the nearest vehicle?" Macy offered what sounded like a reasonable explanation.

"I can't imagine that." Chloe gave the bag a look. "It was in the backseat. And to make things better, he said Russell saw him take it out of his truck."

"What did Russell say?" Tanner asked.

"I guess nothing. He just saw it." She hooked the

backpack over her shoulder. "I'm going, but if you find out anything, let me know."

"I will," Tanner assured her.

When she left, he headed for the barn. "I'm going to get the fishing gear."

He wasn't clueless, but he definitely could use some clues concerning everything going on around this ranch. He would guess the backpack didn't end up in Jay's truck by accident. Someone, other than him, must have the idea that Chloe and Russell weren't a good fit.

The thought was amusing until he realized that the same someone thought he and Macy looked like a couple.

Chapter Ten

They hadn't caught any fish on Wednesday. Afterward Macy had promised they would try again. She would even try baiting the hook. A day later she shuddered to think about it. But, for Colby, she would try. She just hoped today wasn't the day. She had worked at the local library in the morning and the school in the afternoon. Now she was heading to the ranch to help pack.

Some people thought of small towns as slow-paced and lazy. She'd never been so busy.

She pulled up to Cabin One. Eleanor was sweeping the front porch. One of the boys was picking up a few bits of paper and trash that had blown into the yard. Macy joined them.

"Are you here for the joy of packing?" Eleanor asked, leaning the broom against the wall.

"Whatever you need me to do," Macy offered.

"We need to start packing up toys and summer clothes. I have tubs that we can put them in and a permanent marker for labeling. The boys are going through things, deciding what they can do without for the next few weeks. You'd be surprised how much they're willing to give up. And I'm willing to give up all the dishes. We usually eat a few meals here, as a family, but we'll be eating all of our meals at the main house for the next couple of weeks. Until the move."

"The Culpepper place doesn't have cabins. How will that work?"

"There are three wings," a voice, deep and familiar, said from behind her.

Was the man everywhere these days? He was like a sore toe. She didn't used to notice him, but now she couldn't help bumping into him every time she turned around.

She had to face him, or she'd be a coward.

"Good afternoon, Tanner." There, she'd sounded nearly normal.

"Afternoon, Macy, Eleanor. I volunteered with Russell—" he grimaced as he said it "—to take a load to the Culpepper place. Do you have anything to load up here?"

"We do. I have the laundry room piled with boxes of nonessential items."

"I'll back the stock trailer up there and start loading." He tipped his hat, as if that were the end.

Colby came running out of the cabin, letting the screen door bang shut behind him and earning him a warning look from Eleanor. But he wasn't running to Macy. She realized that as he hurried past her to tug on Tanner's hand.

Tanner smiled down at him. "Hey, Colby."

"I dug up more worms."

Tanner chuckled at that. "Did you? Well, now, we'll have to see if we can put those worms to good use. But first we have to work. We're going to move some things over to the new ranch."

The smile on Colby's face dissolved into a frown. "I don't want to move."

Tanner looked from the boy to Macy and then to Eleanor. "Why wouldn't you want to move?"

Colby shot Macy a look and then leaned closer to Tanner. "Because I want to stay here."

"But you can't stay here forever. It's a good resting place, Colby. But you have a home."

Eleanor left the porch and moved forward to do what Macy should have known how to do. But she didn't. She was so consumed in Colby's pain, in his loss, that she didn't know what to do for him.

"Colby, there are changes in life. Some of those changes are harder than others. Some changes are good and even fun or exciting." Eleanor knelt down in front of him. "There's something I want you to do for me."

"What?" He didn't manage to sound happy.

Eleanor ruffled a hand through his hair. "First, try to sound like my friend Colby. You are a tough kid. And that's good because you've gone through some tough things in the last year. But I want you to think about going home."

He shook his head emphatically.

"No, now listen. When you think about going home, think about the fun stuff you and Macy will do. Think about that dog you want. Or a cat. Think about what you'll name it. Think about how you want to redecorate. Or what sports you want to play. Think about the future and everything awesome you want to do. You might want to visit your grandma in Arizona. I heard that the Grand Canyon is amazing."

"Maybe we could visit her in the summer. After school." Macy moved toward her nephew, praying he wouldn't reject her.

He didn't. He looked up when she spoke, and he nodded. "I want to go to the Grand Canyon. And ride a donkey."

She held her arms out, and he gave her a hug. "But to do that, Colby, we have to work on being a family."

His little face fell. "I know."

A hand touched her back, comforting. The touch was strong and sure. "I'll touch base with you later?"

"Yes, of course."

Tanner looked around for his helper, who hadn't shown up. "I guess Russell isn't going to make it."

"Maybe we could ride along with you. Colby would probably like to see the Culpepper ranch. And the two of us are pretty good at moving boxes."

"Sounds like a plan. I'll get my truck and back the trailer up to the back door."

They were loading boxes when Jay showed up.

"Hey, Tanner, I've finished with the boys and their new calves. Do you all need help with these boxes?"

"Since our help skated out on us, that would be good. How did your interview go with the school?"

"I think I'll get the job. High school history and geography. And once I finish my counseling degree, I'll be able to volunteer at the ranch as a therapist."

Macy handed Tanner a box and made eye contact with him. It was easy to see what he was thinking as he looked at Jay Maxwell. He was seeing a young man with potential and comparing him to Russell. She had to agree, Russell would probably break Chloe's heart.

But she also knew from experience that Chloe would have to learn that on her own.

Her phone rang as they were loading the last box. She stepped away and answered it.

"Hey, Macy, it's Avery Culpepper. I wanted to let you know, I've gotten things taken care of here. I'll be in Haven by Sunday."

"Like I said before, I'm not sure that it's necessary to come right away, but you will be able to meet with the lawyer and have a look around town."

"Oh, I plan on staying."

"Well, if you do, we have several options," Macy offered, realizing she wasn't going to be able to talk Avery out of coming to town now. "There's a board-inghouse, a B and B, and just down the road in Field-ton, there's a hotel."

A long pause and then a quiet "Oh."

"Do those not work for you?"

"Well, I kind of thought, since I'm Cyrus Culpep-per's granddaughter, that I would stay at his ranch."

"That might be a problem, and I definitely am not the one to give permission for that."

"I am his heir."

"Again," Macy said as Tanner turned his attention to her and the phone call, "I'm not the one to give per-mission for that. There is a will. And lawyers."

"I see. Well, wasn't my granddad a rich old coot?"

Macy opened her mouth, and she just couldn't get the words out.

"Hello?" Avery sounded young and immature.

"Yes, well, I don't know anything about your grand-father and his finances."

"I guess I'll be getting myself a lawyer, then."

"That's probably a good idea." Macy made eye contact with Tanner. "If you're coming to town Sunday, we'll be at church. If you want to meet me there at noon, I can help you find the boardinghouse or the bed-and-breakfast."

"I'm certainly not going to church," Avery countered. "But, yeah, okay."

"Okay." Macy ended the call. "Wow."

"Avery Culpepper?" Tanner asked.

"Yes, and she's going to be a mess. She wanted to stay at the ranch."

"That is a problem." He motioned her toward his truck. Jay was already inside with Colby. "Climb in. I think we're ready to take the first load."

"Okay." She got in. "I don't know what I expected from Avery."

He started the truck and eased forward. "I guess we expected her to be decent. Old Cyrus was as ornery as they came, but he was a good man. Decent."

"When did his son leave?" Macy asked.

"I'm not sure if I ever knew his son. So I guess long before I ever came to town. Lila at the café said the two of them had a falling-out. She doesn't know if they ever spoke again, but she said Cyrus always regretted the way they parted. He even hired a private investigator to find his son. I guess the PI must have learned about the granddaughter, but he didn't find her before Cyrus passed."

"What a shame."

"Stop!" Colby shouted from the backseat. "Stop talking about Cyrus."

Macy shifted in her seat to look at her nephew. "Colby, what's wrong?"

"I don't want to talk about Cyrus and his son. And I don't want you to talk about him dying."

"No, of course not. And we won't talk about it anymore."

Jay had a hand on Colby's arm, and the two started talking quietly. Macy faced forward again, giving them as much privacy as she could in the cab of a truck. A hand covered hers. She moved, letting Tanner's fingers wrap around hers. It had been a long, lonely year.

Tanner parked with the trailer backed up to the front porch of the Culpepper house. He'd been here a few times, but he was always impressed by the size of the place. Chloe could call his house a castle, but by these standards he lived in a cottage.

"This place is huge," Colby said as he hopped out. "Like a mansion, right?"

"Kind of," Tanner agreed as he looked up at the place. It needed some work, but there was a fund for that. They would need more beds, more food, more of everything.

"Can I go inside?" Colby asked as he stepped up onto the porch.

"You sure can. But stay close to us." Tanner opened the back of the stock trailer. "And grab a box."

Colby grumbled, but he grabbed a box. Jay went next. They carried the boxes inside and up the steps to the floor designated for Cabin One and the Macks. The old place was still in good shape. There were hardwood floors but some carpet. The bathrooms were plentiful, and that was important with an operation of this size.

"Let's use this front bedroom for storage," Tanner

suggested. "I think it will end up being a living room of sorts."

They put the boxes against the wall and then headed back down to the trailer for the next load. As they walked out the front door, Tanner noticed a truck coming up the long driveway. When it got a little closer, he realized it was Flint Rawlings from the Silver Star.

"Flint, did you come to help unload boxes?" he asked the foreman of the boys ranch.

Flint stepped onto the porch. And he wasn't smiling. "No, afraid not. I just got a call from the Lawrence Ranch foreman."

The Lawrence place shared a property line with the Silver Star. Tanner knew the place well. At one time he'd tried to buy it.

"Yeah?"

"They've had a horse stolen. One of their therapy horses."

"Great." Tanner walked away from Macy and Jay. Flint followed. "And I suppose they want to blame the boys?"

"Yeah, they do. In all of the years I've worked at the ranch and lived in Haven, I've never seen anything like this. A community that used to support the ranch now seems bent for leather in shutting it down."

"We'll do some serious PR work in the next couple of months. Katie Ellis is good with fund-raisers and public relations." Tanner rubbed a hand down his cheek. Great, he'd forgotten to shave today. He whistled. "This is all getting a little dicey."

"Yeah, and there's more."

"Of course there is."

Flint pulled him farther away from the others. "Russell was out there the other day. And he had them show him this horse. He said he was thinking about buying it for Chloe. Of course, they told him it wasn't for sale."

"Russell couldn't buy a stick horse for Chloe."

"That's what I figured. I'm not saying he stole the horse. I don't know if he has the brains for being a horse thief." Flint grinned as he said it. "But if not, someone else did. And with everything else going on, I think we have to do more to figure out who is sabotaging the school."

"Local law is getting nothing?" Tanner asked as they headed back down the porch.

"Nope. There just isn't any evidence."

"So what do we do?" Tanner watched as Jay, Macy and Colby grabbed more boxes from the trailer and headed back inside.

"I have a friend who might be able to help. I'll get in touch and get back to you. I'm just not sure if he's willing. He has some history around here and with the ranch."

"I'm not sure if we need anyone else with a vendetta coming into the picture, Flint," Tanner said as he walked into the trailer.

"He won't have a vendetta. I just don't know if he'll want to help. And who has a vendetta?"

"It would seem that whoever is causing these problems does."

Flint shrugged. "The one person I know who has an imaginary beef with the ranch is Fletcher. And I can't believe he'd have the nerve to pick up a gun or a rock."

Fletcher. The name hung between them, and they both shook their heads and said, "Nah."

"By the way, Macy found Avery," Tanner informed the other man as they carried boxes up the steps.

"That's great. One down and four to go. I hope you're having more success than I am."

Tanner shook his head. "Nope. Gabe's grandfather is nowhere to be found. I have one lead, and I don't think Gabe is going to like it."

"Why do you think Cyrus did this? Why couldn't he just give the place to the kids and let it be? Instead he had to attach all of these conditions. Finding people. Having a big celebration. There are kids at stake here."

Tanner set his box down on top of the others that were being stacked against the wall. "I'm not sure. Cyrus could be ornery, but he wasn't a bad old guy. Maybe he wanted people to see how well the boys of the ranch turned out. Fletcher seems to want to stir the other pot, and make the boys all look like juveniles."

"Yeah, maybe that was it. I know that Samuel Teller has sent quite a chunk of cash to the ranch. And Cyrus supported the ranch, too."

Macy reappeared with another box. "Everything okay?"

Flint shrugged and left Tanner to decide if he should tell her or not.

"A horse was stolen from a neighboring property," he said. "And of course it makes the boys look bad. But also, Russell was there the other day, asking about buying the horse for Chloe."

"You think because he wanted to buy it, he might have stolen it?"

"I don't know what to think anymore." He motioned her ahead of him, and they started down the stairs to- gether.

The house was monstrous with big rooms and floor-to-ceiling windows. There was a main wing and then two wings ran back from each end of that main building. The ceilings were high. The woodwork was custom.

"It's going to be expensive to heat and cool," he mused as they walked out the front door.

Something streaked past them, a flash of black-and-white. Macy shrieked and jumped to the side. She let out a pained groan and hopped back to lean against the wall.

"What happened?" Tanner was at her side, a hand on her arm. "Are you okay?"

Stupid question. Of course she wasn't. Her eyes were closed and her mouth tight with pain. Before she could answer, Colby ran at her, his arms going around her waist.

"I'm okay, Colby. I think I stepped on a nail. What was that, a skunk?"

"A cat," Tanner supplied as he took her by the arm and led her to the porch swing. "Let's take a look."

She reached to pull off her shoe. Or what a woman considered a shoe and he considered a scrap of canvas. Blood was already seeping out. From behind him, Jay held out a towel.

"Me and Colby are going to take more boxes upstairs." Jay had Colby in hand. Tanner was glad of that.

"It's fine, Tanner," Macy murmured as she dropped the shoe. "I really liked those shoes."

"I think calling those shoes is using the term *shoe* pretty loosely."

"Be quiet." She grimaced as he lifted her foot.

"It's pretty deep. When was your last tetanus shot?"

"Does it count if I don't remember?"

He wrapped the towel around her foot. "I think if you can't remember, it means you need one."

"I can do that tomorrow."

"I don't think tomorrow will work." He stood and held out a hand. "Come on. Let's take Colby and Jay back to the Silver Star, and I'll drive you to Fieldton to the urgent care."

"You don't have to."

"Oh, you're going to drive yourself?"

"Well, I..." She shook her head. "No, I guess not. I just don't want to be a bother. I'm sure you have other things to do."

"You're not a bother. Let me help you into the truck." He put an arm around her waist, and she leaned into him, her arm around him.

They took a few hopping steps forward, and he realized it wasn't going to work.

"What?" She looked up at him and tried to take another step.

"This," he said. He turned her, and then he scooped her up in his arms, ignoring her protests. He carried her to his truck. "Open the door."

"I could have walked," she grumbled as she reached for the handle.

"And then what kind of knight would I have been? Colby would have been disappointed."

She leaned into his shoulder as he placed her on the truck seat. He tried to think back to the last time he'd held a woman and been tempted to not let go. But with her arm around his neck and her cheek against his shoulder, it was worth thinking about.

Chapter Eleven

"I don't have time to be on crutches," Macy complained as Tanner helped her through her front door that evening.

He didn't say anything, but he flipped on lights and moved her in the direction of the sofa.

"It's a nail hole," she continued. "Who would have thought jumping out of the way of a skunk…"

"Cat," he corrected.

"A cat, then, would have resulted in this."

"Jay said he found the nail and hammered it back through the porch."

"Good. I wouldn't want one of the kids to step on it." She propped her foot up on the coffee table.

Tanner grabbed a throw pillow, lifted her foot and slid the pillow under it. "There, that will be more comfortable. And you're on crutches because the puncture was deep."

"But only for a few days."

He sat on the nearby recliner. "What do you want for dinner?"

"I'll heat up a bowl of soup."

He stood. "I'll heat it up."

"You really don't have to do that." She grabbed the crutches, and he pointed a finger at her.

"Stay."

"Of course." She would stay until he wasn't looking.

He headed for her kitchen. She could hear him banging around in the cabinets. And then the radio came on, and country music drifted through to the living room. She finally did get the crutches under her arms and head for the kitchen. He didn't say anything, just tossed a look back as he emptied the contents of two cans into the pan on the stove.

"Water or tea?" he asked when he finished. "And I told you to stay."

"In school I always got marked down for not following instructions." She patted the chair next to hers. "I really appreciate you helping me today. I could have done this alone, but I'm glad I didn't have to."

"So am I." He sat next to her. Their shoulders brushed, and she could smell the spicy, outdoor scent of his cologne.

It was one of those colognes that made a woman want to lean in close to a man. It might even have been one that would make her want to touch his face, experience his kiss.

As if he knew what she was thinking, he leaned in, cupping the back of her head. And then his lips were on hers, and she was experiencing something she'd convinced herself to be a fluke. But it wasn't. This was real. What she felt when he held her was the most genuine thing she'd ever experienced with a man. It felt pure and good, and it felt dangerous.

He moved back, whistling as he let her go. "I should leave now. Is there anything you need?"

She smiled at the question and reached to touch his cheek, to run her fingers through the thick hair at the back of his neck. And then she pulled back, reminding herself that this wasn't the right time in her life for relationships.

"No, I'm good. And thank you."

He dished out a bowl of soup, placed it in front of her and gave her a spoon.

"I could call Chloe to stay the night with you. Or Josie Markham?"

She shook her head. "I'm really okay. I have some things to do around here. Maybe now I'll stay in one place long enough to do those things."

"I understand. Call if you need anything."

"I will. Thank you."

He left, and she was alone and feeling more lonely than ever before. Funny how that had happened, and all because he'd kissed her and shown her some kindness.

She finished her soup, managed to get the bowl in the sink, and then she headed for the office next to the bedroom she'd claimed when she moved in. She'd avoided Grant and Cynthia's bedroom. It felt like a shrine. In all the time she'd lived there, she hadn't been able to touch anything of theirs. There were shoes by the closet door, discarded by Cynthia; maybe she'd decided the silver sandals didn't match her outfit. Or maybe they'd been uncomfortable. Cynthia's perfume was still on the bathroom vanity.

Macy bypassed the office and headed for the bedroom. Maybe it was time to start letting go. If she let go, maybe she could move forward.

She pushed the door open and entered the room. It still felt wrong, as if she was entering a domain in which she didn't belong. The few times she'd been in here, she'd felt as if her brother and sister-in-law would come home and catch her in the act of going through their belongings. Each time that thought had sent her back out of the room.

And so it had remained, much as it had the night she first arrived in Haven. The night she'd gotten the call from the hospital.

She pulled a chair close to the dresser and sat down. One drawer at a time. She pulled out the top drawer and sighed. Jewelry, notes, mementos. She'd rather go through clothing.

A knock on the front door saved her from going through a box of papers. She grabbed the crutches and hobbled to the living room. It was eight o'clock in the evening, and with everything happening in the community, she didn't open the door the way she might have done a few months earlier. Instead she tiptoed forward and peeked out.

Chloe waved from the front porch.

Macy opened the door to the younger woman and motioned her inside. "You really didn't have to come. I told Tanner I'll be fine."

Chloe looked a little bit surprised. "Tanner?"

"He didn't send you?"

Chloe shook her head. "No. Was he supposed to?"

"Let's get a cup of coffee. And, no, he wasn't supposed to. He took me to the doctor this afternoon, and he thought I should have someone here with me."

"Someone other than him?" Chloe guessed.

"I really don't need anyone," Macy insisted. "It was sweet of him."

"He can be sweet," Chloe said with a tightness around her mouth that took Macy by surprise.

"Tanner didn't send you." She sat down at the kitchen table. "So something is wrong."

"No, not really. Or maybe." Chloe sat down across from her. "My brother is overprotective. He has a difficult time letting go."

"Yes, I told him he should give you space."

Chloe cocked her head to the side. "Did you?"

Heat crawled into Macy's cheeks. "I guess that isn't my place."

Chloe grinned. "Well, it isn't. But it's interesting that Tanner is taking advice. Anyway, I left the house. He was upset about the horse missing from the Lawrence ranch. And of course Russell is being blamed."

"Was he with you today?" Macy asked, pushing herself to her feet. "I'm still hungry. Do you want to share a pizza with me? I'll put one in the oven."

"I'd love to. And, no, he wasn't with me. I'm not sure where he was."

Macy glanced back as she hit the power button on the oven. Chloe looked unsure, but Macy wasn't going to point that out. If the other woman had doubts about her fiancé, she'd work it out.

"You can stay here tonight," Macy offered as she pulled the pizza out of the freezer.

"I'd like that. It looks as if we could both use a friend."

Macy thought that was an understatement. Chloe had an older brother trying to guide her but with maybe too firm a hand. Macy had a room full of memories to sort through.

They both had decisions about their futures that needed to be made.

Friday afternoon, Tanner pulled away from his ranch, the Rocking B, and turned his truck in the direction of the farm supply store. He'd spent the morning separating steers that were heading to the livestock auction. The next thing on his list was to check a shipment that had arrived at the store. Larry had called to tell him there was a pretty good ding on a new tractor.

Chloe was just pulling in as he got there. She'd called last night from Macy's place to let him know she wouldn't be coming home. He'd tried to apologize. She'd told him it wasn't necessary. She understood he was worried about her future. But he needed to let her make her own decisions and trust that she'd make the right ones.

They parked next to one another and met up in front of the building. "Hi, big brother." She looked up at him, shielding sunshine from her face with her hand.

"Chloe. Everything okay at Macy's?"

"She's good. She decided her foot feels better, and she isn't using crutches. I told her she'll be sorry."

She would. But like his sister, she wasn't going to listen to him. Not only that, she wasn't his to order around. Macy would make her own decisions, and either it would work out or she'd suffer for it.

He didn't want her to suffer.

"That's a fierce look," Chloe teased.

He opened the door and motioned her inside.

"I have a lot on my mind. Lane called to tell me

he'd heard the price of cattle is going to drop. And then Larry called to let me know a tractor that was special ordered has a dent."

"That isn't good."

"No, it isn't." He followed her behind the counter. "If you have this, I need to make a few phone calls. I'm afraid I've found a lead on Gabe's grandfather."

"Not good news?"

"No, I don't think it is. And later I'm supposed to go help search for this missing horse."

"Russell didn't take it."

He looked up from the packing list. "Okay."

"I know you think he had something to do with it. He was in Waco. Remember, he has a job."

"I'm sure if they need to check his alibi, they will."

"Okay. But remember to give a person a chance before you start accusing."

"I'm trying, Chloe. I know you don't believe that, but I want to like the guy. For your sake."

"Thank you."

"This is just a tense situation. We have the move for the boys ranch and now someone intent on causing problems in the community. I'll be glad when things are back to normal."

Chloe came around to stand behind the counter. "I was at the café this morning. You know, there are people accusing Fletcher. Because he's so against the boys ranch."

"I know. I'm finding it hard to believe he would go as far as this, to shoot at buildings and put children in danger."

"Yeah, I told them I didn't think he was the person responsible."

"Hopefully we'll catch them before we have the whole town up in arms." He pulled his phone out of his pocket. "Flint just texted me. He heard they found where the fence was cut on the Lawrence ranch."

Chloe didn't look up at him, and he wasn't about to question her. If she doubted her fiancé, that wouldn't be something she wanted to talk about.

When she didn't respond, he filled in the silence. "I'm going to make this call, check that tractor and then head out to the Silver Star. We've got less than two weeks to get these kids moved."

"Let me know if there's anything I can do." Chloe looked up, her expression guarded. "And, Tanner, if Russell did this…"

"One day at a time, sis."

"Yes, of course."

Tanner left his store a short time later. On his way to the Silver Star, he stopped by his place. His foreman, Lane, had called to tell him the buyer for the gray horse, Frosty, was due anytime.

Lane came out of the barn, wiping his brow with a handkerchief. "Hey, boss, didn't expect you back so soon."

"I was driving past and decided to stop and make sure Frosty is ready to meet his new owners."

"I just brushed him out, and he's in a stall waiting. I hope they like that rotten thing."

"He's showy. They'll like him." Tanner closed his truck door. "Just be honest about his temperament. Why don't you bring him out now and work him a little so he calms down? I want them to see him at his best, but also explain that he's dramatic."

"Sure thing."

Lane brought the gelding out of the stable on a lead rope. The animal was a little on the excitable side. It shied at every noise, even at a gust of wind. Tanner didn't think Frosty was that nervous, but rather that he liked the drama of shying and kicking up his heels.

"He's a crazy colt," Lane said. "If he's alone, he never even startles."

"I'm sure he'll settle as he gets older."

"True that. These people have an older daughter. She's an experienced rider, and this horse won't bother her a bit."

"I saw her showing Western pleasure last year. She can handle Frosty, or I wouldn't consider selling him to her. Hey, did you tell me about a neighbor with puppies to give away?"

"You looking to get a dog, boss?"

He ignored the question.

"Yeah," Lane answered when he didn't get a response from Tanner. "The Jacksons have a litter of mutts. I think the mama is a collie, and the dad is a retriever."

"Weaned?"

"Yeah, about ten weeks old. Cute little things. I got one for my niece."

"Thanks. I think I'll go and leave you with this. If you have any problem with the buyer, let me know."

"Will do. Hey, have they found the Lawrences' gelding?"

"Nope." He headed for his truck, checked the time and drove off in the opposite direction he'd planned to go.

When he pulled up to the Jacksons', Melton was outside. The old farmer wore his customary bib overalls, one strap hanging loose. He had on rubber boots up to his knees and a fishing hat.

"Tanner, what brings you to this side of town?"

"I heard you had puppies to give away."

"Yes, I sure do. I've got three left. Do you want them all?"

"No, I think I'll just take one."

With a grin, Melton headed toward the barn, and Tanner followed. The puppies were inside with their mom, a pretty black, tan and white collie. Two of the puppies were fawn-colored; one looked like the mama dog. He picked that one up, and it licked his hand.

"Melton, I think I'll take this puppy off your hands."

"Chloe will like that one, Tanner."

Chloe. He felt a little guilty. "No, this one is for one of the boys at the ranch. For Grant Swanson's son."

Melton Jackson's smile faded. "That little boy ought to have a puppy. That was a bad situation."

"Yes, it was."

"I guess his aunt is going to stay?"

"I'm assuming she will."

Melton hitched up the strap of his overalls that hung loose. "I guess I wasn't sure if she'd stay in our little town. It would be a shame to take that little guy away from his home and everyone he knows."

Tanner nodded at the statement, but he couldn't brush off the way it cut deep, the idea of Macy leaving. He was used to people leaving. But Macy? He guessed he wanted her to be a person who stayed.

For Colby's sake, of course.

The puppies that were left crawled around his legs, sniffing and whimpering. He reached down and picked up one of the pale pups that looked a little like a golden retriever.

"Melton, I think you're right. I think Chloe needs a puppy."

By the time he got to the Silver Star, he was calling himself every kind of fool. Those puppies were all over the cab of his truck, and from the smell in the backseat, one of them had had an accident.

He wasn't surprised to see Macy's car parked out in front of the main house. She was probably packing up the library or finishing up grants.

As much as he'd thought a puppy was a good idea, now he wondered if he'd lost his mind. He reached in the backseat and grabbed up the two menaces before heading inside.

The front foyer and parlor were deserted. Built near the same time as the Culpepper place, the Silver Star had some of the same architecture, though on a smaller scale. High ceilings, crown molding and tall, narrow windows.

"Anyone here?" he asked as he headed through the house. Near the kitchen he heard Bea, and then she stepped out of what had been a storage closet.

"What brings you to the Silver Star, Tanner?" She saw the puppies, and her eyes widened. "I hope you haven't brought me a gift. The last thing I need is to potty train a puppy."

"No, I wouldn't do that to you, Bea."

"Who would you do it to, then?" she asked.

He held up the fawn-coated puppy. "This one is for Chloe."

"For accusing her fiancé of horse thieving?" Bea asked.

"Thanks for not beating around the bush," he told her as he held up the other puppy. "This one is for Colby Swanson."

"I'm sure Macy will thank you for that. She's out at the barn. I guess Flint is teaching her to ride while she waits for visiting hours with Colby."

Flint was teaching her.

Something that felt a lot like jealousy shot through him. He pushed it aside. It didn't matter who taught her as long as she learned.

And after last night, he ought to be glad he wasn't involved.

Chapter Twelve

Macy knew her legs were shaking as she sat atop the big, rusty-red gelding named Bud. Flint had assured her that no other horse could be trusted the way he trusted Bud. The twenty-year-old horse had taught a lot of kids to ride, he'd informed her, including his own son, Logan, who was six.

When they first started, she'd thought Bud shook harder than she did. The horse had calmed down. Macy had even managed to take a few deep breaths. Flint shook his head as she rode the horse around the arena.

"If you want, we could call the local fair and get you a carousel horse," Flint offered from his place leaning against the corral fence. She was glad he was the only witness. "I can ride this horse. Colby is going to be proud of me."

"Of course he will be," a familiar voice said, not Flint's.

She turned, and the horse turned with her. And kept turning. She grabbed the reins, and the horse started moving backward.

"Stop jerking the reins," Tanner called out in a voice

too calm, she thought, for the situation. A quick glance and she saw that he was grinning.

Stop jerking the reins. Easy for him to say, but she didn't know how to stop. Flint had told her, to stop the horse she had to pull back. She was pulling back. Flint moved forward as Bud started to circle again.

"Macy. Stop. Don't pull back. Don't move. At all." Tanner's voice had a healthier dose of concern.

She let the reins go. Bud stopped. Flint was moving back away from the horse, but he didn't do a very good job of hiding his amusement. And then Tanner was there, taking hold of the reins.

"Pulling back like that is a command for him to back up," Tanner explained. "And when you jerk the reins around, you're turning him."

"I didn't jerk," she protested. "Did I?"

He moved his hand over hers. "A light rein against his neck, and he's going to move. Steady back and he'll stop. And use your knees. You'll get it."

The bundle of black, white and tan in his arms whimpered.

"You have a puppy." On closer inspection, she noticed he had two. "Two puppies."

"Chloe is coming out here later. I wanted to surprise her."

She leaned closer, running a hand over the soft coat of the puppies. "Ah, how sweet, bribing her to forgive you for being an overbearing older brother. I had one. He didn't approve of my relationships, either. And in the end, he was right. Amazingly enough, it worked itself out."

"I know that she'll make the right decision."

"Bravo, you can say it, even if you don't believe it."

She unhooked her foot from the stirrup and moved her toes inside the boots that were a size too big. "I'm going to admit something, and you'll enjoy knowing that I was wrong."

"What's that?" he asked, handing the puppies off to Flint.

"I'm sure I can't get off this horse, and I know that when I do my foot is going to hurt."

"I happen to own a castle and have my own kingdom, so rescuing is second nature."

"Corny, but useful." She eased her right leg over the saddle and held out her arms. Tanner reached for her, put his hands on her waist and lifted her off the horse.

"So who is the other puppy for?"

He took the tri-colored puppy back from Flint and handed it to her. The ball of fur wiggled in her hands, and when she lifted it close to her face, it gave her chin a bath.

"It's adorable."

"It's for Colby," he told her, sounding very confident about that fact.

"No!" But she was still holding the puppy, and it was now licking her hand. "We can't have a puppy. I don't know anything about dogs. Or cats. Or—" she looked at the horse that had moved to nuzzle her arm "—horses. I know nothing about horses."

"There's only one way to learn, Macy. Sink or swim."

"Puppies are a big commitment. They take a lot of time." She held on to the wiggling mass of fur with its cold, damp nose and tongue that seemed intent on licking her entire hand and arm. "Even I know they take a lot of time."

"Yes, they do. But it seems that this one likes you."

Yes, the puppy liked her. And she was sure she liked it. She knew Colby would love it.

"What do I do with it?" She cuddled it close. "Does it stay inside or out? What about food? And do I house-train it?"

"It can be inside or out. It eats Puppy Chow. And, yes, it can be house-trained."

She rubbed a cheek against the puppy's head and fought the wave of pain that rolled over her heart. "Tanner, I'm not even sure if I can raise a little boy."

"You are raising him, Macy. You're making the hard choices even when it hurts. I think that's parenting."

"I'm not so sure."

"Trust me."

She did. And now it was time to change direction before her heart got tugged any closer.

"And you're going to help me with this puppy?" She looked up at him, the puppy wiggling to get down and the horse pushing against her arm, begging for attention.

"I'll help you."

"Thank you. Then I guess I should go introduce Colby to his new puppy."

Flint took the reins of the horse. "I'll put this guy out to pasture."

"Thanks, Flint." She gave Bud a final pat on the neck because it hadn't been his fault she didn't know what she was doing.

"For what it's worth, there's nothing like a dog for a young boy," Flint said. "My son, Logan, and his dog, Cowboy, are best friends."

She smiled and said, "Thanks. I think." And then

she shifted her attention back to Tanner. "What are you doing out here?"

"I'm out here to help look for the gelding that wandered off from the Lawrence ranch."

"And here I thought small towns were quiet and maybe a little boring."

"Not lately, it seems." He took her arm and guided her from the arena. "What was it that doctor at the urgent care told you?"

"It seems I can't remember. I'm fine, really. A little sore, but nothing I can't handle.

They exited through the gate, and he turned to latch it. And then they stood there for a moment. In the distance kids played. The puppy squirmed and whimpered in her arms. A soft breeze blew, rustling the drying leaves in the trees. He did love Texas Hill Country.

"Your sister thinks you're trying to end her relationship with Russell." She put the puppy down and watched as it wandered a short distance from them. "Jay called and asked her if she would help him with a horse he's trying to break. Because someone told him she's the best."

"And of course she thought it was me." He whistled, and the puppy trotted back in their direction.

"There, he's already trained."

"I think that was more curiosity than obedience." Tanner reached to pick up the puppy. "I didn't tell Jay anything about her ability to train a horse."

"I didn't think you did." She took the puppy from him. "We should introduce Colby to his new friend, unless you have to leave."

"I've got a few minutes."

She pulled out her phone and looked at the time.

"Visiting hours start in five minutes. We can head to-ward Cabin One."

"Do I need to carry you?" he asked, one corner of his mouth tugging up.

"I think I can make it."

She did take the arm he offered, leaning a little on him as she clasped her fingers around his muscled fore-arm. She liked this rancher, she admitted to herself as they headed across the big lawn in the direction of the cabin.

If only it was a different time and a different place.

Tanner stayed back as Macy climbed the steps of the cabin and knocked on the door. This was her place, not his. Colby was her nephew, and Tanner was the by-stander. He needed to take more than a physical step back. He needed to take an emotional step back from her, and from Colby.

The last couple of weeks had proved that it would be too easy to become involved. And she'd admitted it herself, she didn't fit here in Haven, on the ranch. She didn't know if she could be the person Colby needed.

He couldn't imagine a relationship with a woman who couldn't be a part of his life. He'd seen too many of those marriages, with the man going one direction and the wife going another. Separate interests, sepa-rate lives and with kids somewhere in the middle. It rarely worked.

Eleanor answered the knock on the door. Her mouth dropped when she saw what Macy held in her hands. A minute later Colby appeared. The little boy let out a whoop and took the puppy. Macy glanced back at Tan-ner, including him.

Good intentions fell to the wayside. Her look pulled him forward, drew him in, made him a part of their moment.

As an honest man, he could admit, he liked being in their lives. Colby held the puppy up for him to see.

"Tanner brought the puppy, Colby." Macy reached for Tanner's arm and pulled him close. "Can you tell him thank you? For the puppy and for helping us housebreak it."

"Good one. Very good." He shook his head as she quickly put him in the middle of the situation. "Do you like him, Colby?"

"Yeah, I do. I'm going to name him Sir Arthur. We were reading a story about him in school."

"That's a great name. Can we call him Arthur, for short?" Macy asked.

Colby kissed the puppy's head. "Yeah, I think so. And when I come home, he can sleep with me."

At the mention of home, Tanner noticed tears shimmering in Macy's eyes. She blinked them away and nodded. "Yes, you can sleep with him."

Colby looked up. "I think that's good. I'm used to Sam being in my room."

"I know you are."

Colby hugged the wriggling puppy. "Sam's dad is really mad that he's here. Sam said his dad said mean things."

"I'm sorry, Colby." Macy got down on her knees, putting her close to her nephew. "Life is tough sometimes."

"Yeah, but we're tough and getting tougher." He grinned as he said it.

"You are so right. I didn't realize I was this tough. Did you?" she asked.

Colby shook his head, and then he leaned into her shoulder.

"I want to come home," he whispered close to her ear.

Tanner's throat tightened, and suspicious moisture covered his own eyes. He blinked and looked away. He hadn't cried in a long, long time. He should have known it would take a seven-year-old boy to reduce him to tears.

"I think I'll leave the two of you to get acquainted with your new family member," he said, reaching to help Macy to her feet. "I'll drop supplies off at your house. And I'll see you both at church Sunday, if not sooner."

"Do you have to go?" Colby asked.

"Afraid so, Colby. I have to get work done."

"I'm putting a roast in the Crock-Pot. For lunch after church on Sunday," Macy said, and it sounded like an offer.

"If that's an invitation, I accept."

"It's an invitation." Her hand rested on his arm.

"Then I'll definitely see the two of you Sunday."

Her hand dropped from his arm. "Tell Chloe she's invited, too. And don't forget, Flint has her puppy."

"I'll get him before I head out."

This was all starting to feel a little sticky. As he got in his truck a few minutes later, Chloe's puppy struggling to be free from his arms, his thoughts returned to Macy and Colby. They were filling spaces in his life that he hadn't realized were empty.

He left the Silver Star and headed for the Everett

Ranch. Gabriel was in the equipment barn working on a tractor. Tanner leaned in to see what his friend was doing.

"Anything I can do to help?" he asked, holding tight to the puppy that he had on a makeshift leash Jay had made for him.

"Yeah, you can tell me to stop being sentimental over a piece of metal and buy a new tractor."

"I can help you with that. I have another shipment coming in next week."

Gabriel crawled out from under the tractor. He wiped his hands on a grease rag. "So, what brings you out here today? Seems to me you've been spending a lot of time at the Silver Star."

"Is there a question in that?"

"No, not really. More of an observation. Good thing you have about the best ranch foreman in the state." Gabriel's slight grin set off a warning bell. "And you have a puppy."

"Okay, an observation. What's your point?"

"You and Macy Swanson. Never thought I'd see that. I kind of thought you were looking for a woman who could drive a tractor and pull a stock trailer. Isn't that what you told me?"

"I'm not looking for a woman. Period. And I'm definitely not letting you fix me up again."

Gabriel laughed at that. "I have to apologize. Clarice was not at all what I expected when I introduced you."

"Me, either. I thought I wouldn't get out of that alive."

"She kind of stalked you for a while after, didn't she?" Gabriel looked far too amused.

"A little. Thanks for the reminder. The nightmares had almost stopped."

Gabriel shook his head at that. "Well, I like Macy."

"So, date her." Tanner said it, but he didn't mean it.

"No, I don't poach. And I'm not interested." He led Tanner to an old cola cooler from some bygone-era gas station. "Want a bottle of water?"

"Sure."

Gabriel lifted the lid of the cooler and took out two bottles.

"I know you're not here to sell me a tractor." Gabriel sat down on a bench next to the cooler.

Tanner sat next to him, holding tight to the puppy that plopped down to chew on the rope tied around her neck. "About your grandfather. I'm assuming you want updates."

Gabriel took a long drink of water before answering. "Yes, I do."

"I haven't found him. I'm sorry about that."

"Me, too. But I didn't figure you would. If he'd wanted to be found, he would have shown up a long time ago."

"Maybe so. What I have found is that he had a record. He did a few stints in prison, for petty stuff mostly. Short incarcerations. I haven't found anything recent. The last mention of him is about fifteen years ago when he was released after a year in state."

"We have to find him, Tanner. Not for me. I stopped expecting him to come back about twenty years ago. But the ranch needs for us to find him. I can't let the boys at the Silver Star down."

Tanner got that. The boys ranch had saved Gabriel Everett the same way it had saved Tanner's brother,

Travis. Gabriel had worked long and hard to keep the ranch afloat.

"More beds means more boys having the opportunity at a new life." Gabriel said what Tanner already knew. But he didn't interrupt. "You're not giving up."

It wasn't a question, but Tanner felt an answer was needed. "No, I'm not giving up. We'll find him. And I guess you've heard that Avery Culpepper called Macy."

"I heard. Macy called Bea. And it seems Macy is a little troubled by Avery's behavior."

"A little. I think Avery is under the impression she's an heiress."

"I'm sure once she gets here and we explain, she'll understand."

"I hope so."

Tanner got up to leave. "I have to run to the store and get puppy supplies for two puppies." He grimaced as the words slipped out.

Too much. Gabriel arched an eyebrow and waited.

"Colby wanted a puppy. It's about starting over and…"

Gabriel held up a hand. "You don't have to explain."

No, he didn't have to explain. He picked up Chloe's puppy and walked away. It wasn't his most manly exit ever, with the puppy wiggling and licking his face.

He ignored Gabriel's parting comment, telling him he was getting in deep. He didn't need to be told.

Chapter Thirteen

The two vans belonging to the Silver Star were pulling into the church parking lot as Macy got out of her car on Sunday morning. She waited for them to park and then for Colby to get out. He spotted her, said something to Eleanor and headed her way.

"How's my puppy?" he asked as Macy hugged him.

"He's good. He said to tell you that he loves your bed."

Colby laughed at that. "He didn't sleep in my bed."

"No, he slept in his own doggy bed that Tanner bought him."

"Tanner bought him a dog bed?" Colby took her hand, and they started up the sidewalk to the church.

"He did. A dog bed, food, a collar and a leash. We'll have to take Arthur to Doc Harrow for his shots."

"He has to get shots?" Colby paled a little. "Why?"

"Well, because just like boys, dogs can get sick. We want to protect him from diseases."

"Can I go?"

"We'll see." She turned as a car pulled into the parking lot of the church, the engine of the red convertible loud and rattling.

The woman behind the wheel of the car was a blonde. From the tint, probably not natural. Definitely not natural. As people turned to watch, she got out of her car and combed fingers through dry, brittle hair that had almost a hint of green to the pale shade.

"Uh-oh." Chloe came up behind Macy. "Is that our Avery Culpepper?"

Bea appeared next to them. "Don't tell me."

"Avery Culpepper," Macy and Chloe said simultaneously.

"If that's Avery, she's early." Macy watched the woman dig around in her car. "And she said she wouldn't be here for church."

"She has green hair," Colby whispered.

All three women put fingers to their lips and told him, "Shh."

Avery stood next to her red convertible, her hair now covered by a Western hat with a big feather hatband. Her jeans were tight. Her boots were bright pink. Her shirt was pink satin with fringe.

"Oh, my." Bea chuckled. "That girl found a Western store on her way to town and they had relics from the *Urban Cowboy* days."

"John Travolta called, and he wants his..." Chloe started and then giggled. "Seriously, that's bad. Even Macy didn't try that hard to fit in."

"Gee, thanks." Macy looked down at her own boots. "My boots look just like yours. As a matter of fact, I bought them at your farm supply store."

"My brother's farm supply store." Chloe rolled her eyes dramatically. "Here she comes."

Avery, or they guessed she was Avery, headed their way, arms swinging and mouth chomping on gum. She saw them waiting and grinned big, waving as she climbed the steps.

"Hey, y'all, I'm Avery Culpepper. I got a call from someone saying I'd inherited a ranch."

The ground fell out from under Macy. "I didn't say that."

Bea put a hand on her arm and stepped forward, taking control. "Avery, my name is Beatrice Brewster and I'm so sorry for your loss."

"Loss?" Avery stopped smacking her gum and managed to look a little bit sad. "Yes, when I heard about my grandfather, I knew I had to head on over here. I wish I could have known him."

Her blue eyes, rimmed with dark blue and silver eye shadow, watered in a convincing-ish manner.

"Yes, of course. He was a dear man." Bea patted Avery on the back. "Tomorrow morning you can talk to his lawyer. Harold Haverman has an office here in town. You'll find he can help you with everything."

"And do you have a key to the ranch so I can have a place to stay?" Her gaze landed on Macy. "Are you the one who called me?"

"Yes, I'm Macy Swanson. As I told you on the phone, you'll have to find a place here in town. The bed-and-breakfast might have a room." Macy added a smile to help ease things along.

"I seriously have to rent a room? I thought that was a joke." Avery's sweet sentimental act disappeared. "I was under the impression I had a ranch."

Bea's smile slipped away. "No, my dear, your grandfather had a ranch."

"Which is now mine because I'm his only living relative." Avery turned her attention back to Macy. "You tell this lady I'm his heir."

"Avery, I told you that your grandfather had passed away and you are in his will. If you'll remember, I didn't mention the contents of the will or the stipulations. This will all take time, and we'll have to verify that you are indeed the granddaughter of Cyrus Culpepper."

"If I can't stay at my ranch, where will I stay?"

Macy started to say something about it not being her ranch, but Bea put a hand on her arm. "I'll give you the number for our local B and B."

The church bell was ringing, and Colby was pulling on Macy's hand.

"Church is about to start," Chloe chimed in, her tone far too amused.

They entered the church, and Macy relaxed a little. The interior of this building, with its warm tones, wood pews and the smell of citrus, always did that for her. Chloe led her to a pew near the front. Only as she sat did she realize she was sliding in next to Tanner.

Their arms brushed. He scooted to make a little more room. Colby climbed on her lap. It felt right to have him in her arms. It felt right to be in this church. No matter how complicated things had been, maybe she did have a life here in Haven. Maybe she would become a part of this community.

For the past year it hadn't always felt that way. The majority of the time she'd been more tempted to go than to stay.

Her gaze shifted forward to where the Wayes were seated with their family. The family Grant and Cynthia might have planned for Colby to be a part of if something should happen to them. And yet, here she was. She hugged Colby close, holding him tighter than a boy of seven wanted to be held. But she needed a minute with him in her arms.

The music started; the hymns took the roof off that old building when everyone sang. But even with raised voices, she could hear Avery Culpepper asking someone if her grandfather had actually attended this church. Next to Macy, Chloe chuckled. Tanner shot her a look.

The music ended, and the sermon started. Macy tried to focus, but Colby had fallen asleep, and he was heavy. Somewhere behind them, Avery still commented from time to time. And all around them people were wide-eyed and shocked.

Cyrus had been ornery, a little bit of a hermit, but his granddaughter was something else.

With the final amen, they all stood. Avery was at the back of the church, standing with Fletcher Snowden Phillips. He was nodding as she spoke. And then he took her by the arm and led her out of the church as he pulled his phone from his pocket.

"That can't be good," Tanner said.

"No, I don't think it is. She's still determined to call herself an heiress."

"She's not going to be happy," Chloe offered.

"No, she isn't," Tanner said as he took the groggy Colby from Macy's arms. "He's got a pass today?"

Macy nodded. "Yes. He can't wait to get home and play with Arthur."

"We're still invited for lunch, right?" Chloe asked.

"Of course. I even made a pie." She glanced around

the parking lot for Avery. "Since I found her, should I do something to help her? It feels strange that I was her contact person and I'm not doing more."

Tanner nodded toward Fletcher's car, where Avery stood. "I think Avery has found a friend. It isn't a good friendship, but at least she's being handled."

"I think that's the last person you want her talking to," Chloe offered. "I don't understand that man."

"None of us understand him." Tanner opened the back door of Macy's car for Colby to get in. "We'll just hope his good side overcomes, and he stops fighting the moving of the ranch."

She hoped Fletcher had a good side. But she didn't comment. As they stood there talking, she noticed curious glances directed at them.

People whispered and nodded. They were being seen as a couple, she and Tanner.

But they weren't. Couldn't they just be friends?

Macy's house smelled like roast and baking bread. Tanner followed Chloe inside. He noticed that Macy had taken down a few pictures, replaced throw pillows and added flowers.

"What do you think?" she asked in a quiet, hesitant voice.

"It looks a little more like you." By that he meant warm and welcoming. But he didn't want to say it.

Colby stood next to him, a little wired up. "Want to see Arthur?"

"Of course I do. Where is he?"

"Aunt Macy left him in the backyard. He likes it out there. And Aunt Macy said you brought him a doghouse. That makes him almost like our dog and yours. We can share him."

"I think he should be all yours," Tanner said. But he let Colby lead him through the living room to the dining room and the French doors that led to the deck and the fenced backyard. Arthur was waiting for them.

They played with the dog while Macy and Chloe made the decision that it was too nice a day to eat inside. He watched as they set the table and then brought out the food. Macy had pushed the button on the side of the house, and the porch awning slid out to cover the table area, giving them shade.

On any given Sunday it was just Chloe and Tanner for lunch at the ranch. Sometimes they went to the Candle Light. Every now and then they drove to Waco for lunch and shopping. Lately Chloe had been missing, choosing Sundays to go out with Russell.

"Time to eat," Macy called out. She was filling glasses with iced tea.

Tanner motioned Colby to follow him. "Let's wash our hands."

"Ah, man." Colby looked at his hands. "They aren't dirty."

"No, but you've been playing with the dog."

"He cleaned my hands," Colby said with a mischievous grin.

"Yeah, he did." Tanner put a hand on Colby's head. "You've got me there. But if we don't wash our hands, Macy will pull our ears."

"She wouldn't pull our ears." The boy led Tanner inside. They were alone in the kitchen, hands in the sink, when Colby spoke again. "My aunt Macy is really nice. And I hope you are nice to her. Because that guy Bill yelled at her."

Tanner pulled his hands back and reached for the towel.

"Bill?"

"She was going to marry him, but then he yelled a lot and left."

Tanner knew he shouldn't ask. He definitely knew better than to get involved. He usually knew better, he corrected.

"What did he yell about?"

Colby grabbed the towel to dry his hands. "Me. He didn't sign on to be saddled with someone else's kid."

And then the little boy hurried out of the house, leaving Tanner with more questions than answers.

Lunch was easy. They talked about the Silver Star, about the arrival of Avery Culpepper, and Arthur. Tanner fought the urge to ask Macy about Bill, a man who had made a little boy feel small and unimportant.

And, no, Colby hadn't said it. But the reality had been there in his eyes and his hurt tone. Tanner had to wonder if losing his parents and then overhearing what Bill had said might have been what pushed Colby Swanson to the level of anger that had seen him placed at the ranch.

He would talk to Macy, later. When they could be alone.

He looked up and caught her watching him. Alone. He guessed that was a bad idea. Her lips were pink and kissable, and he couldn't stop imagining the way it felt to hold her.

Maybe he would just mention the conversation with Colby to Eleanor and let her handle it.

No, he wouldn't do that. Macy deserved to know. Even if it put him in the bad position of having to tell her.

"Everything okay?" she asked as they cleared the table.

"No," he responded. She stopped moving, holding the empty meat platter in her arms and waiting.

"What's wrong?"

"We need to talk. About Colby."

"I have to take him back to the ranch soon. I bought posters for him to put on his walls. We're going to do that first. But if something is wrong, you need to tell me."

"It's about the past. Nothing you can fix right now."

She moved away from him, cradling the platter, her shoulders stiff. He followed her inside. He hadn't handled this the right way. Maybe because he didn't want to get involved. He wanted to give her the information and let her do what she needed to with it.

"Chloe, could you take Colby out back to play with his dog?" Tanner asked as they entered the kitchen.

Chloe was washing dishes, and she gave him a look that said he'd lost it. Colby got up off the floor where he'd been sitting with the dog.

"Sure, why not?" Chloe turned off the water and looked at Colby. The little boy grinned, grabbed his dog and followed her out of the kitchen.

"You didn't have to do that," Macy told him as she sat the platter by the sink and rinsed her hands.

"I think I did. I don't want you to be worried all day."

"It scares me that I rely on you so much."

It scared him that she'd just admitted that.

"I guess I never met Bill," he started.

"We ended things soon after I moved here. He hadn't signed on for this, he said. It was supposed to be us starting our lives. We had a five-year and a ten-year plan. A nephew and a move to Haven didn't fit."

"Macy, Colby overheard that conversation."

She shook her head, biting down on her lip. "No. I thought he was in bed."

"I'm sorry."

"Colby didn't say anything. If he had, I could have explained that sometimes things end. They aren't meant to be. And my relationship with Bill was one of those things."

"Tell Colby. He needs to hear that from you."

"I will. I'll talk to Bea and we'll find a time to sit down with him and talk this out. He is the world to me."

Tanner made a move toward her. She stepped into his arms, allowing him to close her in an embrace. Her head rested against his shoulder.

"You've been strong, Macy. Colby is blessed to have you."

She nodded. "I hope so. I hope I'm doing the right thing, and I hope he can come home and learn to be happy with me."

"I think he's already happy with you. He's hurt and angry that his parents left."

"Yes, and someday he'll understand that they didn't want to go."

"I think he already knows that," he assured her. "Sometimes our mind plays tricks on us, convinces us of things that aren't so."

The words settled between them, and she pulled back as if they had been meant for her.

If she'd intended to say something, she didn't. The back door opened, and Colby and Chloe returned, laughing and discussing the puppy. Chloe was telling him about her puppy and about a pony she'd recently bought just because it was cute. She told him maybe Macy could bring him out to see Lucy, the pony.

Tanner pulled at his collar as he watched Chloe, Macy and Colby discussing ponies and puppies. It was definitely time for him to make his excuses and go.

"Chloe, are you heading out with me?"

She looked at him like he'd lost his mind or had three eyes. "Yeah, I guess. Are we going?"

"I got a call from Flint this morning, asking me to come by the ranch and talk to him. He's at the Culpepper place."

"I guess we can go, then, if you're in a hurry."

"I am, kind of. Lunch was amazing, Macy. Thank you." Tanner noticed the flush of pink in her cheeks. He guessed he noticed a lot about her, after having not really paid much attention for the past year.

"Anytime. We enjoyed having company." Her hand went to Colby's shoulder. The little boy was saying something about Chloe's pony.

They left, Chloe shaking her head as she walked to his truck. He'd driven the flatbed farm truck today. She yanked the door open because sometimes it would stick. Slamming it wasn't necessary, though.

"What?" he asked as he backed out of the drive.

"You are so weird. This is why you don't want me to date Russell, because you don't know the first thing about relationships."

"I do." And he did. He'd come pretty close to proposing to a girl he dated in college. And the two of them had realized they wanted completely different things out of life. He talked to Marcia from time to time. She lived in San Diego and worked in fashion.

"Why the rush to leave?"

"We had lunch. It was good. They had things to do. So do I."

"You're afraid." She narrowed her eyes at him, the way she'd done since she was about three.

"Yeah, I'm afraid." He tried to make it sound like a joke.

His phone rang and Chloe laughed. "Saved by the ringtone."

"Not a saying."

"It is."

"Nope." He answered his phone. "Flint?"

"We've got a problem at the Culpepper place. Someone spray-painted the living room walls. I tried to call Gabe but couldn't get hold of him. You're next on the call list."

"I'll be there in five minutes."

He tossed his phone on the seat.

"What happened?"

"Someone spray-painted the walls of the Culpepper place."

Flint was waiting for them on the front steps of the house. The police were just leaving. Tanner greeted the other man and walked inside, following him to the front living room.

"Nice timing, that Avery 'I want the ranch' Culpepper showed up, and today we have these nice murals on the walls," Chloe said as she walked around the living room.

"I hadn't even considered her," Flint admitted. "Yeah, it is a little coincidental."

"Maybe too much of a coincidence?" Tanner offered. "But we've got to get to the bottom of this before someone gets hurt. What are the deputies saying? Any leads?"

Flint shook his head. "Nothing. They see coincidences the same as we do. But whoever this is, they're not leaving any evidence behind."

"Then we've got nothing." Tanner touched the walls. Completely dry.

"I have that friend." Flint walked up next to him and followed his example, touching the paint.

"Who is this friend?"

"Heath Grayson. We were in the army together. These days he's a Texas Ranger. I know he has some history around here, but he might help us out."

"What can he do that local deputies can't?"

Tanner watched his sister walk out of the room, her cell phone to her ear.

"He's just really good at digging and finding things. Better than anyone I know."

"Talk to him. We'll pay him for his time."

"I don't think he'll take money, but I'll talk to him."

That taken care of, they headed back outside. "Anything you need help with out here?"

Flint pulled keys out of his pocket. "No, I'm done. I was checking fence before we bring livestock next week."

They parted. Chloe seemed upset as she got in the truck.

"You okay?"

She gave a quick, jerky nod of her head. "I'm good."

"Anyone I can hurt for you?"

She laughed, the sound watery. "No, I can do my own hurting. Anyone I can help you see as the woman you should marry?"

"You know, Travis needs to come home so you can spend time torturing him." Tanner patted his sister's hand. "I'd do anything for you."

"I know you would." She finally faced him. She wasn't crying, but she was close.

Yeah, he wanted to hurt someone. He wanted to hurt Russell. He wanted to add a guy named Bill to that list. Because Macy hadn't deserved to be hurt, and the fact that the guy had hurt Colby in the process was inexcusable.

Chapter Fourteen

On Tuesday Macy got to the Silver Star early. The boys, including Colby, were in school. She'd planned it that way to give herself a chance to go through paperwork, pack and do whatever else she could to help. Bea peeked into her office just a little after nine.

"How's it going in here?"

"Good. I think there is a lot of this that can be shredded. I don't see moving paperwork that is outdated and won't be necessary for records. Do you want me to box it so you can go through it first?"

"No, I trust you." Bea pulled up a chair. "Macy, I think it is very close to time for Colby to go home. I think we will move him in about ten days. I'm hoping by next week to have the boys at the Culpepper place, or the Triple C, as they like to call it. I guess that's the real name. Since Colby is already packed up, I'm going to let you start taking his things home. He can have a pass to help you put it all away. After that we'll do a weekend pass and see how that goes. I do want him to have a gradual transition."

Macy looked down at the papers in her hand, unsure. Really unsure.

"Macy?"

She nodded. "I'm good. I'm just afraid. For him. For me. What if it's me? He's doing so well here with Eleanor and Edward, and I worry that I'll take him home, and we'll find out it's just that I can't do this."

"You've been doing it. You've been the mom, coming here, doing therapy with him, loving him through this. And now that's he's talking about the conversation with Bill that he overheard, maybe we can resolve all of this stuff he's buried and kept to himself. A little guy shouldn't have to carry these burdens."

"A mom should have known how to protect him." Deep breath. She closed her eyes. A hand rested on her shoulder. "We'll be fine. Of course we will."

"Of course you will, or I wouldn't be sending him home with you. I only wish all of our kids were as blessed as that little boy, Macy. So many of our kids will never go home. We hope and pray that they can, but many will stay here until we can find a home for them. I'd worry more if you weren't a little bit afraid."

Macy sighed. "So fear is a good thing?"

Bea nodded. "A little fear can be good."

Chloe stepped into the office. "Hey, did you need me for anything? I got a note from Russell asking me to meet him in Waco for pizza. Opal's Pizza. I've never heard of it."

"I don't think we need you to do anything," Macy answered. "Bea?"

Bea shook her head and got up from her chair, groaning as she did. "Not that I can think of. I need to keep moving, or I won't be able to move. I hate packing."

"Me, too. I'm going through Grant and Cynthia's room this week."

"I wish you'd done that sooner, for yourself," Bea said, stopping at the door. Chloe moved aside to make room for her.

"Yes, I should have. I guess I didn't want to change their home. Colby's home."

"You don't have to change it. Just make it yours. And let go of their belongings. Let Colby help decide what to keep. Maybe you could make a box for him, of the special things he wants. Help him to learn that memories are good."

"Thank you, Bea."

"You're welcome, honey. And, Chloe, you have a good time tonight. Macy, get something to eat. And if you go to town, bring me back some chicken salad."

"I will. I just need to work a little on the grant before I leave."

"Not a problem. Honey, we just appreciate you so much. Your grants have really helped. And soon I won't have to turn away so many boys. I just can't wait to see that ranch overflowing with boys. I just hope that Avery doesn't do something to delay or to take this away from us."

"I do, too, Bea."

Macy left a few minutes later. She stopped at Lila's first, parking on Main Street. As she got out of her car, she glanced in the direction of the Fletcher Snowden Phillips Law Office. The door opened, and a blonde in a sundress and wearing too-high heels walked out, swaying and wobbling as she turned to say goodbye to the lawyer.

Avery Culpepper looked far too pleased with herself. Macy cringed, thinking of the trouble the young woman could cause. Although Cyrus's will had insisted they find her, Macy wished she hadn't.

Lila's wasn't very busy. Macy glanced at the clock. It was early for lunch. And too late for breakfast. She was headed for the counter when she noticed him sitting with his back to her. Dark hair, broad shoulders, cowboy hat hanging on the chair next to him.

"Have an early lunch with me, Macy?" Tanner pushed out the seat across from his with his booted foot.

"How can I turn down an invitation like that?"

"I would hope that you couldn't. It was charming." He handed her a menu.

"Oh, very charming. Here, darling, let me pull you out a seat," she mocked, grinning at the rancher, who had the grace to blush.

That blush nearly undid her. It was sweet.

"How's Colby?" he asked. And not because it was the right thing to do, but because he cared. She knew that.

"He's good. He's going to come home shortly after the move to the Culpepper place."

"That's good news."

"Yes, it is. It really is." She glanced at the menu.

He leaned a little forward, making her strangely aware of him, of his scent, of the gentleness in his blue eyes. "It is good. You can do this. And he's going to be just fine."

"I hope. I really do." She took a deep breath. "I do worry that he will be okay, but he would be better with someone else. Someone who isn't me."

"You can't believe that."

"I'm not sure what I believe anymore."

"You know I like you." He said it in a gruff voice, taking her completely by surprise.

She put the menu down. "I like you, too."

"Macy, I'm not a man who randomly spends time with a woman. I want to spend more time with you."

Her heart skittered all over the place as she looked into the dark blue eyes of the man sitting across from her. She wanted to spend forever with him. She nearly choked on the thought.

"I'd like to spend more time with you, too."

"But…"

She'd seen that coming. Bill wanted to marry her, but he didn't want to be a dad to Colby. He didn't want to live in Haven. Tanner wanted a wife, kids and someone comfortable on a ranch in Haven.

"Uh-hmm?" Her heart was pounding in her throat. This felt strangely like a relationship in the beginning stages. Or maybe one about to end before it started. She found she didn't want to lose him.

"But I do feel like we're in different places." Yes, that was what she expected.

"Meaning?"

"I'm settled here. I know that, eventually, I'll get married and have kids."

She wanted to be mad at him for being so right and saying it out loud. "And I'm not settled. I still don't know if I belong here. Sometimes I wonder if Colby would be better starting fresh somewhere new. Even in Arizona near my mom."

"I know. And I don't want to miss you if you decide this isn't the right place for you."

"I don't want to miss you, either." She already missed him, and they hadn't said goodbye.

His hands found hers midtable, and he twined his fingers through hers. His hands were suntanned, strong and calloused from farmwork. Dark hair sprinkled on tanned forearms. She looked at their fingers laced together and saw it as a reflection of their lives. They'd started on this journey separate and from different backgrounds and places. Today, sitting there with him, she could see them as a couple.

"I'd like to see where this could take us. And I'm not a man who uses those words lightly."

"I know you're not. Give me two weeks. Let me get Colby home and get our life sorted out, and we'll take another look."

"I think that's a good plan. But sometime this week I would like to take you out to dinner."

"If you ask, I'll say yes."

The waitress approached, and he released Macy's hands. Her heart was another matter.

If Tanner told anyone that he'd practically asked Macy Swanson to go steady, like some green sixteen-year-old boy, they wouldn't believe it. He still didn't believe it.

Even as he drove out to the Silver Star to help move livestock that evening, he was still feeling kind of numb. It had been hours ago, yet he remembered the way she'd looked at him with those green eyes studying him, waiting for something more than what he was prepared to give.

What he should have told her was that he hadn't met a woman in years, maybe ever, who made him think about the future the way she did. Being with her, near her, changed everything for him. He no longer saw himself as the owner of the Haven Tractor and Supply, or the owner of the Rocking B; he saw himself as someone who could have a life with Macy, with Colby.

It was amazing that three weeks could change him this drastically. Amazing. And it scared him silly. Because he knew that she might leave.

When he pulled his stock trailer up to the barn at the Silver Star, Flint was coming out, carrying saddles.

"Grab a load," the other man called to him. "I have boys in there helping pack stuff."

He headed inside, and there was Colby, trying hard to drag a full-size saddle down the dusty aisle of the barn.

"Hey, partner, want a hand with that?"

Tongue out, face tight with focus, Colby shook his head and groaned. "I got it."

"I can see that you do. Let me get the door for you."

"Okay," he said, followed by another grunt as he tugged the saddle, trying to haul it up on his shoulder the way he'd probably seen the older guys do.

"Are you ready for the big move?" Tanner asked, grabbing another saddle and following the little boy out the door.

Colby shot him a look over his shoulder that made Tanner think maybe the kid wasn't ready. "I guess."

"Oh, you just guess? Did you know, I saw your aunt today, and she bought a basketball hoop?"

"Yeah, I don't want to play basketball."

"Why not?" Tanner was lost. He'd seen the kid playing with the other boys.

"Because I don't want to go. I don't want to leave

Eleanor and Edward and the kids. And I know you like her, and you'll just say mean things and threaten to leave."

"Whoa, hold up there." Tanner set the saddle he was carrying on the tailgate of his truck and took the oversize saddle that Colby was dragging. "Let's talk about this."

Colby fought him, but Tanner picked the boy up and carried him a short distance away. "I want down."

"You sure do, and I'm going to let you down in…" Tanner paused, taking a few more steps. "In five seconds."

He put Colby down but held him to keep him from running.

"I thought you were excited about going home."

"I changed my mind. I want to stay here. This is my home."

"No, you have a home in town. With your aunt Macy. And she loves you."

"Yeah, she loves me, and that's why Bill left."

He didn't think of himself as slow to get things, but this time it took a few minutes. When he did get it, everything made sense. "Right, okay, she picked you."

"Yeah. I don't like when grown-ups fight."

"Neither do I." Tanner glanced up as Edward approached. He gave the other man a look, asking for help. This was way outside his realm of expertise. He could teach a kid to ride, even to rope, maybe to ride herd on some cattle. Sometimes he could give decent advice. But Colby had a load on his young shoulders that needed more.

"Hey, Colby, what's up with you? I haven't seen you that mad in a long time." Edward sat down on the ground and pulled Colby next to him. Tanner started to leave, but Edward stopped him with a raised hand.

"I don't want to go home. I don't like it when grown-ups get mad, and then they go away and they don't..." Colby crawled into Edward's lap and cried.

"They don't what?" Edward prodded.

"They don't come back. And it's all my fault."

Tanner ran a hand over his eyes and walked away. Colby's pain pretty near ripped a hole in his grown heart, so he couldn't imagine how the little boy felt. Probably how he'd been feeling for a year, since his parents' deaths.

Near the house he saw Macy talking to Chloe. He headed their way because Macy needed to talk to Edward and Eleanor. She needed to hear this from them, not from him. Whatever "this" was.

"Macy, I think Edward is going to need you. He's over by the barn with Colby."

"What's wrong? Is Colby hurt?"

"Not physically."

Macy hugged Chloe and told her to call later, after her dinner at Opal's.

Tanner waited until Macy walked away. "Are you going to dinner in Waco?"

"Yes, I got a note from Russell to be there at seven." She hesitated and he waited. "I guess from Russell. He mentioned this place to me a week or so back, and the note was signed by him. But the handwriting looked weird."

"I'm not sure if that's a good idea." He backed off, hands up. "I'm sorry, that was none of my business."

"No, it isn't." She pursed her lips and stared him down. "Okay, it is your business because you worry about me. But I have to make my own decisions about the person I date."

"It is your choice. Just be safe."

"I will. Is Colby all right?"

"He will be."

Tanner watched his sister get in her car and leave, and then he returned to the barn. He saw Macy sitting with Colby, saw her fighting tears as Colby cried and clung to her. It was hard to stand back and not charge in. He wanted to hold them both, her and Colby.

Every thought like that one took him by surprise. At thirty-two, he hadn't planned on being knocked off his feet by a woman. And yet, here he was, contemplating this city girl, her nephew and how to keep them both in his life.

Eleanor had joined Edward, Macy and Colby. She reached for the little boy, and he went to her, holding tight to her neck. And leaving Macy looking alone and lost. Tanner brushed a hand through his hair and headed the other way.

"We loaded your trailer with equipment from the barn. Do you want to drive it over to the Triple C?" Jay Maxwell asked as Tanner put distance between himself and Macy.

"Yeah, why not?"

"You okay?" Jay asked, following him.

"I'm good. Tell Flint I'll meet you all over there."

"Will do," he said, but Jay was still giving him a curious look.

"Tanner?" Macy, small voice and waterlogged eyes, stood behind him.

He didn't know what else to do, so he opened his arms. She poured herself against him, heaving sobs racking her slim frame. For a long time he rubbed her back and told her it would be okay. He didn't know how, but it would be okay.

"I don't know what to do for him. He's just broken and so hurt, and I don't know what happened. I wish Grant and I had talked more. If we had, maybe I would have known what was going on. I would have known if they were having problems in their marriage, or if they had a bad night, and Colby felt guilty. I would know how to fix this. I should know how."

"Now that he's started opening up, it's only a matter of time before it all comes out, Macy. And we can pray. For him. For you to know how to help. And for the staff here."

"Yes, I know. I get so caught up in the pain, and I just want to dig our way out of this."

"Understandable."

She leaned into him and sighed. "Thank you."

"You're welcome." He led her toward his truck. "Want to ride along with me?"

"I would like that. I think I can't be here much longer. Eleanor is going to help Colby calm down and put him to bed."

"Let's go. After we get done, I'll take you to dinner."

They were pulling up the drive of the Triple C when Macy's phone rang. Tanner glanced her way as he negotiated the driveway and then the narrow lane that led to the barn.

"Chloe? What's wrong?" She bit down on her lip and avoided looking at Tanner.

Chloe was practically shouting. "He was with another woman. Macy, they were holding hands." Tan-

ner didn't think he heard every word, but he got the
gist of it.

"But he invited you?"

"The note wasn't from him. I think I knew that, but
I wanted…" The rest was garbled. Tanner clenched
the steering wheel and waited for someone to tell him
what was going on.

"Oh, honey, I'm so sorry. What can I do?" Macy held
the phone tight as if she knew he was tempted to take
it. He parked and waited for someone to include him.

He could hear his sister talking. He heard the word
note. And *over*. Macy looked everywhere but at him.

"I'm here. If you want to stay the night at my place
tonight, you can." She cleared her throat. "You should
call Tanner and tell him."

He grumbled about that being a sweet idea.

"No, he'll say he loves you." Macy smiled at him.
"And then he'll threaten to go beat Russell within an
inch of his life."

Another pause, and then Macy spoke again.

"Yes, he is." And she handed him the phone.

He took it, his hand brushing Macy's in the process.
He'd been in control for years. A carefully ordered and
structured life, the antithesis of what his parents had
provided them. And in a matter of weeks, two females
and a boy had turned his life topsy-turvy.

He was okay with that. That was the part that really stunned him.

Chapter Fifteen

A cool wind blew, reminding everyone that it was fall, even though they'd had summerlike temperatures for the past week. It was close to the end of October. In less than a week the boys would be sleeping at the Triple C.

Macy had volunteered to help paint one of the new wings, and Chloe had joined her. Josie Markham was there also, but they wouldn't allow her to help paint. She brought water from time to time and then left again. The surprise helper was Jay Maxwell. When he arrived, bringing a sandwich for himself and Chloe, Macy made a point not to ask questions.

"How is Colby doing?" Chloe asked as she dipped the roller in paint and swiped it down the wall.

"He's better. He's still not really talking. I just know he blames himself for his parents' deaths. He was doing so well, and we were planning what it would be like when we got home, and now he won't talk about it."

Jay set his paintbrush down on the shelf of the ladder and descended to grab a bottle of water. "This happens, Macy. He does want to come home, but there is a fear of not being able to handle it. He probably can't vocalize that at his age, but it happens to older children. The great 'what if' factor. They've been doing so well, but what if when they get home they can't continue their recovery? What if they revert to old behaviors?"

"Eleanor is working with him, trying to get him to confront those fears. We're hoping his trip home this weekend will help."

"And don't be too hard on yourself if there are rough spots." Jay climbed back up the ladder and continued painting.

Macy happened to glance at Chloe and saw the other woman watching him. Interesting. They were finishing up for the day when they heard a commotion from downstairs. Jay stored the paint in the closet and took the brushes to clean.

"That sounds like a woman on the warpath. I'm taking the chicken's way out and using the back door," Jay said as he stepped back into the room. Chloe joined him and the two left.

Josie glanced at Macy. "That leaves the two of us. Should we escape, too?"

They could hear raised voices.

Macy shook her head. "I want to see this."

They walked into the living room to see Avery Culpepper confronting Gabriel and Bea. The younger woman, in her 1970s version of country, was wearing big sunglasses, and her brass hair was pulled back with a headband.

"Miss Culpepper, I assure you, no one is trying to take away what is rightfully yours. And your grandfather was not an elderly man coerced into giving over his property," Bea soothed, but the tone didn't match the spark in her eyes.

"I don't know why you expect me to believe that. Here I am, his granddaughter, and I'm getting nothing but the runaround and questions about my identity. And you all are getting this house and hundreds of acres. For a boys ranch! And I know what the lawyer Mr. Phillips thinks of you all abandoning the ranch that his family donated. He isn't too happy about it."

Gabriel stepped forward. "Miss Culpepper, we're not abandoning the Silver Star. There are uses for both properties."

"Yeah, bringing in ruffians to thieve and vandalize." She flipped her hair over her shoulder. "I have to go, but I can guarantee you, this isn't over."

Gabriel motioned her toward the door. "Might I remind you that when this is over, if you stay here, these people will be your neighbors. So you might want to be careful how you treat people."

She flounced—that was the only word to describe it—out of the house. From the window they watched as she got in her convertible and sped off.

"Well, that was interesting." Josie stepped away from the window. "She does make an entrance. And an exit."

"I wish she would exit the whole area," Gabriel said.

Bea hushed him. "We'll get through this. The law is on our side. And, Macy, you are the person I came here looking for."

"Is Colby okay?"

Bea nodded and motioned for her to follow. "He is. As a matter of fact, we had a good conversation today, and there are some things you should know."

Her heart sank, but she followed Bea, taking some reassurance from the older woman's smile.

Bea led her to the kitchen. They still had some paint-ing and cleaning to do, but the room was big and bright. It would serve the boys well.

"Sit down." Bea motioned to a step stool, and she grabbed one for herself, first putting the paint can on it down on the floor. "It's hard to believe we're days away from moving in here. But I've learned in life to not sweat the small stuff. What looks like a mountain in the distance is often just a bump in the road."

Macy sat and waited. She felt a little like she had in school when sent to the principal's office.

"Stop looking so worried," Bea ordered in a sweet but firm voice.

"But I am worried." So bothered that her hands trembled, and she clasped them together.

"Okay. I want you to know this because Colby is coming home this weekend for a pass. And it is not going to be easy for him, now that we've dredged up the past. Most specifically the night of his parents' accident."

Her heart trembled along with her hands. "Okay."

"Macy, they had a fight, before the babysitter got there. I don't think it was the end of the world, but to Colby it was. His mom was mad at him because he didn't want them to go out. She was mad at your brother, too. She said sometimes she wished she could just go away. It was probably one of those things a mom might say without thinking. But in this case, Colby's mom was mad, and she didn't come back. And then your fiancé, Bill, left."

"With the parting message that he didn't sign on to raise a kid."

"The two situations were just too much for a little guy to process."

Macy put a hand over her face and shook her head. Her poor little boy. "So how do I help him?"

"Love him. Be his mom. Let him talk. When he's afraid, don't discount his fear, just talk openly and honestly."

"I do love him, Bea. Sometimes I worry that I won't be able to help him."

"You're helping him. Being there for him is the way to help move him forward."

"Thank you, Bea. For everything you do for Colby and for the other boys."

"I love these kids, Macy. And their parents. That includes you."

She was a parent. Colby's parent. She reminded herself of that as she walked out the front door a short time later. She hoped she didn't let him down.

As she pulled her keys out of her purse, she became aware of someone standing on the porch. "Tanner."

"I've been waiting for you. I wanted to see if I could fix you dinner." He stepped out of the shadows, wanting to see for himself that she was okay.

"I..." She closed her eyes, took a deep breath and nodded. "I would love that."

"I thought you might not want to be alone."

She took his hand and he led her down the steps. "I would love for life to be less complicated. Just for a week or two."

He opened her car door for her. "It will be. And in the meantime, you're still moving forward."

"I am still moving forward," she agreed.

Instead of Tanner cooking, they stopped on their way back to town and took a pizza to Macy's. He parked his truck behind her car and followed her inside. The house had changed. Gone were the dark pictures on the walls. She'd replaced them with brighter colors. It was starting to feel like her home.

"Do you like it?" she asked.

"I do. It fits you."

He eyed the tubs and boxes. "Things you're getting rid of?"

"Yes. It's been difficult. I still have a drawer or two in their dresser that I just can't bring myself to open and look through. It feels too personal."

They walked into the kitchen, and she flipped on a light. Somewhere in the house he could hear the puppy barking. "Do you want me to let the puppy out?"

"Please. I have him kenneled in the spare room. Down the hall on the left."

He returned a few minutes later. "I put the puppy in the backyard. And, Macy, if you want help sorting through things, I can do that."

"I know. And thank you. My mom is coming up in a few days. She said it is to see the new ranch and to help Colby with the transition back home. I think she's coming to see if she can talk me into bringing her grandson to live near her."

He opened the pizza box and took the plates she handed him. It wasn't the first time she'd mentioned Arizona. He had brushed it off, thinking it was just out of frustration, but saying it twice told him it meant something.

"Don't look at me like that," she said as she reached into the cabinet for glasses.

"Like what?"

"Like a storm cloud about to erupt." She poured him a glass of tea and then got herself water. She didn't ask, he noticed; she just knew.

And that troubled him, that she knew him so well, but she was thinking about leaving.

"I'm not erupting. I'm just hoping you don't go. I don't want you to go."

She opened the pizza box and put a slice on each of their plates. "I don't know what I want."

That didn't sound promising to a man who thought he'd like to be a bigger part of a woman's life.

"I don't mean it like that," she said. "I don't know, Tanner. I know what I want, but I'm afraid of what will happen. I'm afraid for Colby and myself. I'm afraid that I'll fail. I never planned to put myself in Cynthia's shoes. Even though we had discussed that they wanted to make me his guardian, I hadn't considered the reality of it. It wasn't supposed to happen this way. A guardian is a 'just in case.' And in this case, they had also considered the Wayes. And I wonder if they'd meant to change the will, to make them Colby's guardians."

"It's no use second-guessing the situation. You are Colby's guardian."

She leaned in close. "And I want to be his guardian."

"Life is messy," Tanner said. He picked up a napkin and wiped her chin. "And so are you."

She laughed and took the napkin from his hand. "I am a mess."

"Yes, but I kind of like the mess."

She pulled back and smiled up at him. "I kind of doubt that. I see you as a man who likes everything in its place. I'm chaos, at best."

"Chaos can be good." He leaned over, cupping her cheek in his hand as he lightly touched his lips to hers. The kiss was easy and sweet. He pulled back. "Yes, I like chaos. More than I ever dreamed possible."

His lips lingered over hers, and he pulled her close. They ended up standing, her arms around his neck as he held her.

He didn't want to let her go. He wanted to convince her to give them a chance. But he also knew that she had to make her own decisions. As much as he'd like to sway her to stay, she would do what was best for her and Colby.

He'd never seen himself as the dramatic sort, but he kind of thought that their kiss felt like a goodbye.

Chapter Sixteen

Colby walked through the front door of the house on Friday afternoon, his overnight bag in his hand and an apprehensive look tugging at his mouth. When he saw his grandmother, he lost a little bit of that look and ran to her, letting her grab him up in a hug.

"Why, Colby, I think you've grown!" She held him up for inspection. "Yes, definitely a guy that could hike the Grand Canyon with me."

"Mom!"

Nora Lockwood smiled at her daughter. "Macy, I meant for a vacation."

"Thank you."

"But I did bring Colby a gift from Dr. Lockwood." Nora spun Colby around again.

"You mean Granddad," Colby chided her. "That's what he likes to be called."

"Yes, Granddad."

But Macy's mom liked being a doctor's wife and so she often referred to William by his title. Dr. Lockwood.

"Oh, Macy, the title to the car."

Macy had forgotten. The minivan that had been Cynthia's. Her mom planned on selling it, and Macy had forgotten to look for the title.

"I think I know where it is." The drawer she hadn't wanted to deal with.

"Why don't you look while you're thinking about it? Colby and I have to plan a Grand vacation."

"Love the play on words, Mom." Macy kissed her mother's cheek and hugged Colby. "When you're done with the vacation planning, why don't you let Colby show you his room? We've been redecorating."

"I see that in the living room. Very colorful."

"Yes, I like color."

As she walked away, she heard Colby telling his grandmother about the new ranch. They were beginning the moving process. His cabin was being transitioned that weekend. But he wouldn't be there, because he was at home on a pass.

He sounded okay. She took a deep breath and prayed he would continue to move forward.

She headed to the back of the house and the bedroom she'd tried to avoid. In the top drawer of the dresser were papers she really needed to go through. She had to. And why not now?

There were bank papers, receipts. As she dug through, she found the car title. Simple. Easy. She should have done it months ago. She just hadn't wanted to do this. It seemed too final.

She started to put everything back, and she found a typed letter. She opened it and sat back to read. And reread.

The letter was typed on letterhead from Grant's office at school. There was no signature. But the desires of her brother and his wife were clear. Macy folded the letter and left the room. As she walked through the kitchen, she handed her mom the title of the car, and she grabbed her purse.

"Where are you going?"

"To town. I have to go to town." She shoved the letter in her purse.

"You can't just leave." Her mom stood, leaving Colby on the sofa, staring at the book on the Grand Canyon, his eyes big and luminous.

"Mom, I'm going to town." She gave a pointed look at the little boy. "I'll be right back. I'm not upset with anyone."

"Don't go, Aunt Macy."

She kneeled in front of her nephew. "Colby, when people leave, they also come back."

"Sometimes they don't," he whimpered.

"Of course they do. I'm coming back. Most important of all, I'm not upset with you or Grandma. I am a little upset about something I read, but that isn't your fault. You see, sometimes people are upset and say things, but they're not as mad as their words sound."

"God should have taken care of my mom and dad," he said.

"I agree. I wish He would have. And maybe He took care of them in a way we don't understand." She kissed his forehead. "Why don't you take Arthur outside? I'll be right back. And I'll even call in a few minutes to see if we need anything from the store."

Colby leaned his head on her shoulder. He was hers. No one would take him away from her. But what had her brother wanted? Had they meant to change their will and appoint the Wayes as guardians?

As she expected, her mom followed her to the door. "Where are you going?"

"Mom, I found something, and I need to find out if it is recorded anywhere."

"What?"

She pulled the letter out of her purse and handed it to her mother. "It was in the dresser. I guess I should have cleaned it out sooner. I would have known sooner. But it makes sense."

Her mom shook her head as she read through the letter. "No, it doesn't. You saw the will. It named you as guardian. It gave you this house and the care of a child your brother and sister-in-law loved to distraction. They knew you would love him, as well. So, where are you going with this?"

"To the attorney in town, Mr. Haverman."

"Why? This isn't signed."

"But if he knew about it? What if they planned on changing their will and hadn't gotten around to it?"

Her mom put a hand on each of her shoulders and shook her head. "Mr. Haverman would have said something."

"Mom, I have to know. Maybe they hadn't talked to him yet."

"Okay, go, then. Just remember that you have a little boy counting on you to make choices that are best for him."

That took her by surprise. "I think having a real mom and dad would be best for him. So, Mom, what do you think is the best thing for Colby?"

Her mother smiled a secretive smile. "I'm not going to tell you, because I want you to make the decision you think is best."

"Okay, and thank you."

A few minutes later she pulled up in front of Mr. Haverman's office. She got out, dreading what she'd discover. This letter could change everything. So why didn't she just throw it away and forget she'd ever seen it?

Because she wanted an out? She shook her head at the thought. No, she didn't. Maybe in the beginning when the speed bump looked like a mountain. But now? She'd adjusted. She could live in Haven. This could be her life.

She reached the door and pulled. It didn't budge. Of course it didn't. She found the hours posted and groaned. The hours showed that he went home early every Friday and he wouldn't be back until Tuesday.

"Problem?"

She turned, smiling at Chloe Barstow. "Yes. No." She shook her head.

"Maybe the problem is that you don't know the right answer."

"I found a letter."

She handed it over, and Chloe read it, not once but three times. "The Wayes?"

"Yes. I don't know what to do."

Chloe handed the letter back to her. "You take that to the nearest trash can and throw it away. It wasn't signed. It isn't legitimate."

"But is it what they wanted? What if that is what they were planning, and they just never got around to giving it to their lawyer?"

"What would it matter, Macy? You are the one who has been here for him. He needs you."

"But am I the best thing for him? I've watched the

Waye family. They love each other. They love Colby. They have four kids and a minivan."

"But what does Colby want?"

"I'm sure he would pick a family with two parents and siblings. He always wants to be with them on Sundays."

"Why don't you ask him what makes him happy? I think he'll say you." Chloe walked with her back to the car. "And while you're asking, you might ask my brother. I think he would give you the same answer."

Macy called her mom and Colby on the way back to the house. They were laughing and talking about the puppy, and they informed Macy the only thing they needed was for her to not do the cooking.

On Saturday Macy and Colby sat down in the driveway to put together a new basketball goal. They had no idea what they were doing, but the picture on the box showed the base that would be filled with sand, the pole and at the top the backboard and hoop. Somehow it would all come together. Macy's mom was sitting in a lawn chair supervising. Arthur ran around the three of them, picking up pieces of paper and chewing them to bits.

"Shouldn't we read directions?" Colby asked. "My dad always told my mom to read the directions."

Macy drew in a breath, surprised by Colby's mention of his parents. "Did she ever read them?"

Keep it light, she told herself. *Make it easy.*

"No, she never did."

"What happened?" Macy moved parts around, hoping she knew what went where.

"She could never put things together. Not even the

Christmas tree. My dad laughed at her for putting it all wrong."

Memories. She smiled because Colby had them and they were good, and eventually he would learn to share them, and to treasure them.

"Did they get a picture of that tree?" Nora asked from her lawn chair.

Colby thought about that for a minute. "I think there is a picture."

"We will have to look for it," Nora pushed on. "I do love to look at pictures."

"I don't think I like pictures." Colby picked up a part to the basketball goal.

"Maybe when you decide, we can look for them."

He nodded and reached into the box for the instructions. "This looks complicated. You should read the instructions or call Tanner."

Heat crawled up her cheeks, and she put a finger to her mouth. Colby's eyes narrowed, and he shook his head.

"What?"

"Who is Tanner?" Nora asked.

"He kisses Aunt Macy," Colby supplied, all the while looking at the directions and pretending he wasn't causing trouble.

"He's a friend."

"Sounds like a friend," her mom said with a grin.

"So, back to this basketball goal." Macy handed a few parts to Colby. Maybe if she kept him busy, he wouldn't tell more than he had.

They worked for fifteen minutes, and what they had at the end of that time was…nothing. Macy sat back on her heels and stared at the mess. It looked like her life at this point. She couldn't do what needed to be done. She couldn't be a mom and a dad to Colby.

"I know that look on your face," her mom warned. "It's a basketball goal, Macy."

"It's something Colby wants. And I don't have a clue how to do it."

"You could call Mr. Waye," Colby offered. "He knows how to do all kinds of stuff like this."

Macy shot her mom a look. "Yes, I'm sure he could. Mr. Waye is good at a lot of things, isn't he?"

"Yeah, but he can't cook. Mrs. Waye says he burns water."

"They're a pretty great family, aren't they?" she asked. And she wanted him to say they weren't. But she'd met them, and they were good people with a sweet family.

"Yeah, they are. My dad and mom used to like to eat dinner with them."

Macy's mom tapped her foot and then moved out of her chair to sit on the ground. "Grandma is going to have to show you all how to put this basketball goal together. You know, a long time ago I was all by myself, raising your dad and your aunt Macy."

"How come?" Colby asked.

"Because your grandfather, their dad, died. It was really tough. But we had each other."

"Like I have Aunt Macy?" Colby asked, fitting pieces together.

"Exactly like that." Nora handed him a part and took the directions from him. "Let's show your aunt what we can do."

"Hey, that's Tanner's truck coming up the road."

"Is it really?" Nora sat back and watched as the dark blue truck parked out front. "Maybe he can help us."

"Maybe." Colby jumped up and ran toward the parked truck and the man getting out of it.

Macy was tempted to do the same.

Tanner wasn't sure what to say to Macy. Chloe had let it slip about the letter she'd found. He couldn't believe she'd even think about handing Colby over to the Wayes. Even if she thought it might be best or what her brother had wanted. She had to know that her nephew had been through enough, and the person he wanted was her.

As he headed up the driveway with Colby talking a mile a minute about the basketball goal, his gaze tangled with hers. Once tangled, it was hard to disengage.

"Hello, you must be Tanner." An older woman with graying blond hair, clear green eyes and a mischievous smile stood to greet him. "I'm Nora Lockwood, Macy's mother."

"Good to meet you, ma'am." His gaze again clashed with Macy's. "Colby said you can't do this without me."

He leaned to pick up a part of the basketball goal.

"Help would be nice." Nora Lockwood moved from her chair. "And I think I'll go inside and see if we have lemons to make lemonade. Colby, come help me."

"We're going to make lemonade?" He jumped up to follow his grandma.

"I don't think we have lemons, Colby." Macy touched her nephew's arm. "But maybe you can find something in there."

Tanner started putting the pieces of the goal together. Macy sat back and watched.

"You know about the letter?" she asked.

"Chloe didn't mean to tell me. She was upset, thinking that you might consider giving Colby over to another family."

"The family my brother and his wife thought were better suited to raising him. Tanner, the letter was written just two months before…" She glanced away and swiped at her eye. "Before they died."

"I'm sorry." He kept working on the basketball goal. It was something he could do for her. Something he knew he could fix.

"They didn't want me. They wanted another family. People I didn't even know until I came here. And maybe they wanted the Waye family because they knew I wasn't ready for this. I'm not a mom. He needs a mom and a family."

He kept working. "You are his mom. I've watched you with him. And you are his family. You have your mom. You have the church and this community."

"What do I do with the letter? Pretend I didn't find it?"

"I guess you have to make that decision."

It *was* her decision to make. Not his. If it was up to him, she would never leave. She would stay and build a life for herself and her nephew.

He could admit, though, that he was a little selfish. He also wanted her to stay because he wanted her in his life.

"I do," she said quietly. "And it won't be easy. I never thought I would be in this place, making these decisions. What hurts is to think that you believe I'm being selfish, that this is about me, what I want. It isn't. It hasn't been about me since that night I stepped into this house and held my nephew as I explained that his mommy and daddy weren't coming home. It wasn't about me when I took him to Silver Star and left him. And this is not about me, because I want him to have the best home. Even if it means giving up."

"I know," he answered. The basketball goal was almost finished. He stood it up and finished the last pieces. "And maybe that's what you haven't considered. You are willing to give him up if that's what it takes to make him happy. I think that's the definition of a mother."

She lowered her head as tears streamed down her cheeks. "I would give up more than him."

"I guess you have decisions to make." He held a hand out to her, and she took it, allowing him to pull her to her feet. "I know this isn't where you expected to be. But I hope that you decide it's where you want to be."

He rested his forehead against hers and held her loosely.

He moved, dropping a kiss on the top of her head. "And now I have to go, because I'm not going to stand here and beg you to stay in our lives."

The front door banged shut. Nora Lockwood came down off the porch, lips pursed and eyes narrowed. Macy stepped away from him, the distance between them feeling like miles instead of feet.

"What have you two done?" Macy's mom asked.

"We put the basketball goal together?" Macy responded, glancing at him, questions in her eyes.

"No, what did you say? Colby is inside upset because the two of you are fighting and it's his fault."

"It isn't his fault," Macy assured her mother as she headed for the house. "I'll talk to him."

Tanner watched her walk away. He felt a touch on his arm, hesitant and questioning.

"She can't give that boy up," Nora told him.

"I know. But she has to believe she can be a mom. And she has to know that Grant and Cynthia picked her because they knew she was the best person to love their little boy." He pulled off his hat and brushed a hand through his hair. "If she doesn't believe that, there isn't much I can do to change her mind."

"I somehow doubt that," Macy's mom said as she picked up cardboard and packing materials.

He nodded and left, because he didn't know what else to say. He hadn't expected to be in this position, wanting her to stay and wanting to keep her in his life.

Chapter Seventeen

Macy had never suffered through such a long, agonizing weekend, followed by a longer Monday. She'd fought the urge to call Tanner. She'd avoided him by staying home from church. She'd spent the weekend talking to Colby about adults not always agreeing but that didn't mean they didn't still… She'd stopped herself from saying love.

Instead she told Colby how much she loved him.

She loved him enough to give him up if that was what was best for him. She sat in her car looking at Haverman's law office. She didn't want to go in. She didn't want to face the truth. Her brother and sister-in-law had intended for someone else to raise Colby. The thought settled deep inside like a lead weight.

What would she do if Haverman told her that she needed to honor what had been Grant and Cynthia's last wish? All of this time she'd thought someone else would be better as Colby's mom. As his parents. She'd seen the Wayes with him, and it had seemed natural and loving.

But now, in her heart, Colby was hers.

Someone tapped on her car window. She jumped and then put a hand to her throat where her pulse beat at a crazy pace. Tanner motioned for her to put her window down.

She did. And then she couldn't speak. Her throat clogged with emotion, and tears burned her eyes.

"You're not really going to do this?" he asked, his mouth a tight and disapproving line.

"It isn't me doing this, Tanner. I want to know what my brother intended to happen."

"He intended for you to raise Colby. His will reflected that. This letter you found is not a reason for you to give up. You and Colby are a family. The two of you have bonded over the past year."

"I'm not giving up. I'm trying to do what is best for Colby."

"Is this about what is best for him?"

"You had to put the basketball goal together because I couldn't. Because my brother isn't here to do the things a dad should be doing. I'm not sure I can be a mom. I know I can't be a mom and a dad." Her heart cracked a little, thinking about all the things Grant wouldn't be there for. The things that Colby would miss out on with his dad.

"Yes, and I was there. Don't forget that part."

"I won't."

He backed away so she could get out of the car.

"They didn't sign the letter or give it to Haverman."

"Maybe they didn't have time?"

"Maybe they decided you were the best person to love him."

He walked away, and she whispered to his retreating back. "I think I might love you, too, Tanner."

She loved Tanner. She loved her nephew. So why in the world was she walking into a lawyer's office, intent on giving them all up? Because she wasn't sure her love was what they needed?

In the past year she'd felt like a failure on so many levels. Colby had needed her and she hadn't been able to help him. He hadn't felt safe with her. It made her question her ability to be a mom. If she couldn't rescue one little boy and make him feel loved, then how could she commit her life to being a mom?

She could let Colby go to the Wayes, and she could return to Dallas and visit him on weekends. Maybe he would be happier?

The receptionist in the wood-paneled office looked up, smiling from behind the glass partition. "Can I help you?"

Macy stood there wondering what to say to the question. Yes, she needed help. She needed answers. She needed to know that she was doing the right thing.

"I'm Macy Swanson. I'm here to see Mr. Haverman about my nephew, Colby Swanson. I don't have an appointment, but if he could just answer a question for me?"

The receptionist looked at her appointment book and nodded. "I'm sure he has a minute. Have a seat."

Macy wandered to the waiting area. Instead of sitting, she stood in front of the magazine rack. She closed her eyes and prayed, because she knew she couldn't do this on her own. She wanted to make the right decision. She wanted Colby to be healthy and happy.

She wanted to run after Tanner and tell him she was afraid, she couldn't be the person he wanted or needed.

She didn't know anything about cows or horses, and it seemed that she didn't know much about children.

She knew books and libraries, how to teach and how to avoid the traffic during rush hour in Dallas.

She didn't want to let anyone else down. Her mind flipped back in time, to the past year. To holding Colby during the funeral and then at night when he cried. They'd gotten through some tough times, she and that little boy.

They'd gotten through. The thought melted into her heart, chasing away the doubts that had plagued her for months. Her brother and sister-in-law had known. They hadn't taken this letter to Haverman. They hadn't changed their will. They had trusted her to raise their son. Maybe she was the one who needed to trust a little. Trust their decision. Trust her own abilities.

Maybe, rather than turning Colby over to the Waye family, she could invite them into her life.

It all made sense. She closed her eyes, thanking God for this answer when she needed it.

She pulled the unsigned letter from her purse, crumpled it and tossed it in the trash. As she walked out the door, the receptionist asked if she'd changed her mind or did she want to reschedule.

She shook her head and kept going. She'd not only changed her mind about seeing Haverman, she'd changed her mind about herself. She was much stronger than she'd given herself credit for.

Tanner walked back to Lila's, entering the crowded café and bakery and not really knowing why he was there. He saw Flint at a corner table. Flint waved Tanner over to join them.

"Flint?" Tanner pulled up a chair and sat down.

"I wanted you to know, I talked to my friend Heath Grayson. I think he's going to help us out with our vandalism."

A waitress hurried to their table, menus in her hand and a pot of coffee. "I just want coffee," Tanner told her. "I'm glad to hear that. We've got to do something before people start to believe Fletcher."

The waitress poured him a cup and hurried off.

"They found the Lawrences' horse this morning," Flint told him as they drank their coffee. "Grazing alongside the road about a mile from where the fence was cut."

"Glad they found him. Still doesn't explain how he came to be on the wrong side of the fence."

"No," Flint said, "it doesn't. But we're going to figure this out. It might take a while, but we'll get to the bottom of it."

"Before someone gets hurt, I hope." Tanner looked at the now-empty cup and searched for the waitress. She spotted him and headed their way to refill their cups. "About this friend of yours. Why hasn't he been around?"

Flint started to say something, but the waitress reappeared with two plates and more coffee. After she'd left, Flint dumped ketchup on his eggs.

"Just some old baggage. But I think he'll be fine. By the way, I saw Avery going into Fletcher's office. I think she's visited him a couple of times, and she's looking pretty proud of herself. If it was just her, I wouldn't worry." Flint stirred his eggs up and piled them on his toast. Tanner was starting to feel a little bit sick. Flint gave him a challenging look and then continued. "I worry that Fletcher will use her as a pawn to do his dirty work."

"He might, but we have a will and community support on our side. Fletcher might want to think about the fact that this community is his livelihood."

"I hope he is thinking," Flint said. "Bea has already taken a few new boys. We moved Cabin Two over to the Triple C. They're set up in their wing and we're moving Cabin Three today."

"That's good. Anything you all need over there?"

"Not that I know of right now." Flint forked up a big bite of the concoction.

"Then I think I'm going before I lose my appetite." Tanner pushed back his chair and stood. "I think I'll run out to the Triple C and look things over."

"We're having a dinner this weekend, a big cookout for the kids and the community." Flint leaned back in his chair.

"If you're making that public knowledge, then I would suggest you have the police on hand." Tanner didn't like thinking that way. But if someone wanted to cause problems, the cookout would be the time to do it.

He left and headed out to the ranch. When he got out of his truck, Colby, on a tire swing that hung from a big tree next to the house, saw him and came running. Another boy trailed along behind him.

"Tanner, we have new kids. And I have a cool room."

"Do you? How are you liking it here?"

"I like it a lot." Colby motioned the other kid forward. The boy was younger than Colby and obviously shy. He stayed back a few feet, dark-haired and dark eyes. He had a bruise across his cheek that was starting to fade.

"What's your friend's name?" Tanner asked.

"His name is TJ. He doesn't talk much. And we have another new boy named Danny. He's older than me. And he can ride a bike."

"Can't you ride a bike?"

Colby shook his head. "No. I just got a bike."

The boy didn't finish, and Tanner wasn't sure what to say.

"I'm sure you'll learn to ride it when you go home."

Colby shrugged, as if it didn't matter. "Yeah, I guess. I think Aunt Macy can teach me. I guess. If she stays. I think she wants to be in Dallas."

"I don't think so, Colby. I think she loves being here with you." And he was going to have a talk with her and let her know what her nephew was thinking.

"I like it okay on the ranch. I would miss Eleanor and Edward. And Miss Bea." Colby looked back at his new friend. "And TJ needs me around."

"Yeah, I'm sure he's glad you're here." Tanner patted Colby's shoulder and made an attempt at smiling, because a little boy shouldn't be okay with not going home. "You're a good man, Colby."

"Thanks, Tanner." The little boy beamed and suddenly looked older than his seven years. "I should go now. I have to show TJ all the stuff."

"Okay. Later, Colby."

Tanner headed for the barn. He knew Jay and other hands would be working, getting everything put away. He could help them out before he headed to his store. This would give him a chance to get to know Jay a little better, since it seemed he might be dating Chloe.

He had to give one to whoever was doing the matchmaking. They'd saved his sister from a bad relationship, and they'd fixed her up with a decent guy.

That brought to mind a book and a note. The matchmaker's attempt to fix him up with Macy. It seemed they had failed when it came to Tanner and Macy. As much as he thought he might like her, he wasn't going to chase after her or beg her to stay in Haven.

He'd done enough begging in his life. Most of it before he turned ten.

What surprised him was how much he didn't want to walk away from her. All of the things he'd thought would be important in the woman he someday met didn't seem to matter. City or country, kids or no kids, he wanted Macy in his life.

But it seemed to him she was putting more distance between them, and that distance meant something. Maybe it meant she'd changed her mind about them. Maybe she meant to take Colby and go to Arizona.

Macy wasn't surprised to see Tanner's truck at the Triple C when she got there. She hoped she didn't run into him. Not now. Maybe after a few days, or a few weeks, she'd be able to talk to him, to tell him she'd made the right decision, throwing the letter away and choosing to stay.

She hadn't spoken to him since they met up outside Haverman's office.

Maybe he'd decided it was best to let her go, for them to go their separate ways. After all, they were two different people in different places. She had Colby to focus on. That had to be her priority. She'd received a call from Eleanor, telling her that today was the day she should move Colby home. He was getting too comfortable at the ranch and using it as a way to avoid his pain.

Macy understood wanting to avoid pain.

She walked into the ranch that smelled of new paint, something good cooking in the kitchen and fresh country air. Eleanor met her in the front living area. The other woman, her red hair held back with a headband, paint spattering her top, smiled and motioned her outside.

"He's on the tire swing with TJ," Eleanor told her as they walked down the front steps. "I didn't tell him that you were coming. I didn't want him to worry and get himself worked up."

"I understand. I've been working myself up on the drive over."

"Macy, you can do this."

"I know I can. I doubted myself for a while. But I'm not running."

As they crossed the yard, Colby waved and told Aunt Macy to come see the swing and meet his new friend. She smiled big, and when she got close, he ran to give her a hug.

"Colby, it looks like you're having fun." Macy waved to his friend TJ. The little boy, head down, started for the house.

"I didn't know you were coming to visit." Colby had her by the hand, pulling her toward the swing.

"Actually, this isn't really a visit, Colby," Eleanor cut in. "Aunt Macy is here to take you home."

Colby shook his head and pulled away from her. "I'm not going home. I want to stay here."

"Sweetie, what happened? I just don't know what to

do. Grandma doesn't know what to do." Macy knelt in front of him, but he wouldn't look at her.

"I don't want any more people to get mad and go away. I don't want to go home. I can stay here, and you can go to Dallas if you want."

To Dallas. "What does that mean?"

"You told Tanner you don't think you can be my mom."

"I'm not going away," she said as firmly as she could. He had to believe her. "I'm here, and we're a family."

"You're not my mom." He cried as he said it.

She picked him up and sat him on the tire swing. "No, I'm not. I'm a poor substitute. I can't make chocolate chip cookies without burning them. I couldn't put together the basketball goal. I can't sing like your mom. But I love you. I'm not trying to take her place. I just want to be here with you."

He jumped down off the tire swing. "No, you don't!"

And then he ran off. Eleanor kept her from going after him.

"We'll try again."

"I don't think it's just about trying again," Macy said, watching her nephew round the corner of the house. "I think he needs to realize that I'm here and I'm not going anywhere."

"That's exactly what he needs from you."

"The two of us are a team, Colby and I."

Eleanor hugged her tight and released her. "We'll try again this weekend. And make sure he knows that."

"Thank you."

Dazed, she walked away. She had a cake at home and streamers hanging from the ceiling. She had bought the ingredients for his favorite casserole. Her mom had bought Colby a cool leash for Arthur.

And she was going home without him.

"Are you okay?" Tanner appeared at her side.

She shook her head, feeling okay with the honest answer. "I will be. Colby isn't ready to go home with me. But I'm not giving up."

"Time," he started.

She cut him off. "I know, give him time. I will."

She wanted to ask if he would give her time and second chances. Maybe she didn't deserve either. And Colby needed her. Her nephew didn't need to be second in her life right now.

"Did you talk to Haverman?"

She shook her head. "I threw the letter away."

"Okay."

That was it. She didn't know what she expected him to say. But surely he could do better than that.

"I need to get home. My mom is waiting. We had a little family party planned. Balloons, cake, everything."

"The party will happen, Macy."

"I know it will. We've gone through so much and we'll go through more. But I think we're getting somewhere, and I do believe he'll come home."

He nodded and let her go.

She drove off with him in her rearview mirror. She didn't know what she'd expected. For him to declare his love and beg her to stay in Haven? To stay in his life?

He wasn't the kind of man who begged. And she wasn't the kind of woman who begged. She'd learned more than just that she could be a mom. She'd learned that she was strong. She'd realized what she wanted for her life.

Chapter Eighteen

Saturday, the day of the party, was warm but breezy. Macy and her mom arrived early. They'd seen Colby every day since Tuesday. Each day he'd seemed to come around a bit more. He had seemed a little more sure of himself.

The cookout was being held on the big patio behind the house. The giant grill was going, and Flint and Jay were cooking burgers. Miss Bea waved and hurried their way.

"How are you, ladies?" Bea asked as she gave Macy a hug. "I have the best news. Samuel Teller will definitely be here for the reunion in March."

"That is good news. Two down, if we count Avery, and three to go. Has Flint made any inroads?"

"Not that I know of. But he does have a friend who is going to help out around here, making sure we don't have any more problems and trying to find the person responsible for all of our incidents."

"Who is his friend?" Josie Markham approached, her hand on her rounded belly.

"A Texas Ranger from Waco," Bea offered. "And speaking of Avery, that girl is a mess."

"I know," Macy confessed. "I almost wish I hadn't found her."

"But we had to. We'll let God take care of the rest," Bea assured Macy. "Now, you ladies go find something to eat. I think Colby is playing on the swings with some of the others. And we have boys who are giving their parents a tour of the new facility."

"How is Colby?" Macy asked. She'd seen him the previous day during counseling. It had been tough for both of them, but when she'd left, he'd given her a hug.

"He's good, Macy. We talked again this morning about trust. It's going to take time, and I think we should keep with our plan for him to have weekly counseling for a month or two."

"Thank you, Bea."

Macy left her mother with Bea and went in search of Colby. She'd been praying for him, that today would be the day. She knew the timing would eventually be right. She knew that Colby's heart would heal.

"Aunt Macy," Colby shouted and waved. He was on a board swing hung from a tree. "Want to swing with me?"

She did. Very much so. She approached, and he got up and gave her his spot. And then he climbed on her lap. She exaggerated a groan as he sat down. "Colby, you've grown."

"I know, I'm getting older and more mature. That's what Edward said. He said I would be a fine man and that you need me to be the man of the house. I told him I thought Tanner would be the man of the house. He laughed at that and said someone should tell Tanner."

"Oh, Colby." She buried her face in his back. "I'm so glad you're going home with me." She was so glad she was staying here with him.

A weight had been lifted this week. It had felt as if her heart had been waiting for her to come to terms with everything and to make a decision to stay in Haven with Colby. She felt more peace. She felt stronger.

Her mom had told her she'd been worrying too much about things that couldn't be changed and not moving forward with the life she had been given.

"You do like him, don't you?" Colby pushed with his feet, forcing her to set the swing in motion. "Because I think he likes you. And I don't want the two of you to fight."

"What?" She was yanked back to the conversation.

"Tanner," he said, as if it was a given. "I don't want the two of you to be mad at each other."

"Colby, people have disagreements sometimes. Remember when you were upset with me the other day?"

"Yeah."

"I came back."

They continued to swing in silence for a while. Finally Colby sighed and leaned back against her.

"Yeah, you came back."

"That's because I love you. Your mom and dad loved you, too."

"I keep waiting for them to come back. But they're not going to. It's just you and me now. And you aren't going anywhere, are you?"

"No, I'm not."

"For a while I thought you might." He broke her heart with those words. "I don't want you to go. Someday I'm going to call you Mom. Eleanor said I can."

"Of course you can." She squeezed her eyes closed, and it was just her, Colby, the autumn breeze and…

Tanner's cologne. She opened her eyes, and he was

standing by the tree, one shoulder against the rough bark of the big oak.

Colby stopped the swing and hopped down. "I have to go tell Grandma that I'm going home. Arthur will be glad."

"Yes, Arthur will."

Tanner moved away from the tree to the swing. He stood behind her, catching hold of the ropes and pulling back to set the swing in motion. They didn't speak. He continued to push. She flew through the air, every now and then catching his scent and the scent of autumn combined.

"I'm a little bit like Colby," he finally said. And he stopped the motion of the swing, pulling her back so that her head rested against his chest.

"How so?"

"I don't like to feel abandoned. I close off when I think people are walking away from me. And I won't beg someone to stay if they don't want to be in my life."

"I'm not going anywhere. Haven is Colby's home. It's my home," she said softly.

"That's the best news I've had, maybe ever." He moved to the front of the swing and reached for her hands to pull her to her feet. "Because I didn't know how empty my life was until you became a part of it. You and Colby."

He lowered his mouth to hers and kissed her long and sweet, holding her close and safe in his arms. She dug her toes into her shoes, needing to know the earth was still under her.

"Macy, I love you," he whispered close to her ear.

She grinned, turning her face into his neck. "That's the best news I've had, maybe ever."

"That wasn't the response I was looking for."

"I love you, too," she said as she closed her mouth over his for a brief moment to punctuate her words. "And I'm not going anywhere. I talked to Mr. Haverman this week. He said Grant approached him about the Wayes and had even talked to them, but then they decided to leave things as they stood because Colby is my nephew. He said they knew it would be tough, but that I could do it. Of course, they hadn't expected anything to happen."

"You're a good mom. It hasn't been easy, giving him space and adjusting to your new life here. I hope you know you're not in this alone."

"I know. I have my mom, Bea, Eleanor, the church…"

He pulled her close. "You have me."

"Yes, I have you. And I love you."

Tanner held Macy close for as long as he could. Because he loved her and she loved him. He hadn't expected to be sappy. He'd never been sappy in his life. But this woman changed things. She made him want to write bad poetry and sing love songs.

He planned on telling her that. But not today. Today was about the ranch and about taking Colby home.

"Someday I'm going to ask you to marry me," he said as they walked back toward the house and the growing crowds of people.

"I think when you do, I'll say yes."

That was the way he wanted this day to go. He held her hand, and they found Colby telling his grandma that Tanner kissed Macy. And then he ran to tell Eleanor and Bea.

No one seemed too surprised.

* * * * *

THE RANGER'S
TEXAS PROPOSAL

Jessica Keller

Dedicated in memory of those who made the ultimate sacrifice in the line of duty. To the guardians of peace and civilization. The heroes.

Our thanks and honor will never be enough, but it's yours.

May the God of hope fill you with all joy and peace as you trust in Him, so that you may overflow with hope by the power of the Holy Spirit.
—*Romans* 15:13

Chapter One

"A forced vacation," Heath Grayson grumbled and tightened his grip on the steering wheel. He loathed speaking on his phone through his car speakers. It felt unnatural.

"You need time off. You won't take it. Where does that leave me?" Chuck, the major who oversaw the Texas Rangers out of Company F, was starting to lose his patience.

"It leaves you with a man who wants to work. Why not just let me keep working?"

"Rules are rules, Ranger. The handbook says I'm not supposed to let you carry more than one hundred and sixty vacation hours into the next year."

"I know this is only the start of my second year as a Ranger, but the Department of Public Safety hasn't ever enforced that on me." He'd carried hundreds of vacation hours with him when he became a Texas Ranger. Hours he'd never used during his years working in the investigative unit of the state troopers. "My paycheck comes from them. We're still under their umbrella."

"Unfortunately, the Ranger unit is a little stricter

with time usage. Now…even if you stay away all of November—which I'm ordering you to do, hear me?—you'll still be carrying over four hundred hours into next year. I can't believe they let you bring that time with you when we hired you."

"It's all the same branch of the government." He tried to keep the grumble out of his voice this time but wasn't successful.

"I'm aware of that. But the Austin office is going to mince me if you don't start whittling these hours away."

"Fine. Sorry. I don't want to cause you any trouble. I'll stay away." Heath swallowed hard. Worked his jaw. Still, after all these years, why was it so hard to talk about it? "But do I have your permission to look into that cold-case file we talked about…on my time?"

Chuck sighed. "I won't stop you from looking into your father's murder, if that's what you're asking. But, Heath?"

He glanced down into the footwell on the passenger's side of his truck, where a box of file copies on his dad's murder rested. "Yes, sir?"

"That case has been cold for fifteen years. Arctic cold."

Heath sucked in a breath. "I'm well aware of that, sir."

Fifteen years.

Heath had now been without his father for just as many years as he'd known the man. The hero. The Texas Ranger who had lost his life on the job. Heath had followed in his father's footsteps—at least in choosing the same profession. Heath tapped his badge, resting in the compartment near the driveshaft. However, he wouldn't make the same mistakes his father had. Heath wouldn't get married. Wouldn't drag kids into a situation where they might lose their dad like he and his sister had. He couldn't do that to people he cared about.

Chuck cleared his throat and Heath got the sense that the major was about to try to talk him out of his mission, but instead he said, "Best of luck, and rest up. That last case… You've done a lot of good, son. I wish we had more awards to hand you for that one."

Heath dragged his hand over his short dark hair. The last case had worked him raw. "I don't want awards. That's not why I do this job."

"All the same. There are twelve kids out there safe today because of your work these past few months. Allow yourself a moment to celebrate that while you're enjoying vacation. For me. That's an order."

"Will do, sir."

Heath had been the lead Ranger on a statewide bust that had started as a drug-smuggling investigation but blew up to uncover a dirty underground of child trafficking. It took months of covert and often stomach-turning investigation, but Heath and a few other officers had been able to bring charges against the seven top guys in the criminal ring. They'd arrested six more on lesser offenses. And twelve kids had been set free. He'd never forget their faces when he broke into the room and ushered them to safety.

That was why he did this job, even though it was inherently dangerous. Bringing about justice, seeing people free and safe again…that was why he wore the badge.

And now he had one more kid to help out. His teenage self. Ever since his father's murder, there had been a weight, a binding around his chest. If he could close the case, perhaps he could move past the anger that still bubbled inside that boy who'd lost his dad. The boy who'd fought with his dad the last time he saw him. The boy who'd never gotten to tell his hero *I'm sorry* or *I love you* one last time.

Which was why he was keeping his vacation local. Haven, Texas…home of the boys ranch where his father had been murdered.

First, though, he had to investigate some mischief that had been occurring at the boys ranch, where his buddy Flint Rawlings now worked. Flint had asked him to look into a string of minor offenses. Not exactly normal Ranger-type work, but Heath was desperate for an excuse to plant himself in the middle of the boys ranch in order to poke around about his father's case anyway. He'd investigate some calves getting out of their pens and some petty thefts if it served that purpose. Besides, Flint and Heath had been friends since basic training, back when they'd both served as soldiers. Heath wasn't one to turn his back on the few friends who had stuck with him over the years.

Heath adjusted his visor, blocking the midmorning sun from blazing directly into his eyes.

Flint had explained that the troubles at the ranch had escalated last night. A female volunteer by the name of Josie Markham had witnessed someone running out of the barn, calves following in the person's wake. No one knew how the perpetrator broke into the barn. But they had a firsthand account from a witness, so at least there was a starting point.

More than Heath had to go on about his father.

Was the mischief at the boys ranch a coincidence?

Doubtful. At the moment, Heath would guess everything amounted to pranks or the frustrated acting out of a disgruntled resident. It was a home for troubled boys after all. But Heath wasn't a guessing sort of man. He believed in hard facts and logic. Everything had an answer if a person was willing to dig far enough to find it.

He'd built his life on information and facts, and currently Josie Markham was in possession of both those things.

Josie Markham took a deep breath as she stopped for a moment to lean against her late-model truck. Morning sunlight traced through the unkempt field behind her home. Next year she'd plant something there. This little patch of land would be a working ranch with crops, too. She clenched her fists. No matter what, she was determined to see her dream through.

"I can do this." She rubbed her hands over her arms, trying to warm up.

Even in Texas, early November mornings carried a chill. A shiver raced down her spine, but it could have more to do with exhaustion than the weather. Josie sighed.

There wouldn't be time to relax today.

The animals needed to be cared for, she had to make something to eat, and by the time those things were done, she'd have to head to the boys ranch across town for her volunteer shift. Bea—the director at the boys ranch—had already urged Josie to begin cutting down her hours serving there, but she didn't want to. As a new member of The Lone Star Cowboy League, the organization that ran the boys ranch, Josie felt a responsibility to be there whenever she could. But it was more than that; Josie loved working at the boys ranch. She thrived on the animal-husbandry classes she taught and the hours she spent in her role as mother's helper inside the large home on the property.

Chores. She needed to finish her chores before she could think about anything else.

Josie started to move, but then decided to allow herself the small luxury of one more minute watching the sunrise before heading into the barn. Fingertips of sunlight outlined the stable and a fenced-in pasture area. Golden and pink light sketched into the fleeing night sky, making the world glow with possibility.

If Josie lived to be a hundred, she'd never get over the beauty that was the rise and fall of the sun each day. A reminder that everything had a beginning and an end—a marked-out time—that she had no control over. But God did. He knew and nothing happened outside of His care. Didn't the Bible say there was a time for everything? A time to cry, to laugh, to rejoice. God was in control.

Some days she almost believed that.

Josie traced her fingers over the large dent and scratches along the side of her truck; most of the bronze paint had started to peel off in that area. It didn't look pretty, but she wasn't going to waste money fixing it. Not that she would have had the money even if it desperately did need to be fixed.

When they'd purchased the truck as newlyweds, Dale had often kidded her that the bronze clashed with her auburn hair. Foolish man. He never did understand what the word *clash* meant in a fashion sense. She shook her head, suppressing the smile that pulled on her lips whenever she thought about their early days together. The good times.

Don't think about Dale. Don't cry.

Her throat clamped and she blinked back the burn in her eyes. Texas dust. That was all it was. The dust.

After paying off the gambling debts and back taxes she'd discovered after Dale's funeral, she'd had to sell their home and most of their married belongings. All but the truck—she got to keep it because it was paid off. The vehicle was all she had left of her and Dale's life together.

Her hands automatically dropped to her expanding midsection.

The little person growing and moving inside of her begged to differ about the truck being the only piece of their marriage left. Tears found their way to her chin. The irony of her situation—almost six months pregnant and a husband buried just less than that—tore at her heart. The week before he was gunned down on the job, Dale had started packing to leave her. He'd wanted a son—a child—and in ten years of marriage, Josie hadn't gotten pregnant.

She hadn't been enough to keep Dale happy.

Now none of that mattered. He was gone and they were having a child. A child she'd raise on nothing. With no husband, no man to help with chores or bring in a paycheck or hold her when she wanted to fall apart and cry.

For the rest of her life...alone.

"We're going to be okay, lima bean." Her voice broke on the nickname. "Hear that?" She rubbed her belly. "Don't mind your mama's tears here and there. The doctor tells me that's all part of being pregnant.

Emotions. Lots of 'em. So don't let them worry you at all. They don't mean anything. You and me are going to be just fine."

If she kept repeating that, maybe it'd be true.

Heath glanced at the screen on his GPS. Almost there.

Over the phone, Flint had given him the name Josie Markham along with her address and sent Heath off to "go along, now, and do your investigating." Knowing Flint, Heath was fairly certain the man hadn't given Ms. Markham a heads-up that a Ranger was on his way over. No matter. It wouldn't be the first time he'd shown up at someone's home unannounced, and it sure wouldn't be the last. It went with the job.

Wind whipped through his windows, carrying the scent of dirt and cattle and something musty—stale water. Decay. A low river. They'd had a dry summer and not much more rain so far that fall, either. Later in the day, the high would sit in the upper sixties. Cold by Texan standards, but Heath liked the fresh air. He'd always choose fresh air over the vented stuff.

Heath pulled onto a small dirt road, dust swirling behind his truck. At the end of the road, the ranch that greeted him left something to be desired. Could it even be called a ranch? A small cabin perched on the edge of a meandering river. Cattails encircled the opposite side of the water from the cabin and there was a tiny dock, good for launching a rowboat or canoe. It would also make an ideal fishing spot. Too bad Heath wasn't much of a fisherman.

There was a large SUV-type truck parked beside the cabin. It sported a dent almost big enough for a person to hide in along the passenger side. No way that door opened anymore. Recent crash? The lack of rust said so. Was someone still driving around in that thing? It couldn't be safe.

Behind the cabin was a barn that had seen better days. Heath parked his truck, stepped out and ducked past the cabin to get a better view of the rest of the land. Scratch his original thought—the barn had seen *much* better days. The thing looked liable to fall down in any stiff wind, probably smashing whatever poor animals called that place home in the process.

Right when Heath was about to turn toward the cabin, he spotted a petite woman coming out of the barn, struggling as she huffed and puffed behind a creaking wheelbarrow.

His long stride ate up the distance quickly. "Here. Let me help."

The woman set down the handles, balanced the wheelbarrow in the soft earth near a grassless pen and swiped sweat from her forehead. One of her fingers poked through a hole in her worn-out work gloves. The nail polish on it was chipped, but purple. Her hair color fell somewhere between red and brown. She had it pulled up, but it must be long to make that gigantic bun on her head. He never understood how women were able to get it to look that way, all piled on top... Didn't it hurt? Wasn't that much hair heavy?

The woman—Josie Markham, according to Flint—set her hands on her hips and scowled at him as if Heath were a spider on her wall. "What can I do for you, Officer?" Her tone said she didn't really want to do anything for him. Ever.

He raised his eyebrows.

She heaved a sigh. Her cheeks were flushed from exertion. She grabbed at the collar of the light green shirt she wore, fanning it to cool herself down. "White hat. Boots. White starched shirt. And that belt's the type they only issue to Texas Rangers." She gestured toward his holster. "I hope you weren't trying to be undercover."

"Good eye." He extended his hand. She narrowed her gaze but shook it. "Heath Grayson. I'm a friend of Flint's."

In the space of a heartbeat, her hesitant expression vanished and was replaced by wide-eyed concern. "Did something else happen at the ranch?" Her lips parted to suck in air and her skin went paler than it was naturally a moment ago. Josie had one of those the rare types of faces that didn't age—she'd look young forever. Even though she was probably nearing thirty, she could pass for eighteen.

She shifted from around the wheelbarrow. "What are we waiting for? If something's wrong, let's go." She started toward her truck.

Once she moved away from the wheelbarrow, he saw her stomach. Pregnant. Very pregnant. That fact wasn't a maybe or a possibly—it was a certainty. Flint had mentioned Josie was widowed, but he'd left out the little detail that she was with child. So, a recent widow.

Had she been in the barn alone...doing chores?

Heath imagined his sister, Nell. She'd been married to a fireman a few years back. Bill. A loser. He'd cheated on Nell and left her alone, pregnant with their daughter, Carly. Even the reminder of the man caused Heath's hands to bunch into fists. Heath had always wanted to march up to Bill and give him a piece of his mind, but Nell had forbidden any such nonsense. His younger sister was a strong, determined woman. The set of Josie's chin hinted that she might have that in common with Nell.

"Let me help you with your chores," Heath said.

Josie's jaw dropped. "What about the boys ranch?"

"The ranch is fine."

"Why didn't you say so? You about gave me a heart attack." She laid her hand on her chest and took a few deep breaths. Then her eyes skirted back up to capture his. "If the ranch is fine, why exactly are you here, then?"

She fanned her face and dragged in huge amounts of oxygen through her mouth as if she was having a hard time getting it into her lungs.

Now he'd done it. Gone and gotten a pregnant woman all worked up. Did he need to find her a chair? A drink of water? Rush her to the hospital? What a terrible feeling, being out of control. It was disconcerting. With his training as a Ranger and his years as a state trooper before that, he was far too used to knowing what to do in whatever situation he was placed in.

"Are you all right, ma'am?" He took hold of her elbow and steered her away from the barn, toward the cabin. She felt so small and breakable. There wasn't much meat on her arm. "What do you need?"

"I'm fine. Just fine." She laughed. "You should see your face, though." She pointed up at him and covered her mouth, hiding her wide grin. Her warm brown eyes shone with mischief. "Now *you* look like you're the one having a heart attack. Relax there, Officer. It was only a figure of speech." Her laugh was a high sound, full of joy. Josie laughed with her whole self, without holding anything back.

Heath wanted to hear it again.

She even smelled nice—a mixture of sunshine from the outdoors and something sweet, almost like the scent that used to drift through his childhood home when his mom was making caramel chews.

"You still haven't answered my question."

Had she asked him something? Heath scratched his chin.

Josie crossed her arms, resting them on top of her protruding stomach. "So, then, Heath Grayson, Texas Ranger, what brings you to my ranch?"

He toed his boot into the parched earth. How on earth was this tiny woman making him feel as if he was the one under questioning, not the other way around? Off-kilter. That was the way to describe how he felt.

"Flint wants me to speak with you about the incident last night. About the calves."

"Funny." She inclined her head. "I didn't take this for something that required the intervention of the Texas Rangers."

"You're right. This isn't exactly official business." He made finger quotes around the last two words. "I'm on vacation. Only doing Flint a favor."

"Ah, so you're a do-gooder, then? The married-to-the-job type. Poking around for petty criminals on your off time?" The tug of her lips let him know she was teasing him again.

Silence usually worked when he was locked in a room with his worst offenders. Perhaps the trick would get the firecracker that was Josie Markham to stay on track, as well. Heath locked his jaw out of habit.

"Okay. I see. That's your confession look." She pointed at his face. "That's the stern one that gets the bad guys to give in. Fine. Be that way." She pulled off her gloves and wiped her hands on the thighs of her jeans. "Well, let's get it over with quickly, then. I've got a lot that needs to get done today." She jutted her thumb over her shoulder, pointing at the barn.

Heath's gaze traced back over the patched-together ranch. If Josie was all alone, she needed help. That should take precedence over an investigation about some loose cows. It wasn't exactly like anyone was in immediate danger. Not from what Flint had shared.

Unlike the danger that had plagued the boys ranch fifteen years ago.

"How about I go ahead and help with your chores first?" Heath crossed his arms and widened his stance, ready for the fight he was sure this woman would put up. He'd spent enough time on his uncle's ranch over the years, especially after his father's death, that Heath knew his way around a barn and wasn't shy when it came to manual labor. He was just as much at home mucking stables as he was on the shooting range.

Her lips pinched as if she'd bitten into something sour. "Absolutely not."

No one could say he wasn't a good judge of character.

"I insist."

Josie blew out a long stream of air. "Listen, Officer Grayson—"

"Heath is just fine." He took a half step closer.

"Heath, then." She patted her hair. "I make it a point not to spend too much time around lawmen anymore."

Anymore?

"Interesting." He held his ground. "We're at an impasse, then, because I make it a point not to leave pregnant women on their own to do any heavy labor."

"*Labor*, really?" A muscle twitching on her cheek said she was fighting the upward tilt of her lips. "That's the word you're going with?"

"Let me help you. Please?" He softened his voice.

Why was he pushing this issue so hard? He didn't know Josie, but her condition twisted his gut and it tugged at him... She could be Nell. He'd been with the state troopers, stationed clear across the state when Nell fell on hard times. The distance had made it impossible to help her at all when she was alone and pregnant with his niece, Carly. Heath would always regret not being there for them. But perhaps lessening Josie's load—if only for a month—could be a small way to atone.

Besides, she was a witness to a recent crime. Even though Flint didn't believe there was an immediate threat, depending on what Heath's investigation uncovered, it could mean Josie was a target. Especially if she had been seen or if her information led to someone's capture.

He couldn't leave her on her own.

Heath had a month off... Why not help around her ranch? He needed something to do with his time and he wouldn't be able to spend every second of his vacation at the boys ranch investigating his father's murder. Not without people becoming suspicious. He didn't want them all to know that was what he was doing there. There was a chance he'd solve nothing. That he'd fail. He definitely didn't want them to feel sorry for him, the way people often did when they found out about his father's death.

Helping take care of Josie gave him an out…an alibi. He could help on her ranch and then drive her—because her truck was not safe in its current condition—to the boys ranch for her volunteer hours, which would give him a believable reason to hang around so much. Because he knew Flint would get annoyed if Heath trailed him around at the ranch. Hopefully, Josie wouldn't.

He yanked off his hat and laid it over his heart. "My mother would be ashamed of me if I left your ranch without pitching in. Say yes…for my mother's sake."

Josie popped her fists onto her hips and let out another loud laugh. "Well, if you're going to guilt me by bringing your mom into things, I guess a girl's going to have to accept your help." She shook her finger at him. "But mark it in the books that I am accepting begrudgingly and slightly under protest."

"Under protest." Now Heath was the one who couldn't help but smile. He wasn't used to that. "I'll be sure to mark that down."

The woman was definitely a bit of a spitfire. And not even an inch of her was intimidated by his being a Texas Ranger, which was refreshing. The instant respect that often came with the office was nice, but it tended to keep everyone at an arm's distance.

Heath rolled up his sleeves and got to work.

This November, Josie Markham wouldn't be alone. Not like Nell had been.

Not if Heath had anything to do with it.

Chapter Two

At first Josie followed Heath around. "My ranch may look like a mess. I know it does. But I'm only starting out. This has been mine for the last five months. I haven't had time to turn this place into what I've envisioned. But I will."

Heath nodded. "I'm certain you will."

He moved the cows out of the barn and into the pasture. After the cows were cleared out, he wrangled the three large hogs into a separate penned area, away from the cattle. The man spent an hour mucking out the stables and refreshing them with clean straw. While he worked, Josie minded the chickens, hunted for eggs and milked her dairy cows along with the two goats that rounded out her animals. Heath lunged for the metal buckets when Josie made a move to lug them toward her house.

"I got them." He scooted over and made a grab for the pails.

"I'm perfectly capable of bringing them in, Officer Grayson."

"Heath. And while I know you're capable…remember…my dear old mother." He winked at her.

She rolled her eyes, but moved out of his way. "Fine, then. Follow me, *Heath*."

"Lead the way." Heath grabbed the pails and inclined his head. "I'll follow you wherever."

I'll follow you. He'd meant it about the pails, but the words made her heart speed up just the same. Foolishness. Josie had only ever dated Dale, and Dale didn't believe in chasing a woman in order to win her. She'd never been followed…pursued. Not when they were dating and definitely not after they had married. Dale had referred to romance as a "mind game."

But as Josie made her way toward the cabin with Heath trailing her, the Ranger's hard-won smile and teasing wink flashed through her mind.

Oh, this was bad. Very bad. Mayday bad.

Most mistakes started in the form of a good-looking man.

She peeked a glance at him over her shoulder.

Definitely a mistake.

In those leg-hugging jeans, boots and with his sleeves rolled up until they were snug around his tanned forearms, the man was far, far too handsome for his own good. And when he'd taken off his hat and invoked his mom, his almost-black hair, messy and sticking out at weird angles from wearing the hat, about did her in.

Josie had always been attracted to the tall, dark and handsome type. Heath Grayson definitely fit the bill. He had dark, wide eyebrows, and his eyes were black coffee—hold the cream.

Don't forget tall. The man had a foot on her, maybe more.

Josie had met her late husband, Dale, when they were in high school, and they'd started dating soon after. He'd never grown beyond the five foot seven he was when they'd met. And Dale's face had been rounder—softer around his edges. Whereas Heath had sharp lines, as if his face had been chiseled from stone by some great, ancient artist.

She shook her head, releasing her wayward thoughts.

There was zero reason to compare the two men. None whatsoever. So they were both in law enforcement? Big whoop. That didn't mean she needed to pull out a chart and make a pros-and-cons list of whom she was more attracted to. Goodness... Dale was her husband. *Her husband.* At least, he had been her husband and he hadn't passed away that long ago. She was still working through the grief of losing her first love, losing the man who would have been the father to the child kicking in her stomach.

The attraction she felt for Heath—a man she'd only just met—had to be her pregnancy hormones talking. The doctor had said her emotions would do silly things in the next few months leading up to the birth. That must be the reason for her rapid heart palpitations, and the way her gaze kept tabs on Heath all morning and memorized the way his dress shirt pulled across his shoulders... It was crazy pregnancy stuff. End of story.

Besides, Heath Grayson was a lawman. Not just any lawman—he was an officer who worked the most dangerous and high-stakes cases in the state. A Texas Ranger. If Dale, who had been a sheriff's deputy, could die in the line of duty, Josie imagined the target on a Ranger's back was even bigger.

Especially these days.

Her front porch made a horrible moaning sound under their combined weight and Josie grimaced.

The old fishing cabin had belonged to her father and had fallen completely out of use after his passing several years ago. Dad had left it to her, and Dale hadn't wanted to care for the property. Once she'd moved out of her and Dale's old home, the fishing cabin was all she had to her name. She'd been proud of the little space. It was hers. One hundred percent hers. It was the first time ever that she'd lived alone, which she discovered she didn't like, but that was a different issue altogether. The fact was, now she knew.

But for as much pride as she had in the small patch of land that she was trying to turn into a functioning ranch and the tiny two-bedroom cabin that was going to be the perfect amount of space for her and her baby, worry lanced through her. She tried to see the place through Heath's eyes. Would he consider it shabby? Think her poor and tragic?

Josie lifted her shoulders, filled her lungs and held up her chin as she opened the door. This was her home. She refused to care what anyone else thought about it. She was determined to craft this cabin into a welcoming place filled with love. One her baby would enjoy growing up in. She wouldn't waste worry on what a passing-through Texas Ranger thought. No matter how much the muscles in his arms popped when he carried in her milk pails.

Josie stepped around Heath and opened up her green secondhand refrigerator. "Just set them in the bottom there."

He did so and then turned to face her, almost as if he was waiting for her to issue his next marching orders. She couldn't allow him to work on her ranch for a few hours and then send him on his way. That wasn't good manners. Besides, she still needed to fill him in about the incident she'd witnessed at the boys ranch.

Josie clasped her hands. "Why don't you wash up and have a seat? After that many chores, I have a feeling you've worked up an appetite." She rubbed her palms together, hesitant. Was this a good idea? Too late. "Bathroom's the second door in the hall there."

"Ma'am, there's no need—"

She held up her finger in that scolding way she used to do when she worked as a nanny years ago. "Ah. I won't hear it. Now's my chance to invoke *my* mother on you. She wouldn't hear of me sending away an honest, hardworking man without so much as offering a scrambled egg or two, so I won't listen to any arguments. Scrub your hands and have a seat."

"Yes, ma'am." He tipped his hat.

"And no more *ma'am* stuff," she called after him as he made his way to the washroom. "I'm probably younger than you are."

"I'm sure you are," he called back.

Josie mentally cataloged what ingredients she had and settled on biscuits and gravy with a side of cheesy scrambled eggs. She'd made a batch of her favorite biscuits from scratch the other night and there were plenty left over. They were always a huge hit when she shared them at the boys ranch. She popped a bunch of them onto a pan and set her oven to warm.

After she wiggled the knob on the stovetop, it finally clicked and the flame went on. She set a skillet over the flame and crumbled breakfast sausage into the pan. Grease sizzled and popped. Josie licked her lips. She was hungry and loved cooking. These days, though, she often skipped making what she considered real meals because there was only her.

Making food for one was no fun.

She scraped the skillet and then sprinkled in the flour, keeping an eye on it while the grease soaked it all up. Next the milk and then the rest of the flour and seasonings. The mixture would have to be stirred frequently now so it didn't get too thick or burn on the bottom. Josie juggled cracking the eggs and starting to scramble them along with stirring the gravy with finesse.

When breakfast—she glanced at the clock and saw that it was ten in the morning, so it was closer to brunch now—was done, she arranged both their plates and then turned toward the table. Heath sat there, his hat off and resting on the pole on the back of his chair. His dark hair was doing that adorable messy, sticking-up thing again. Josie tried not to stare, but it was hard not to.

"That bad?" Heath's cheeks reddened and he patted his head. "Should I put the hat back on?" He swiveled around to grab the Stetson.

He had noticed her staring? How embarrassing.

Josie swallowed hard and forced her eyes down to their plates. "No. You're fine like that. Just fine." She set the plate with double the amount of food in front of him and then took her seat across the table. "Would you mind saying grace?"

"Of course." Heath nodded and bowed his head. "Father, we thank You for the people we meet and the adventures You take us on. Bless Josie and her baby, keep them both in good health. Bless this food to our bodies, that we'll use the energy to go out and do things that glorify You. And bless our conversation. In the name of Your Son, Jesus, we ask all these things. Amen."

"Amen," Josie whispered. "Thank you."

"Sure." Heath shrugged and gave her a look that said it was strange to thank someone for saying a prayer. They both dug into their food. Heath passed a compliment her way after every bite.

"I haven't eaten that well in…" He leaned back and rested his hands on his abs. "Well, suffice it to say it's been a long time since this bachelor has had a good meal. I don't think I've ever used the oven back at my apartment for anything beyond frozen pizza."

Living off frozen pizza? Josie shivered at the thought. "No Mrs. Grayson, then?"

"There's my mother?" He shook his head. "But no, she hasn't been Mrs. Grayson in fourteen or so years. She's Mrs. Nye these days."

"Dating?" Why was she grilling him?

"No, ma'am. I'm not exactly the dating type."

She pointed her fork at him. "What did I say about the *ma'am* business?"

He ran his hand over his hair. "Force of habit, I'm afraid." Then he rocked forward, pushed his plate to the side and rested his hands on the table. "How about you tell me what happened at the barn last night—go ahead and go into detail, if you will."

"Right." Josie clasped her hands in her lap. "It was just past sunset last night. I know that because the boys were in the dining room with their house parents—there are couples at the ranch who serve as counselors and role models for the boys living there. They had just finished dinner. I was heading out to my truck."

"That one out there?" He jutted his thumb toward her driveway.

"The only one I have."

He laid a hand on the table, giving off a relaxed air that Josie knew—from Dale's training—was all part of the tricks of the trade when it came to getting a witness to feel comfortable in an interview. "Is it safe to drive?"

"Is this pertinent to my story?"

"No." He shifted in his seat. "I apologize. Continue, please."

"Well, I was about to unlock my truck but I froze because I heard a clanging sound, and I know that sound because it's very distinct. I hear it every day." Josie stopped clenching her hands together. *Relax.* She wasn't on trial. Heath was here to help.

She took a deep breath and continued, "It was the side door to the calf barn. The one I personally had locked before dinner. I'd asked one of the ranch hands—Davy—to grease the door so it wouldn't frighten the calves anymore, but I guess he hadn't gotten around to doing that yet. Good thing, too, because if he had, I might not have seen all of this and the calves would be lost."

"You're positive it was locked?"

"Absolutely. I sent the boys in to wash up for dinner and I stayed back and locked all the doors before I headed in."

"So you heard the door open?" he prompted.

"Yes, and then I saw someone charge out of the barn."

"Could you describe them?"

Of course he'd ask that. She should have used the

past few hours to try to draw a better, clearer image from her memory.

She shrugged. "Medium height, medium build. I'm sorry...that's all I've got." She blew out some air. "They were wearing a hooded sweatshirt and it was dark out. I never got to see his face."

"His? Are you certain it was a man?"

Questions... Josie took a deep breath. It was Heath's job to pick apart her story. That was how he found the truth. Josie knew that, but even still, it made her want to shrink. Dale had never been able to turn off his police brain. He spoke to Josie the same way he would a suspect. Maybe that was an across-the-board thing for all people in law enforcement.

She picked at a chip in her table. "I guess I'm assuming that part."

"Do you have any idea who it might have been?"

"No. I mean, at first I thought it might be one of the older teens from the ranch. They have setbacks sometimes. But it wasn't one of them."

His chair creaked. "You're positive?"

"Absolutely. They wouldn't do something to put the calves in harm's way. Even if one of them were upset."

"Did the person recognize you?"

"No. Maybe? How would I know? I didn't recognize them. But I talked... I said my name." She licked her lips, remembering that detail. She'd called out to the person... *It's Josie.* If one of the boys had been in distress, she'd wanted to be able to help them.

Heath leaned forward.

Josie pressed on. "The person took off toward the open pasture and I couldn't chase them." She gestured toward her abdomen. Pregnant women didn't run. Hopefully, Heath picked up on that without her stating it. "And as they took off, all the calves spilled out of the barn and started running around the ranch—into the darkness. I couldn't catch them all, so I called for help and all the boys and the house parents came out and helped corral the calves. We caught them all and were finally able to locate all the boys, too."

"Locate the boys?" His head tilted, just by a fraction. "So someone was missing?"

"Stephen." Should she have told Heath? She didn't want him to grill the teen. Stephen had been aloof recently, but he was still on track to go home next month. "He's seventeen. But he's a good kid. He didn't do it."

"How can you be certain?"

"He had a book with him. He'd been out reading."

Heath frowned. "Outside? In the dark?"

"It wasn't him."

Heath's brow dived. He used his pointer finger to rub under his chin. "How long were you outside before this all happened? Roughly."

"Fifteen…maybe twenty minutes maximum."

"Alone?" His eyebrows inched closer together with each question. "What were you doing out there for so long?"

She'd been focusing on how lonely she was. She'd been crying, not looking forward to the quiet back at her cabin. She'd foolishly asked God for a second chance at life and love.

Josie hid her shaking hands under the table. "Does that matter to the case?"

"It might."

Calm down. "I was thinking. Thinking and watching the sunset. That's all."

He touched the tips of his fingers together. "I ask because I have to determine the suspect's most probable time of entry into the barn. You didn't hear someone accessing the barn before then?"

"Not at all. I'm the one who locked it. All the doors were locked. And that was at least an hour before then."

Heath rocked forward. "More than likely the perpetrator was camped inside already when you locked the doors."

"He was in there with me?" That idea made her skin crawl. She'd locked up alone and it wasn't like she walked around the boys ranch armed.

"That's my guess. It could change depending on other information." He leaned back in his chair again and tapped one finger on the table a few times. "Then again, it's most likely one of the boys, so there was probably no danger."

"It wasn't one of the boys. They were all accounted for." *Besides Stephen, but it wasn't him.*

Heath pressed back from the table and crossed his arms. Leveled her a doubtful look. "Those boys are at that ranch because they're trouble. They wouldn't be there if they weren't. I wouldn't put it past any of them to cause problems. They've done worse."

Josie pressed back from the table. How could Heath say those things? Peg the boys as bad eggs before he'd even met them? Was he one of those cops who had seen so many horrible things that he automatically assumed the worst about everyone? She had watched Dale grow bitter about the world, more so each year on the job.

She shouldn't press Heath. Then again, Josie had promised herself after Dale passed away that she wouldn't allow anyone to push her around ever again.

Not that Heath was being pushy. But from now on, she was going to be strong. Ask questions. The old Josie always swallowed her thoughts and opinions… No longer.

A breath. "I'm sorry, but your tone. You…you don't like them—the boys—do you?"

"I don't know them. I've only been to the ranch a few times and last time was years ago at the old location."

"Yet you're judging the boys anyway." She shouldn't be talking to him like this. Heath was almost a stranger, and here she was challenging him. But it grated on her to hear someone misjudge them, and so quickly. The Lone Star Cowboy League had worked hard to try to weed out the rumors in town that the boys at the ranch were trouble, yet still some of that belief lingered.

Heath scooped his hat off the back of the chair and worked it around in his hand. "See, that's where people get it wrong, though. Using good judgment isn't the same thing as being judgmental."

A fire lit in Josie. She wanted Heath to see the boys differently. But how to do that? "How long are you around, doing this favor for Flint?"

"For November."

She had a month to change his opinion, and she knew just how to do it. "You should volunteer at the ranch. Get to know the boys." It would be good for him. Besides, the boys would be floored if a big, important Texas Ranger started hanging around them.

Heath's eyebrows formed a V. "Why?"

Think like a lawman… What will convince him?

She took a deep breath. "For starters, your presence will prevent anything else from happening. Also, if you really think it's one of them, that'll put you in close proximity. You'll be able to get to know them and talk to them. Someone might even confess. Or you may see that they're wonderful and realize you were wrong to judge them."

Heath rubbed his thumb over his nose. "You know what, that's not a half-bad idea. It would help my... investigation. You're right about that. I'll talk to Flint about it tomorrow."

Josie's heart tripped over itself at the thought of spending more time with Heath. Of course she wanted him to change his opinion about the boys, and time at the ranch was the best way for that to happen. But what if it changed her opinion about men in law enforcement?

Her eyes skirted over the lines of his strong jaw, his shoulders. He'd given up so much time to help her this morning and he hadn't talked down to her at all. Maybe he wasn't like Dale. Maybe...

The baby inside of her moved, rolled. Josie loved that feeling. She hugged her stomach. Above everything, she had to protect her child from hurt. That was her duty as a mother.

No lawmen.

If God did choose to give her a second chance at love, He'd have to bring a nice insurance agent or IT man her way. Someone who worked a boring, safe job all day, tucked away behind a desk. One whose greatest career danger was an ink stain.

Not someone who carried a gun for a living.

Chapter Three

The loud noise outside sent Josie reaching for the closest heavy object.

A frying pan.

She pulled back the curtain over her sink and peered
outside. Heath's large Ford pickup was parked near
the river, dwarfing her vehicle. He'd unlatched and
opened the barn—which explained the noise—and had
already headed inside. A minute later he was leading
out the cattle.

"That man," she grumbled and set the pan back onto
the stove. "What is he up to?"

He'd left soon after their brunch yesterday. Said even
though his apartment was only forty-five minutes away,
he needed to check into the Blue Bonnet Inn in town
because he preferred to stay close during an investigation. He explained that if something happened at
the boys ranch, he wanted Flint to be able to call him
and be only minutes away. Which made sense. Flint's
place at the boys ranch wasn't that big and his young
son lived with him—so asking Flint to host him for a

month, even though Heath and Flint were close friends, was probably asking too much.

Josie had to chuckle, though. The Blue Bonnet Inn was an upscale place inside an old historical home. The rooms were decorated to match Texas flowers. It was better suited for a granny on vacation than a lawman. Heath Grayson would stick out there like a rooster in a henhouse.

She rested her elbows on the counter and cupped her chin in her hands. Today she'd have to ask Flint exactly how long his friend was going to stick around and be a pest in Haven. Heath had given her the vague answer of November, but she had a hard time believing that an investigation into a few missing items, a lost therapy horse last month and the calf incident would hold the attention of a Texas Ranger for long. At least after speaking with Flint, Josie would have an end date to look forward to. Not that she particularly minded Heath—not him personally. Oh, he was nice enough and not bad to look at.

But he was a Texas Ranger. They sought out danger. That was their job. Even if he insisted on stopping by her ranch and doing chores in the morning, which it looked like was his plan, she couldn't get used to it... to him. Heath would leave soon and rush off somewhere that meant risking his life. It was best not to get attached to him in any way, even simply as a friend.

Really, it would be better if she got rid of the overly helpful man. At least in her personal life.

After changing into fresh clothes, braiding her hair and straightening the kitchen, Josie made her way outside and entered the barn. She found Heath sitting on a stool, hunched over the water troughs, scrubbing them out with all his might.

He glanced her way. "Animals are fed. Bedding's changed. I spotted a few fence posts that could use re-inforcing."

How did he know how to take care of a ranch? It wasn't like a Texas Ranger had a lot of free time on his hands to care for animals and land and everything that went along with ranching.

"You don't need to do that." She paused in the door-way. "Actually, you don't need to be doing any of this." She crossed her arms. "Why are you here?"

"I thought I could help."

She propped her shoulder against the doorjamb. "I don't need any help."

Straw dust danced between them in the morning rays of light bleeding into the barn. Heath's eyes met hers across the space and he held her gaze. Raised his eyebrows.

Josie shook her head and walked forward. "I don't need *your* help."

"What if I said I was hoping to get more breakfast out of the deal?"

Even though he said it with a straight face, Josie was smart. She knew the man was trying to save her pride. Allow her to hang on to the idea that he was working for a good meal instead of pitching in because she was a lonely, pregnant woman. He could get a huge break-fast at the inn every morning if he wished and he was choosing not to.

Fine, then. She'd play along. Because that was bet-ter than admitting the truth.

"Oh. I see how it is." Josie clucked her tongue.

"You're like some homeless dog. I made the mistake of feeding you and now you'll just keep on coming back?"

He dragged the first trough back to its corresponding enclosure. "Something like that."

Josie spun around and called over her shoulder, "Wipe your boots before coming into my house."

"Will do."

She went back inside and muttered to herself as she set the griddle on. She leaned her hip into the counter and braced her hand along her side. It was a blessing not to have to do all the chores this morning. Over the past week, her lower back had been hurting more often than not.

When the griddle was warm enough for a pat of butter to sizzle its way across the surface, she mixed the liquids and soaked six large pieces of fluffy bread. French toast and bacon. She'd make him some food, explain to him that he couldn't just show up here and take care of all her chores every day—even though she really did appreciate it—and then she'd ask him to leave again. No getting attached. Easy peasy.

Heath entered as she was filling cups with orange juice.

"All set." She gestured to the plate.

"Looks great. Smells even better." He nodded. "Let me just wash my hands."

Once he was back at the table, he said grace for them again and they both dug into their food. This morning Josie was glad to be heading into her third trimester—no more morning sickness. Food was her friend again.

"I didn't get to mending the fence posts today. But I will by the end of this week."

Josie's curiosity was piqued. She had to find out how

he knew so much about ranching. "To be a Ranger, you'd have had to have worked for the state for a long time before then, right?"

"Eight years in investigations with the state before you're even allowed to fill out an application."

"So your entire adult life has been dedicated to police work?" He sounded a lot like Dale. Living…breathing the job.

His head bobbed. "I served as a soldier right out of high school and then went straight into the force."

"Did you ever see action?"

He looked down at his plate. "A tour in Iraq."

"Was it scary?"

Heath shrugged. "To be honest, I didn't have a lot going for me at the time and I wasn't afraid to die. I know that sounds bad." He moved his cup in a slow circle so the orange juice swirled around and around. "My father had passed away a few years before that, and my mom remarried pretty quickly. I'm afraid to say my stepdad and I butted heads from the get-go. More than anything, I joined the service to escape."

Heath wasn't afraid to die? She wanted to ask him about that statement, but she didn't really have a right to. Policemen and soldiers were alike in that way, weren't they? They always knew that not coming home was a possibility. But that didn't mean they weren't afraid of the possibility. Did Heath enjoy an adrenaline rush? Or was it something else?

Josie laced her fingers together and looked down at her palms. She didn't need to know because she wasn't getting involved with him. Not even as friends. He'd be around for a month and then be gone.

Ask him something else. Anything else.

"Did you grow up on a ranch?"

"No, a quiet patch of suburbia." He stretched out his legs under the table. "My dad was in law enforcement."

"Ah." Josie nodded. A lot of families were like that… Being on the force seemed to run in the blood. She cradled her belly. *Not you, little one! I won't allow it.* "Well, when did you learn all this stuff?" She motioned over her shoulder, in the direction of her barn. "How to take care of cows and pigs and fix fences? Last I checked they don't teach that on the force or in the army."

"They sure don't." He chuckled and set his napkin on the table. "My uncle Blaine has a ranch not far from here, near Waco. I moved in with him when things went south with my stepdad. Blaine put me right to work." Heath rubbed his hand over his smile. "He says there's no such thing as hands that aren't working on a ranch."

"Good for your uncle."

"I'm glad he did." Heath steepled his fingers. "If he hadn't done that, I wouldn't be any help to you now."

"What are you doing in Haven anyway?" Josie asked between bites. "Besides bugging me at my ranch, that is. And the calves mystery." She rolled her eyes. Not because she wasn't still scared about the possibility of a stranger having been hiding in the barn with her, but because it still seemed silly that a Texas Ranger was working the case. "We both know you didn't take a month off to investigate *that*."

Heath finished a piece of bacon. "Visiting Flint, mostly. And checking out the boys ranch, of course."

"Do you know someone who might need to go there?"

"Having resources for troubled youth stored up

here—" he tapped his forehead "—is good in my line of work." He rested his forearms on the table. "How about you? Why do you volunteer there?"

Josie shrugged. "Everyone in Haven pitches in."

"Did your husband?"

Not at all. Dale always gave the place a wide berth. "Why do you care—"

"I'm sorry." He held up a hand. "Forget I asked."

Josie plowed on anyway. "I'm a member of the Lone Star Cowboy League. We support the boys ranch. I'm there because I want to be, but also because it's my duty as a member of the League. My husband wasn't a member. You have to be a rancher to be involved... Dale wasn't one. I only just joined. After." She looked down.

"You didn't have to answer," Heath said. "My question was out of line. Job hazard. I'm used to asking whatever I want to know." He smoothed his hand down his jaw. "How about this... Who's your favorite kid on the ranch?"

She shifted her cup around and around in her hands. "I don't have a favorite."

"Of course you do." His voice was gentle. "Who is it?"

"I guess, if I absolutely had to pick... I'd probably say Diego. He's had a hard road in life. He's this bright little guy who always has a serious expression on his face. Like he's working out a math puzzle at all times." Josie pulled a face, imitating Diego. Heath answered with a soft grin.

"His hair is almost black and his eyes are dark and soulful." Josie found she was smiling but couldn't help it. "He and I get along really well because he loves the cattle. He's always the first one at the barn waiting for me and wants to pitch in on anything having to do with the calves. You could say I have a soft spot for him."

Heath leaned forward. "What's Diego in for?"

"In for?"

"All the boys there, they're troublemakers. They wouldn't be sent to the ranch if they weren't. What's Diego's issue? What'd he do wrong?"

Josie bristled. There was nothing wrong with Diego. Nothing at all. Sometimes a child needed special attention. Sometimes they needed a change from normal life in order to work through something. But living at the ranch certainly wasn't a punishment.

"You still don't think well of them. Even after our talk yesterday?"

Heath's expression became unreadable. "I know good, well-adjusted kids don't end up there. Normal kids are at their homes…with their parents. I know bad things have happened at the boys ranch in the past."

"With that attitude, it's a wonder you're willing to help Flint solve his case at all." She scooted out of her seat and collected both of their plates.

"Attitude?" Heath turned in his chair so he could continue facing her as she moved to the sink. "That's not attitude. It's the truth."

Josie dropped the dishes into the sink with a loud clang and turned around. "Those boys are flesh and blood with feelings and dreams and they just want to be loved and accepted. Same as you and me." She laid her hand along her collarbone. "If you can't see that, Officer, then you aren't that great of a detective after all."

"I'm sorry." He looked down, studied the table. "Perhaps you're right. After everything, I guess it's hard to see them any other way."

"After everything? What's that supposed to mean?"

"My dad was a Texas Ranger. I don't think I told you that before. But he was."

He'd said his dad worked in law enforcement…but they were both Rangers? That was amazing. "You followed in his footsteps?"

Heath nodded. "I wanted to honor his sacrifice." He looked down at his hands as if the lines on his palms were the most interesting things in the world. "Fifteen years ago, my father was working a case at your boys ranch."

Josie's heart sunk. She sucked in a loud breath. As someone who'd lost a loved one to the thin blue line, she knew where his story was going.

"They found him dead. Three bullets. Near the main barn on the old property."

"Oh, Heath." Josie crossed the kitchen and laid a hand on his shoulder. She squeezed. "I'm so sorry." She blinked against the burn of tears, his words dragging up the ache of her loss.

"My dad's murder is still a cold case. Unsolved."

His hand came up and covered hers. It was warm and comforting. Josie's throat spasmed. She missed the friendly touches of her past life…a quick hug, a shoulder brushing against a shoulder, holding a hand. She missed it so much she ached.

She drew her shaky hand out from under his. "Now that you mention it, I remember hearing about it on the news when it happened. It was a big deal in a town like Haven."

He swiveled in the chair in order to make eye contact. "I'd like to solve the case, if I could."

"That's why you're here, isn't it?"

"Among other reasons." He shrugged. "But I'd like to keep that private as much as I can, if you don't mind."

"Of course." She nodded. "My husband was a deputy." Josie dropped into the seat beside Heath. Close enough that their knees bumped. "It started as a routine traffic stop and turned into him never coming home." She got the words out before her throat clamped up again. But her voice pitched higher at the end, betraying her.

Heath reached over and took her hand. He held it between both of his. For a minute they sat in silence. Allowing each other to deal with their loss. Finding comfort in the fact that someone else understood.

Finally, Heath cleared his throat. "I'm sorry you had to go through that. No one should have to lose a loved one that way."

She dabbed at her eyes and nodded. Staying in the pain, reliving everything, wouldn't help her or her child. If Heath was still hanging on to the pain of losing his father, he needed to move toward letting that go, as well. But Josie knew how hard that could be. Still, she racked her brain for a way to encourage him.

She squeezed his fingers. "I know you said you would yesterday, but this is one more reason why you should volunteer at the ranch. There are ranch hands still working there who would have been working fifteen years ago. Someone might know something, Heath. Don't you see?"

Heath looked off to the side for a second. Josie had noticed he did that when he was considering something.

"Some of the ranch hands are still there?" He captured her gaze again. His dark eyes swirled with questions. "Are you sure about that?"

"Very sure. I'll have to talk to some of the old-timers, but I think I can get you a list of the names of people who still live in town who worked or volunteered when it happened."

Heath rose to his feet. "Get your shoes on, Josie. Let's head to the ranch."

One hand on the steering wheel, the other cocked on the open window, Heath maneuvered his truck toward the boys ranch.

He stole a glance at Josie.

She'd wriggled more personal information out of him in the past two days than he'd told his coworkers in the nine years he'd worked for the Texas Department of Public Safety. They were the branch of the government that the Rangers functioned under. In order to be considered for the position of Ranger, Heath had worked as a state trooper for eight years first, in their investigative unit. Still, he was one of the youngest guys to be made a Ranger in a long time. He had a hunch that those in upper management remembered his father and that had paved his way. After all this time, he should be used to keeping a tight rein on his personal life, but Josie had somehow slipped under his defenses.

The woman should consider going into detective work.

She caught him looking at her and hugged her stomach. "My truck *is* just fine, you know. I could have driven myself."

They'd gone toe-to-toe over her truck. She'd called him overbearing and he'd insisted on having the vehicle checked out before she continued to drive it. Texan winters weren't bad, but still, anything could happen.

And that thing wouldn't be able to handle another accident if she did get caught in bad weather at some point. She'd said that was what caused the last fender bender, a storm. It was raining and she missed the stop sign. Ended up broadsided by a sedan.

Heath's stomach tightened. The idea of Josie and her baby in an accident didn't sit well with him. Not one bit.

He forced his fingers to relax his grip on the wheel. "Like I said before, let me take a look at it tomorrow. I know a little about cars."

"You know a little about everything, don't you?"

He popped his gaze back to her for a second, fighting a grin. This woman had exercised his smile muscles more than he cared to admit. "I've picked up things here and there."

"I don't like it." She looked out the window.

"Let's make sure it's sound before your baby comes," he added softly.

That did her in. She sighed and ran a hand across her stomach. "I guess that makes sense. If you're sure you don't mind."

He threw on his blinker to turn into the ranch. "Have you had someone install a car seat for you yet?"

She laughed. "I still have three months."

"They usually suggest doing it before…before it's too close to your time. Just in case. Babies have a way of appearing whenever they want to."

"And how do you know so much about babies?" She poked him in the arm a few times as she talked. The way his little sister used to when she was trying to be annoying. Although, when Josie did it, the action felt endearing.

"Not babies." *Those* he knew nothing about and

never would. "Car seats. I was trained as a car-seat technician when I worked with the troopers. I could teach you how to install one, if you'd like."

"I'll think about it."

Josie had the door open and jumped down to the ground the second he put his truck in Park. She had told him on the way over that she needed to meet up with the minister who volunteered at the ranch. She'd catch him later or maybe find a ride home with someone else. He'd make sure he found her before she wanted to go home. Because her place was on the way back to the inn where he was staying... That was the only reason he should drive her home, of course.

Heath shook his head. She *was* trying to shake him. Poor woman. Did she really understand what he did for a living? Once he made his mind up about something, he could be pretty stubborn. The trait came in handy in his profession.

Still...what must she think of him for showing up at her house two days in a row? He'd do it tomorrow, too. And the day after that. The woman was alone and pregnant; she shouldn't be managing the ranch on her own. Besides, she was the eyewitness to a possible crime. If the wrongdoer had spotted her, then Josie could be in danger. He wouldn't scare her with that notion, but he'd stick close until things were sorted out.

Heath spotted Flint straightaway. He was near the heavy machinery, but when he saw Heath's truck, Flint came striding across the yard. A big black dog yapped circles around his feet.

Heath grabbed his white Stetson, pushed it onto his head, then tucked his badge into his back pocket as he stepped down from his truck. He took in the barn, the fence posts, the large home—it was impossible for Heath to turn off his investigative eye. His brain seemed programmed to constantly log information, and look for weaknesses or issues. Things to fix, help, protect.

The black Lab bounded toward Heath, its tail smacking his legs while it used the running board on Heath's truck to jump up into the driver's seat, which put the animal at head level to lodge a full lick attack on Heath's neck and face. Heath groaned and good-naturedly shoved the dog's nose away so he couldn't lick him any longer.

"Cowboy, down." Flint reached around Heath, grabbed the dog's collar and tugged him out of the truck. "Sorry about that." Flint finally looked at Heath. The two men were about the same height, but that was where their similarities ended. Where Heath's eyes were dark, Flint's were blue; same for the hair—Heath had black to Flint's blond.

"He's only two," Flint apologized. "Still learning his manners."

"It's fine." Heath used the sleeve of his white button-down to sop the worst of the drool from his neck. "He still has better manners than most of the people I deal with." He adjusted his hat. All the Rangers wore them for work, but he'd gotten so used to the feel of it on his head, Heath usually wore the Stetson at all times.

"Got a minute?" Flint released the dog and it took off toward the barn where a group of school-age boys were working a few ponies in the arena. Flint set his hands on the edge of his belt.

"Right. Down to business."

Flint laughed.

Neither of them was a chitchat type of guy. That was probably why they'd gotten along so well during basic training.

"I've been meaning to ask you about something," Flint said as Heath came over.

Heath propped his hand on the edge of his holster. "I have all the time in the world right now."

Flint leaned against the giant wheel of a tractor. "I told you about the gentleman who died and left us this new property. Didn't I?"

"Cyrus Culpepper."

"That's the one." Flint shook his head. "I forgot about how good you are at remembering things—facts."

"That's what they pay me for."

"Well, I got some more facts for you, then." Flint hooked his thumb in his pocket. "Culpepper left terms in his will. You know how our ranch used to be located on the other end of town?"

Heath nodded. The boys ranch had moved into their current location—the land from Culpepper's will—only a week ago. Before then, they'd been located on a smaller piece of land.

"Well, it turns out Culpepper was one of the original residents from when the boys ranch was first started. One of his stipulations for us to keep the property and everything else he left is to have the original boys from the ranch back for the anniversary party in March."

Heath waited for the punch line. There was always a punch line.

Flint shifted his weight, obviously uncomfortable with whatever he had to say. "I was tasked with tracking down a man by the name of Edmund Grayson.

Maybe it's a long shot, but I was wondering if you might be related to him. Does that name sound familiar?"

Edmund Grayson? But it couldn't be…could it?

Heath sucked in a rattled breath.

Of course he knew that name—but no, it wasn't possible. He wouldn't believe it. Heath straightened his spine. Kicked his boot against one of the tractor tires to shake free of the dirt.

He cupped his hand along his jaw. "That's my grandfather's name, but he was never a resident at any of these ranches."

"Is he from the Waco area?"

"He is that." Heath nodded. "Born and lived in this area most of his life. He was a state trooper until he retired and moved to Florida."

"Edmund's not a common name," Flint said gently.

It wasn't, but there had to be two of them. If his grandfather had lived at the boys ranch, Heath would know. Wouldn't he? That was something his father or grandfather would have mentioned at some point.

"I'm telling you, you have the wrong guy. My grandfather never went to one of these ranches. I'd know if he did. He would have told me. Especially after what happened to my dad, that would have come out at some point."

Flint shuffled his feet. "It's imperative that all four of the original residents are found and reunited at the celebration in March. If that doesn't happen…we'll lose all of this." He raised his hands to encompass the land. "Edmund Grayson is a unique enough name. I haven't been able to find another one with ties to the Waco area."

"It's not my grandfather."

"Ask him. What's it going to cost you to ask?"

An olive branch and then some.

Heath hadn't spoken to the man in years. He'd received a congratulations card in the mail when he'd been appointed a Ranger, but that had been their last contact. Maybe he'd ask Nell, see what she thought before poking at the old bear.

"Please?"

Heath sighed. First investigating the incidents at the ranch and now possibly reaching out to his estranged grandfather. Flint was sure getting a lot of favors out of him this visit.

He gave Flint one stiff nod. "I'm not promising anything, but I'll see what I can find out."

Chapter Four

◦◦◦

Josie shooed Heath away when he tried to help her down from his truck. One would think he'd have caught on by now that she liked to get down from the cab on her own.

They'd been following the same routine for a week now. Every day he showed up at her house just after sunrise. He did all the chores and then polished off whatever food she placed in front of him, praising her cooking the entire time. Then he drove her to the ranch, and while she worked her volunteer shift, he poked around and talked to people about possible leads for the incidents that had occurred there. She'd given him a list of names of ranch hands to talk to who would have worked at the ranch when his father was murdered and she'd noticed him engaging each of those people in conversations, as well. The boys ranch was blessed to have so many people who either volunteered or continued working there faithfully for so many years.

After talking with Flint, a few days ago Heath had started leading an after-school club for boys interested in learning how cops investigate crimes. They called their little club *detection class*. A majority of the older boys had instantly jumped at the chance to spend time with a Texas Ranger. Josie couldn't blame them; Heath was good company.

On her way toward the office, Josie spotted a few of the boys in the pen with the calves, trying to put a lead line on one of them. As she drew nearer, she recognized Riley, one of the oldest teen residents at the ranch, and his ever-present shadow, ten-year-old Morgan, as they moved to corner the skittish dairy calf everyone called Honey. She was a favorite among the kids because she had a marking that looked like a heart on her forehead.

Morgan was a shy kid who was sometimes easily discouraged. If Honey kicked one of the boys, Morgan would probably not want to be around any of the calves any longer.

Josie stepped into the pen and secured the door again. "Careful, now. She scares easily." Josie held up her hands. "Shh, Honey. It's okay, girl."

"Be careful, Ms. Markham." Riley's eyes went right to Josie's pregnant belly. "How about you let me get up close to Honey instead? If she kicks, I'll be fine." At seventeen, the boy towered over Josie.

Right. She'd forgotten how protective the older boys were about her. There was no way Riley was going to let her get close to Honey until he had her tethered.

As small framed as she was, Josie's pregnancy had showed almost immediately. Once the older boys noticed, they'd taken it upon themselves to try to ease her load. They were always offering to carry things for her or go in with the bigger animals when needed or pitch in when her truck got a flat the other week.

All their gestures were sweet, but sometimes the

extra attention grated on her all the same. The whispers of Dale's repeated instructions to her—*don't do this, you can't handle that, no I won't let you have a farm, my wife won't smell like cattle if I have anything to say about it*—were never far behind whenever she let one of the boys help her.

She had to remind herself the boys' intention wasn't to control her—they weren't trying to tell her she wasn't capable of doing those things. They were showing they cared about her.

Josie stayed and encouraged Morgan as he led Honey around the pen a few times. She headed toward the office housed at the ranch once the boys left the pen on their way to their next lesson. The director had left a message for her earlier in the day. Bea, the director, had said she wanted to speak with her about how long Josie planned on volunteering…*considering her condition.*

Josie held her head high as she strode past the blond receptionist, Katie Ellis, who was talking animatedly on the phone to someone about an electric bill. On a normal day, Josie would have stopped to say hi to Katie because the two women were good friends, but Josie didn't want to interrupt Katie's conversation. Instead she gave a little wave and the receptionist rolled her eyes and pointed at the phone. Josie stifled a laugh.

Josie went over again what she had decided to tell Bea. She wanted to volunteer as long as she was able, although the pains in her back told her that it might not be too much longer. But she still had three months until her due date. Plenty of women worked right up until they went into labor; surely Josie could help around the ranch until then.

Be brave. Be strong. Speak what's on your mind.

The director's office was empty.

Josie swiveled back toward Katie, who was just hanging up the phone.

"Bea's not in?"

Katie sprang from her seat and came over to Josie, offering a quick hug. "You seriously just missed her. She had to run into town." Katie motioned for Josie to follow her to the front of the office near a set of wide windows, her bouncy hair swishing as she walked. "She shouldn't be long. Do you want me to have her find you?"

Josie pressed her shoulder into the wall for support. "Heath has to leave early to run some errands today. I leave when he leaves, so I might not be here when she gets back. And I'll be late tomorrow because I have a doctor's appointment."

It had been a week of Heath stopping at her ranch in the morning, helping with chores and then sharing breakfast. He'd discovered some problems with her truck and declared it unsafe to drive for the time being. Something about her radiator and, even more concerning, he explained that the main rail for the frame of the vehicle had been weakened by the accident and needed to be replaced. He'd told her to call her insurance agent and have the truck junked, but Josie couldn't do that. Not yet. She simply needed to have the rail fixed...and figure out how she'd pay for that. Surely that would be less expensive than buying a whole new car. She'd been a housewife for ten years and all of their bills and credit had been in Dale's name. No one would give her a loan. She had to build up credit before she could buy a new car.

Katie's green eyes danced with mischief. "Well done there, with Heath. You snagged a good one. He's a looker."

Josie rolled her eyes. Katie was young and single and had her radar set to locate and catalog all single, attractive men. Josie knew for a fact that there were at least three ranch hands who were suffering from crushes on Katie, but Katie didn't seem to have eyes for them.

"I snagged nothing. Nor do I want to." Josie hooked her hand on her purse strap. "*Snagging* isn't in my repertoire any longer."

Katie gave her a deadpan look. The younger woman was hopelessly determined to see everything through romance-tinted glasses.

Josie let out an exasperated breath. "Heath has a strong protective streak. Most guys in his line of work do. The man saw a pathetic pregnant woman all on her own and turned keeping an eye on me into a mission. That's how these types of men function. Everything's a mission." Josie popped her hands onto her hips. "Mark my words, come end of November, he'll be gone on a new one and will have long forgotten us here."

"You're hardly pathetic." Katie's eyes grew wide. "You know that, right? You're one of the strongest people I've ever met."

"Thank you for saying that," Josie whispered. She didn't feel very brave. She was fighting tooth and nail to survive and hang on to her dream at the same time. Was that brave? Or was it foolish? Could the two be the same thing?

"I mean it."

Josie glanced out the window and her gaze landed on Heath. He was near the doors of the learning center, a small building behind the main house that held a library and had tables for the boys to do their homework on. A group of boys surrounded him.

Katie nudged her elbow. "You like him." *Nudge. Nudge. Nudge.* "Admit it."

Josie turned away from the window, but only slightly. She still wanted to keep an eye on...outside. She sighed. "He's a pest. That's what he is."

"The kids already adore him. That didn't take long." Katie jutted her chin toward where one of the young boys hung on Heath's arm as he talked to an older boy. "They were all raving after his first lesson in...what are they calling it? Investigation? No. It was...*detection*." Her voice took on a dramatic flair. "That night the boys put together this large-scale spy game that went all over the house. Whenever an argument broke out, they'd end it with 'Tomorrow we'll ask Heath. Heath will know. Heath knows everything.'" She laughed.

Thinking about the impact that Heath was already having on the boys in only the few days he'd spent on the ranch, Josie felt her lips tugging into a smile. "He does seem to have a way with them. I've been volunteering at the ranch for five months and haven't been able to connect with the boys the way he has in less than a week."

"Well, I mean, he does have an unfair advantage." Katie tapped the pocket on her pink shirt. "Shiny badge."

"And I'm a pregnant lady." Josie laid her hand over her abdomen. "That counts against me for coolness points."

"No way. The boys are so excited about your baby."

That was true. The boys were always asking what they could do or if they could be invited to the baby shower.

Josie tapped the glass, pointing at Heath. "Still not as cool as a Texas Ranger."

"True. Very true. But then again, none of us measure up to that. We can't. Not in a boy's mind." Katie crossed her arms and leaned against the edge of the window. "So are you going to fess up that something's going on between you two or not?"

"We hardly know each other and he leaves in a few weeks." Josie walked away from the window. Enough staring. It wasn't kind to her heart to watch him so much. "For good."

"His company's out of Waco. That's not exactly far, Josie."

"Sure, Waco's not that far away. But he said he doesn't live in Waco proper. A distance outside of that. And it doesn't matter whatsoever if he lives five minutes away or ten hours away because the second his vacation is over, we'll be out of his mind. As we should be."

"You two have already talked about how far away he lives?" Katie smiled excitedly. "Oh, this is promising."

He lived forty-five minutes away…too far for her to want to think about keeping up a friendship while trying to juggle her ranch and the baby who would be arriving soon.

"He's a Texas Ranger." Josie's voice went up a little, just a little. Why didn't anyone understand what a big deal that was? "Do you know what kind of cases they work? The sort of danger they're in?" Josie hugged her stomach. "After what happened to Dale…" Her voice broke.

Katie's eyes went soft and she placed her hand on Josie's arm, offering a squeeze.

Josie swallowed hard. "I don't want any connections to law enforcement. Not ever again. I don't want to care...even a little bit...for someone who could be killed as part of their job."

"Couldn't that happen to any of us, though?" Katie said softly. "Not just a lawman. But... I could get in a crash on the way to work. One of the ranch hands could get thrown from a horse and land wrong. Someone could be stampeded."

"That's not the same." Josie shrugged away from her touch. "It's not the same as willingly knowing that part of your job requires you to have a gun pointed at you at any time of any day. Freak accidents are very different than dealing with criminals."

"But doesn't that say something, I don't know, something really great about a man's character when he's willing to do that?" Katie started to pace. "That he's willing to stand in the gap between society—people they don't even know—and the dangerous stuff? I mean, in a way it's a lot like how Jesus stands between us and the worst possible fate. It's very Christlike, being ready to lay down your life for someone."

Josie adjusted the strap on her purse and inched toward the door. "And there. You just made my point for me. They killed Jesus."

Katie's face fell. "That's not at all what my point was."

She had to get Katie off the topic or else they'd go around in circles. Josie wasn't going to change her mind. "Moving on..."

"Okay, but please admit that he's cute. You can do that at least, right?" Katie pointed over her shoulder out the window. "He's got that tall, dark and handsome thing working for him. Not to mention he has that *I'm here to rescue you* vibe, as well."

She was trying to make right for having upset Josie. That was Katie's way. She was kind, a peacemaker. Josie sighed. She would ease Katie's conscience by making light of everything. "He is handsome. I'll agree with you there." That was part of what made him so dangerous.

"He's here until the end of the month?"

Josie nodded.

"Are you bringing him to the Thanksgiving celebration?"

"I didn't think to ask him."

"Please do." Katie's phone started to ring and she headed back to her desk. "I need a head count, and the boys who are sticking around for the holiday will want him there. They already look up to him so much. They'll all try to sit at his table."

"I'll ask him."

Her hand hovered over the phone receiver. "As your date?"

Josie walked backward through the doorway. "Absolutely not."

Katie shrugged. "Hey, you can't blame a girl for trying. I wish someone would get Pastor Walsh to ask me, but it's like he doesn't even notice I'm here." She sighed and then picked up the phone, answering it in her cheery voice.

Everyone at the ranch knew that Katie had her heart set on the young pastor. Too bad Andrew Walsh was just about clueless when it came to women. He was a great preacher, but started to fumble and grew shy whenever the younger women in the congregation tried to speak with him. Pastor Walsh volunteered at the boys ranch, often holding lessons with the boys under the large tree in view of the office window near where Katie sat.

Josie laughed as she walked down the hall, making the connection for the first time.

Maybe Pastor Walsh wasn't so clueless after all.

Heath slowly paced in front of the row of boys. They were all at attention, soldier straight as their eyes followed him. He'd led them into the barn—the "crime scene"—so they could start collecting clues.

"Now, I've roped off the area so that our evidence won't be disturbed. Take some time to study the scene and then we'll talk about what we see."

The boys inched forward, craning their necks.

Heath had locked them out and set up the crime scene. Shoe impressions on the dirt ground, areas where the suspect would have stumbled under the weight of what they stole and a clear area where the item was stolen from. Those three things should be enough to tell them who'd committed their make-believe crime.

If only his other investigations—the real ones— would go as smoothly. He'd started to move down the list of people Josie had given him, people who had worked at the ranch when his dad was murdered. Talks with the first four on the list had only produced people who said they were sorry for his loss and knew nothing. Heath scrubbed his hand over his jaw. She'd given him the contact information for a few people who still lived in the area but no longer worked at the boys ranch. Those were his next leads. His only leads.

So far there was no news on the mischief at the ranch, either. Everyone claimed they hadn't seen or heard anything suspicious, although a few people suggested a man by the name of Fletcher Snowden Phillips as a suspect. Supposedly he had a grudge against the boys ranch. Heath would look into that next.

But first, his detection class.

Heath shook away his thoughts so he could give the boys all his attention. "So what do you see?"

A boy with a mop of brown hair raised his hand. "Footsteps." He pointed.

"Good eyes." Heath nodded. He crossed to where he'd set up a pail and then motioned the boys over. He'd made sure to wet the dirt earlier, until it was muddy, and sank the borrowed shoes in deep so they'd leave solid places to cast impressions. "I need two very detail-oriented helpers."

All hands shot up. He pointed to an older and younger boy, probably sixteen and ten respectively, and jerked his head for them to come closer. Heath hadn't learned all the boys' names yet, but he meant to. Whenever he got a name right, they beamed like they'd just won a prize.

"We always try to collect as much evidence as we can, but we have to balance that with being as careful on scene as possible." He squatted near the pail, all eyes following him. "In this profession, we live by the motto 'Do Right the First Time' because we don't get second chances. Not with a crime scene, and often not when questioning people."

"Do right the first time," Stephen, one of the older boys, muttered. Heath had made certain to learn which one was Stephen right away because the teen was on his list of suspects for the string of incidents that had occurred at the boys ranch. "That seems like a tall order. Almost impossible."

A female voice cleared her throat near the doorway. *Josie.* Her auburn hair cascaded over her shoulders and the sun shone behind her, lighting her petite frame.

Heath's throat went dry. He couldn't take his eyes off her.

"That's a good point, Stephen." Josie stepped into the barn and joined the boys. "It's really difficult to do right the first time. At least, in life it sure is. I know I usually mess up before doing something right. I don't know about all of you, but I'm really thankful that Jesus has grace on us when it comes to our lives."

She draped her arms around two of the shorter boys' shoulders. "But that's not what Heath is talking about. He's talking about using your God-given gifts and talents to bring glory to God. By Heath doing his best to get everything right and not miss a thing when he first arrives at a crime scene, that's a form of worship for Heath. He's honoring God. See, God cares about justice. God cares about what Heath does…about what you guys do in your lives, too. I hope y'all understand that."

A couple of the boys nudged each other and looked back and forth between Heath and Josie, but Heath couldn't pay too much attention to what that meant yet. Josie's words thundered through him. Was she right? While he had been raised in the church, Heath had intentionally distanced himself from God after his father's murder. What else could he do? As a young man, he'd pleaded with God to bring about justice for his father and it never came.

Because God didn't care. Not about his family. Not about him.

But deep down, Heath had decided that he could *make* God care. If he caught enough wrongdoers, if he solved enough cold cases, if he served enough victims…perhaps then God would care about him, perhaps God would answer his prayers.

A foolish notion, but he'd held on to it for so long.

Was it possible, like Josie said, that his police work—the normal tasks he did every day—brought glory and honor to God? If so, it made all the late nights and striving worth it. Maybe he wasn't as far from God as he thought he was.

It was something to think about.

The kids were staring. Waiting for him to say something.

Heath found his voice. "When we find deep shoe prints, we always try to make a cast of it as quickly as possible." He explained how they used a mixing powder called dental stone. "It's the same stuff the dentist uses to make impressions of your mouth." He eyeballed the amount of powder and then had his two helpers measure water into the pail. "Looks great." Heath rose to his feet. "Stir it until it looks like pancake batter. It'll take about five minutes. Take turns. Believe me, that's a long time to stir something."

He handed talcum powder to another student. "Dust this into the shoe prints. Go ahead and do all of them and we'll pick the best one to cast."

When the dental stone was ready, he helped them pour the plaster-like substance into three of the best prints and then gave his helpers high fives. "Well done. We'll let those set until tomorrow and then we'll pull them up and try to find the shoes that match them. Normally I'd photograph it all first, and if these were muddy prints indoors on carpet or hard floors, the process would be a little different."

He was losing the younger ones. Too many details. He had to remind himself these weren't recruits. That was who he was used to training. Heath roped off the crime scene. "That's probably enough for today. You guys are dismissed. We'll start back here tomorrow and solve this crime."

Josie chatted with a couple of the boys, ruffling their hair and laughing with them, while Heath packed up his things.

Stephen found him a few minutes later. "I wanted to tell you that I really like your class. I'm learning a lot."

"Knowledge is great, son. But more important than learning something is using the information for good. Will you promise to do that, Stephen? Use this training for good?" Heath hooked his hands on his belt. "Someone who wanted to commit crimes could learn how police investigate in order to do things without getting caught."

Stephen's face fell. "You think I'd do that?"

"I didn't say that. Not at all. But you have a responsibility, everyone in our class does, to use what you've learned to help people."

"I plan to." Stephen nodded solemnly. "I wish... I mean, it would be so cool if I could be like—" He shook his head. "I look forward to whatever we're doing tomorrow." Stephen hurried away, almost as if he was embarrassed.

Josie wandered over to Heath. "They like you and I'm starting to think the feeling's mutual."

Heath could say the same thing about whatever was happening between him and Josie. He cared about her—that was undeniable. But what did that mean? He knew it was stronger than his normal desire to protect those when his station demanded it. With Josie, he *wanted* to protect her. If someone else offered to, he'd argue with them for the right.

He swallowed hard. "I'm still keeping my radar up around Stephen."

"He didn't do anything wrong."

"Then there's nothing to worry about."

Her face dropped. "Heath."

"Josie. You realize what I do for a living, correct? Sometimes the least likely person is the guilty one. Some people are good at hiding their real self. I've seen a lot of really bad...really messed-up stuff. Okay?" He hated bursting her bubble, but he'd seen too much in his life to think otherwise. "All of these boys here are capable of the worst sins imaginable. We all are. That's the hardest part in law enforcement. Crime isn't one size fits all. Have a little faith in me? In my process?"

"These boys are here to heal." She placed her hand on his arm. "Are you? That's the entire purpose of this place."

He pressed his teeth together—wanting to fight what she was implying but finding himself at a loss for words. He wanted answers about his father's death. He wanted to write *Case Closed* on the file. Would doing that heal him?

He sure hoped so.

Chapter Five

Sunshine blazed through the wide front windows in the waiting room of Josie's doctor's office. She narrowed her eyes and adjusted how she was sitting, fighting nausea. Sometimes the oddest things—like bright light—could make her feel sick since becoming pregnant.

The receptionist at the front desk tapped away at her keyboard. It sounded unnaturally loud. A nurse in scrubs behind the front desk was taking a personal call, arguing with someone about how expensive her daughter's orthodontia was.

Josie ran her fingers over her forehead.

Heath rose from his seat beside her and crossed to the windows. He adjusted the blinds so the light didn't hit them in the face any longer and then came back to his seat. Josie's heart tightened at his ability to read a situation and take care of needs without asking questions. Heath Grayson was a man of action.

Too bad action often led to danger.

Josie swirled the sticky orange drink around and around in her cup. The nurse had explained that she had five minutes to down the highly sugared liquid and then they'd have to wait an hour. After the hour, the nurse would do a blood draw and they'd be free to go. A normal test for gestational diabetes, everyone assured her.

Even still, Josie couldn't help but worry. If the test came back positive... No, she couldn't think about that right now. She couldn't take one more disappointment this year or one more setback on her dream. All of Dale's life-insurance money had gone to paying off his debts, leaving her and their child with nothing to live on. If she was told to stop working, her ranch would go belly-up and she'd have no way to provide for her child. The only job Josie had ever worked was as a nanny while she and Dale dated, but he'd wanted her to stop after their wedding. And she wouldn't be able to take on a nanny position with a newborn in tow, now, would she?

She wrapped her free hand over her stomach.

Lord? I know I don't have much to give in return. Less than much. I have nothing to offer You. Nothing at all other than a heart that wants to learn to trust You. I'm penniless and in need and I don't like being like this. But...please take care of us.

Heath laid down the magazine he was flipping through. "Feeling any better?"

Josie swallowed another gulp of the horrible orange liquid. "Yes, thank you. The sunlight's intense today."

He chuckled and leaned back in his chair. "You could sure say that."

The air-conditioning kicked on, swirling the leaves of the potted tree in the corner of the office.

A nurse in maroon scrubs popped her head through

the door near the reception area that led to the exam rooms. "Jenny Price?"

There were three other ladies in the waiting area. The one wearing purple, who looked like she might be past her due date or possibly carrying twins, slowly got to her feet and headed into the back area.

"Listen, Heath." Josie laid her fingertips on his forearm. "They said this'll take an hour. I'm sure you have better things to do. Thank you for the ride, but you don't have to wait here. I can call you when I'm done."

He traced a finger over the design on the side of his boot. "I don't mind waiting."

"It's an hour."

"I've sat patiently at stakeouts that lasted for ten. No worries."

She should know by now how stubborn this man was. Besides, it was nice to have company in the waiting room, even when they weren't talking. Simply knowing someone else was there with her was enough. She'd attended every other appointment alone. Not that Heath would come into the room for the blood draw or to listen to the heartbeat. She wasn't about to let that happen. But still…he was here and he didn't have to be.

Josie forced down the rest of the drink and then brought the cup to the front desk so they'd know to start her hour. She eased back into her seat and rubbed her palm back and forth over the fabric covering her thigh. "So, stakeouts? Those are dangerous, aren't they?"

Heath shrugged. "Only if they spot you before you spot them. Which doesn't happen often. Not being seen…that's the nature of a good stakeout after all."

Sure, but every stakeout carried the possibility of

being seen. Being ambushed. Being murdered. "Do you have to do them much?"

He nodded. "More now as a Ranger than I did when I was a trooper."

Josie sighed and moved to lean away from him. She needed the few inches of distance she could get in the chair. It was far too easy to start depending on Heath. Come December she'd miss him, miss the breakfasts they shared as they discussed ways to improve her ranch, miss the sweet way he equipped the boys and made them feel capable, miss how he read her mind when she needed something and seemed all too willing to put her first.

Pain radiated underneath her collarbone. She pressed her fingers into the spot. Heartburn. Probably just heartburn. That happened these days.

Heath angled toward her. "Did your husband— Dale, right?"

She nodded.

"Was he an investigator? Or...?"

She allowed a moment before answering to take a few deep breaths while the pain in her chest subsided. "A sheriff's deputy. On their truck-enforcement division."

His eyes went to her stomach and then came back to meet her gaze. "I said it before, but I'm real, real sorry for your loss."

They fell into silence. Heath flipped through a magazine about birds and Josie had to bite her tongue because she wanted to ask him if he was a nature-lover. Did he enjoy camping? Hunting? There was so much about Heath she wanted to know, but she swallowed down the questions. Knowing him would make her care more.

Still…the quiet felt too heavy. Perhaps it was the glucose drink she'd just put into her body, sending her heart into overdrive, but she couldn't sit without fidgeting and wanted to talk.

Josie cleared her throat. "The boys ranch has a huge Thanksgiving dinner buffet that a lot of the families come out and attend. Most of the boys and the staff will be there."

Heath set down the magazine and rested his elbows on his knees. "I know about the Thanksgiving celebration."

"Oh, that's great. So will you come?" *With me?* "Katie—she works in the front office—asked me if I knew if you were going to attend. She needs a head count."

"I…ah." Heath pressed his hands together and touched the sides of his pointer fingers to his lips, deep in thought. His gazed was fixed on a carpet stain shaped like a running dog. "Thanksgiving…" He sat up slowly. "I don't know. Thanksgiving's not a good time for me."

Her heart sped up and her gut tightened. Or maybe the baby kicked? "Are you planning to leave before then?" Why did her voice have to go up like that?

He shook his head and pulled his phone from his pocket. "I'm here until the end of the month." He got up. "Will you excuse me?" He started backing toward the door. "I'm late returning a call."

Josie watched him walk out of the lobby and stand outside the front doors. She'd scared him off by inviting him to the Thanksgiving meal.

"He wants nothing to do with the boys ranch," she mumbled to herself. How had she forgotten that? A week with the boys hadn't changed his opinion. Not if Heath couldn't even stand the thought of sharing a holiday meal with them.

With her.

Josie fanned at the burn in her eyes.

"Dumb hormones." She blinked away her tears.

It would be silly to cry over Heath, a passer-through who had made it perfectly clear that he didn't respect the boys ranch and, come the end of November, had no intention of staying involved in anyone's life beyond his friendship with Flint.

What did she even want from the poor man? For him to attend the Thanksgiving dinner and decide he wanted to move to Haven and keep doing her chores and driving her around for the rest of his life?

Even if—it was outlandish to entertain the thought— he developed feelings for Josie beyond friendship, she wanted nothing to do with a lawman. So picturing a friendship lasting past November was foolishness on her part and she only had herself to blame for these emotions, because Heath had been up front with her from the get-go.

No more letting her hopes get out of hand.

It was in the low fifties outside. Heath felt ten times better with the sun on his face, away from the freezing-cold office. He knew medical offices were purposely kept cold to discourage germs from multiplying, but running the air-conditioning in November felt like a stretch.

Things had gone topsy-turvy in the past week. He

wanted to keep the boys from the ranch at a distance, but then again, each one of them made him smile in their own unique ways. So far he'd found them to be good kids, respectful and hardworking. But that didn't fit with the image in his head. Fifteen years ago they'd found his father bleeding out near the barn after he'd taken on an assignment to protect one of the residents. Heath had always secretly assumed the youth turned on him.

Still believed that was the case.

He let out a long sigh. Trying to solve his father's case was foolish. Every night, he'd gone over the paperwork in the files, looking for a clue the investigators might have missed, but he found nothing new. Nothing besides plummeting hope. But that wasn't new, either.

Beyond all that, confusion reined in his thoughts for another reason. Heath had long ago decided he would never marry. Never get involved with a woman because he wasn't about to leave a family in the same position his father had. Heath couldn't do that. It was easier to care about no one than to start to care and realize the best thing for them would be for him to fade from their life.

He was playing with fire when it came to his friendship with Josie Markham. Hopefully, neither of them would walk away at the end of the month burned. Then again, it might be too late for that where he was concerned.

Advice. That was what he needed. A voice of reason.

Heath leaned against the brick building, pressed the button for his saved contacts and pulled up the first number. Nell.

She answered on the second ring. "Long time, no hear, big bro."

"Sorry about that. The last few months have been busy." Heath pushed away from the building and paced the length of the parking lot.

"Last few months?" She laughed. "Don't kid yourself. You're always too busy." Her voice was warm, kidding, but her words hit a soft place in his heart. They stung with truth.

He bunched up his free hand and glanced back through the front doors at Josie. So small and fragile and yet brave despite it all. So alone.

His throat went dry. "Nell? I'm sorry—all those years ago when Bill left— Would you forgive me for not being there for you?"

"Where is this coming from?"

"Just thinking." He ran his hand over his hair. "I wished I'd been there for you."

"It wasn't your responsibility."

He hooked his free hand on his belt. "Doing something out of love is more important than out of responsibility, don't you think?"

"Don't beat yourself up about it. You were stationed out of Lubbock at the time. That's a five-hour drive, Heath."

For Heath's entire career, he'd thought himself selfless—spending his time helping victims, seeing that justice was served—but in reality, he'd been selfish. He'd used his positions as soldier, trooper, investigator, Ranger...all of them to feel like he mattered. To convince himself that he was a good person. All the while, not investing in the people who actually knew him, like Nell and his mother. Never going out of his way for them.

When was the last time he'd called his mom?

He paced down the parking lot again, his boots clicking over the pavement. "I should have taken a leave from work. I had the time. But it never even crossed my mind to do that. It was selfish of me not to. I see that now."

"Heath. Seriously. Stop. I'm fine. Carly's fine. There's nothing to forgive."

"I could have been there." He kicked a rock into the abandoned yard in between the medical office and a small strip mall.

"But you weren't. And know what? I'm over it. I moved on. I'm with Danny now and I have this hunch he's going to propose around Christmas and you'd better be there for the wedding."

His feet stilled. Nell married? Danny was a good guy.

Heath felt a smile tug at his lips. "I wouldn't miss it."

"You promise?"

"Yes. And I love you." He ran the toe of his boot over a patch of tar covering a crack in the road. "I don't really ever say that, do I?"

"Not ever." Her voice hitched a little. "I love you, too. And I definitely like this warm and fuzzy version of you, but I have to ask, where is this change coming from?"

"The anniversary of Dad's death is coming up." November 22 would mark fifteen years.

"Two weeks from now." Her voice sobered. "Is that... Are you okay?"

"I'm in Haven for the month. Investigating it."

"Are you sure that's a good idea? You had such a hard time when…well, you know."

"I was fifteen. Dad was my hero."

"Not was. He is. Dad's still your hero. Mine, too."

"I want closure." Nell would argue that they had closure at the funeral, like she always did, so Heath pressed on, "More than what we have."

"So investigating Dad's death has led to you thinking about the past?"

"Not just that. There's this lady here." Heath cupped his free hand around the back of his neck. "Josie. She's in a situation like yours except her husband was a policeman. He lost his life in the line of duty."

"Oh, Heath. You have a soft spot for her, don't you?"

He debated denying it, but Nell knew him too well for that. "You could say that."

"Have you told her?"

"Her husband of ten years died six months ago." He spoke slowly so his sister would understand how impossible the situation was. "No. I haven't told her that I care about her. It wouldn't be appropriate and I don't think the attention would be welcome." Josie often brushed away Heath's offer to help her out of his truck and fought him when he tried to lighten her load. The mix of being standoffish yet sweet was messing with his head.

"But you care about her?" Nell squealed. "This is huge. I haven't heard you talk about a girl since high school."

"I've been busy."

She clucked her tongue. "Not anymore, though. Not this new and improved Heath Grayson." There was a smirk in her voice.

"How'd you do it…all alone, with Carly?"

"I just did, because I had to. But it was hard. I wouldn't choose to walk pregnancy and birth and caring for a child alone if I had to. I thank God every day for Danny strolling into my life last year. He's already such a help." Carly was singing along to something loud and high-pitched in the background. Nell and Heath both shared a laugh over it. "Heath…you could be Danny in Josie's life. You realize that, don't you?"

He wanted to argue with his sister, but that would just lead their conversation in a circle, so he didn't. "She invited me to the Thanksgiving dinner at the boys ranch."

"Tell me you're going."

He started to head back toward the doctor's office. "Since Dad, well, you know. Thanksgiving's never been my thing."

"So change that. Go. I want you to go."

"There's something else I want your opinion on."

"Shoot, Ranger."

Leave it to Nell.

He chuckled. "Flint's trying to locate all the original boys from when the ranch opened. They're looking for someone by the name of Edmund Grayson… They think it might be Grandpa."

She gasped. "No. It can't be, can it? He would have said something. We'd know, wouldn't we?"

"That's what I thought, but should I call him? Make sure?"

"I wouldn't. He's such a grumpy old man. I'd be afraid to ask because he might get offended. You know how he can get."

Of course he knew; that was why Heath hadn't made the call yet.

He noticed Josie fidgeting inside, so he tied up the conversation with Nell with a promise that he'd be around to celebrate Christmas with them and he couldn't wait to see how much Carly had grown. He also found out what Carly's favorite shows were so he'd have a better shot at picking a gift she'd enjoy. From now on he would be more involved in his niece's life. Next year, he wouldn't have to ask Nell for suggestions because he'd know what Carly wanted.

At least, that was a goal to aim for.

When he went back inside the waiting room, he smiled at Josie and they sat together without talking while they listened for her name to be called. Heath liked that. Just sitting near her, knowing she was safe.

How would he ever go back to his old life next month? The life where he was just as alone as Josie had been, but hadn't ever realized how lonely he really was? His five-hundred-square-foot apartment would feel like a solitary prison after this.

After the doctor's appointment, Josie walked beside Heath on the way back to his pickup truck. Because of construction taking place in the parking lot, they'd had to park in the strip mall next door.

"I can go get the truck," Heath offered again.

"Walking is good for me." She charged ahead and shooed away the offer of his arm, although it would have helped to lean on him as they picked their way across the yard spanning the distance. But she'd decided to put space between them.

As they entered the strip-mall area, the door to the

first store flew open—the nail salon—and a lady with brass-blond hair and French-manicured fingers cut in front of them. She wore skintight jeans and a shirt bearing a bedazzled cowboy hat and the words *Everyone Loves a Texas Girl*. Josie would know those sparkly high-heeled sandals anywhere.

Avery Culpepper.

Despite her decision moments ago to not touch Heath, Josie grabbed his arm and gently tugged so he'd slow down. "That's Cyrus Culpepper's granddaughter," Josie whispered. "She came after the reading of the will. A real troublemaker."

Heath bobbed his head slightly. "I've seen her a few times at the Blue Bonnet Inn. She made a ruckus over wanting poached eggs the other morning." Heath eyed the woman as they got closer. "Culpepper? The man who left his property to the boys ranch?"

"The same."

Avery had her smartphone in her hand as she tottered toward her aging red convertible. "I can't wait until I can shut down that ranch. Turn out all those bratty little children and sell the place for some real cash. I have so many plans for that money. You have no idea."

Josie dug her fingertips into Heath's arm. He wrapped his hand over hers and offered a sympathetic look.

"Of course I think I'll win!" Avery smacked away at her gum. "Ain't it my right?" Her car chirped when she hit the unlock button. "What claim do those snivelers have to it? I've got the name. They've got sad stories." She dropped into her driver's seat and adjusted the rear-view mirror. "Sad stories don't win lawsuits and I aim to sue." Avery peeled out of the parking spot, veered around an elderly woman pushing a shopping cart out of the grocery store and tore down Main Street.

Heath worked his jaw back and forth as he held the passenger door open for Josie. She climbed in and waited for him to slowly round the front of the truck and enter on the driver's side.

But not a moment longer.

"She can't take the ranch away, can she?"

Heath shoved the keys into the ignition, but then let them dangle. He leaned back in the seat and took in a long breath. "I don't know. I hope not."

"But you know laws."

"I know crime codes. Not inheritance laws."

"The will named the Lone Star Cowboy League for the property, not her. She can't do this to those boys." Josie swiped at tears.

"Shh." Heath's face twisted when he saw she was crying. He reached over and squeezed her hand. "Don't cry. Please don't cry. I'll talk to Flint. I'll help however I can."

"Why? You don't even care about the boys ranch." She shot the words at him because she was frustrated and needed an outlet for the emotions that threatened to drown her. They had never affected her like that before pregnancy.

Heath kept his voice soft, calm, as if he was speaking to one of her orphaned calves. "Just because I don't trust every single person there, doesn't mean I want the place shut down. The work being done at the boys ranch is valuable. I'll tell Flint what we heard and—"

"No. Gabe." More tears. "He's the president of our

chapter of the Lone Star Cowboy League. We have to tell Gabe."

"All right, we'll tell Gabe. Hey. Everything will be okay." He squeezed her hand again before letting go. "We'll fight for this place if we have to."

Not trusting her voice, she sucked in a rattling breath and nodded.

Heath wrapped his arm over the steering wheel and turned on the engine. He backed out of the parking lot and headed in the direction of the boys ranch. "I'm sorry about how I acted earlier, when you asked me about Thanksgiving."

She gripped the armrest, just to have something to hold. "I shouldn't have assumed you'd want to attend."

"It's not that. It's only…my father was murdered a few days before Thanksgiving. At the boys ranch—at the old location. So, this is all a mess for me right now. If that makes any sense."

"Oh, I didn't know." She placed a hand on his shoulder, not knowing how else to comfort him. "That makes complete sense. Why didn't you say something?"

"I'm saying something now."

Josie shook her head. Men.

Heath turned down the music and glanced her way. "What I'm trying to say is, I'd be happy to come to the Thanksgiving dinner, that is, as long as you promise to sit at my table." His smile lit up every angle of his face.

She wanted to say she'd sit beside him at every meal for the rest of their lives if he was willing.

Careful, heart.

Act like it's no big deal. Because it's not.

Josie removed her hand and rolled her eyes at him.

"Are you sure there will be room? My guess is all the boys will be fighting to sit at your table."

"I'll save a seat." He winked at her. "Right beside me."

Josie swallowed hard. "Then, sure, I'll sit at your table."

And she'd probably regret it once December started...but she'd do it for the sake of the boys at the ranch. They'd be ecstatic once they learned Heath would be there.

Okay, maybe it wasn't just for the sake of the boys, but she wouldn't give hope wings by dwelling on the feelings stirring in her heart. Because truth be told, if that hope sprung wings, the only ending for it would be a crash landing.

Chapter Six

Neither of Heath's real-life investigations were going so well.

Despite talking to several staff members who had worked at the boys ranch while his father was there and going over the case files every night back in his hotel room, he wasn't any closer to figuring out what had led to the murder.

Could a resident at the ranch really have committed the crime and then been able to cover it up? Unfortunately, he'd encountered crazier scenarios during his course of duty. Heath's gut twisted. It was impossible to imagine one of the boys who currently lived at the ranch engaging in such an act. The very thought made him feel ill.

Then again, there had been different boys there fifteen years ago. Who knew what they'd been like? Other than his father. And Heath could hardly ask him.

When it came to the recent happenings at the boys ranch—a missing therapy horse last month, some minor thefts and the person Josie had witnessed setting the calves loose—he didn't have much to go off

of there, either. Although, his hunch was still that one
of the boys had a penchant for pranks—nothing sinis-
ter. So far, there hadn't been any more incidents while
he'd been volunteering. Heath guessed—if someone
local *had* been committing crimes—his presence was
enough to keep wrongdoers away. Haven was a small
town. Everyone knew a Texas Ranger was loitering
around the boys ranch by now.

They'd wait until the guard dog went home to strike
again.

So don't leave.

He sighed and scrubbed his hand over his jaw.

At least the made-up investigation his detection
class was working on was going better.

Since a few new boys had joined the boys ranch in
the past week, Heath had put off going back to the fake
crime scene. He wanted to give the new boys a chance
to catch up before bringing the group to solve the case.
But today he'd led them back to the makeshift crime
scene in the calf barn. They'd pulled up the shoe im-
prints and were passing them around for inspection.

Most of the boys were staring at him, waiting. Had
he been silent so long?

He cleared his throat. "So what else do you notice
about the crime scene?"

Heath passed in front of the row of students. He
paused in front of Joey and Damon, two of the new
boys to arrive at the ranch that month. Joey's red hair
stuck out at odd angles, making it look like he'd just
woken up in spite of the fact that it was already mid-
day, but he'd been smart as a whip during his talk about
interviewing suspects. Damon was smaller, shier. His
deep brown eyes matched his skin tone.

"Damon, notice anything?"

Damon squinted and tilted his head. "Maybe the person was shuffling?"

"Great eye." Heath stepped across the yellow crime-scene tape and squatted near the shoe prints. "Damon's correct. Does everyone see how some of the prints are dragged together and spaced closer?" He pointed so they could see exactly what he was talking about. "These little details are real important when it comes to identifying the suspect. It's also the sort of thing that'll help you win a case in court."

Stephen raised his hand. Heath still needed to find a time to speak with the young man about the calves getting loose. He made a note to do that before he and Josie left for the day.

"Yes, Stephen?"

The teen stood at the back of the pack and rose up a little, probably on his tiptoes, to gesture toward the back wall. "It looks like the shoes went deeper into the mud way over by the wall there."

"Excellent." Heath rose to his feet. "Any ideas as to what would cause that?"

Joey licked his lips. "The ground could have been muddier there. Wetter?"

Heath nodded. "That's definitely a possibility. However, the ground slopes toward the drain in the center of the building, so it's unlikely that moisture would pool near the walls. But I really like the way you're thinking. The deeper impressions mean something..."

Stephen crossed his arms, narrowed his eyes and tilted his head a fraction. "The person was carrying something heavier when they stepped there."

Heath winked at him, letting the teen know he was correct. "Which raises the question...what's missing?"

Riley, one of the older boys, looped his arm over a shorter boy Heath had noticed was always his shadow. "I got this one. I asked Josie. She said the old hand-crank ice-cream maker used to be on that ledge there." He gestured toward the back wall near the footprints. "And now she can't find it."

"Sought out and interviewed a victim." Heath whistled. "I'm impressed. You just might be a future Ranger." He grinned at the boys, surprised by how much fun he was having teaching them. "So here's what we have so far." He used his fingers to tick off the clues. "A stolen ice-cream maker, someone who might have shuffled and the knowledge that the ice-cream machine might have been a struggle for them to carry."

"And this." Stephen wiggled the plaster cast of the shoe impression. "The print doesn't have any logos on it, and most of the bottoms of tennis shoes have that. Right?" He looked off to the left. "So I think it's someone who doesn't wear shoes like that. But most everyone else around here wears cowboy boots, and it doesn't look like that, either. It's too wide...almost like a loafer or something."

Joey laughed. "It looks like an old-lady shoe."

They were so close to cracking the case. Heath almost gave in and told them, but he bit his tongue. They'd piece it together soon enough and the ranch cook, Marnie Binder, had a surprise waiting for them when they did.

Stephen's eyebrows rose. "You know, now that you said that...it looks like Marnie's shoes! She makes sense with the ice-cream maker, too." He took off running out of the barn and banked a hard left toward the big house. Heath motioned for the rest of the boys to follow. Moving as a pack, they sprinted past the learning center and barged into the back of the big house, where all the boys lived.

Marnie was waiting for them in the kitchen, a huge smile plastered across her face.

"You're the thief!"

"It was you!"

"Give the ice-cream maker back!"

The younger ones were jumping up and down, excitement pulsing around the room.

Marnie threw back her head and laughed as she raised her hands in the air. "You caught me, all right." She grinned back at Heath. "I see you've got a whole brood of junior detectives on your hands."

"My future boss is somewhere in this crowd. The next generation of Rangers, right here." He spanned his hands to include all the boys. Each one looked so proud of himself, proud and confident. Heath's chest swelled, although he couldn't brush away the pang of sadness he felt, too. He would have benefited from a father figure to encourage him after his dad passed away.

Nell had said he could be someone like that for Josie. But what about for these boys? Was it possible God had placed Heath here for a reason far beyond his father's case?

He shook away his thoughts.

Heath had a job to do. An important one. As a Texas Ranger, he had one mission, one goal—to uphold the law. That duty put him at risk daily. Attachments slowed an officer down...made him go soft when difficult, snap decisions needed to be made.

"Well, now." Marnie popped her hands onto her hips. "Looks like I got a bunch of junior Rangers here who can help me whip up some ice cream."

The boys clapped and whooped and took turns scrubbing their hands in the sink, the older boys monitoring the progress of the younger ones. Marnie pulled the ice-cream maker out of hiding and sent a few of the boys to gather the ingredients from the fridge, where she'd set them to chill.

"You." She pointed at Heath. "Rock salt. Back porch."

"Yes, ma'am." He tipped his hat and then fetched the heavy bag from the rack on the porch.

Marnie lined the boys up and had them take turns churning the hand crank. "You, too, Ranger." She motioned Heath forward. "Only those who crank get to eat it."

"Then by all means." Heath rolled up his sleeves and worked the crank for a few minutes. It took more strength to do than he'd figured, but the boys cheered him on. After his turn, he backed away from the group in order to observe everyone.

When was the last time he'd spent an afternoon smiling this much?

Months? No...years had passed.

He worked his jaw back and forth, trying to piece together the puzzle of his own life. Somewhere along the way, Heath had stopped experiencing joy. Perhaps it was because in his profession, he saw more of the bad side of humanity. He'd been a firsthand witness to so many horrible situations because of the cases he investigated, he'd forgotten how to or even felt guilty if he enjoyed life.

Experiencing joy shouldn't make him feel guilty, though. If memory served him right, the Bible said something about joy being a by-product of someone knowing God. Somehow he'd forgotten that along the way.

Who knew how long the joy would last? Nothing in life was guaranteed. But for now, he'd savor it. Store it up so he had enough to last him all the lonely years for the rest of his life once he left the ranch and Josie.

Josie reached for the next pile of T-shirts to fold.

Part of her role as mother's helper was to assist and sometimes take over the day-to-day tasks that needed to be accomplished in order to keep the house at the boys ranch running. All the boys had household chores, but they also had responsibilities outside of the house. Josie was there to help fill in the gap.

For as long as she could during her pregnancy.

"Didn't we just do laundry the other day?" She laughed as she tapped the top of the leaning tower of folded shirts. "How do these boys manage to go through so many outfits?"

The three housemothers who were folding alongside her all shook their heads and smiled good-naturedly. Dark-haired Laura was on her right; the woman was kindly and served as a sort of grandmother figure in the house. Abby giggled on Josie's left. She was Josie's age and full of life. The two had become fast friends when Josie started volunteering. Across the folding table stood Eleanor, who wore her red hair pulled back in a low ponytail.

Eleanor sighed. "Just wait until your little one arrives. You'll be amazed how someone so tiny can make so many messes. When my first came, I remember doing a load of laundry every day and not being able to understand where all the towels and blankets were coming from."

"Here, Josie." Laura pressed a basket full of clean kitchen rags and towels into her hands. "Go ahead and bring these to Marnie and then you can head to the barn." She nudged her with a grin. "We all know you didn't get to take a peek at your calves yet today."

"What are you going to do when those calves all grow up?" Abby joked.

Josie felt a smile bloom on her face. "Get new ones. Believe me, ladies, there are always orphaned calves to be had." She did a little bow and then propped the basket on her hip as she headed down the hall. Although she loved catching up with the housemothers, Josie really did miss the calves whenever she didn't get to see them, and because of her doctor's appointment that morning, she hadn't made her way to the barn yet.

She maneuvered out of the way as the door to the office opened and revealed Gabe Everett, president of their chapter of the Lone Star Cowboy League and liaison to the boys ranch. His broad shoulders ate up all the room between the doorjamb.

"Just the man I needed to see." Josie wedged the laundry basket against the wall because it was getting heavy.

Gabe's blue eyes cut her way. He was a powerful figure in town—a single, wealthy rancher who was more handsome than any cowboy had a right to be. Josie always found herself intimidated around him, but she forced her lips to move anyway.

"Will you be around awhile longer?"

"I can be if you need me." Gabe hooked his hand on the top of the doorway.

"Okay, let me just find Heath and we'll be right back."

Thankfully, the man in question wasn't difficult to locate. Josie turned the corner and found Heath with a bowl of melting ice cream in hand, surrounded by a bunch of chatting boys.

Diego sprang to his feet and rushed toward her. "Ms. Josie!" He bounced beside her and she couldn't hold back her laugh. She'd admitted to Heath when she first met him that Diego was probably her favorite. He'd won a special place in her heart because of their shared interest in cattle, his infectious smile and his cheerful spirit to match. Sure, the boy had baggage—the years before he came to live at the ranch had been difficult ones—but he was growing every day. Josie had a connection with Diego that none of the other adults working at the ranch seemed to have obtained. Her friendship with the boy was one of the things that had confirmed for her that all the extra volunteer hours were what God wanted. Not only that, the time had blessed her, too.

"Want to taste the ice cream?" He thrust a bowl under her nose. "We made it ourselves. Heath let us after we solved the crime."

"Looks delicious, but maybe later."

Diego's eyes went wide. "See how many of us there are?" He solemnly shook his head. "There won't be any later."

While Diego was talking, Heath set down his bowl, got to his feet and crossed the kitchen to her side.

"Here. Allow me." He eased the basket from Josie's

hands and passed it over to the counter near where Marnie was leaning. "You might want to take them up on the ice-cream offer. It's the best I've ever had."

"Homemade is the only way to go," she agreed but still passed. She'd overdone it on the burritos at lunch. But they'd been delicious and she was pregnant. So there.

Heath rested his hands on his stomach and nodded. "The only thing that would make it better would be a side of pumpkin pie."

Josie chuckled. "Is that your favorite?"

"It is. And I've yet to partake in any yet this fall."

Diego's gaze shot back and forth between them like he was watching a tennis match.

She really shouldn't kid with Heath so openly in front of the boys, but she was having too much fun to stop. "We'll have to rectify that."

Diego wedged himself closer to them. "Do you know how to make pumpkin pie?"

"I have a secret recipe and everything." She tapped the tip of the boy's nose. He gave her an impulsive hug and then dived back toward the table for seconds.

Josie scanned the room, happy to see Heath engaging with so many of the residents. Her gaze landed on the tiniest boy in the room, a small blond boy. Tucked between Riley and Stephen, Flint Rowling's little boy, Logan, shoveled spoonful after spoonful of dessert into his mouth. Logan was only six, younger than most of the boys in Heath's class. He and his father lived on the property, but Josie knew Logan was supposed to be with either Flint or his nanny. Neither person was in the room.

She stepped closer to Heath. "Does Flint know Logan's here?"

Heath rested his hand on the right side of his belt. Josie noticed he did that a lot. Probably a reflex of carrying a gun there his entire career. He was used to something being there to set his hand on.

"His son?"

She inched so she was right beside Heath and the boys couldn't hear. "The little one. Over there."

Heath frowned. "I didn't notice him before. Is he not supposed to be in here?"

"Not unless his nanny is with him." She held out her hand. "Give me your phone." Heath quirked an eyebrow, but handed over his phone. "Thanks. I forgot mine at home today." She swiped at the screen. Heath's screen had a plain, boring solid color background and a couple of icons. She found Flint in his recent calls, just like she'd guessed. She pressed the green button.

Flint answered right away.

"Hey, it's Josie."

"Heath all right?"

"Yeah, I stole his phone. I just wanted to make sure you knew Logan was up at the big house."

"He's *what*?" Flint's voice rose.

Josie turned away from the group. "He's okay." She kept her voice soft in an effort to calm Flint down. "He's in the kitchen here eating ice cream."

"I can't believe this." Something clanked in the background. Had Flint thrown something? "That child will be the death of me."

Josie turned a little, immediately seeking out Heath's gaze for comfort. Why was Flint getting so worked up over Logan being at the big house? "I only wanted you to know where he was. He's not causing any trouble. That's not why I called."

"He'd best not be misbehaving. He's in plenty of trouble for wandering off again as it is."

"He's only a kid," she pleaded. "I'm sure he simply enjoys spending time with the others. No harm done."

"Oh, harm's done, all right. Disobeying's not okay. Not on my watch. I'll be there soon." He hung up. From his tone, she expected him to come barreling through the door any second.

What was going on between the boy and Flint? Every interaction she'd seen between them in the past had been positive, but Flint had sounded really upset. Logan was only six. Surely Flint knew that a six-year-old boy would try to get up to the ranch to hang out with the other kids every chance he could.

Calm down. Flint was on his way and he was Logan's father. It wasn't up to her to judge. Perhaps Flint was having an off day. Even still, she silently prayed for God to soften Flint's heart toward his son and give him compassion and the imagination to remember how it was to be so young.

She reached out to touch Heath's arm. "When you're done, I need you. Gabe's here and I want you to come with me to tell him what we heard."

Heath wiped his hands off on one of the clean towels. "I'm done now." He dumped his bowl into the wide kitchen sink and instructed the boys to wash up. "Marnie's taking the watch from here."

Relieved of his duties, he followed her back to the office and Katie pointed them toward a small room where Gabe waited. Josie made introductions and then launched into the details about seeing Avery Culpepper earlier in the day.

"She said she's planning to sue for all of the property and then she's going to kick the boys out. Can she do that?" Josie wrung her hands over and over again as she talked.

Heath reached across and laid his hand on top of hers. A silent message to relax, take a breath. He was there to fight beside her.

Gabe leaned back in his chair. "Unfortunately, Avery has bite behind her threats. She met with our leadership last week and tried to cut a deal. We give her one hundred thousand dollars and she'll sign something that forfeits her ability to sue for the land, but if we refuse to pay, she says she'll hire a lawyer and battle us in court for everything."

Josie gasped. Tears pricked in her eyes. "I can't understand how someone could be so coldhearted toward this organization."

Gabe rested his hands on the desk. "I hear she's been telling anyone in town who will listen that Cyrus did her wrong."

Heath nodded. "I've heard her griping some back at the inn. I never realized it had to do with Culpepper or the ranch, though. She didn't say any names. Only that she's been treated poorly by her family and they'd pay for it."

Gabe scrubbed his hand over his jaw and exhaled loudly. "Not only did he deprive her of a relationship with him, but he left her only that run-down cabin where he was raised. And we all know the old property isn't worth much."

It was better than the ranch Josie was scraping out at her father's old fishing cabin.

Josie balled up her hands. "We make out of this life what we put into it. Some of us fall on hardships or get a bad road of it, but that's no one's fault. That's life. We can't wait for or expect handouts to make it all better."

Gabe's eyes softened with understanding. "I know that, Josie. Believe me, I do."

Heath's spine straightened. "Don't give in to her threats. It's not lawful, her trying to manipulate the League that way."

Gabe frowned. "No disrespect, Ranger, but I'm not so sure it's that easy. Avery has a proper claim to the land if we can't meet *every* stipulation in the will. If we don't find *all* the original men for the reunion, we can't keep the ranch anyway."

Josie ran her fingers over the worn fabric of her jeans. She swallowed hard. "Is there... Would there ever be a situation where the League would pay her?"

"I can't say what we'll do if we end up with our backs against the wall. If we're forced to..." He shook his head. "All I know right now is we stand no chance unless the anniversary celebration is a success. That has to be our focus."

Josie leaned forward. "We'll find the men. We have to."

Gabe tilted his head, glancing Heath's way. "Flint mentioned you might be related to Edmund Grayson. Has anything come of that?"

Heath stared down at the toes of his boots. "Nothing yet. But I'm planning to call him."

Gabe tapped the desk. "It's imperative that all four original residents of the boys ranch are reunited at the ranch in March." His words were slow, deliberate. "If we don't meet the demands of Cyrus's will, we'll lose the property."

"I understand." Heath hooked his ankle onto his knee and rested his hand on top of his boot. "I'll check with him."

"Soon?" Gabe urged.

"You have my word."

Josie turned to face Heath, but he wouldn't meet her gaze. Why hadn't he told her he might be related to one of the original boys? What was he hiding?

Chapter Seven

Heath probably shouldn't have left the ranch right after their talk with Gabe, but he'd needed air. Space. Time to think. Still, he shouldn't have walked out of there without letting Josie know his plans.

Gravel churned under the tires of his truck as he steered it back up the long drive to the boys ranch. He hadn't been gone long, but the daylight hours were growing shorter. The sun's last tips of light blazed orange over the far field, but it would dip away to darkness soon.

If he wasn't on vacation right now, if he was home—as much as his tiny, sparse apartment could be called that—the streetlights would give a sense that there was still time to accomplish something more that day. Out in the country areas like Haven, the sun dictated the work hours. When it went down, it was time to relax.

But Heath couldn't relax just yet.

"You left her. You just…left." He worked his jaw back and forth as he popped the truck into Park. Everyone who lived on the ranch would be inside of the large house by now. Josie among them, no doubt. By this time, dinner was long over.

His phone vibrated in his truck's console. Maybe it was Josie. She'd spotted his truck and was headed out to join him. Wishful thinking. She'd mentioned earlier that she'd forgotten her cell at home today.

He grabbed his phone and glanced at the screen. Nell. He hit Accept.

"I figured I'd start calling and checking in on you," she said.

"I'm glad you did." He filled her in on everything that had happened since their last conversation, including his failed attempts at coming up with leads for the happenings at the boys ranch and their father's murder. Many interviews, but no possible suspects. He told her all about Josie, too.

"So you're just going to keep this girl—this Josie—at a distance?"

He pinched the bridge of his nose. "It's for her own good. I stay away from people because of my job. You know that."

"That's selfish, Heath. You've got to let people make their own decisions. If they want to love you and risk losing you, then that's their choice to make. Not yours. You hurt more than just yourself doing that."

"But, Nell, I could die. If... I... Like Dad. No." He braced his hand on his dashboard. "I chose to become a Ranger, and this is part of the price. I stay away from people to protect them. If I was around you and Carly all the time and then something happened, wouldn't it be harder?"

"Harder than going to your funeral and thinking, *He's gone and now I'll never get the chance to actu-*

ally know him? No, actually, it wouldn't. At least we would have known you fully. We'd have a storeroom of happy memories to cling to. Instead of *Well, I never really knew him—I wish I had, but now there's no hope of that.* See the difference?"

He'd never considered that. It hurt losing his dad, but they'd been close. He missed him so much *because* he'd been such a present father. Heath swallowed hard. "Painfully so."

"Then stop being such a mule and do something about it. You know what? You go right on ahead and call Grandpa."

"You said not to."

"I changed my mind. You're going to become just like that grouch unless you make some drastic changes in your relationships. I love you, but you've really got to get over this stubborn self-isolation thing you've got going on."

Heath groaned, but Nell was right. "I love you, too." He promised to call her after he talked to their grandfather.

After hanging up, Heath scanned the buildings beyond the house and spotted Flint's outline near the horse corral. The two hadn't spent as much time together during Heath's vacation as he originally thought they would, and the month was half over already. Heath jammed on his Stetson and headed toward his friend.

"You seen Josie around?"

Flint's shoulders went rigid and he turned around slowly. "We've known each other a long time now, haven't we?"

Heath froze. Was Flint angry? Frustrated? Flint's tone sent off warning alarms in his mind.

Heath forced himself to relax. "That we have."

"How long?" Flint folded his arms over his chest and speared him with a hard look.

Huh. Heath had seen that look before. Ten years ago at boot camp to be exact. Determination mixed with an equal measure of indignation. But now that look was honed in on him. Was this about Logan eating ice cream with the boys? Heath hadn't even realized Flint's son was there.

Just answer the man's question. "Ten years, or thereabouts."

"Ten years seems long enough to know someone." Flint cocked his head. "To decide if someone's trustworthy."

Where was this coming from? The two men had watched each other's backs during boot camp, during their time in Iraq. Heath trusted Flint more than anyone else in the world. To think his friend didn't return that conviction...

Heath widened his stance. "You saying you don't trust me?"

Flint shook his head once. "That's not what I said at all. I'd trust you with my life. Have before."

"Then what *is* this about?"

"Josie."

Her name, the way Flint said it, felt like a punch to the gut. Heath's mouth went dry. Muscles in his legs and arms tensed, ready to spring into action. "What happened? Is she okay?"

"Don't know." Flint slid his thumbs into his pockets and rocked forward on his boots. "I think that's something I ought to be asking you."

Heath couldn't stand the idea of waiting for Flint to

get on with the conversation. Evidently he wanted to confront Heath on something. *So do it.*

Heath rolled his shoulders. "Go ahead and spit out whatever wants to be said so bad it's clawing its way out of you."

Flint lowered his voice and stepped closer. "What are your intentions where Josie Markham is concerned?"

"You sound like her father."

"Well, Josie's father is dead." Flint's stare remained hard. "In fact, she's got no blood family left. All she's has is us on the ranch and those in the League. While I might not be family, someone's got to watch out for her."

Heath stepped an inch closer. He and Flint might have fought as soldiers together, but Heath had gone toe-to-toe with the roughest folks in Texas for the past ten years while Flint had hidden away at the boys ranch. Hold up. It was wrong of him to think such a mean-hearted thing about his best friend. Acting on momentary indignation never served him well. Flint wasn't hiding at the ranch, he was devoting his life to something good. Something worthwhile. However, Heath wasn't about to let Flint attempt to intimidate or talk down to him.

"Funny, considering I'm the one watching out for her." Heath thumped his own chest. "That woman was struggling on her ranch and working herself to exhaustion and still would be if I wasn't doing the chores over there." He gestured off in the general direction of Josie's ranch across town. "You were all letting her and her unborn child drive around in that death trap of a vehicle before I insisted on picking her up every day. She's gone alone to every doctor's appointment. None of you have bothered to go and sit with her there." Heath took another step closer to his friend and dropped his voice low. "So don't talk to me about you being there for her if it's only going to be in word and not deed."

Flint's arms went slack beside him. "Maybe there's more we all could have been doing to pitch in for her. Plenty I didn't think about. She's stubborn and doesn't let anyone know when she needs help." He took a deep breath. "But that's beside the point."

Heath backed off, giving them both some breathing room. "I'm struggling to see what the point even is."

"Are you leaving at the end of the month?"

Heath took another step back. "If by leaving you mean going back to work, yes."

"Exactly." Flint grabbed a bucket off the ground, sending a puff of grain dust into the air, and started for the barn door, signaling the motion-detecting floodlights to turn on.

Heath captured Flint's arm, jerking him to a stop. "Exactly, *what*? What's that supposed to mean?"

"It means that you're leaving and you need to remember that."

"I'm a bad person if I go back to work? That makes no sense whatsoever." Even as he said it, Flint's words rang true and echoed Nell's. Of course Heath had to go back to work in December…but that had been an excuse to keep people at a distance, too.

Flint made a *tsk* sound with his tongue and shook his head in a slow, sad way. "For a man who has spent his life unraveling crimes, you sure have a hard time reading people."

Heath's throat went dry. He knew what Flint was getting at... Josie. Was Heath setting them both up for heartache? But it wasn't like that. He was helping her because she was alone and he'd want someone to do the same for Nell. She was also the witness to a crime, be it a petty one that didn't seem to amount to much danger, but still...

He pinched the bridge of his nose. "Josie's my friend. That's it, Flint. She and I both know that."

"Tell yourself that if it helps you sleep better."

Enough. He didn't want to fight with his best friend. Not anymore.

Heath let go of Flint's arm. "Is she in the house? I'm supposed to drive her home."

"Josie's gone." Flint rested his hand on the door handle, his back to Heath. "Macy Swanson—the tall blonde who reads stories out loud to the boys in the learning center—she drove her home after Josie saw your truck was gone."

"I was going to come back."

Flint glanced back at Heath over his shoulder. "Josie looked upset."

No wonder Flint had launched into an argument with him.

An ache spread through Heath's chest. He shoved the heel of his hand against the center of his rib cage. "She did?"

Flint turned to prop his shoulder against the door-jamb. "I saw her crying."

If Heath was a man given to cursing, now would have been a time to use one, but he'd long ago given up that bad habit. Instead, he kicked at the ground.

After they had finished speaking with Gabe earlier, Heath had made an excuse to leave the ranch for the rest of the afternoon. All to avoid Josie—only for a few hours. He had taken a drive, got his head together before seeing her again, because he'd noticed the way she'd looked at him after Gabe mentioned Edmund Grayson.

Josie would ask.

Did she know how much her examination made him mentally squirm? He couldn't stop wondering what she was thinking. No one had ever had that effect on him before, but Josie was a singular woman. Sharp and quick to figure something out, bold enough to ask questions, yet empathetic and kind when the answers were difficult.

The problem was Heath didn't want to answer her questions. Not today. Not when he knew she'd ask about his grandfather. She would have prodded into why he hadn't called the man yet. Josie had a way of making Heath crack wide-open with information.

Heath blew out a long puff of air. "I didn't mean to hurt her."

"Since you've been my friend a long time, I'm going to level with you."

It's about time.

"If you have no intention of sticking around past November, then stay away from Josie. Plain and simple." The bucket swung beside him. "The woman lost her husband this year, she's pregnant, had to leave her home and her entire life has changed. She doesn't need another setback." Flint looked away, toward the ground. "Don't...don't lead her on."

"Flint. I wouldn't—"

"Don't make her hurt."

"That's not my plan." But then…what *was* his plan? Once he was back to living at his apartment, he couldn't stop at her ranch every morning to take care of her. He wouldn't get to kid with her over breakfast or encourage her while she shared her dreams about her ranch.

Flint's nostrils flared. His knuckles went white around the bucket's handle. "Listen. I know what it feels like to think you're in a relationship. Think the other person cares about you. And then have them disappear as if you're nothing more than dried dirt on their shoe."

Realization popped in Heath's mind. Of course Flint's thoughts would automatically go to Logan's mom and her betrayal. Her name was usually off-limits, but Heath saw no way around it.

"I'm not like Stacie. I wouldn't do that. Making someone think, hope, and then leave…" Heath shook his head as words failed him. He envisioned the end of the month, driving away and never seeing Josie again. His heart sank into the toes of his boots.

But, he'd visit. They'd stay friends. Wouldn't they?

"Abandoning someone." Flint nodded slowly. "It's the worst thing you can do to a person."

"I'm sorry." *For what Logan's mom's did to you.* Flint didn't want to hear that.

Flint blinked a few times, almost as if he was refocusing. "Don't be sorry. Be smart. You head back to your apartment and your career in two weeks and we'll all stay here. What you've done to help Josie would be great if you were sticking around, but now you've simply given her something to lose again. So let her be between now and then. That's the best thing you can do."

"But what if…" Heath couldn't meet his friend's eyes.

"What if, what?" Flint set the bucket down by the barn door so he could use his hands to talk. "I know you. Being a Ranger is your life. That's the most important thing and there isn't room for much else."

"But—"

"Oh, you may think you care about Josie now. She's pretty and nice and depending on you. Any man would like that. But once December hits, you'll get assigned a case and that'll become your priority. Promises to visit will lag into months of getting pushed back until finally it's summer and Josie hasn't heard from you in six months."

Heath tugged off his hat and then scrubbed his hand over his hair. "I'm not that bad."

"You are. You forget people the second you don't need them."

Everything came to a screeching halt. Was Flint mad at Heath for not being a more present friend? Come to think of it, Heath hadn't been there for Flint at all when Stacie left him. How many people had he failed without realizing it?

"I… Am I really like that?" Hadn't Nell accused him of the same thing? Letting too much time pass between contacting her and not staying engaged in her life? Did Heath have any friendships that he kept up with? Sadly…no. He partially blamed his police work. There was so much about his job he couldn't discuss outside of work. Heath had watched that put strains on a lot of the married Rangers' relationships.

But it wasn't all police related. Most of the blame fell squarely on his shoulders. Heath kept people at a distance—for their safety, of course. If he wasn't so connected to them, then if the worst happened, they wouldn't need to miss him or mourn him at some point.

None of his relationships would be like when Dad died. That had been his plan.

Nell had challenged him to let people choose if they were willing to take that risk. Heath didn't know if he was capable of doing that, though.

"You don't want to depend on others," Flint said. "I get it. I think it's what makes you so good at your job."

Heath shoved his hand against the barn and hung his head. "But it makes me a bad candidate for being a friend or anything more in someone's life."

"Bingo."

"Ouch." He ran his hand down his face.

"Well." Flint grabbed his shoulder and gave it a quick squeeze before letting go. "I'm still willing to be your friend."

Heath nodded and stepped away from the barn. "I'm sorry I wasn't there for you. During everything."

Flint shrugged. "It happens. I'm not losing sleep over it. Don't you, either."

His friend's words tumbled around in his head as Heath took the long way back to town. Driving often helped him straighten out his thoughts. What Flint said made sense. He should stay away from Josie, but Heath didn't know if he could. Even when she wasn't nearby, he wondered how she was and where at the ranch she was and pictured her smile.

Flint was right about Heath being a bad friend, too, and he wanted to change that. But how could he if he was supposed to pull away from Josie? Wouldn't that be making the same mistake again—the same behavior that had led to his hurting Nell and Flint?

What was he going to do?

The long drive didn't help at all.

Heath ducked his head, hoping to avoid Gabe as the man strode purposefully toward the ranch house the next day. When he'd stopped off at Josie's house in the morning like he usually did, she was nowhere to be found, and she hadn't answered her phone, either. Heath had gone so far as to send a text message, not something he was given to doing seeing as he had very few people in his life to text with. Still no answer.

If something was wrong, if she was sick or had an emergency or there was something the matter with the baby, she would have called him. Of course she would have.

Still, Heath walked a little faster.

Despite Flint's warnings, Heath needed to find Josie and apologize for leaving her stranded yesterday. As long as he dodged Gabe, he could duck into the calf barn and catch a moment with her before she went into the big house to help with the housework for the day.

"A minute of your time, Ranger?"

Too late.

Gabe spotted him and motioned him forward.

"Of course." Heath trailed Gabe to a rough picnic table situated under one of the large trees by the ranch house. "What's on your mind?" Not that he needed to ask...

"Were you able to get ahold of your grandfather?"

No surprise there.

Heath exhaled and looked up to examine the way the branches on the tree wove into one another—like they existed to support each other and if some of them weren't there, the whole tree would start to die.

"Yesterday wasn't a good day for me to do that, but I'll have an answer for you by the end of the week." Three days to work up the nerve to make the call. Less than a week until the anniversary of Dad's murder. Last night he'd crossed off the last name on Josie's list of people who had worked at the ranch fifteen years ago. All dead ends. No new answers...only more confusion.

"There's something more." Gabe leaned against the edge of the tabletop and crossed his arms. "I hear you have some reservations about the boys here."

Heath snapped his gaze back to Gabe. "Josie told you?"

"She didn't have to." Gabe's face remained unreadable. If he ever got tired of ranching, the man would make a top-rate investigator. "But word gets around in a tight-knit place like this."

"It appears so." Heath rubbed the back of his fingers under his chin, then straightened his spine. "Whatever you heard, know that I think you all are doing a great thing here for these boys."

Gabe adjusted his arms a little. He had the build of a man who might best Heath in a takedown if he was a criminal. Good thing Gabe was about as noble as a person could be. Honest and hardworking, the man ran one of the most successful ranches in the area and spent all his free time volunteering. Heath admired the man for everything he was doing to help others.

"You think the boys here are all bad news, though, don't you?"

"I guess you could say that." Heath tried to choose his words carefully. "Normal kids are home with their parents. You get sent to a place like this because you're having issues or are too much trouble for your family to handle. That's a fact, and I'm the type who works in facts."

"You're not wrong about what *starts* the process of them being here. However, I find it hard to believe that you still consider these boys capable of putting one of our therapy horses at risk, endangering Josie's beloved calves or stealing from the staff that they care about."

True. After spending almost two weeks getting to know the boys in his detection class, Heath found it impossible to suspect any of them. Even Stephen—especially Stephen.

But the training that came with so many years in law enforcement told him there was always a chance. "I believe anything—often the most unlikely—is possible. I have to."

"Do you think these boys will leave here and go back to their troublemaking ways? That they're destined to be bad eggs, or however you want to phrase it?"

"Not all, but some will."

"So lasting change isn't real? It's not something we can actually accomplish?"

Heath bit back a groan. He didn't want to get into this discussion with Gabe. Not when he wasn't sure what he believed anymore. "I know that bothers you to hear, but I'm a realist. I don't think a person can do what I do and see what I've seen and not be."

Gabe propped himself up so he was sitting on top of the table. His demeanor said he wasn't bothered at all by what Heath had said. Or he was very good at holding his emotions in check.

"I don't think you know, but when I was young I used to be a resident at this boys ranch."

"You?" Heath stumbled over the short word. Gabe was capable and prosperous, the president of the area's Lone Star Cowboy League—and he'd been a troubled kid? The two facts didn't seem to fit, but Gabe had no reason to lie about such a thing.

"Me." Gabe nodded. "I turned out better for it, just like the current residents will."

"What years?" Heath licked his lips. "How long ago were you here?"

"Not—" Gabe scooped off his hat and tapped it on his leg "—when your father was murdered. That was a good seven years after I left. I know it was a long time ago, but I'm sorry for your loss. It's why you came here, isn't it?"

"Originally, yes."

Gabe studied him for a moment before saying, "But not now?"

"I'm just on vacation." Heath held his hands up in a stop motion.

"Watch out, Ranger." Gabe hopped down from the table. "You might find you don't want to leave. This place has a way of healing people." He stopped beside Heath.

"Funny." Heath shook his head. "Josie said the same thing."

Gabe pointed at him. "Smart lady, that Josie." Then he headed toward the ranch house.

And Heath went to search out the woman he'd spent half the night awake thinking about.

Chapter Eight

The sweet smell of banana bread flooded Josie's senses. She swallowed. Hungry. Wasn't that always the case these days?

Then again, it could be because she'd skipped the larger breakfast she'd grown accustomed to. Leaving the ranch before the usual time Heath arrived meant she hadn't whipped up a hot meal. No matter. Josie had never enjoyed cooking for one. When Macy offered to pick her up for the day, Josie couldn't turn her down. Not when she wasn't sure if Heath would be stopping by.

You could have called him.

Absolutely not. She wasn't desperate. She had friends outside of Heath Grayson she could depend on. And she definitely didn't *need* that man.

She stretched and pressed her hand against her lower back as she adjusted how she was sitting. Abby, one of the housemothers, sat beside her, and Marnie, the ranch cook, occupied the other side of the table. The three women had spent the past hour decorating mason jars so they could be used as lanterns on the tables at the upcoming Thanksgiving celebration. Each one was covered in a strip of lace and then a Bible verse on linen was affixed on top of that. Twine circled the rim to form a rustic bow. Complete with flickering votive candles, scattered across the outdoor tables at the event as the sun sank lower, they'd be beautiful.

The rough wooden chair creaked under Josie's movements.

"Why don't you take a break?" Abby urged. "At least let me grab you another pillow to pad that seat. I can't imagine how uncomfortable crouching over all this small stuff is for you."

"I'm fine." Josie flexed her fingers and then reached for the next jar. "Let's get this done so we can cross it off the list."

"We have a week." Abby sighed. She snagged two more jars and the hot-glue gun.

Josie cut a length of lace to fit around the outside of the jar. "*Only* a week. I saw the list. It's long."

Marnie opened a second bag of votive candles and spread them along the center of the table, where they'd be easy to grab. "Speaking of lists, I'm finalizing the menu and compiling what I need for the final grocery run this weekend. Can I still count on your Ranger to be there?"

He'll never be my Ranger. Even though it was true, the words lodged themselves in Josie's throat. She looked down and fiddled with the strip of lace in her hand. So beautiful. So delicate. So easily destroyed if it was handled incorrectly or glued on wrong.

She ran the slightly frayed edge back and forth over her fingertips. "I'm… I'm not certain. I think so. He said he was, but…" She shrugged.

When she and Heath had met with Gabe to relay the story about Avery, Josie's heart had swelled. They were a team—a good one. Hope had surged through her veins like a galloping horse set free in a new pasture. He'd taken her hand when she was upset. Reached over and had known that was what she needed without her even looking his way.

Dale had never acted like that.

For more than two weeks, Heath had done the chores around her ranch, shared her breakfast table and acted as her personal chauffeur. He'd sat beside her for the long haul in the waiting room yesterday.

Then disappeared last night after they talked to Gabe.

Why?

The piece of lace trembled in her hands.

It didn't matter. Heath didn't matter.

How had she let herself get so involved? So attached? When push came to shove, what did she really know about that man? Not much, other than his role in law enforcement, which was enough to make the achy feeling over his absence yesterday completely irrational. Also, he was great with kids, kind, patient and honorable.

Josie blinked away the heat of tears.

Marnie pressed her lips together and watched Josie for a moment. "Oh, honey. You're allowed to care about him," she whispered.

Marnie was known to fancy herself a matchmaker when it came to the ranch staff and volunteers. The woman wouldn't be happy until all the singles were paired off. She could often be found bending the ears of the ranch hands, urging them to have some courage

and ask one of the women on a date. Lately a mysterious matchmaker had been leaving notes and gifts.
Whoever it was had successfully paired up the librarian, Macy, and the vice president of their chapter of
the Lone Star Cowboy League, Tanner. They'd also
had a hand in breaking up Tanner's sister's engagement and finding her a more deserving man. There
was a rumor that Marnie was behind some of the obvious matchmaking attempts, but Josie wasn't so sure
the cook would go as far as writing fake love notes or
splitting up couples.

Then again, who knew?

If the woman was behind the hoopla, Josie would
make sure Marnie understood she shouldn't involve
her at all.

She took a deep breath.

"No, actually." Josie let the lace flutter to the
ground, where it would end up covered in dust. Unus-
able. She fisted her hands and pressed them into her
thighs. "I don't care about him. I won't let that happen."

Abby laid her hand over one of Josie's fists.

The cook jerked back in disbelief. "Why ever not?"

Because a good wife would still be devastated over
the loss of her husband. Because Heath was a Texas
Ranger, which meant every single day spelled danger
for him. Because already her heart throbbed with deep
pain when she thought about him leaving.

"A million reasons."

Marnie shook her head real fast a few times. "Child,
do you honestly believe you're not allowed to be happy
in this life?" She ducked her head to catch Josie's gaze.
"That God wants you to only know suffering? That
you're allotted one go around at love and once that's

done you're put on some back shelf for the rest of your life? 'Cause if you believe that, you're wrong."

"My husband was killed." Josie usually tried not to say that out loud because it sounded like she was asking for pity, but sometimes there was no way around it.

"I know, honey. I'm so sorry you had to live through that. But—*living*—that's the point. Despite what has happened, God is not done working in your life." She tapped the table a few times as she spoke. "Praise Him for that, honey. He's still doing a work in you. Don't make the mistake of punishing yourself for what happened, or holding back the growth God wants to bring into your life because you somehow believe you're undeserving of it." Marnie leaned over the table. "Don't go missing the blessings and opportunities He's laying out before you. They don't always come around again after we ignore them."

Josie cradled her stomach. "It was only six months ago."

The oven pinged. Marnie pressed up from the table and hustled over to pull the banana bread out. "There's no time stamp on these things. No rule books."

The baby moved. A foot or elbow pressed against Josie's hand. Hope and responsibility declared war on each other in her heart. She had to make wise choices for her child's future.

She took a shaky breath. "If I do end up falling in love again, it won't be with a Texas Ranger. That's for sure. I'm not risking my heart or my baby's future like that."

"Well, now." Marnie eased the steaming bread from the pan and set it to cool on a wide cutting board. "The

Lord does often choose to work in mysterious ways. His ways aren't ours. Not ever."

Abby sorted through the stack of verses she'd carefully been writing on the linen sheets in her calligraphy-like handwriting. "Here it is. I think this is the one you need on your next jar." She handed over a verse.

Josie stared down at the strip of fabric.

The joy of the Lord is my strength.

Could that be true? Lately, Josie felt more beaten down than strong. What if her feelings were a result of her lack of joy? But no, it was natural to feel as she did after what she'd been through. Of course it was.

Josie set down the verse and slid back from the table. Her chair scraped along the ground. "You know, I think I do need to take a break and will stretch my legs a little after all."

Knowing she probably couldn't bend to pick it up anyway, she sidestepped the ruined piece of lace on the ground and tried to ignore the worried glance that passed between Marnie and Abby as she walked out the back door.

Heath poked his head through the opening in the barn door in search of Josie, but he spotted a lanky teen instead.

"Stephen?" Heath stepped into the room.

The teen startled and spun around to face him, a book clutched in his hands. "Wow. Okay. It's just you." Stephen gave a nervous laugh. "You scared me."

Heath scanned the area. Alone in the calf barn, Stephen had one of the pens unlatched. He'd been inside with the littlest calf, the one Josie liked to baby. The animal had markings that made it look like it had a white heart on its forehead. Everyone called it Honey.

What was Stephen up to? Simply reading? Heath hoped so. After spending time with the teenager, Heath's gut said Stephen was a good kid. But his police training demanded that he question the young man anyway.

"Where's Josie?"

Stephen gave Honey one last pat on the head and then stepped out of the pen. "Don't know." He checked the latch, making sure it was secure.

"She wasn't in here with you?"

"Just me." Stephen slipped the small paperback he carried into one of the back pockets of his jeans and then brushed his hands off on his thighs.

Heath strode forward, eating up the distance between them. "I never did get to ask you about the night someone set the calves free."

Stephen's eyes narrowed. "What would you need to ask me?"

Heath crossed his arms and widened his stance. "How I hear it, you were the only person unaccounted for that night. No alibi means you're the most likely suspect. At least, that's what it usually means."

The teen shoved his hands into the pocket on the front of his black hooded sweatshirt. "You've taught us enough in detection class—I know there has to be a motive. So, Officer...or whatever it is I should call you...what's my supposed motive? Why would I do something like that?"

"Because you..." Heath's eyes locked with the lanky teenager's and his tongue went dry. Anger, confusion, frustration, desperation—all there. Louder than all of it, though: *Believe in me.*

"Just say it. You know you want to." Stephen stalked forward. "I'm a bad person. I wouldn't be at this ranch if I wasn't. Right? And people like me will always do bad things. Since I got the label now, that's all I can be for the rest of my life. This is a place for bad seeds." He made finger quotes around the last words.

"Who told you that?" Heath asked gently.

"My stepfather." He jammed his hands back into the front pocket of his shirt. "It doesn't matter. You think it, too. Everyone thinks it." He jostled past Heath in the narrow area between the calf pens, shoulder checking him. Well...as hard as a scrawny teen could shoulder check a fit, thirty-year-old man.

With quick reflexes from ten years of needing them, Heath caught Stephen's arm and turned him back around before Stephen could take off. "Hey, listen. I don't think you're a bad person."

Stephen looked up at the ceiling, toward the wall, down at the floor, back up at the ceiling, anywhere in an attempt to hide the fact that he was about to cry. "Then what's my motive?" he ground out. "Why would I put our calves in danger? Huh?"

Heath laid his hand on Stephen's shoulder. "People do things when they're upset. Sometimes we're hurting and the pain takes over and we make choices we wish we hadn't. Because we're struggling and because life is hard. If that's what happened—it doesn't make you bad, okay?"

"How would you know anything?"

Heath hadn't been around for Nell or Flint when they needed him, and he had spent fifteen years closing off from everyone around him so they couldn't know the intimate parts of his life. From *knowing* him at all. But he could do this for Stephen. He could be there for him because opening up would be the brave thing to do.

And Heath didn't fancy himself a coward.

"My father died when I was fifteen. My mom remarried pretty quickly and my stepfather and I locked horns from day one." He dropped his hand from Stephen's shoulder. "He told me to buck up and stop moping about my dad."

Even fifteen years later, his stepfather's rejection still stung.

Heath leaned in. "Between you and me... I might have done some things to him that didn't help the situation. Nails in his tires, salt in his coffee when he asked for sugar, that sort of thing. I had a lot of anger and I just didn't know what to do with it." He straightened back up.

Might as well tell everything.

"In the end, he gave my mom an ultimatum—me or him. She chose him and I got shipped off to live at my uncle's ranch until I was old enough to join the army." He scrubbed his hand over his jaw. "So that's how I know. I made some choices fueled by hurt that I wish I hadn't. Things I can't explain the rationale behind, even now."

Stephen's Adam's apple bobbed. "Do you and him— your stepfather—are you two friends now?"

Heath shook his head. "I'm afraid we'll never be friends, but we can tolerate each other if we have to. So we do for my mother's sake. I wish I had a better picture to paint for you."

The teen toed at the ground. "My stepfather hates me."

"*Hate*'s a strong word." Heath sighed as he searched for the right way to explain things. "Men feel like a failure when they can't automatically fix something. A lot of men—we don't know how to connect and we're more afraid of failing than anything, so we don't try to work at a relationship, because walking away feels like a choice, whereas working at it and struggling feels like failing. It's not logical. But we men seldom are when it comes to relationships."

"So you're saying they point at us and say we're the problem so they don't have to invest and then feel like they can't fix us? It all comes down to pride?"

Heath nodded slowly. "I believe that's the case, and I'd be lying if I said I wasn't guilty of doing the same thing with people in my life."

Stephen finally made eye contact again. "Do you think the boys here are bad seeds?"

"Not anymore."

"I didn't set the calves free that night. I wouldn't do that."

"I believe you."

"I'm supposed to go home next month, for good." He fiddled with the cuff on his sleeve. "I don't want to. I don't want to live with him."

"Does your stepfather—does anyone lay a hand on you?" The muscles in Heath's back bunched up, tense. He'd fight tooth and nail to protect Stephen if he found out his stepfather was abusive.

"It's not like that. He doesn't hit me. He just makes it very obvious that he doesn't like me and doesn't think I'll measure up to anything."

"You're seventeen, son. One year." Heath held up a finger. He wished he could promise the teen that life would be wonderful when he went home to his parents. That they'd all get along great and make a ton of memories and his stepfather would be supportive. But Heath couldn't promise those things. False hope caused more pain in the world than outright punches. "You only have to stay for one year and then you'll be considered an adult and can strike out on your own if you have to. That's what I did."

"Will you... It's probably too much to ask." Stephen studied the toes of his gym shoes.

"Ask anyway."

"Would you help me? Mentor me, kind of...even after this month?"

A burning sensation filled Heath's chest, but it wasn't unpleasant. It was more of an ache than anything. A pain that had always been there but he hadn't recognized until that moment. Heath wanted to be a part of something—something more than just his career. He wanted to be actively involved in someone's life.

Heath coughed a little, clearing his throat. "Yeah, son. If you want me to, of course. I'll be in your life as long as you want me to be."

"Well, if that's the case." Stephen's face lit with a conspiratorial grin. "Want to help me get some hay down from the loft in the big barn? Flint asked me to do it an hour ago and he's going to come searching for me soon if I don't have that done before the next time he looks."

Heath laughed. "Oh, I see how it is." He turned to join Stephen but froze when he spotted Josie. She was leaning in the doorway. With her red hair braided and wearing jeans and a flannel shirt, she was the most beautiful person he'd ever laid eyes on. Every cell in his body told him to go over and hug her—at least apologize and make things right between them. But she might not appreciate having that talk in front of Stephen.

How much had she overheard?

She looked at Heath. "Will you come back here when you're done?"

Always. I'll always come back to you. For as long as you'll let me.

Where had that come from?

"Yes, ma'am." He tipped his hat. They had so much to say to each other, but none of it needed to be said in front of Stephen.

The teen slapped Heath on the back. "I'll send him back with hay for your calves, Ms. Josie."

She waved them out.

They headed toward the barn and climbed up into the loft. Heath scaled the huge pyramid of hay bales and passed the rectangles one by one to Stephen, who tossed them through the hole in the loft down into the main section of the barn.

Stephen moved, making the loft's floorboards groan. "You know, since I started your class, I notice things all the time. A lot more than I even realized there was to notice." Breathing heavy, he pointed at the tower of hay. "We probably only need one more."

Heath hefted the last bale toward Stephen. "And it's hard to turn your mind off once it starts."

"That's so true," Stephen grunted and tossed the bale down through the hole. "Like right now." He dusted off his hands. "This floor. The noise it makes."

He stomped across the loft. "It's so different than the barn loft at the old ranch."

Heath stepped down from the hay, his legs suddenly wobbly. "How so?"

"That old one sounded…" Stephen screwed up his face. "I don't know…almost hollow."

"Hollow?" Heath's heartbeat sounded in his ears.

"Like there was space in between the levels." Stephen headed toward the ladder so he could climb down to the main level. "I'm probably wrong."

Heath licked his lips. Dare he hope? "Which barn, now, are you talking about?"

"The main one back at the old ranch."

The one where Dad was murdered.

Chapter Nine

Josie prepared bottles for the calves and called over a few of the boys to move them out into the small pasture and take turns giving each calf a bottle. The boys were ecstatic—they always begged for the opportunity to do the bottle-feeding. By the time Heath strolled in with a bale of hay propped on his shoulder, Josie was alone again.

"Are they old enough to eat this stuff yet?" Heath swung down the bale and set it beside the cabinet where she stored the other food items.

She smiled and shook her head good-naturedly. Sure, Heath had told her he'd spent time on his uncle's ranch, but the man definitely had more city in him than country when it came to animal knowledge.

"We start them on hay at four days old. But they're mostly still on the bottle. If you must know, I end up sneaking most of it over to the goats." She pointed in the direction of the goat enclosure. "They're so cute and I've always wanted one. It's impossible to pass up their sweet little cries, so I feed them."

Heath tilted his head, wearing a soft smile. "You've always wanted a goat?"

"Or two." Josie laughed lightly. "I can't justify spending money to buy one now, but they're on the dream list for my ranch. Someday."

They stood for a moment, staring at each other. The man in front of her looked so capable, handsome and strong. She fought the powerful urge she felt to melt against him and beg him to change her mind about falling for a lawman.

What should she say? *Why did you leave yesterday without saying anything? Do you care about me? If not, why do you act like you do? Will you leave me... us...and never look back? Can I trust you?*

Heath cleared his throat. "I'm real sorry about leaving you stranded yesterday. That wasn't my intention. I was going to come back for you, but I should have told you that."

"Why'd you go?"

"To clear my head."

Of what? Of her? Of the ranch? "Did it work?"

A slight grin tugged at the corners of his lips. "Does it ever?"

Josie propped her hands on her sides. "I overheard what you said to Stephen."

He adjusted his hat. "All of it?"

"Most," she admitted. Okay, all. She happened to step through the doorway right as Heath began questioning the boy about the calf incident. "It was sweet of you to say you'd mentor him after November, but will you be able to do that?"

Say you love it here. Say you're moving. Say you'll stay.

"I don't live all that far. When assignments don't

take me away, I could swing by here in the evening if I wanted to." He propped his hand on the side of his belt.

"Stephen's scheduled to go home in December. He won't be here at the ranch any longer."

"Right." Heath scratched the back of his neck. "Cell phones and computers are wonderful inventions, as well."

"True, but they don't replace face-to-face interaction."

"I agree." He stepped closer. His voice was somewhere between a whisper and a breath. "Josie?"

Only her name—but the way he said it made her want to believe anything was possible.

She looked away. "You haven't told me much about your family. Will you?"

He stepped back and leaned against the wall. "What would you like to know?"

"Everything."

"You know more than most people already. I told you about my father. About my mother remarrying. You know about Nell and my niece. And you heard me tell Stephen about my stepfather."

Josie's heart twisted for the teenage boy who had lost his entire family in such a short time—his father in the line of duty and then his mother and sister because his mom chose his stepdad. Heath must have felt such anger toward the man. Suffered the slice of betrayal from his mother's actions. Known loneliness after being separated from his younger sister. All while mourning his hero. At least he and Nell had mended their fence.

"I can't believe your mother allowed him to kick you out." She laid her hand on his arm. The muscles under her touch were so solid and firm, much like the man, but she wanted to get past that to find out what drove him. "It wasn't fair of him to make that ultimatum."

He sighed. "She was still in mourning, too. My mom, she's not a strong woman—she's not like you. She'd never worked a day in her life and when my father died, she latched on to the first available man she could find. For security. Just to have someone to pay the bills and take care of her…at least that's how I saw it go down. I'm sure she figured she was doing it for us kids' sake, too. For me and Nell to have a father figure. It just didn't work out that way." He looked off to the side.

Josie squeezed his arm. "You're a good man, Heath. You've been through so much and were treated poorly by people who should have loved you and yet you're still so honorable. I don't know how you do it."

He looked down at her hand on his arm and exhaled. "Because of all that happened with my family, I don't… I don't know how to *show* people I care. A man my age should be able to do that. I'm starting to wonder if perhaps I'm not all that honorable after all."

She slid her hand down his arm to take his hand. "Hey, don't say that."

He wrapped his fingers over hers, clinging as if she was a lifeline. "What if everything I've done has been to prove my own worth? To prove that my dad would be proud of me and that my mom should have kept me? What if my drive has been wrong all along? Do you think that discounts everything I've done?"

She placed her other hand around their joined ones. "You're a good man. Do you hear me? Is that sinking in? I'll keep saying it if you need me to. I think you might be the best man I've ever known."

His deep brown eyes captured hers as he searched her face. A hundred questions creased his brow. "I want to know you. Really know you. Tell me about your family, too."

Josie traced her thumb over his knuckles. "I'm an only child. My mother passed away when I was eleven. Brain tumor."

"I'm sorry," Heath whispered. He gently tugged her closer so they were sharing air as they spoke. The scent of fresh pine soap and hay dust enveloped her. If only he'd wrap his arms around her. She missed the feeling of being held more than she realized.

Josie took a deep breath, continuing, "Dale and I met my freshman year of high school. We never even officially dated—we met and he became my world. I was very young. I didn't know what I was looking for."

I should have been searching for you.

"My father was a truck driver, all over the country. He was gone a lot. I was lonely." She stopped tracing Heath's knuckles and let her hand rest on top of his. "Dale proposed the day after my eighteenth birthday. That same year my father's truck hit an icy patch in Colorado. His eighteen-wheeler went off the edge of the road into a ravine. They assured me he didn't feel any pain at the end."

With hesitation, Heath cupped his free hand around her shoulder blade. A fierce protective look crossed his face. Almost as if he never wanted to let go.

"You're all alone now, then, aren't you?"

"In a sense." She dipped her head. "But I'm not alone. Not really." Feeling bold because of their proximity, Josie tipped her face to his and whispered, "I'm not alone right now."

He sucked in a ragged breath. His gaze moved from her eyes to her mouth, asking a question she didn't know how to answer.

She bit her lip. Change the subject. Before they both wound up doing something they'd regret. "Why won't you call your grandfather?"

Heath dropped her hand and turned, slipping around her from where he had been cornered between her and the wall. He yanked off his hat and tossed it on top of the feed cabinet, which made his hair stick up in adorable angles. He wrapped his hand over the back of his head. "When my mother remarried, we lost all connection to him, and when Nell and I tried to contact him later on, he hung up on us. I'm not so sure he wants to hear from me now."

"But you're going to try?"

"I promised I would, so I'll keep my word." He snatched his hat back up and worked it around and around in his hands. "Well, if you don't need me anymore, I better head out. There's something I need to go take a look at."

"Thanks for the hay," she called lamely as he left. The whole time holding back the words that desperately wanted to cross her lips.

I need you, Heath Grayson. Wait. I'll always need you.

Heath was afraid his heart was going to pound its way right through his rib cage.

Calm down. Treat this like any other case.

Impossible.

He turned his truck down the driveway that led to the area across town where the boys ranch had been located before Cyrus Culpepper left the Lone Star Cowboy League all his land. Heath knew this area of the old boys ranch well. He'd combed over it a handful of times during his friendship with Flint. Never in an official capacity before, because he'd only recently obtained clearance from his boss to investigate his father's cold case, but that hadn't stopped him from poking around. After all, it wasn't against the law for him to stumble upon clues off duty.

What had he missed?

Probably nothing. No doubt he was chasing the wind, but after Stephen's observation, he had to come back to check the barn.

What if...?

Heath had wanted to head to the old location right away, but talking with Josie had been more important. Before today, the crime scene sat for fifteen years—another half hour wasn't going to hurt it.

But a few more seconds with Josie? Oh, that would have changed everything. Heath groaned. He would have kissed her. Would Josie have responded favorably? She'd tilted her face up to his, as if to grant permission. He crammed his hat on. Focus. Right now he couldn't process all that. Not when he might finally have a lead after fifteen years of unanswered questions. He slammed the gear shift into Park and was out of his truck a second later, tearing his way toward the large barn. Flint had lent him the keys to the buildings, so getting through the locks wouldn't be a problem. He fished the ring of keys from his pocket.

For a minute he froze outside the side door. From the photos and case files back in his room at the inn, Heath knew he was standing exactly where his father had been murdered. They had found his body right here. No murder weapon. No reason for the killing.

Just gone.

The anniversary of his death was only four days away.

You might be the best man I've ever met.

"That's because you didn't know my father." Heath cupped his hand over his jaw. "He was the greatest man I've ever known." He squatted and pushed his fingertips into the hard ground. He blinked against a burning in his eyes.

Being at this location had never affected him in this way. Maybe Heath was going soft. Everything— the boys at the ranch, his family, realizing what a junk friend he'd been to Flint, and Josie, especially Josie— was making his chest sore from aching with emotions he'd never wanted to sort through before. From longing for a life he didn't know if he had the right to want.

He pressed his palm into the earth. "What did they do to you? Why did they do it?" But verbalizing questions wouldn't assist his investigation. His earthly dad was long past the point of being able to help him, but God—another Father—might be willing to help him, if only he'd ask.

Heath's knees hit the ground and he bowed his head. "God, I've left You out of all of this—haven't I? For the past fifteen years, I've set up cones around my dad's murder and told You to keep out. I *wanted* to hang on to that hurt. That's all I knew. It defined me."

He took a rattling breath. Might as well admit it all; God knew anyway. "And I've made every choice in my life to date because of it instead of seeking Your guidance. Forgive me, Lord. I've been so boorish. I've walked around saying I care about protecting people, when all I've done is make choices to protect myself— my heart. Because of that, I've been a terrible witness for You. Haven't I? I've claimed Your name, claimed to follow You since I was a teen, but it was mostly in word and not deed. Exactly what I accused Flint and the League of doing in Josie's life. Well, no longer."

No one was around to see, so Heath tipped back his head and spread his arms as if he was opening them up to God. "I am Yours." He slowly rose to his feet. "My life is Yours. Guide my hands in this investigation. If there is justice, let it be because of You. I'm handing over my desire for vengeance to You. Heal me, Father. Please... I don't want to just exist anymore. I want to know a joy that comes from You. I want to live in a way that pleases You. In the name of Christ, I pray all these things." He opened his eyes and whispered, "Amen."

"Over here. This barn." Heath waved at Finn Brannigan, another Texas Ranger from Company F. On duty, Finn wore the normal Texas Ranger uniform—khaki pants, boots, a white button-down and his white Stetson. The gun on his hip glinted in the late-afternoon light.

Heath was surprised Finn answered the phone when he had called an hour ago. The man had recently gotten married and had taken an extended honeymoon, but apparently he was back to work now.

"Thanks for coming out so quickly." Heath extended his hand for a handshake. "How's married life?"

"If you get the opportunity, I highly recommend it." Finn pumped his hand once. "Amelia reminded me to thank you again for the wedding presents. She's planning to display both of them year-round."

Once Heath heard Amelia loved and collected Christmas decorations, he had enlisted his sister to pick out a wedding gift for them. Nell had tracked down a special Texas star for the top of their tree as well as an ornament in the shape of a pug in honor of Amelia's dog—Bug—who had played a role in bringing the couple together. Heath had felt cheesy giving the decorations to Finn and his bride, but the thoughtful gifts had struck a chord with Amelia. So far she'd thanked him three times in person, once in a thank-you card and had Finn thank him whenever their paths crossed.

"Come on in." Heath held open the barn door. "Let me show you what I found."

"What type of drugs?" Finn specialized in undercover drug work, which was why Heath had called him. As much as Heath wanted to take the lead on his father's investigation, with what he'd uncovered in the barn, Finn was the better-trained man for the job. The best option was to let go of his desire to run the case and allow Finn to take over.

"Once I found them, I wasn't going to touch anything without another officer here. I didn't exactly bring evidence gloves and bags on my vacation. Let me show you." Heath climbed into the loft and walked to the far end until the sound the floorboards made changed. Slightly dull and hollow, just like Stephen had pointed out.

Finn's boots clomped behind him. "False floor?"

Heath nodded. "I don't know how it got missed in the original investigation." Then again, Heath had missed it the dozen times he'd scoped out that barn, as well.

The county offices were closed for the day, but with Finn's permission, tomorrow he would head over and uncover when the last building permits for the ranch had been submitted, and by whom. Of course, the perpetrator wouldn't have included the details about the false floor in whatever plans had been submitted for approval, but the boys ranch was frequented too often to alter the buildings without building permits. If they did, anybody could have reported them, and the drug-smuggling happening there would have been uncovered right away. Someone would have had to fake improvements or roll the false floor into approved plans to seamlessly achieve what they did. Heath would examine the building permits from fifteen years ago and follow the trail of names attached to the paperwork.

"Right here." Heath knelt down and pulled up the board that served as the way into the cubbyhole. The only difference between it and all the others was a slight, faded indent on the wood.

Finn crouched beside him and ran his hand along the floor. "No wonder it was never found. I can't say I would have spotted this. They constructed it in such a way that you can't tell from the lower level that there are two layers of floors up here. It's ingenious. I'm impressed. And with what I see every day, that's saying a lot."

"I thought the same thing." Heath lifted the board, revealing what looked like rows of tightly bundled bricks and a dusty Smith & Wesson .38 revolver.

Finn whistled and then pulled out a camera to begin photomapping the scene. "I'm itching to catalog everything, but I'm not about to risk muddying up the crime scene. We're going to have to call in the evidence crew to remove and package everything. The gun will have to go to the crime lab for prints. We won't know right away."

"I know. I do this all the time."

"For other people…not for the murder weapon in your dad's case."

Heath stared at the gun for a moment. That was what took his father's life. He was sure of that fact. Fifteen years without leads and all the answers had been here all along. A powerful feeling of peace and certainty pulsed through his veins. These items would lead to the killer. The angry teenager who still kicked around in his mind from time to time could finally rest.

Finn watched him. "Are you all right?"

"Relieved, more than anything. I want to move on from this." Heath gestured to encompass all the drugs. "If you had to guess, how much would you say is there?"

Finn cocked his head. "I'm assuming by the looks of it, there's both heroin and cocaine here. Combined, I'd say thirty to thirty-five kilograms." He narrowed his eyes, running a calculation in his head. "When all that's broken down for street use, it could be worth anywhere from a half million dollars to upward of one and a half million dollars. You're looking at what may end up being the biggest bust in my career."

A wave a nausea slammed into Heath as he rocked back to sit on his heels. "That… All of this… That's why they killed him. He must have been about to blow their cover." Heath swallowed hard. It was all so point-less. Drugs for his father's life. "But why leave it all here for fifteen years if they thought it was worth taking a man's life to hide?"

Finn punched a message into his phone, alerting the dispatch center to send the evidence technicians to their location. Neither man would disturb the possibly evidence-rich scene until the whole team was present and the correct tools were there.

"My assumption would be that whoever placed this here, and whoever killed to protect it, must have disappeared very soon after and hasn't been able to return since."

Unable to return for fifteen years? The obvious answer. "Jail?"

Finn nodded. "Either that or fled the country. There's also the possibility that the person could have died soon after killing your father. You need to prepare for that, should it be the case. Those are the only logical conclusions for abandoning a haul of this magnitude. At least it gives us a place to start."

Hopefully, it gave them not only the start—but the end, too.

Chapter Ten

The baby was having a field day kicking at Josie's internal organs.

Josie braced her hand hard against her lower back. "I think the first lesson we'll focus on after you make your grand appearance is going to be manners. We don't kick vital organs that Mom might need later on. Hear that, lima bean?" She ran her hand over her stomach. The movement and subsequent pain subsided as she spoke. "There, now, isn't that so much better? Get some rest so all that energy can go into growing."

That morning Josie worked alongside Laura, one of the housemothers, changing all the bedsheets in the house before handing them over to the group of boys in charge of laundry that week.

Light as a butterfly, Laura touched Josie's shoulder. "Honey, maybe Bea's right. Maybe you should take it easier the closer it gets to your time. No one would blame you."

Although Josie recognized the wisdom and care behind Laura's words, the sentiment implying that Josie couldn't handle her load still ate at her. Sometimes in the evening when she was home alone, Josie would put on a documentary—one of her favorite pastimes. Pioneer women made meals and helped hoe fields *while in labor*; surely Josie was made of the same mettle. But she also recognized that people asked her to take it easy because they cared—not because they thought she was incapable.

It would take a long time to get over the beliefs Dale had spoken into her heart for years—ideas Josie now understood were wrong. *You can't do that. If you work, that makes me look bad. Even if we had a ranch, you wouldn't be able to handle the workload. It would fail.* Josie relaxed her hands. Dale had not been a horrible man. In fact, she'd loved her husband, but looking back objectively, she could recognize how controlling he'd been.

Now that she knew that, his leaving made sense—in a way. Dale had been a man who knew what he wanted in life and had done everything within his power to work toward a certain outcome. He cared deeply about what people thought of him. He loved wearing a badge because it made people instantly respect him. He hadn't wanted his wife to have a job because it might imply that he wasn't making enough money. And he'd wanted a family, a son to carry on his name…but he couldn't control if they became pregnant. That must have bothered him immensely.

The only thing within his control was the woman he was trying to have a family with. Josie had proven herself incapable of getting pregnant during their marriage, so Dale took control again and planned to leave.

Josie huffed and straightened her spine. "I still have three months. My doctor says I'm fine. It's not like I've been put on bed rest or something like that. A pain here and there is pretty normal, at least so say all the books and websites I've been reading."

"I understand. I was the same way with mine." Laura smiled at her. "But please, speak up if the tasks become too much for you."

They headed toward the kitchen area in the back of the ranch house and dark-haired Diego pounded through the back door. The second he spotted Josie, a smile overtook his face.

"There you are, Ms. Josie!" He crossed the room and hugged her middle.

She ruffled his thick hair. "I see someone's ready to check the calves."

"Ah, not just that." He grabbed her hand, tugging her toward the back door. "I like you a little, too."

Josie laughed. "So reassuring." She waved to Laura. "I guess this is my cue. See you later."

Outside, Diego let go of her hand and ran ahead of her by a few feet and then spun around. "I saw Ranger Heath today."

"Me, too."

"I know." Diego nodded, his eyes dancing. "You two show up together all the time." He stopped in front of her. "Are you two married?"

Josie let loose a nervous laugh and peeked around, hoping no one had overheard the loud boy. "No, of course not. Come on." She passed him.

He jogged to catch up. "Well, then, *when* are you two going to get married? Can I come to the wedding? Can I *be* in the wedding? I'll be so well behaved. If I have an itch or something, I won't even move. I promise. I'll stand still in all the pictures. I won't sneeze or anything. You'll be so proud, Ms. Josie. Will I still call you Ms. Josie after you get married? Or will it be Mrs. Josie…? Mrs. Heath? That don't sound right."

Exasperated that she couldn't get a word in, Josie let out a groan.

Diego stopped. His eyes went wide. "You okay, Ms. Josie? Is it the baby? Want me to go get Heath? He's just over by Flint." He pointed in the direction of the horse barn. "I'll get him."

Josie caught Diego's arm before he could take off. "No. Diego. Come back here. I'm fine. Completely fine." She—slowly—got on her knees so she could place her hands on the boy's shoulders and be eye level with him. "Ranger Heath and I aren't getting married. Okay? Whatever made you think we were?"

The boy scowled. "But don't you love each other?"

Did she…? She couldn't. She wouldn't let herself. But neither could she deny feelings, either.

Josie sighed. "I don't know how Heath feels."

The little boy's face went slack as if he was surprised that she didn't know something so obvious. "Then ask him."

Josie sat back on her heels. She'd regret getting on the ground later when she tried to stand. "Girls don't come right out and ask boys things like that."

"Then I'll ask him." Diego laid his hand over his heart.

Josie shook her head. "That's not how these things are done."

Besides, over breakfast Heath had told her about finding the drugs and revolver back at the old ranch site. A huge step toward solving his father's murder. If he was successful, Heath would be able to leave at the end of the month with that checked off his list. Done.

No need to ever return.

"Don't you like him?"

"I like him very much, but there's more to being married than just liking a person." Josie folded her hands in her lap and looked down at her fingers. "You have to think alike, have personalities and goals that complement each other, and more."

Diego crossed his arms and his eyebrows inched closer together. "It sounds like you're making it all harder than it needs to be. I seen how he looks at you and how you look when he's around. That's love, Ms. Josie. I think that's all you need."

Enough. She shouldn't involve an eight-year-old in her love life anyway. Or lack of a love life. She struggled to her feet. Diego offered her a hand and she held on to his shoulder as she stood.

Josie dusted off her jeans. "We aren't getting married."

"But your baby needs a daddy." Diego pointed at her stomach.

"Is that what this is about?"

"A lot of the boys here, we didn't grow up with dads." Diego kicked at a small rock buried mostly in the hard dirt. "You don't want your baby to grow up like that." He looked back up at Josie, eyes hopeful. "Heath would make a good dad."

Heath would make an excellent father and husband for a family someday. Some woman would be blessed to win his heart and devotion. Just not her.

Josie nodded slowly. "I agree with you there."

"But not for your baby?" The boy frowned and it twisted Josie's heart.

"He would have to want to be a daddy first." Josie opened the door to the barn and held her hand out, inviting Diego to go in first. "He's pretty focused on his job, and his job is very dangerous."

Diego brushed past her. "That makes him a hero."

"I think so." She headed toward the feed cabinet.

"You don't want to marry a hero?" Diego leaned down and gathered a few cattle brushes and combs into a bucket and then headed in the direction of the calf pens.

"Not don't. Can't," she whispered. She fanned her face, blinking away tears.

Stupid pregnancy emotions.

Josie reached to open the cabinet but stopped when she spotted a small bundle sitting on the counter. It hadn't been there earlier.

The printed label on the envelope read *For Josie*.

She tugged at the envelope, but it was heavily taped to the tissue-paper wrapping, so when she lifted the envelope, it ripped the paper open. Setting the card to the side, Josie ran her fingers over the pale yellow fabric poking through the hole in the tissue paper. Delightfully soft. Baby soft. She couldn't resist and tore off the rest of the paper. Two small stuffed animals tumbled onto the counter. A black-and-white grinning cow and a small brown goat with curly horns. Josie lightly touched the top of their little heads, one at a time. So adorable.

Whoever had left the gift knew about her love for cattle and goats.

Or perhaps they were an excellent guesser.

She pulled the yellow baby blanket from the package and snuggled it to her chest. Perfect. Josie imagined carrying her baby into her home in the blanket—safe and warm. She couldn't hold back her tears any longer. People at church and in the League had told her they were planning a baby shower, but this was the first gift she'd received for her baby. Everyone wanted to know the baby's gender, but Josie had chosen not to find out. She planned to decorate the tiny bedroom back at her dad's old fishing cabin yellow and gray. A barnyard theme had been on her mind, as well. It was almost as if whoever had left this gift knew that. Funny, though, she didn't remember ever telling anyone.

Josie set the gifts down and moved the tissue paper aside, searching for the envelope. Her fingers closed around the hard cardstock and she opened the clumsily taped-together seal on the back. A typed note fell out: *For your baby. From Heath Greyson.*

She bit back a smile.

As much as she wished it was from the man in question, Josie was fairly certain Heath would spell his own last name correctly. Which meant the ranch's mysterious matchmaker had their eye on Josie and Heath. Was the matchmaker Marnie Binder? Probably not. Marnie would have known how to spell Grayson. If Josie could figure it out, she'd loved to thank whoever had given her the thoughtful gifts.

Regardless, despite how much Josie fought her attraction to the man in law enforcement, imagining Heath giving her something like the stuffed animals and blanket made her smile even bigger.

Such foolishness.

Josie shook her head, folded the blanket into a tiny square and sat the stuffed animals on top.

Apparently she was spending too much time with Diego. He was filling her head with hopes, dreams and echoes of joy that were better left locked away, deep within her heart.

Heath trailed the boys in his detection class as they headed toward the learning center. They were done for the evening, but a handful of them had left their bags on the tables after finishing their homework assignments required by their teachers at the schools they attended in town.

He checked his phone for the seventh time.

No missed calls.

Last night, Finn and Heath had stayed on scene while the evidence technicians worked the area. Insisting that because Heath was on vacation, he shouldn't run around for the case, Finn had decided he'd follow up with the city's building department today to check on permits. Heath's coworker promised to call the moment he had news.

Letting go of his father's case might prove to be more difficult that Heath had originally thought.

He filled his lungs with the crisp, late November air. The sweet smell of cinnamon drifted from the kitchen. Marnie must be cooking up something amazing for dinner. Heath's stomach grumbled.

He pushed through the door and was met on the other side by five grinning boys.

Stephen slung his backpack over his shoulder. "Can I have a piece of your pie?"

"It looks really good," another boy chirped.

Heath swiveled his head to where they were all pointing. At the front of the reading area was a wide table. It was usually full of towering piles of books and paperwork, but presently it had been cleared off of all but a pie and a sheet of paper. Heath zigzagged through the group of boys to get to the table.

Not just any pie—a pumpkin pie, his favorite. Someone had gone through a lot of work baking it and then decorating the top with swirls and cutouts of crust. He reached for the piece of computer paper beside it.

Stephen appeared at his elbow. "It's from Josie. Sorry. We already looked."

Heath raised an eyebrow at the boy.

Stephen shrugged. "Just putting our detection skills into practice."

"Investigating crimes and snooping in people's personal affairs are two very different things." Heath nudged Stephen in his ribs good-naturedly.

Stephen grinned wickedly. "Maybe I want to be a PI. Can't you see it?" He spread out his hands as if envisioning his name in Broadway lights. "Stephen Barnes, Detective for Hire."

Heath pulled a face. "Most PIs are retired cops."

"Dream killer." Stephen playfully nudged Heath back. "Way to spoil my fun."

"Use your powers for good, Stephen." Heath winked at the teen.

Stephen laughed. Picking up on the hint, he rounded up the rest of the boys and ushered them out of the room. As he closed the door, he hollered, "But I was serious about you saving me a piece of pie, okay?"

"For good, Stephen."

"Pie, Heath. Remember my enduring love for pie."
Stephen shut the door.

Heath chuckled. He'd sure miss ribbing with that
kid once the calendar changed to December. He turned
back to the table and flipped the page over: *For Heath.
Enjoy. —Josie M.*

It was impossible to hold back his grin. So, the lady
did like him. After a near-silent ride to the ranch this
morning, Heath was beginning to wonder if he had
completely imagined their almost kiss yesterday afternoon. When he told her he thought he was close to
solving his father's murder, she'd been downright icy.
Why wasn't she happy for him?

But perhaps the pie was a peace offering. Or a window to her true emotions.

Josie had a justifiable reason for having reservations
about getting involved with a Texas Ranger, but Heath
was beginning to feel like all the risk was worth it.
Why not? No matter how long he searched, he'd never
meet another woman with such a mix of determination, strength, compassion and beauty.

He tucked the note into his back pocket and picked
up the pie.

Yes, stubborn man that he was, his heart had be-
trayed his tough resolve to never get involved with a
woman. Heath was falling for Josie Markham. And if
the pie was any indication, she just might feel the same
way about him.

Chapter Eleven

The goats called to Josie with wavering bleats as she passed their enclosure.

"Not now, sweethearts." She shifted the blanket and stuffed animals she was carrying into one arm so she could go down the row and pet each one. The smaller goats had their heads at odd angles, completely rammed through the wires of the fence, while the larger ones braced their front hooves on the groove of the fence, making them tall enough to stick their heads over the top line. The coarse hair of their whiskers tickled her skin.

"I'll sneak you goodies later, though. I promise."

Thankfully, bucks weren't kept with the herd, so Josie didn't have to contend with the reek of the male goats, which was worse in the fall. Her pregnant nose couldn't have handled the bucks right now. However, the wethers and does were delightful. Each one nuzzled at her hand, their large eyes following her every movement as if she might still have treats on her somewhere and she was holding out on them. Dale used to say goats creeped him out because their eyes looked like something out of a science-fiction movie, but their strange eyes, with the rectangular pupils, were one of the reasons Josie found them so charming.

"Those are cute." Katie Ellis, the receptionist at the boys ranch, pointed at the stuffed animals and blanket in Josie's arms as the two women met halfway up the walk to the back door of the giant ranch house. Her curly blond hair looked extra bouncy today, and was it only Josie's imagination, or was Katie sporting some new makeup? Her green eyes really popped.

"Not the goats. The stuffed animals. Where are they from?" Her face read blank and Josie knew she wasn't that good of an actress. Katie Ellis was definitely not the mystery matchmaker.

Should Josie bother with telling her about the fake note? Sometimes Katie had a way of over-romanticizing situations. After Diego's questions about marriage, Josie wasn't sure she was up for more matchmaking talk.

Josie shifted to cradle the items in both hands. "I was hoping you might know. Someone left them for me."

"No tag?"

Not a tag Josie believed. "You could say that."

Katie glanced at the stuffed cow. "Aww. That's supercute." She handed over a canvas shopping bag. "Here. Take my bag. I insist. I was using the excuse of tossing this in my car as a way to get a breath of fresh air anyway." Katie pivoted to face the side yard as she talked.

Josie followed her movements to where Andrew Walsh, the extremely young but devoted senior pastor of Haven Community Church, was teaching a group of boys how to tend the compost heap—all in the name of a hands-on Bible lesson. Earlier he'd led the boys around the ranch until they returned with wheelbarrows loaded down with fallen leaves and plant debris. Usually Josie gave the compost area a wide berth. The musty, rotting smell that wafted from the heap was enough to make her nauseous for the rest of the day.

"That's expertly done, Sam." Pastor Walsh clapped one of the quieter boys on the back in an encouraging manner. "Dry materials, green matter, a shovelful of soil and a sprinkling of fertilizer. Mix. Repeat. You remembered that all on your own."

Young Jasper—who was known as the ranch prankster—snickered beneath his mop of sandy-brown hair. "And by fertilizer, he means horse—"

"Now, now, Jasper. We all know what it really is." Andrew intercepted the conversation before it went south. The pastor excelled at redirecting the boys. He turned back to the others waiting in line. "Fertilizer actually teaches us an important spiritual lesson."

More of the boys joined Jasper's laugher.

"Believe me, I know. I know." Andrew shook his head in a commiserating way. "As funny as it sounds, sometimes it's a good thing when we can draw spiritual parallels from the most mundane items. If we connect something we see or experience daily with a spiritual lesson, it teaches our minds to see God's hand everywhere." Andrew didn't look fazed by their continued stream of giggles.

"Even with—" Jasper doubled over before he could finish his question.

"Even with fertilizer." Pastor Walsh ruffled the boy's already unruly hair. "Because fertilizer teaches us that it's not where we begin that matters—we all have the power to work toward enriching the future. You do." He laid his hand on top of little Morgan Duff's head. "And I do, too." He placed his hand over his chest and kept moving. "It's our job to discover the skills and passions God has placed within us and then use those to better and grow His Kingdom. That's something each and every one of us is called to do. No exceptions. Even if in the beginning of our journey we feel like we have the potential of…fertilizer."

"Even me?" Sam asked. "Or is that just for pastors?"

"Especially you." Pastor Walsh's voice was warm. "Isn't that exciting?"

Jasper draped his arm over Sam's shoulders. "Yeah, it starts as hay and ends up as—"

Andrew cleared his throat. "I believe it's your turn, Jasper."

Josie adjusted her hold on the canvas bag and then reached over and squeezed Katie's arm. "So by *fresh air* you really meant you needed an excuse to venture outside to spy on poor Pastor Walsh?"

Katie gasped. "Am I really that obvious?"

Josie shook her head in an *I can't believe you don't know already* way. "Only to everyone."

Katie tilted her head and smiled dreamily. "Isn't he so wonderful with the boys?"

Josie nodded. "He really does have a way of connecting with them and I've never seen him get exasperated with any of them…not even Jasper. I don't think anyone else on the ranch can say that for themselves."

The younger woman sighed. "I wish he would ask me out already. Better yet, I wish the ranch matchmaker would start trying to pair us up."

Josie looped her arm through Katie's and turned her to walk away from the ranch house, in the direction of the red barn. "Speaking of the ranch matchmaker... any rumblings? I haven't heard the latest hypothesis. Do we have any idea who it is?"

"Are you kidding? If I knew, I'd be begging them about Andrew."

"Right." Of course.

"Oh!" Katie's eyebrows shot up toward her hairline. "You think the matchmaker sent you that gift?"

"I don't think. I know." Josie fished the typed card from the bag and handed it over. "See." She tapped the card. "His last name is spelled wrong. I doubt Heath would do that."

"*E* and *A* aren't *that* far from each other on the keyboard."

"Far enough."

Katie fanned the card. "You know, whoever the matchmaker is...he or she has been successful with every couple so far. You might as well give in and pick a date for the wedding."

Leave it to Katie.

"Don't start." Josie snatched back the card. "Anyway, so far it's only been Tanner and Macy, and they complement each other well. I'm sure they would have ended up together without the matchmaker's interference."

"Not true." Katie pursed her lips and wagged her head back and forth. "The matchmaker also broke up Chloe's engagement."

Josie couldn't argue that point. Tanner's sister wouldn't have discovered her fiancé's cheating ways unless the matchmaker had steered her in the right direction.

"But Chloe's fiancé was a creep. That would have come out sooner or later." Or not...but it burned Josie to give the matchmaker any more credit now that whoever was behind the letters was twisting her heart with hope about Heath.

"Well, well, lookie who we have here." Katie winked at Josie and then jutted her head to the side. Heath was cutting his way across the barnyard, heading straight toward Josie.

"I'll take this as my signal to go back to my desk. But between you and me—" Katie leaned closer, speaking at a loud whisper "—I may or may not walk *really, really slowly* past the compost bin."

"You're incorrigible," Josie called after her retreating figure.

Heath stopped a pace away and chuckled. "Me? Or her?"

Josie sighed in a good-natured way. "Probably both of you."

She met his deep gaze and rocked forward onto her toes. Looking into his eyes gave her the feeling of tipping over, headfirst, diving. And she found, in the moment, she didn't mind that feeling.

Not one bit.

Josie's brown eyes were warm and inviting as she joked with him.

Not just falling...nope... He was 100 percent, entirely in love with her.

There.

Had that been so hard to admit?

Heath should have kissed her yesterday. He wanted to right at that moment, but they were out in the open, and even if Josie welcomed the advance, she probably wouldn't want a display of affection to happen in such a public manner.

At least not the first time.

Heath had the pie balanced in one hand. He looked down at the pie and back at Josie. Then back at the pie. *Well, talk already.* But he wasn't quite sure how to start the conversation. The past few days had felt like they were playing tug-of-war. One second he thought Josie cared about him and the next she was silent and withdrawn. Then the pie.

He lifted the pie so it was right between them. "I know over the past few days we've experienced a couple of miscommunications, but I wanted to say thank-you. I really appreciate this gesture."

Her brow formed a V. "I'm sorry, but what gesture? I have no idea what you're referring to." Josie crossed her arms, a reusable grocery bag hung around one of her wrists so it dangled over her stomach. "And it's not even noon—why are you carrying around a pie?"

He jerked his head back. Was she joking? If someone was pulling a prank on Heath, they were cruel. He'd taken the pie to believe she cared about him. Apparently he was a fool.

Heath looked down at the pie as if it held the answer. "Because you gave it to me?"

"I didn't."

Suddenly the pie felt very heavy. He lowered his arm. "You left it for me, but you didn't make it. Is that it?"

"I have never seen that pie before in my life."

"Color me confused, then." Heath pulled the printer paper with Josie's note from his back pocket and handed it to her.

Josie glanced at the page and then tipped back her head and belly laughed. Not exactly the response he had hoped for. It would have been better if she'd looked at it and said, *Oh, this? I'd forgotten I wrote it. Yeah, it was me. I'm actually in love with you. Want to eat pie and be together forever?* If a man didn't have hope, he had nothing.

A stiff wind ripped across the ranch, shooting dust like pellets against Heath's back. Hopefully, the wind meant rain was in the air. The ground could use it. So could everyone's sinuses.

Josie groaned. "I should have known."

Heath rocked forward in his boots. "I'm usually pretty quick on the uptake…but I feel like I'm missing something here."

Josie's lips quivered as she tried to hide a teasing smile. "Are you completely certain you're a trained detective? Because…" The grin that tiptoed across her lips was downright mischievous. Heath loved seeing Josie's playful side. If he was going to be the butt of a joke, at least he got to flirt with Josie in the meantime.

"Give me that." He snatched the page back.

Josie held up a finger. "One, why would I type a note that short?"

"Maybe because you have terrible handwriting."

She opened her mouth and her eyes went wide.

He held up his hand. "Oh, I've seen it. With that handwriting, you could be a doctor, sweetheart." He folded the page into a small square and tucked it safely into the back pocket of his jeans.

"Two," Josie continued, obviously enjoying the back-and-forth jabs, "why sign it with the initial to my last name? I'm the only Josie here."

"I don't know." He tossed up his free hand. "I saw pie. I thought, *That's really nice*. My mind was clouded by pie."

She giggled. "Three, there's this." She fished a small card out of her bag and handed it to him. It was a note from him…a fake note. Heath hadn't written it. Although, now he wished he'd been smart enough to have the idea of giving her a gift.

"Well, now, this is downright ridiculous. They spelled my name wrong." He raised his voice in mock offense.

It was her turn to snatch back the card. "That's how I knew it was a fake right away."

"So what did I supposedly give you?" He craned his neck to try to look into the bag.

Josie showed him two small stuffed animals and a tiny blanket. "Isn't this little goat the cutest thing?"

"I'm not an expert in cute—they don't train us on that in the academy—but I will say, are you sure that's a blanket and not a washcloth? It's almost nonexistent."

She traced her fingers over the plush fabric. "Babies are exactly this size in the beginning. You'll see."

Babies were awfully small when they first entered the world, weren't they? Heath's gut bunched into a knot. Josie would need someone helping her more than ever once March hit. He imagined her and him relaxing on the couch back at her ranch after a full dinner, a tiny yellow blanket spread between them with a baby sleeping soundly as they both watched on.

She had said *You'll see*… Did she mean it?

Heath cleared his throat as well as the image from his head. "It was very nice of me to give you that."

"Incredibly thoughtful." She tucked the stuffed animals back into the bag.

She hadn't given him the pie. So what? He could still try to find out if she had any interest in him beyond someone who was fixing the fence at her ranch for free. Besides a chauffeur.

Heath balanced the pie on the top of a fence post and then touched Josie on the arm. "If you have a second, I think we need to talk."

Josie's smile dissolved. "Aren't we talking now?"

Although they were out in the open, Heath closed the distance between them so no one could overhear. "I understand—it's only been six months. I know you're still in love with your…with…"

"My late husband," Josie offered.

Heath swallowed hard. Nodded.

Josie bowed her head. "He was planning to leave me," she whispered. "That's the twist no one knows about." She angled her face a bit to be able to meet his eyes. "Just me, and now you. The day before…before he was shot, that's the day he told me he was walking out on our marriage."

The word *twist* couldn't have been used more appropriately.

Heath had a hard time wrapping his head around the idea of a man being stupid enough to leave a woman as amazing as Josie. "Are you sure?"

"He'd packed up all his belongings." Josie suddenly gripped Heath's arm, as if without him she might not be able to stand. "He already had a divorce attorney lined up."

Heath caught Flint eyeing them from across the barnyard. No doubt, his friend would have some severe words for him after seeing them together. But Flint didn't get it. It was impossible for Heath to stay away from Josie.

"Josie." Heath fought the desire to wrap his arms around her.

She pulled her hand away from him and tucked it against her side, giving herself the hug he wanted to offer. "I hear it happens to a lot of spouses in law enforcement."

"Not everyone. I know countless guys in happy marriages who adore their wives. Guys in my company."

Josie shrugged and blinked a whole bunch of times. "He wanted a child. That's the real kicker to my sad little story. He said I couldn't give him what he wanted. I was pregnant, Heath." She laughed once, but it held no humor. "I didn't know it yet, but he was leaving me and I was standing there crying with our baby growing the whole time." She hugged her stomach even tighter. "At least I know this little one was wanted. Even if I wasn't."

I want you. I'll always want you.

Heath fisted his hand. His muscles screamed for an outlet—something to punch—some way to burn off the anger he felt for how Josie had been treated. He forced his fingers to straighten, flex again, straighten. No fists, but his voice shook. "I mean no disrespect to your husband's death or his office, but in this, he was a fool."

"I'm not in love with Dale anymore," she whispered. "That's all I meant to say."

"Josie." His voice was only a breath. A breath that held every hope for the future. Could she hear it?

She turned so he could no longer see her face. "You had a breakthrough on your father's case yesterday. If you solve it, will you be leaving before Thanksgiving?"

"Flint still wants me to look into the run of incidents happening here. The thefts and the animals being set loose."

Josie gave him a look that said *level with me.* "You've been poking around and asking everyone questions all month. No offense, but I think we both know that investigation is going to come to nothing."

Heath ran his fingers over his jaw. "Some people are suggesting I should question a man named Fletcher Snowden Phillips."

Josie rolled her eyes. "Fletcher's a pain, but I doubt he'd do anything illegal. Besides, this isn't what I wanted to talk about—you were always here for your dad's case. If you solve it, will you leave?"

Did she want him gone? "Do you want me to?"

"That's not what I asked."

He came beside her. "I'm more interested in that answer, though."

"You're a pest." She looked up and shook her head, but she lacked the smile that usually completed the gesture. "You know that, right?"

"I believe you told me so on the first day we met," he added softly.

"My opinion of you hasn't changed, then."

For a man who specialized in reading conversations and directing them so he got the answers he needed, Heath was having a hard time knowing the right words to say. Josie seemed to want to steer all talk away from where he'd been headed. She didn't want a relationship with him, did she? They could tease each other, they could help each other, but she was putting a stop on any paths toward romance. Every time he hinted at caring about her, she brought up the fact that he was leaving soon. As if she wanted to constantly remind him that there was no hope for them as a couple.

Fine. He was man enough to respect that. His heart wouldn't, but he could keep his distance, for her sake.

Heath worked his jaw back and forth. Took a deep breath. "I'll consider that a good thing, then. At least your opinion of me hasn't gotten worse. So there's that."

"How long, Heath?" She faced him. "How long will you actually be around?"

What do you want? Just say what you want. Give me a clue. He searched her face.

His phone rang. He automatically yanked it from his pocket and glanced at the screen. Finn. It would be news about Dad's case. He looked back at Josie.

She sighed and batted her hand. "Take the call. That's what you're here for. Take it."

He hesitated, but pressed Accept. "You got news?"

"Better than news. I think I found our guy."

When he hung up, Josie was already halfway up the walk to the ranch house.

Chapter Twelve

A hard wind shoved against Heath's door as he stepped out of his truck and scanned the parking lot at the McLennan County Jail facility for Finn. The building, with its tan stonework, stood like a sentry, tall, cold and imposing.

So this was it.

Finn waited near the front of the entrance used by law enforcement. He'd set up a meeting with an inmate by the name of Kane Grubbs. Heath had glanced over Grubbs's arrest record. The man was serving time for a string of both financial and physical crimes. His original arrest dated back to the week after Heath's father was murdered. Each time Grubbs was released, he committed another crime and quickly returned to prison. During his latest arrest, he'd battered an officer and removed his weapon during the altercation—not something authorities took lightly.

In the past twenty-four hours, Finn had poked around for more information and everything he'd learned pointed to Grubbs being their man. It turned out Grubbs had worked at the boys ranch off and on during the time that Heath's father was murdered; he'd spearheaded the renovations to the barn and insisted on doing the construction work on his own for free.

Finn had his smartphone pressed to his ear and his voice carried. "That sounds good for tonight. I shouldn't be long. I love you, too."

Heath hung back until Finn was done, but when he overheard his coworker's conversation, Heath couldn't help thinking about Josie again. It would be nice to be able to talk openly with that woman, but Finn and Amelia were married, vowed to each other, so they had the right. Heath didn't.

Maybe it was for the best that Heath told himself long ago that he'd never get involved with a woman because of his job. Better that way. Because women and love were more confusing than any case he'd ever worked. He wasn't cut out for romance.

Finn stowed his phone. "You ready?"

Nope. Not for the interview or for Josie.

Heath stayed rooted in his spot. "Before we go in, can I…ah…can I ask you a personal question?"

Finn stretched his back, making his shoulders pop. "If it was my father, I'd want to know."

"It's not about the case." Heath almost lost the nerve to ask him, but he had to. No telling how much time would pass before he had another opportunity to ask a married lawman for relationship advice.

"Sure…go ahead and ask."

"Even with our job being as dangerous as it is, you were married before—and chose to marry again." Heath rested his hands on the edge of his bulky Ranger belt. "I guess I wonder why. Each day we walk into situations we might not walk out of. Why take the risk?"

Finn's chest lifted with a huge breath. He looked off at the clouds for so long, Heath began to wonder if he'd answer him at all. Were his questions offensive?

"I lost my first wife and my daughter," Finn said. "That was… Going through that is unimaginable and it's impossible to explain that kind of pain." Finn held up his hand. "But I don't regret having loved them for a second. They're gone and I—with the dangerous job, as you put it—am the one who was left behind."

"But level with me." Heath pushed the issue—he needed a solid answer. Something to help order his thoughts. "It crosses our mind every time we rush into a warehouse with our guns out. What-ifs are there for all of us, but I have to imagine that a married man has double the what-ifs to consider than someone like me."

"You're not wrong, but the real question is—are the what-ifs worth it to you? A married man and a man with children carry much more into a battle, but if you think about it, they're also fighting for something greater, too." Finn frowned a little. "Do you trust God, Heath? Do you believe He has a hold on your life and cares about the people you love?"

"I… I *want* to trust God like that."

"If Amelia and I get one more day together or sixty more years, we'll treat each one as a gift. Because we're not guaranteed tomorrow in this life, Heath. And that's true no matter if you're a butcher or a baker or a rancher or a Texas Ranger." In an uncharacteristic move, Finn rested his hand on Heath's shoulder. "I'll say this and then leave it be—if you love someone, do something about it. Today. Having that love today is worth the risk of having it ripped away tomorrow. I promise you that."

* * *

On the way back to the ranch, Josie would buy a cupcake for Katie at the bakery in town to thank her for the use of her car.

Josie parked on the edge of the path. That was the thing about cemeteries, they didn't have parking spots. People weren't meant to stay long.

Pastor Walsh had advised her to go to Dale's grave site and make peace with his death. He instructed her to talk out loud if she needed to. And to pray.

It would be her third visit since the funeral, but that day rushed back all at once. Bagpipes playing "Amazing Grace," the entire sheriff's department saluting in their dress blues, huge displays of fresh flowers crowding the funeral home—the smell of the bouquets mixing with everyone's over-applied perfumes.

Why did people feel the need to wear perfume or cologne to a funeral? Who were they worried about impressing? The deceased didn't care how they smelled and the family wouldn't even notice. Josie shook her head.

She could still feel all the hugs and hear the whispered *I'm sorry for your loss* from strangers who would never speak to her again or be there with her as she tried to piece her life back together. She could still hear the final call for Dale's badge number over the loudspeaker, a call that would forever go unanswered—a law-enforcement tradition.

On shaky legs, she stepped out of the car and headed toward Dale's headstone. Josie stopped a few feet away and crossed her arms. It felt futile, coming to speak to a grave, but she knew she needed to get the words out. If she didn't process everything she'd been feeling over the past six months, she'd never be able to move on.

And Josie wanted to be able to do that—move on—desperately. For her child's sake, if not her own.

"I don't really know what I'm supposed to say right now." She traced her fingers up and down her arms, but it only left her feeling colder. "I'm pregnant. We're going to have a child."

Josie took another step closer. "Actually, I do have something to say. I'm mad at you. I'm as mad at you today as I would be if you were standing here alive." She clenched her hands into fists. "I'm mad because you wanted to leave me. Because I wasn't enough for you."

Her throat caught with tears and she couldn't see through the blur in her eyes anymore. "I'm mad that you didn't love me enough to stay even if we were never going to have a child. You never believed in me—never encouraged my dreams. How hard would that have been?"

She took another step closer, her words tumbling out faster. "I'm furious about the financial situation you left me in. Why were you gambling? What were you trying to prove by racking up so much debt? Why didn't you pay our taxes? I trusted you to do that. You were an officer! Not paying taxes is illegal."

Her chest ached. It was best not to ask questions. She'd never get the answers she wanted. "But I'm also mad that you died. I'm mad that you're gone and I'm alone. I'm mad I didn't get to see if we could have saved our marriage."

Her arms were shaking now. Her voice, too. "But now I'm done being mad." She swiped at her cheeks. "For the past six months, I've carried around guilt—as if I was to blame for you leaving. As if I should be ashamed for not being *enough* for you." Her voice broke on a sob. "But you know what? Leaving was your choice. Not mine. You promised to love and cherish me forever, but instead you gave up. I won't blame myself for that anymore. I am not responsible for carrying your mistakes."

Josie rested her head in her hands and took a few breaths. While she did not regret the years she was married to him, she'd come to the realization that Dale had made all the choices in their life—in her life. Forgiving Dale was the final step to no longer being controlled by him.

"You were my husband—my first love—and I miss you," Josie whispered. "I forgive you for giving up on us. I forgive you for everything."

Feeling light-headed, she staggered back to the car and dropped into the driver's seat. If she wasn't pregnant, she would have stayed and prayed at the grave site, but getting up from the ground was difficult.

"God," Josie prayed as she rested her head on the steering wheel. "Renew my heart and my spirit. I feel like I've been an old, threadbare version of the woman I'm supposed to be for a long time. I've been running on spiritual fumes, and I don't want to live like that anymore. I want to be full of Your love and joy. I want people to meet me and automatically see You in how I act and speak. I don't know what my next step is, but I know You do. Guide me? Show me what to do where Heath is concerned. I'm afraid to be a mother alone, but if that's Your will for me, I know You'll equip me for the task. No matter what I've walked through or who has left me, I know You've always been there. Thank You, Jesus. Amen."

Josie turned the key and headed toward town.

Even with forgiveness, many of Dale's bad choices

still affected Josie's life. But she was no longer going to allow the wrong he'd done to have power over her.

She gripped the wheel tighter as light rain started to patter against the windshield.

Now Josie was in charge of the choices in her life—which also meant that she would be to blame if she made the wrong decisions. What was she going to do about Heath? She hadn't wanted to be involved with a man in law enforcement again, but whether or not they admitted to it, weren't they already involved? She looked forward to every minute spent in his company. But what if those minutes ended tomorrow because of his job? She had to think of her baby. Her baby needed a father who would be there to dance at his or her wedding, to hold grandchildren.

Then again... What if—like Dale—Josie was walking away from someone without realizing the life and joy that was already growing between them?

No matter where Heath traveled, every prison was the same.

Poured-concrete floors made footfalls sound hollow. There was the constant shriek of metal grating against metal and the smell of stale, humid recirculated air. Finn was ahead of him, talking with one of the guards as they passed down a long corridor on the way to the interview room. A strong bleach smell did very little to cover up a lingering trace of grease, dirty mop water and, oddly, an overwhelming scent of corn chips that permeated the space.

The guard showed them into the interview room. "I'll get Grubbs."

Finn joined Heath at the steel table in the center of the area. "Are you ready for this?"

"I don't think not being ready is an option."

A buzzer sounded, letting them know the guards were bringing in a prisoner. The door opened and Heath looked up—meeting the eyes of the man who most likely killed his father, or at least knew who killed him.

Over the years, Heath had wondered how he'd react if he ever found the murderer. He thought he'd feel rage. He thought he would want to slam the guy against a wall.

But it was pity drying the back of his throat, making it difficult to swallow.

Thin, bald and pale, Kane Grubbs needed a guard on either side of him, holding his arms, to help him shuffle in. The prison-issued jumpsuit, which looked like it was the smallest size they probably offered, hung off his body. One of the guards wheeled an IV unit beside Grubbs, and a woman wearing scrubs filed into the room.

Heath glanced over at Finn, but his face remained unreadable.

Grubbs slowly eased into the seat across from them. His shoulders shuddered violently as he hacked a few times. Heath studied him, trying to place his age. Grubbs wheezed in a breath, folded his hands on the table and then looked up at Heath. The whites of his eyes had a yellow tint to them.

"I know why you're here." He coughed again.

Finn nodded and pulled paperwork out of his manila folder. He read Grubbs his Miranda rights and then slid the sheet across the table. "Please initial each line and sign at the bottom, saying you understand. Also, I need to remind you that this room is being both video and audio recorded at all times."

Grubbs nodded by a fraction and signed the sheet. Then he looked back at Heath. "You look just like him. Your pa."

Heath's heart pounded as loud as a metronome. He opened his mouth. Closed it. "You... Did you know my father?"

The prisoner cradled his arms together. His chair creaked loudly as he rocked back and forth. "If you can't tell, I'm dying. Stage four. They say the cancer's everywhere. Two months left, if that. Being that I'm here, it could be tomorrow."

Heath's stomach rolled. "I'm sorry to hear that."

"Are you, now? We'll see if that sticks." Grubbs stopped rocking. For a few moments, the only sound in the room was the tick of his IV. "I have nothing to hide. Death on your back will do that to a body. I know you look like your pa because I was the last one to see him. I pulled the trigger. I killed him. If you located my hiding spot, you'll find my fingerprints on the gun."

Although Heath had suspected as much, hearing it confirmed ripped through him with a sharp, physical pain. He hunched his shoulders and shoved his fist against his chest.

"*Why?* He had two children. I was fifteen." His tone wasn't professional, but that was because the Texas Ranger wasn't talking; the boy who'd lost his hero was.

Grubbs flattened his hands on the surface of the cold metal table. "He got in the way of my lucrative business. It's as simple and complicated as that."

Finn cleared his throat. "Heath? A minute, please?" He motioned toward the doors and told the guards he'd be back shortly.

Legs trembling and heart blasting in his ears, Heath followed Finn out into the hallway. The second the door closed, Finn faced him. "This was a bad idea. Your being here. I'm going to get his written confession and finish the interview. I want you to be done with this case."

Heath's back hit the wall as his knees went wobbly. He bowed his head and pinched the bridge of his nose. "What does it matter? We're too late. The man's dying. It doesn't even matter anymore."

"You may not get retribution, but having an answer means closure. We'll change the cold-case label to Case Closed. *That* matters."

"The man's body is killing itself." Heath slammed his eyes shut and tipped his head back. He would not cry in the middle of a prison. "I don't need retribution. I just... I want to be done."

"And you are. I'll take it from here. I promise to treat this case as if it was my own family." Finn reached for the door handle, but then hesitated. "Are you all right to drive?"

"I'm fine. I just need a minute."

"Your father would be proud."

Not trusting his voice, Heath simply nodded. Finn headed back into the interview room, leaving Heath to slide down the wall until he was sitting on the floor.

It was done. He was done searching. Done making decisions for his life based on what happened to his father. Done living in fear, because if he was being honest, that was what most of his problems had been rooted in. Fear that he would never measure up to the man his father was. Fear that he'd never solve the case. Fear that his life didn't matter. Fear that he'd die, too. Fear that no one would miss him.

No more fear.

It was time for Heath to finally live.

Chapter Thirteen

Heath sat in his truck, watching the workings of the boys ranch through the front window. He squinted. That was Tanner and Macy in the horse arena with a couple of the residents.

"Just call." Heath stared at the phone in his hand.

Today he was supposed to give Gabe an answer about his grandfather. Too bad he hadn't called yet.

Even if his grandfather chewed him out on the phone—it was only a phone—Heath could end the conversation at any time. The worst the old man could do was hang up, and he'd done that before, so Heath had nothing to worry about. He finally pressed the call button.

His grandfather answered by clearing his throat over the phone. "If this is one of you charities calling about donations, we aren't giving."

"Grandpa? It's me. Heath."

"I didn't recognize your number. Is it new?"

Would he have answered if he'd known who was on the other end?

Heath worked his jaw back and forth. "I've had this number for six years."

"I guess it's been a while since we talked."

"That it has."

"Did you get my card? I sent it a ways back."

"I did. Thank you." Heath collected his thoughts. What to address first? "I called for a couple of reasons, but mostly because I wanted you to know that my company solved Dad's case."

"You did? I don't know what to say." The curmudgeonly old man actually sounded choked up. "Son, that's tremendous. After all these years. Did it... I always suspected it was someone related to that boys ranch. Was it?"

Heath eased back into his seat. He should have cracked the window. Gotten a little fresh air. "It was one of their part-time ranch hands. He was using the ranch as a location to run a drug and gun ring. Dad was about to blow the case and arrest him."

His grandfather breathed over the line for a moment. "Your father would be proud."

Are you?

Heath propped his elbow against the window on his door. "There's something else I want to ask you. I don't really know how to ask, though."

His grandfather was silent for a minute. Heath was about to ask if he was still on the line when the man finally spoke. "Just ask, son. There's a lot of years and troubled water between us. We don't need to beat around the bush."

Heath wanted to ask what he meant by *troubled waters*, but thought it best—considering his grandfather's temper sometimes—to stick to the information he needed first. "The boys ranch was left land in the will of a man by the name of Cyrus Culpepper. However, one of the stipulations for the Lone Star Cowboy League to secure the property is that all the original residents must return for a reunion in March."

"That so, now?"

Keep going... "Interestingly, someone by the name of Edmund Grayson is listed among those original residents. With the same spelling and he'd be around your age. People keep asking me if it's you but I said—"

"That you'd know if your own grandfather had been a troubled youth?"

"Exactly." Heath opened his eyes; he didn't remember shutting them so tightly.

"However," his grandfather continued, "it's not surprising that you don't know a lot about me or my past since we've never been close, not since your mother refused to let my son's death be honored as it should have been and then she remarried, and that's my fault. Entirely mine."

Heath had addressed his father's murder and the boys ranch. With his grandfather still on the line, it was time to finally get answers for himself. "Why did you disappear? Dad died and you... We never heard from you again and when we tried..."

"I hung up on both you kids," Grandpa finished. "I regret that more than anything else in my life. The fact is, after that shoddy funeral she gave for your father, your mother tried to get money out of me. She said it was my fault your father died—that I put the expectation to be a cop in his head since that's what I'd devoted my life to. She refused to let me see or speak to either you or Nell unless I gave her money. And you know how bad she is with money. She would have wasted it all. You and I both know that. Not a cent would have been saved for you or Nell."

Could that be true? Heath knew his mother had been desperate but... "I had no idea."

"By the time both of you contacted me, I thought she'd gotten to you. That you were calling to ask for money as well or you'd try to get close to me with the intention of asking later on. I figured you'd hand it all over to her. Looking back, it was foolish to isolate myself. I couldn't see beyond the anger of losing my son. Guilt factored in there, too."

Heath ran his free hand over his hair. "I think isolating ourselves runs in the family."

"Oh, I hope not. I hope you're never as foolish as this old man."

"Would it be okay..." *Just ask.* "Now that we cleared the air, would you be open to the idea of us starting to get to know each other more?"

"Of course. And I'll need a place to stay in March. Can I stay with you?"

"You're coming in March?"

"For the reunion, Heath."

"Wait." Heath grabbed the steering wheel, leaned forward. "Are you telling me you *were* one of the original boys?"

"Has anyone ever told you that you're pretty slow for a Texas Ranger?"

"Lately, yes, I'm afraid I've been told that a lot."

"If it's a woman, that's the type to keep around."

Heath laughed but quickly sobered. "But why didn't I know about you being a resident here? How come you never told us?"

"I...well... I've always been a bit ashamed that I

needed a place like that to set me straight. I wanted you to see me as the state trooper who caught bad guys for a living, not the boy who very well could have become one of the criminals. I'd planned to tell you both when you were older, but then your father was murdered there and I was so ashamed to share any connection to the place where my son was killed. We stopped talking and it seemed a moot point."

"I'd love to give you a tour of the new place. They do amazing work here."

"I look forward to seeing the old and the new location."

They made plans to talk again next week, then Heath hung up. This time when he stepped down out of his truck, he glanced around and felt a deep connection to the ranch. It might not be the same location, but it was the same organization that had set his grandfather on a straight path; his father had given his life on a mission to protect the residents at the time, and it was the place where Heath had learned that he was allowed to experience joy—he could live.

The place he'd fallen in love.

Josie picked up a mini clothespin, dipped it into a bowl of white glue and then pressed it into a huge pile of gold glitter. She and Abby were inside at the large dining table making name placeholders for the upcoming Thanksgiving buffet. A few of the boys had traced and cut out hundreds of leaves on orange, yellow, brown and red card stock. The mock leaves that weren't used as name holders would be scattered down the centers of the many tables that would stretch outside for the event.

Marnie was nearby, banging around with pots and pans in the kitchen as she prepared dinner. "You girls spend so much time and effort making things look pretty. I don't think those boys even notice."

Abby's eyes went wide. "They deserve to have a memorable Thanksgiving, and I aim to make sure every detail is taken care of so that they do."

"Suit yourself." Marnie opened the fridge and started piling ingredients onto the counter.

Josie glanced back over the instructions craft-loving Abby had ripped from one of her favorite magazines. She rested one hand on her stomach. The baby had been moving less than normal today.

Abby touched the pile of burlap she'd trimmed into squares. "I set them in order—burlap goes on the bottom, the leaf with their name written on it is glued to the burlap and then the glitter clothespin will clip on the bottom when we're done."

"If it's glued together, does it even need the clothespin?"

"I thought this out already." Abby pointed a white permanent marker at her. She was going down the guest list and writing names on the leaves with her beautiful handwriting. "With us eating outdoors, the clothespins will weigh down the cards. We don't want all of them to blow away before people can even enjoy them."

"You think of everything."

Footsteps echoed from the hall that led to the office area. Diego and Stephen were walking side by side, their heads bent toward each other, deep in conversation.

"Why do I think the two of you look suspicious?" Josie asked.

A smile blossomed on Stephen's face. "Can you keep a secret?"

"Depends on the secret." Usually secrets and rumor-spreading were discouraged at the ranch, so Josie didn't want to encourage the boys down a path they shouldn't go.

"It's one that Gabe and Bea approved," Diego said.

"Then sure."

"On Tuesday we're going to have a surprise for Heath." Stephen snatched a leftover muffin from the counter. Marnie shooed him away but looked pleased all the same. "But you can't tell him."

"What type of surprise?"

Diego bounced his way forward. "We're not telling."

Josie winked at them as they filed out of the house. She touched her stomach for the seventh time in as many minutes.

Abby caught the movement and cocked her head. "You've been doing that all day. You're starting to worry me. Is something wrong?"

Josie pressed on her abdomen again, trying to shift the baby to cause movement. Sleeping. The baby was probably only sleeping hard. Still, her heart pulsed in her temples. She *had* been feeling dizzy a lot lately.

She licked her lips. "Can you… Would you go find Heath?"

Marnie set down a pot on the oven with a loud clang and wiped her hands. "You both stay put. I'll fetch him." She crossed to the back door, tossed it open and then yelled at the top of her lungs, "Heath. Ranger Heath."

Josie sighed. *I could have gotten up and hollered.* The whole point had been *not* to cause a ruckus.

Marnie kept yelling, "Grayson. Right there. You're needed. Make those boots run."

She was so loud that Gabe wandered out of the office where he'd been meeting with Bea. "What's all the commotion?"

Heath crossed over the threshold, breathing hard. "You called?"

Gabe clapped his hands and strode forward. "Just the man I was hoping to see."

Josie opened her mouth to speak. *I called. Me! I need you.* But there were so many people gathered in the kitchen and it would feel weird to draw all the attention toward her. Especially over something medical...something she wanted only Heath to know. Too late for that.

"I have great news," Heath said, zoning in on Gabe. "I talked to my grandfather this morning. He *is* the Edmund Grayson you've been looking for and he promised to be here in March."

Gabe whooped. "One down." He reached to shake Heath's hand. "You just made my day."

Josie wound a piece of burlap around her fingers. *Speak up.* Heath wasn't like Dale; he'd want her to interrupt his conversation if she needed something, right?

Gabe pumped Heath's hand. "Tanner and I have been trying to track down my grandfather, Theodore Linley. He was an original resident alongside your grandfather." He leaned his hip against the counter and crossed his arms. "Problem is, he walked out on our family when I was eight and we've never heard from him again. His last known whereabouts was prison, but we've had no luck there, either. I wanted to pick your brain—ask your advice about hiring a PI."

Heath glanced around the room until his gaze landed on Josie. When it did, their eyes locked and everyone else faded away for a heartbeat. "Is that why I got called in here?"

Marnie slapped a dish towel onto the counter. "I called you in here because Josie said she needed you. You'd know that if you and Gabe hadn't gone straight into jawing."

Heath brushed past Gabe, sidestepped Abby and dropped to his knees beside Josie's chair. He wrapped one arm over the back of her chair and laid the other across the table in front of her. It was the closest he'd ever come to hugging her.

"What's wrong? You don't look okay." His voice was soft, intimate. In a room full of people, his words and attention were solely hers. He was doing the *Ranger thing* she'd noticed him do before—his eyes roved quickly over something…her—looking for problems, weaknesses, ways to help.

She twisted in her seat so she could place a hand on his shoulder. She needed to feel the muscles there—needed his strength to chase away her fears. The fabric was soft, worn. She leaned closer. "I haven't felt the baby move all day. I'm scared."

"When I first…? Why didn't you? I would have…" His cheeks lost some of their color and his brow creased with worry. He looked at her stomach. "Do you need me to call an ambulance? Take you to the hospital? I can carry you. That's not an issue." He started to get up.

She applied pressure to his shoulder. "No. Stay. I want you to talk."

"Talk?"

Josie grabbed his hand from the table and placed it on her stomach. "The baby moves more when you talk."

His hand was warm on her belly. His nostrils flared

as he took a deep breath as if to calm down, but his eyes still looked a bit frantic. "When *I* talk or is that a royal 'you' meaning anyone?"

"You. Heath Grayson. When you talk." She'd noticed the baby kicked and changed positions more whenever he was nearby, when his voice carried. However, she hadn't planned on ever mentioning that to him. Desperate times. "Say anything."

Heath nodded and dragged some air through his mouth. "Hey…you're scaring your mom and me. Could you do us a favor and have a dance party in there?" He stared at his hand on her stomach as if he could will the baby to move.

"Just talk."

He sat back on his heels. "Let me tell you about your mama. She loves goats and baby cows, so you better be okay with that. She's beautiful. The most beautiful woman you'll ever see. Not just that, she's determined. As stubborn as a Texas summer. But it's because she cares about people so much. So don't worry about that, she—"

The baby rolled. Josie gasped. Her hand automatically went on top of Heath's. "Did you feel that?"

His mouth hung open. "I did."

Josie leaned back in her chair and closed her eyes.

Heath removed his hand slowly as he got back to his feet. "You should still call your doctor. I'll drive you over right now if he'll see you."

Josie pulled out her phone and pressed the button for her doctor.

The baby was fine. Heath was here. Everything would be okay.

Chapter Fourteen

At the last stop sign before their turn, Heath looked over at Josie. "Are you sure you're okay to serve at the ranch? The doctor said to take it easy for a few days."

She tipped her head back and smiled up at him. "I'm not one to sit around. Besides, I don't want to miss what's happening at the ranch today."

Her hair was pinned back in a way that made her look like one of those royal princesses with their picture splashed on the front of the magazines in the checkout lane in the grocery store. The ones the internet went wild about whenever they stepped into public. Josie had the same grace and kindness about her.

He hit the button for his window, allowing chilly morning air to blast into the truck's cabin. Josie always complained about being hot anyway.

She patted her stomach. "Relax, Officer. I took it easy all weekend and yesterday, too. I feel fine. And you heard the doctor—it's only anemia. Iron supplements for the rest of my pregnancy and up my steak quota. Which—since we live in Texas—let's be honest, is not exactly an issue. I'll be good as new."

"If—even for a second today—you feel dizzy again or light-headed—"

"I know. I know." She put her hands up as if to say *Don't shoot.* "Sit down and tell you right away."

Heath tightened the grip on his steering wheel as he turned the truck past the large horseshoe-shaped metal sign announcing The Lone Star Cowboy League Boys Ranch, Founded 1947.

He ground his molars, causing a bolt of pain to blaze into his temples.

Relax. It's not even the same location. The case is closed. Done. Get over it.

Josie skirted a nervous glance his way. "Please tell me what's the matter. You haven't been yourself all morning."

Heath had made peace about the boys ranch when it came to his father's death. And after spending time with the boys in his detection class, and discovering his grandfather was an original resident of the place, he'd grown to view the boys ranch in a positive light. But he still had no desire to show up today.

Not on the Tuesday before Thanksgiving.

Not on the anniversary of his father's death.

"I'm fine." He craned his neck. Squinted. Up a ways near the barns...were those police cars?

"I see." She grabbed on to the door handle as they bumped down the quarter-mile-long driveway. "But that was a Ranger *fine*, which actually means something is terribly wrong."

At the end of the driveway, police cars from multiple agencies lined either side of the road. Even some of the undercover vehicles that belonged to Company F.

"Wow." Josie's whisper held a hushed awe. "So many of them came."

Did she know what was going on? Why hadn't she told him about danger at the ranch?

Adrenaline flushed hot through his veins and the muscles in his back coiled as he tossed the truck into Park. If someone had done harm to the boys or destroyed property, they would have to answer to Heath. His heart pounded. His hands shook.

If he had to—if duty called—he'd die for this place. Without hesitation.

As his father had exactly fifteen years ago, to the date.

He shoved his gun into his holster and threw open his door. "Stay here. I don't know if it's safe."

"Heath." Josie reached across the cabin and latched on to his wrist. "Take a breath. Nothing's wrong."

Couldn't she *see*? Law enforcement didn't show up in mass when everything was dandy.

He was so focused on Josie and trying to make sense of her words, Heath startled when he heard Stephen speak behind him. "There you are. I'm here to escort you to the service."

Josie let go of him and scooted out of the passenger side.

Heath pivoted to face Stephen. "What's going on?"

Red crept over Stephen's pale cheeks. "We found out that there was never a service for your dad. After everything. Your mom had a private ceremony. No big honors?"

Heath's mouth went dry and refused to form words, so he nodded, only once.

"Today we've changed that," Stephen said.

A dull ache spread through his chest. "You've what?"

Josie slipped her arm though his and place her hand on his forearm. "Come on. Everyone's waiting for you." She propelled him forward.

Rows of officers in their dress blues saluted as the three of them walked down the center of the aisle. At the front of the large gathering of people, which included all the boys from the ranch, the staff, many of the members of the Lone Star Cowboy League and a few familiar faces from around town, stood the major of Company F alongside Finn and his new wife, Amelia, and Heath's sister, Nell, her boyfriend, Danny, and her daughter, Carly.

Stephen went to stand beside Diego and Pastor Walsh.

Nell handed Carly to Danny and ran to Heath, wrapping her arms around his middle in a fierce hug. "Can you believe this?" She was crying already. "Your friends are amazing."

"Did you know?" He hugged her back.

"They told me last week, but they wanted you to be surprised."

Surprised was putting it lightly. Heath was overwhelmed to the point of having a hard time stringing together words.

Heath took her hand and slipped it through his arm so he had Nell on one side and Josie on the other.

Chuck, the major of Company F, made a motion for everyone to sit. "Last week I was contacted by two exceptional young men who wanted to right a wrong that had been done to one of the heroes from our very own Company F. Fifteen years ago a Ranger laid down his life while he was protecting the boys ranch and his sacrifice was never properly honored. Well, today, thanks to the dedication of his son—" Chuck gestured toward Heath "—to not let the case go cold, and to two boys—" at this he wrapped his arms to include Diego and Stephen "—who worked tirelessly to see this memorial happen, we can finally pay honor to a man we will never be able to thank enough and, moreover, will never forget."

Chuck motioned forward the honor guard, dressed in their pressed uniforms and white gloves. They marched until they were standing in front of Heath and Nell. They did an about-face and held a salute toward both siblings.

Chuck stepped down from the small stage. "Customarily we would present you with the flag from the burial, which we do not have. However—" he motioned Stephen and Diego forward "—the boys ranch was able to produce the flag that has been flying at the old site for the past twenty years."

Stephen and Diego handed a huge, faded, torn and beat-up flag to the honor guard. When they started to walk away, Heath snagged both boys and had them stand in front of him, one of his hands resting on either of their shoulders.

How could he have ever though badly of the boys here?

God, forgive me. I misjudged this place—these kids. I was wrong.

Chuck took a ragged breath over the microphone, evidently struggling with emotions, as well. "So you see, this very flag was flying fifteen years ago on the very day—this same day—that Ranger Marcus Alan Grayson paid the ultimate sacrifice."

In the distance, taps started to play as the honor guard turned and began folding the flag into a perfect triangle. Taps—even when he didn't know the downed officer—always pulled at him…but being played for his father? Emotion balled and lodged itself into Heath's throat. He swallowed a few times, but it wouldn't go away. His eyes burned with tears—tears the fifteen-year-old boy had refused to shed.

The honor guard turned to attention and held the flag out to Heath. "On behalf of the great state of Texas and the Department of Public Safety, please accept this flag as a symbol of our appreciation for your loved one's distinguished service." The man pressed the flag into Heath's hands. "God bless you and your family, God bless the state of Texas and God bless the United States of America."

"Amen." Pastor Walsh took the stage. "Today we honor the sacrifice of a remarkable man, but may it also remind us that those who love God are all called to do the same. In the Bible, the book of John tells us 'Greater love has no one than this: to lay down one's life for one's friends.'"

Diego turned around and looked up at Heath. "But you don't have to *die* to be a hero, do you?"

Heath bent a little and whispered, "I don't know, son."

"I think you're a hero. I don't want you to die. That doesn't have to happen."

Not knowing what to say, Heath put his hand back on the boy's shoulder and straightened to his full height again.

The pastor stepped off the small stage and continued down the aisle. "How much more so a man like Ranger Marcus Grayson, who was willing to lay down his life for people he didn't know? Men like his son, our friend, Heath Grayson, who still answers the call by going into law enforcement." The pastor stopped in front of Heath.

Sacrifice.

Lay down one's life.

From the beginning, that was what Heath had committed to, hadn't he? He should be ready to lay down his life any second. Moments ago he'd been willing to do just that when he thought he'd have to protect the ranch.

He shifted in his boots, moving closer to Nell and placing a gap between himself and Josie.

Andrew climbed back onto the stage. "Jesus tells us that a good shepherd will lay down his life for his sheep. These men and women in uniform here today have taken a pledge stating they are willing to do that, but if you claim to be a Christian, that means you have also taken a pledge. One that says you are willing to sacrifice whatever you need to in order to honor God and point people toward Him. Please join me in prayer and then the boys have something to present to Heath." Pastor Walsh bowed his head, but Heath's ears were roaring so loud, he couldn't make out the words to the prayer.

I've taken a pledge to be willing to lay down my life.

Both as an officer and as a Christian.

Heath filled his lungs with a rattling breath. He'd asked God for guidance, and this was it—wasn't it? He had no right being involved with Josie. Especially not with her being pregnant. She deserved a man who would be around for the long haul. He would not allow Josie or her child to suffer another loss. Flint was right. Leaving her—letting her be so she could find another man—was the only loving, sacrificial option on his table.

After the seven-gun salute, the boys presented Heath with a box they had decorated and filled with notes each of them had written saying what they admired about him and how much they appreciated what his father had done.

Heath left her side to mingle with some of the officers in attendance, but Josie kept an eye on him. Something was off, but perhaps he was simply feeling mixed emotions because of the significance of the day and, being a man, it caused him to clam up instead of process. Even though she'd known what he was struggling with, on the drive over she'd given him multiple opportunities to confide in her, and he'd chosen not to. That hurt, but Heath seemed to need to work things out alone for a while before he spoke. It wasn't how Josie was wired, but she could respect that.

As the crowd thinned and staff members began heading back to their daily chores, Josie found her place at Heath's side.

His smile was false. Frankly, he looked exhausted. "I wanted to thank you." He didn't meet her eyes. "From the get-go you told me this was a place of healing and I didn't believe you. But you were right."

"Heath," she whispered his name and stepped closer. After the other day at Dale's grave site, where she'd prayed for God's guidance…she'd known the truth. How she felt about Heath… Those kind of feelings shouldn't be fought. They were worth every risk and danger in life.

No one else was around. *Go ahead, tell him now.*

She slid her hand onto his chest so it rested over his heart. "Heath Grayson, you deserve to know, I think I'm falling in love with you."

"Please. Don't." As if she had sucker punched him instead of professing feelings, Heath's face fell. He stepped back, removing her hand from his chest. "Please don't say that." Anguish laced his voice. "That makes what I need to say really difficult."

Did she hear him wrong?

"I don't understand." The baby rolled. Josie hugged her stomach. "All this time. Me and you. I thought…"

"I can't be with you." The muscle that ran along his jaw popped. "You shouldn't want to be with me."

"Why not? Don't you care about me? What's wrong? Why have you been so kind if you didn't have feelings?" She was tossing out every question she could think of. "How you've been acting, it sure feels like you care."

"I *do* care," he said loudly, then lowered his voice. "But don't you see? That's why this can't ever happen. I could die today. Tomorrow. Just like my dad."

"So could I. So could all of us. I could die in childbirth."

"Don't say that."

"Please, Heath." She didn't even care if her tone came out like a whine. Every action had proven that he was in love with her. Why was he denying it?

Heath grabbed on to the fence and looked away. One of the goats trotted over and nuzzled him. He jerked his hand away, as if the goat offended him, too. "Josie, you're wonderful and you're pregnant and you deserve a man who—"

"I want you."

The goat bleated long and low.

Heath's shoulders slumped. "We can never be together. Don't you see that?"

"Is it because I'm pregnant?" Irrational, but at the moment she was willing to toss out anything.

"I can't have a family. I've always known that. I lost sight of it because…" He closed his eyes and shook his head, unwilling to go on.

She started sobbing. She couldn't even blame pregnancy emotions this time.

"Josie." His voice broke. He made a movement to reach toward her, but then fisted his hand and let it drop back to his side. "Please. It'll be okay. I just— You were right. All along. You need a man who doesn't work a job like mine. This is my fault. I shouldn't have let us get close. This is best for you. For your child."

Now there were three goats with their heads rammed through the fence links watching them.

"Are you leaving?" Josie choked out. If he didn't want her, if he wasn't in love with her, she couldn't bear being around him.

"At the end of the—"

"I think it's best if you leave. Now."

The chorus of goats bleated along.

Heath glanced down at the goats and then back at Josie. "Now?"

"Now."

"Yes, ma'am. If that's what you want."

"It is."

He hesitated, but then tipped his hat and headed straight for his truck and left. Along with her heart.

Chapter Fifteen

Josie yawned and rubbed at her eyes.

Unable to turn off her mind and uncomfortable both because she was pregnant and because her heart ached about Heath, sleep never came last night. Not for long anyway. When Katie swung by her house in the morning to pick her up, she'd urged Josie to stay home for the day and rest, but Josie hadn't wanted to be alone.

Alone would be the rest of her life.

Sure, there would be her baby, but Josie realized that raising a child on her own might be even lonelier and more difficult than being a hermit. Her child was a blessing, of course, but a child asked questions about a missing parent. Questions that would remind her again and again that she wasn't meant to be alone. One day—a day that would come sooner than she wanted to acknowledge because that was how time worked—after her baby grew up and moved out, Josie would truly be on her own. Forever.

Because she didn't want to fall in love again. Not unless she could be with Heath.

Admittedly, Josie wasn't much help at the boys

ranch today. Diego had side-eyed her until he finally got Abby to convince her to come inside and talk. He promised to see to the calves if she stayed and visited with the ladies until she felt better.

Sweet child. She wanted to hug him and promise that everything would be okay. That his calf buddy would be smiling again soon. But a woman didn't just say a few words and feel better when her heart had driven off with a lawman in a truck the day before.

Josie scooped up the decorative pillow on the couch and held it to her. It wouldn't make the sharp pain in her chest go away, but it did help to hold on to something.

Abby scooted closer, wrapped her arm around her shoulders and tipped her head so their temples were touching. "I don't know what to say, but we're here. We're all here for you."

Marnie eased to the front of her chair so she could rest her hand on Josie's knee. "Maybe he'll still come tomorrow for the buffet."

Josie loosened her hold on the pillow so she could swipe at her eyes. "I told him to leave. I don't think he'll be back. I don't even know if I want him to come back."

"What can you mean, sweetie?" Marnie asked.

"I'm in love with him." Wow. That hurt to say. Would it always? "And he doesn't want me. I don't think it gets much worse than that."

Abby lifted her head. "Did he say that? Those actual words? Did he say he wasn't in love with you?"

"He didn't have to."

"Because sometimes men do strange things," Abby said. "Before John and I were married, we once broke up for a week because he decided I should be with a man who made more money since my parents are wealthy and that's how I'd grown up. Silly man. It was the worst week of my life."

"I think this is different." Josie hugged herself again. She hadn't felt this badly broken since finding out about Dale's death on the heels of his saying he was leaving their marriage. Was that how her life would be? Men leaving her?

First Dale left because he didn't think she was capable of giving him a family. Now Heath was gone because she *could* give him a family.

"He...he doesn't want a family. Because of his position. He doesn't want to be attached to me and the baby and have us face him dying in the line of duty like his father and Dale did."

Marnie picked up the teakettle sitting on the coffee table and refreshed Josie's half-gone cup of mint tea. "Well, I'm no expert in these things, but that right there sounds a whole lot like love to me."

"Him leaving? That's love?"

"No." She batted her hand. "That's plain foolishness. But the thought behind it—he cares about you and your child so much that he is willing to hurt himself in the present to save you from possible pain in the future. That, honey, is what we call sacrificial love."

"If that's love... I don't like it."

Abby moved to snag her cup of tea. "What I think Marnie is trying to say is that Heath's actions are not love—he's going about it wrong and he's confused— but the motive behind them proves his love."

"Mmm-hmm." Marnie pursed her lips. "*Confused* is a good word for that man. He somehow thinks he can tell the future and that's something only the good

Lord is capable of doing. Heath's borrowing tomorrow's troubles instead of treating today as a gift. That's the wrong I see."

"Can this year just be over already?" Josie closed her eyes tightly. "I'm *so* sick of hurting. That's all this entire year has been."

Marnie clucked her tongue. "When all is said and done, don't let temporary situations allow you to question God's goodness or what He's been doing in both your and Heath's lives. I know this year's been tough on you—between Dale and finding out you'd have a baby alone and now this mix-up with Heath." She narrowed her eyes, pursed her lips and wagged her finger at Josie. "But I've watched you both over the past month. God has done great work in both your hearts. I believe He brought you two together for a very special purpose. What is that purpose? That's not for me to know or say."

"I wish it was for you to say." Josie stared at the ceiling as if she could find answers there. "It would be easier if the answers would fall into my lap."

"Maybe we'll never see Ranger Heath again. There's a chance of that. But how God moved in your heart because of that man? *That* you will always have and you're responsible for holding on to and continuing the growth that started in your heart and spiritual walk."

"The joy of the Lord is my strength," Josie whispered the verse. Putting together those lanterns felt like a lifetime ago.

Abby cupped her hand over Josie's arm. "Hold on to joy. Whatever you do, no matter what, keep holding on to joy."

Marnie rested back in her chair. "You, more than

anyone here, know how fragile life can be and how quickly plans can change. We humans are finite and have no business counting on tomorrow. Which is why we have to cling to the joy of the Lord. That's not some trite saying. No, it's the only hope and only true and lasting thing in the world…the knowledge that God loves us and has sacrificed all to save us so our relationship with Him can be right. That, child, is what the joy of the Lord means."

Josie nodded, but her heart still ached. "I get that. I do. But knowing that…is it wrong to hurt about Heath still?"

"No, sweetie. It's not wrong at all. We're created to be in relationships, with God, yes, but with other people, too. I don't know what tomorrow holds, but today, today is a time to mourn for what feels like the end of a relationship that you had hoped would be more."

Josie dropped her head into her hands and let her tears fall. Abby rubbed circles into her back and started praying out loud. But Josie was having a hard time focusing.

Was it wrong to hurt more over Heath's departure than she had over her husband's death? She mourned Dale, but this was different. With Heath—pain sliced through her in a way that felt like the wound would never heal. It was more difficult knowing the man she loved was out there in the world but she couldn't be with him, than dealing with the fact that someone had passed—gone forever and there was no chance of talking to them again.

Katie Ellis charged down the hall. "I feel so bad interrupting, but something happened. Something really bad. You guys need to head to the church. Everyone belonging to the League needs to go."

Marnie was the first to her feet. "Josie, why don't you stay here? Abby and I can go see what it is."

Josie set aside the pillow and straightened her shirt. "I'm a member of the League." She lifted her chin. "I care about this ranch." She swiped under her eyes. "I'm going."

No matter what they said and despite the personal pain she was wading through, she would fight to go along if she had to. Because if Josie Markham knew one thing with certainty, it was that no matter what happened in someone's private world, life kept going. She could choose to sit in her problems, or she could get up and be a part of something and be useful in the midst of her mourning.

With God's help, she hoped she'd continue to be the type of woman who would always choose the latter.

He didn't even own a kitchen table.

Never before had Heath noticed how empty his apartment was. How empty his life really was. Not until he realized that this—his lonely, bare apartment—was his future stretching out in front of him. Years and years of this place, a fridge, a bed, a couch, TV and coffee table.

And him.

"You eat in front of the TV." He walked past his spotless fridge. No Christmas cards with smiling families adorned it. Shouldn't he have friends who'd want to send him those? At the very least? "You have everything you need."

He fished his keys from a bowl near his front door

and headed outside. Nell's condo wasn't a far drive. An hour.

After everything with Josie the day before, Nell had invited him to spend Thanksgiving with her and Danny and Danny's family. A part of him wanted to say no. Wanted to hole himself up in his apartment and shut out the world—shut out life. But he'd promised himself, promised God, this past month that he'd knock off the isolationism.

So he turned his music up as loud as he could handle without making his ears hurt and made it to Nell's in record time.

She met him at the door and thrust Carly right into his arms. "Come in. I'm so glad you could come a day early. I need you to help chop vegetables."

"Nice to see you, too, sis." He bopped Carly on the nose.

"Put me down! I have to get my ponies." She giggled, squirmed out of his arms and took off down the hallway in the direction of her playroom.

Nell chucked a dish towel at him. "I don't need pleasantries with you. Besides, I just saw you yesterday."

"Wow, you sure know how to make a guy feel loved." He rubbed his chin and dropped down into a seat at the kitchen table. There was a cutting board, a few knives and a pile of vegetables waiting for him.

Nell slipped her apron back over her head. "Love? Ha. You don't deserve to talk about love. Not after what you pulled yesterday."

"Can we not get into that?" He should have known Nell would force him to talk about Josie. It wasn't in her nature to beat around the bush.

"Oh, we can and we will. Right now." She jabbed her finger a couple times into the kitchen island so hard he felt bad for the countertop. "What on earth are you thinking?"

He grabbed a carrot. "How do you want these sliced?"

"Chopped. Cut." She threw up her hands and huffed. "Shaped into little triangles or trapezoids. Who cares? Just make them smaller and don't change the subject."

Heath grumbled and started to slice the carrots. The knife made a loud thudding sound with each cut. Might as well give her an answer. "I was thinking that I don't need Josie or her baby losing someone again and I'm a Texas Ranger. People point guns at me. People ram their cars into our trucks. People—"

"People. Die. Every. Day." Nell spit out each word as she yanked the garbage bag out of the can.

"You don't get it."

"Oh. I don't, do I?" She swung around the island to stand in front of him. Her hands on her hips. "Because you were the only one hurt when Dad died. Only you had to suffer through that, right?"

He set down the knife. "That's not what I'm saying."

"But isn't it?" She sighed as she yanked out a chair and sat down. She rested her hand on top of his. "I lost my hero, too. I know what that feels like. But you know what? I would rather have gotten thirteen years with Dad than none. And that's really what this boils down to."

"Love is sacrifice."

"Is that what this is about?" She jerked her head back in a show of disgust. "That preacher got into your head and jumbled everything around?"

He ran his fingers along the grooves in the table on either side of the cutting board. "You were there yesterday. He said loving means being willing to lay down your life."

"Yeah, I was there and he didn't just mean dying for someone. Come on, Heath." She bumped her knee against his. "Process what you heard a little more instead of just letting fear lead you down the easiest path."

"Easy? Walking away from Josie was the hardest thing I've ever done in my life."

"No." She shook her head. "Staying and being in a relationship. Taking a risk that today may be the only day you're afforded and loving someone with everything you've got. *That* would be the harder, braver choice. Can't you see?"

"That verse he shared said—"

Nell held up her hand. "I don't need a play-by-play of the sermon. I was there. But, Heath, come on. Sacrifice doesn't always mean dying in the physical sense. Sacrifice could mean dying in your need to be the greatest Texas Ranger in the history of the world."

"I don't—"

She rolled her eyes. "Sacrifice could mean giving up anything that you're holding on to tightly—sometimes that means the shield you're using to keep everyone away or the lifeboat you've climbed into to set yourself adrift at sea." She scooted her chair closer to his. "Sacrifice could mean that you love Josie and her baby for the rest of your life and you work hard at your job but mentor those boys in your spare time and live in a way that points everyone toward the Lord."

"But that wouldn't be a sacrifice… That would be the greatest life I could picture having."

"Maybe—" she lowered her voice and looked him in the eye "—you need to sacrifice your pride. The part of you that whispers your life isn't worth squat unless you make yourself miserable and isolated and keep love at bay. Sacrifice the part of you that says you're selling out on your cause—your passion for law enforcement—if you let yourself love someone."

Lord, help me see reason. Is Nell right? Guide me.

Heath stared down at his hands. "I think… I think I've been living in fear my whole life. I prayed recently about it. I thought I'd let it go, but it may still have a hold on me."

She took his hand and held it between both of hers. "Things like that take a while to work through. I wouldn't expect success at letting it go to be automatic. You may battle fear your whole life. But keep fighting."

He pushed his hand against hers. "When did you get so smart?"

"I don't know. I have a pretty awesome big brother who took me under his wing."

"I love you."

"I love you, too." She let go of his hand and swatted at his chest as she rose. "But you're an idiot if you let that woman go."

"She told me to leave, Nell. Josie opened up to me and I all but walked on her heart. She might not want to see me again."

"I have a hunch she does. But…take it from a girl who had her heart stomped on before, if you're strolling back into her life, you'd best be ready to sweep her off her feet. Don't mosey back halfheartedly."

What if he'd already messed up too big? What if Josie didn't forgive him?

Heath grabbed at his hair. "She kept asking me if I was going to leave. All month. And then I did."

Nell grabbed a bowl and a spoon from her cabinets. She whirled around and pointed the spoon at him. "Then you better do something big to show her that you're never going to leave her again. Catch my drift?"

"It's hard not to catch it when you're lobbing it directly at my head." Heath got up, crossed the room and pulled his sister into a hug. "Will you forgive me if I miss Thanksgiving?"

She hugged him back and then shoved him toward the door. "Go, Heath. Go get your girl."

Red, white, and blue flashing police lights bounced off the church's white clapboard.

Townsfolk, members of the Lone Star Cowboy League, boys-ranch staff and officers on scene all stared at the three-foot-high black graffiti marring the walls of Haven Community Church and the busted row of windows.

Boys Ranch Was Here.

Josie covered her mouth. "Who would do this?"

Marnie wrapped her arms around Josie and tugged her into her side. "Someone who wants to make our boys look bad."

The mayor, Elsa Wells, adjusted her horn-rimmed glasses as she pursed her lips. "We've never had something like this happen. To our church, no less. Not under my watch."

Avery Culpepper crossed her arms and smacked her gum. "My granddaddy leaves the boys all that property and assets and this is how they repay the community. Seems awful ungrateful, if you ask me. I know I would never act like this."

Fletcher Snowden Phillips—the only living relation left of the founder of the boys ranch—tipped his hat to the mayor and moved to stand beside Avery. "I've been saying they need to dismantle the boys ranch for years." He thrust his hand toward the broken windows and graffiti. "Do you know what vandalism like this does to the property value in a town?"

Tanner Barstow scowled at Fletcher. "Nobody asked for your opinion. We all know how you feel about the boys ranch. You tell us every chance you get."

"And I'll keep telling everyone until that place gets shut down and dismantled," Fletcher boomed. "I'm a lawyer."

"We know," someone in the crowd groaned.

But Fletcher didn't seem fazed. "I will find a way to sue the League. My family set up that ranch and I *will* see to it that I'm responsible for taking it down. That's a promise."

Josie turned away from Marnie and looked at Gabe, who stood next to her. "Our boys wouldn't do something like this. You don't believe they would, right? Then again," she said, lowering her voice, "we all know Heath's father was killed by a staff member. That's been confirmed now. So anything is possible."

But in her heart she couldn't believe one of the boys would harm the church.

Gabe shook his head. "This is the work of someone

who wants to make the boys ranch and our organization look bad. That's all this is."

Tanner and Macy joined their little circle.

"Did you see Fletcher smirking at the graffiti? I hate to falsely accuse someone...but could he be responsible for the string of mischief we've had the past few months?" Tanner looked over at Josie. "Did Heath come to any conclusions about the thefts and calves being set loose?"

Maybe Heath had been right to suspect that Fletcher was possibly behind the string of bad things that had happened at the boys ranch in the past two months. The lawyer had always seemed harmless, but perhaps he disliked the place enough to delve into illegal activity to ensure it would be closed down.

But Josie shook her head. She couldn't talk about Heath. She was doing her best to focus on the task at hand and that was already taking all her reserves.

Marnie rubbed a circle into Josie's shoulder. "The Ranger's gone. It's up to us to solve this puzzle now."

Gabe nodded. "Whoever did it stands to gain something by turning the town's opinion against us. We need to brainstorm. Who would benefit from our doors closing?"

Tanner angled his head closer. "Fletcher just left with Avery Culpepper to take her to lunch. Even if they aren't involved with this incident, I have to believe the two of them teaming up can only mean trouble for the ranch."

Josie finally found her voice. "Heath mentioned that some of his interviews hinted that Fletcher might be to blame for some of our troubles, but there's no solid proof."

"I'll store that information away." Gabe clapped his hands. "Tomorrow is Thanksgiving—I don't want this casting a shadow onto the festivities. How about we leave here, keep thinking of possibilities, but focus on making it a great, carefree Thanksgiving for the boys who aren't going home for the holiday. This weekend we'll all pitch in to repaint the church and replace the windows. On Sunday, no one will even be able to tell this ever happened."

Josie wrung her hands. If only Heath was here. He'd know what to do. He might have found clues at the scene that the local police could have missed.

Stop trying to factor Heath into everything. He's gone.

Right… She would do as Gabe suggested.

Focus and rebuild.

Chapter Sixteen

Light wind whistled through the cracked door of the horse barn Heath and Flint were momentarily holed up in. The rainstorms that had threatened to unleash a few days ago never ended up doing anything more than drizzling. Probably for the best. Rain would have meant mud and mud wouldn't have made for the best outdoor meal.

Heath tried to see through the crack in the door. He'd stashed his truck out of the way, near Flint's cabin where no one would spot it. Although, he might have been able to hide it among the fifty or more vehicles parked in the makeshift lot on the front field. Some of the boys had gone home to enjoy Thanksgiving with their families, while other families came to the boys ranch to celebrate. However, Flint explained that some of the boys were alone, so most of the staff members attended the buffet and sat with the kids without family that day.

Adrenaline buzzed through Heath's system, making it impossible for him to stay still for too long. Two baby goats—kids, as they were called—butted heads near his feet. The brown one tripped over his boot and tumbled to the ground with a tiny, offended bleat.

Heath leaned over and righted the animal. "Hush, now. You're liable to get us found out."

Outside, seventeen tables were lined in a row, heavy with place settings. Candlelight flickered from jars evenly spaced between orange and mint-green-painted pumpkins. The women had gone all out making the place look nice. Heath hoped Josie hadn't overworked herself. The thought pulled a smile to his face. Josie was bent on doing her share, so he imagined she had fought to work alongside the others.

The woman would always be a stubborn spitfire. He'd fallen for her on day one because of that trait.

Flint slapped Heath on the back. "I'm not trying to discourage you, so don't take it that way. But after everything, are you sure showing up here unannounced is the best idea?"

Heath straightened his shirt for the tenth time. "It's not unannounced. I told her I'd be here for the Thanksgiving buffet. I'm keeping my word."

Flint cocked his head and smirked.

Heath held up his hands in surrender. "I hear you. I do. Believe me. But I think doing it this way is for the best." He crossed his arms. "While we're at it, I also wanted to thank you for your warning earlier."

"The warning I gave you to stay away from Josie?" Flint picked up the white goat and held it like a football. "The one you didn't listen to? That one?"

"The very same." Heath grinned but his gut kicked with nervous energy. "And you didn't tell me to stay away—you told me to stay away if I couldn't commit. Well, I'm committed, buddy."

"So it would seem." Flint chuckled. "Are you sure you don't want to wait until you have a ring and a better plan?"

The plan was to walk out of the barn, find Josie and ask her to marry him. That was as far as he'd gotten.

"Stores are closed today." Heath shook his head. "I don't want to let one more day pass before I ask. That's the biggest thing I've learned lately—we only have today. So I plan to use it."

"I have to say, I never thought I'd live to see the day you'd settle down. It didn't seem to be your thing."

"Meet the right girl and it suddenly becomes your thing."

"That's how it tends to work for everyone else." Flint set the wiggling goat back down. It tromped off to butt the brown one again.

"Your day will come. I'm sure it will."

"Me? No." Flint pulled a face, as if he was offended Heath would broach the topic with him. "I have my hands full keeping Logan in line. I've been down that road. I'm not going down it again."

"You may change your mind."

"I won't." Flint rubbed his hands together. "But we're talking about you here. Are you ready?"

"I think it's time." Heath pulled both the goats out of the stall they'd weaseled into, holding one in each arm. "Will you pray for me?"

Flint pulled a face. "That's not really my thing anymore. Besides, even if it still was, I don't believe you'll need it."

Heath sighed. With all Flint had been through, the man had fallen away from God, hadn't he? Heath should have picked up on that before now. He should have been praying for his friend, encouraging him and talking to him about God more. He'd do so going forward. "We always need it."

"Then, sure. Although I don't believe anything I say will make a difference."

Heath took a big breath and pushed the door open with his foot.

This was it.

The mingling scents of cinnamon, nutmeg and cloves heating in the busy kitchen made Josie's mouth water. People hustled around her as she fit bowls full of baked sweet potatoes topped with brown sugar and pecan crumble onto large trays. A line of older residents who hadn't gone home for Thanksgiving waited to take the trays to the tables outside.

Thankfully, the vandalism from the day before wasn't the topic of conversation—yet. Josie prayed that the troubles they'd experienced over the past two months wouldn't overshadow all the good happening at the boys ranch.

Please let people see the good. The positive. And please let us catch whoever is trying to make the ranch look bad. Work on the wrongdoer's heart, Lord.

"Hot rolls coming through. Fresh from the oven. These are hot, hot, hot." Marnie held a tray above her head and bustled through the kitchen.

Bea, the director of the boys ranch, tapped Josie on the shoulder. "I think we're about set here. You can head outside and help corral people toward the tables."

Josie braced her hands on the counter and dipped her head. "Thank you, I think I'll take you up on that." A handful of them had been working in the kitchen since six o'clock in the morning, and when they weren't busy mixing and chopping, Abby had them out beautifying the tables and eating area. All of that amounted to one pregnant woman in a dress with very sore feet and an equally achy back.

Stephen slung open the back door. "Ms. Josie, I think you better come out here quick. There's something you need to see." He held the door for her and moved his hand in a circle, silently asking her to move faster.

Despite the sadness she felt about all that had happened, Josie smiled. "Sorry, Stephen, this is as fast as you're going to see this pregnant lady move today."

Stephen's grin was wider than she'd ever seen it. "I wouldn't be so sure about that."

Odd. The boy had been downright moody earlier, upset that his family wasn't bothering to come to the celebration even though, all things considered, they lived pretty close to the ranch.

Josie stepped outside and shielded her eyes from the early afternoon sun.

Diego came running up the walk. "Look! Heath's back!"

In the past, Josie had listened to people talk about moments when time stood still for them. She'd always brushed off their stories as overly sappy. She'd known love, been married and had never experienced what they were talking about. Time didn't stand still. Time moved on, dragging a person to the next second, even if they didn't want to go.

But when her eyes landed on Heath Grayson…handsome as the day was long with his wide shoulders, tight button-down and adorably hesitant smile…everything else in Josie's world faded away. The more than one hundred guests milling around the yard didn't exist. Stephen and Diego chatting about goats vanished, too. Heath cut down the yard, a baby goat bobbing under each of his arms, and headed straight toward her.

There was only Heath and Josie and for one irrational heartbeat, she wished life could stay that way. Wasn't she supposed to be angry with him?

But all she wanted to do was toss her arms around his neck and never let go.

"You're here," she breathed.

Heath's eyes took her in and his chest puffed out. "I told you I would be."

"You brought goats?" Really? That was the best she could do?

"For you. A peace offering." He lifted them up a little, but instead of handing them to Josie, he passed one to Diego and one to Stephen. "Well, *peace offering* isn't correct, either. I need to say this right." Heath stepped forward and took both her hands. "I brought those for you because I want you to know that I believe in you. I support your dream of running a successful ranch and I want to do everything I can to make all your dreams come true." His lips parted and he exhaled softly. "I'll do everything within my power to make your dreams come true for the rest of my life, if you want me to."

"The goats mean all that, huh?"

"You said you wanted goats, so I brought you goats." He took another half step closer. She had to tilt her head up to keep eye contact. "Anything you want, I aim to see that you have it. If you'll let me."

She swung his hands a little. "I just want you."

"I love you, Josie Markham. I was a fool to walk away from you the other day. I never want to spend another day without you in my life. Forgive me for being so stubborn and blind. I don't have a ring with me but I had to come and ask right away."

"Heath."

He drew as close as he could and lifted her hands so they were cradled in his, resting on his chest. "I've learned that I can't promise tomorrow, but I can promise you that I will love you completely, with everything I have, every single day the good Lord gives me. You have my life, if you want it. You are my life."

"I love you so much."

His eyebrows rose and he whispered, "Marry me?"

"Are you sure?"

He touched her hair, and his fingers slipped between her auburn strands. "I've never been more sure of anything in my life."

"Heath, I'm pregnant."

With one hand he cupped the side of her head and the other he laid over her stomach. "Let me raise this child with you. I'll be her father. I want to be there when the baby's born. Be there for both of you every day I have."

"Her?" Josie couldn't resist teasing him. Even in the midst of a special moment. "So your guess is a girl?"

His lips twitched, hinting at a suppressed grin. "Doesn't every dad want a little princess to spoil?"

Joking aside, Josie had to know. "You're willing to raise this child as your own?"

"I'll raise this child as ours, because if we're married—" he moved his fingers ever so lightly across her stomach "—this is our family. My family. I'll do anything for both of you."

Josie walked her fingers up his chest, his neck, up

until she could guide his face down to hers and kiss him soundly. His arms came around her and they sealed the promise she hadn't yet answered. Because a kiss spoke louder than any words she could manage in the moment.

They might have enjoyed each other longer, but a huge cheer rose around them.

Heath and Josie parted, laughing breathlessly.

Heath pressed a quick kiss to her forehead. "I forgot about all them."

"Me, too." She laid her head on his chest. "Ranger, I know you've been slow on clues lately, so if you didn't get that one, my answer is yes."

His shoulders tightened when she said *Ranger*. "You don't mind that I'm in law enforcement? We didn't discuss that. I'm still a Texas Ranger."

"Being a Texas Ranger...that's who you are. Protective, caring, always looking for ways to solve problems. It's one of the reasons I fell for you." She circled her arms around his neck again and rose up on her toes to kiss him again. "Getting to love you is worth any risk."

Heath pressed his hands to his stomach and groaned when Josie placed another helping of corn casserole onto his plate.

She winked at him. "Oh, stop your complaining. We all know you're going to eat three more helpings anyway."

She looked so beautiful when she teased him. It took every ounce of self-discipline he possessed not to lean over and kiss her. Again. But the boys sharing their table had started grumbling after their second, or perhaps it was their third, peck during dinner, so he reined in the affection, for now.

"Besides." Stephen elbowed Heath in the ribs. He was sitting on Heath's other side. "You can't be out of room just yet. There's still pie. And Josie even made it this time."

"For me?" Heath grinned at Josie. He couldn't stop. There was a chance he would never wipe the grin off his face. Josie loved him. He was getting married. He was going to be a dad.

"Sorry, Ranger." She pouted her lips and wagged her head. "I didn't even know you were coming."

"She made it for me." Stephen talked around a spoonful of sage stuffing. "I guilted her into it because my family refused to attend."

Heath sobered. "I'm sorry for that. Real sorry. I would have liked to meet them."

And given the teen's stepfather a talking-to. Maybe in December.

Stephen shrugged. "Whatever. I'm not letting it ruin my day." He turned to address the five other boys sitting at their table. "None of us are going to let the fact that our parents didn't show wreck today, right? There's pie and John set up hay bales in the formation of a bowling alley, and I could probably scrounge up some water balloons." He rubbed his hands together like a movie villain. "We can ambush ourselves a Ranger."

A blond boy at the end of the table stared at his plate as he pushed some green beans around with his fork. "Some of our parents can't show up. It doesn't mean they don't want to."

Josie pressed her fingers to Heath's wrist and whispered, "Visitation rights."

Heath nodded. Because of what he saw in his line of work, he'd already figured court paperwork played a role in many of these boys' lives. However, like Stephen pointed out—it was within their power to not let those circumstances affect today. After dessert, Heath would do everything he could to make certain that the boys had a good time. The hay-bale bowling alley sounded like it might be fun. He made a mental note to keep an eye on Sam and try to involve him in whatever activity Heath ended up participating in.

Heath finished the additional helping of corn casserole and then shoved his plate toward the center of the table. No more. At least, not until dessert.

He leaned back in his chair, wrapped an arm around Josie and observed everyone else at the celebration. The candles in the decorated jars wavered a little. All around them, hundreds of people mingled, laughed, shared food—all coming together to give thanks for today. And he got to be a part of it. Despite years of isolating himself, God had drawn him into a community. A community that had been waiting to welcome him—God's timing was amazing in that way.

Thank You for blessing me, despite the fact that I was living in fear. Help me use my life to bless others now.

Stephen laid down his fork and turned in his seat. "So I noticed that you didn't argue about the water-balloon fight—does that mean you're game?"

Heath dropped his hand onto the teen's shoulder and shook it a little. "Yes. I'm game. But first—" he pushed back his chair and offered his hand to Josie "—I'm going to take my gorgeous soon-to-be bride on a romantic walk."

Josie slipped her hand into his and beamed up at him.

Wes Corman, one of the newer residents, pulled a

face. "Right now? But you two are getting married. You have *forever* to spend time with her."

Heath laced his fingers through Josie's and pulled her close. "Time's precious and not guaranteed. I have right now and I'm going to spend this moment with the woman I love." He tucked a strand of hair behind Josie's ear as her gaze captured his. "Besides, I forgot the yellow roses I was going to give you in my truck."

Stephen folded his hands on the table. "But should you have time—say—a half hour from now?"

Heath laughed. "It's yours."

* * * * *

WE HOPE YOU
ENJOYED THIS

LOVE
INSPIRED®
BOOK.

If you were **inspired** by this

uplifting, **heartwarming** romance,

be sure to look for all six Love

Inspired® books every month.

Love Inspired®

*Read on for a sneak peek at
the first heartwarming book in Lee Tobin McClain's
Safe Haven series,* Low Country Hero*!*

They'd both just turned back to their work when a familiar loud, croaking sound cut the silence.

The twins shrieked and ran from where they'd been playing into the little cabin's yard and slammed into Anna, their faces frightened.

"What was that?" Anna sounded alarmed, too, kneeling to hold and comfort both girls.

"Nothing to be afraid of," Sean said, trying to hold back laughter. "It's just egrets. Type of water bird." He located the source of the sound, then went over to the trio, knelt beside them, and pointed through the trees and growth.

When the girls saw the stately white birds, they gasped.

"They're so pretty!" Anna said.

"Pretty?" Sean chuckled. "Nobody from around here would get excited about an egret, nor think it's especially pretty." But as he watched another one land beside the first, white wings spread wide as it skidded into the shallow water, he realized that there was beauty there. He just hadn't noticed it before.

That was what kids did for you: made you see the world through their fresh, innocent eyes. A fist of longing clutched inside his chest.

The twins were tugging at Anna's shirt now, trying to get her to take them over toward the birds. "You may go look as long as you can see me," she said, "but take careful steps by the water." She took the bolder twin's face in her hands. "The water's not deep, but I still don't want you to wade in. Do you understand?"

Both little girls nodded vigorously.

They ran off and she watched for a few seconds, then turned back to her work with a barely audible sigh.

"Go take a look with them," he urged her. "It's not every day kids see an egret for the first time."

"You're sure?"

"Go on." He watched her run like a kid over to her girls. And then he couldn't resist walking a few steps closer and watching them, shielded by the trees and brush.

The twins were so excited that they weren't remembering to be quiet. "It caught a *fish*!" the one was crowing, pointing at the bird, which, indeed, held a squirming fish in its mouth.

"That one's neck is like an S!" The quieter twin squatted down, rapt.

Anna eased down onto the sandy beach, obviously unworried about her or the girls getting wet or dirty, laughing and talking to them and sharing their excitement.

The sight of it gave him a melancholy twinge. His own mom had been a nature lover. She'd taken him and his brothers fishing, visited a nature reserve a few times, back in Alabama where they'd lived before coming here.

Oh, if things were different, he'd run with this, see where it led…

Don't miss
Lee Tobin McClain's Low Country Hero*,*
available March 2019 from HQN Books!

www.Harlequin.com

PHLTMEXP0319

Looking for inspiration in tales
of hope, faith and heartfelt romance?

Check out **Love Inspired**® and
Love Inspired® **Suspense** books!

New books available every month!

Love Inspired®

LIGENRE2018R2

Inspirational Romance to Warm Your Heart and Soul

Join our social communities to connect with other readers who share your love!

Sign up for the Love Inspired newsletter at **www.LoveInspired.com** to be the first to find out about upcoming titles, special promotions and exclusive content.

CONNECT WITH US AT:

Facebook.com/groups/HarlequinConnection

 Facebook.com/LoveInspiredBooks

 Twitter.com/LoveInspiredBks

LISOCIAL2018